Outstanding praise for the novels of Holly Chamberlin!

THE SEASON OF US

"Fans of Elin Hilderbrand will adore this genuine exploration of family bonds, personal growth, and acceptance." —*Booklist*

THE BEACH QUILT

"Particularly compelling." —*The Pilot*

"Beautiful and heartbreaking . . . a novel that resonates with readers." —*RT Book Reviews*

SUMMER FRIENDS

"A thoughtful novel." —*ShelfAwareness*

"A great summer read." —*Fresh Fiction*

"A novel rich in drama and insights into what factors bring people together and, just as fatefully, tear them apart." —*Portland Press Herald*

THE FAMILY BEACH HOUSE

"Explores questions about the meaning of home, family dynamics and tolerance." —*The Bangor Daily News*

"A dramatic and moving portrait of several generations of a family and each persons place within it." —*Booklist*

"An enjoyable summer read, but it's more. It is a novel for all seasons that adds to the enduring excitement of Ogunquit." —*The Maine Sunday Telegram*

"It does the trick as a beach book and provides a touristy taste of Maine's seasonal attractions." —*Publishers Weekly*

Books by Holly Chamberlin

LIVING SINGLE

THE SUMMER OF US

BABYLAND

BACK IN THE GAME

THE FRIENDS WE KEEP

TUSCAN HOLIDAY

ONE WEEK IN DECEMBER

THE FAMILY BEACH HOUSE

SUMMER FRIENDS

LAST SUMMER

THE SUMMER EVERYTHING CHANGED

THE BEACH QUILT

SUMMER WITH MY SISTERS

SEASHELL SEASON

THE SEASON OF US

HOME FOR THE SUMMER

Published by Kensington Publishing Corporation

last summer

holly chamberlin

KENSINGTON PUBLISHING CORP.
http://www.kensingtonbooks.com

KENSINGTON BOOKS are published by

Kensington Publishing Corp.
119 West 40th Street
New York, NY 10018

All Kensington Titles, Imprints, and Distributed Lines are available at special quantity discounts for bulk purchases for sales promotions, premiums, fund-raising, and educational or institutional use. Special book excerpts or customized printings can also be created to fit specific needs. For details, write or phone the office of the Kensington special sales manager: Kensington Publishing Corp., 119 West 40th Street, New York, NY 10018, attn: Special Sales Department, Phone: 1-800-221-2647.

ISBN-13: 978-1-4967-0800-7
ISBN-10: 1-4967-0800-8
First Kensington Trade Edition: July 2012
First Kensington Mass Market Edition: June 2017

eISBN-13: 978-0-7582-7985-9
eISBN-10: 0-7582-7985-X
First Kensington Electronic Edition: July 2012

10 9 8 7 6 5 4 3 2 1

Printed in the United States of America

As always, for Stephen.
And this time, also for Hannah Jane.

Acknowledgments

First and foremost, thanks to John Scognamilio for his perception, foresight, and guidance. Thanks also to Hannah Jane for sharing with me the sometimes puzzling but always interesting world of today's young person.

Thanks also to Margaret J. O'Connell and Katherine J. Wilder for sharing with the community of friends and family their wedding at the Cathedral Church of St Luke's, Portland, Maine.

This is for anyone, young or old, homosexual or heterosexual, girl or boy, who has ever suffered at the hands of a bully. You will triumph. I did!

This is also in memory of Maureen Wall Bentley and of Elizabeth Wasserman.

This is a work of fiction and is in no way meant to present a complete picture of the many successful anti-bullying campaigns and educational programs at work throughout the great state of Maine. Similarly, the story of Rosie Patterson is just that—a story. It is unique to the character and not intended as a representation of every victim's experience.

Life appears to me too short to be spent in nursing animosity or registering wrongs.

—Charlotte Brontë, *Jane Eyre*

1

Fourteen-year-old Rosie Patterson stood at the window in the living room of her family's house on Pond View Road in the town of Yorktide, Maine. She didn't know why the road was called Pond View, as there was no pond anywhere in sight. She guessed there must have been one years and years ago. And maybe a developer had filled it in to build a house or even two houses. It seemed that every year more land that had been beautiful, wild woodland was being bulldozed or blown apart so that someone "from away" could build a huge house with big white columns out front (like anyone would really think it was historical!), a four-car garage, and an in-ground pool.

The Patterson house had been built sometime in the 1930s. At least, that's what Rosie's dad had told her. It wasn't a tiny house, in fact, it was the second-biggest house on the road, but Mrs. Patterson had decorated it so that it felt cozy and welcoming, even on the coldest day of the year. And in Maine, even pretty far south where the Pattersons lived, close to the New Hampshire border, that could easily mean temperatures below freezing.

On the first floor were the living room and a small den. In the living room there was a big fireplace with a wide stone mantel on which Mrs. Patterson displayed portraits of the family, including those members long gone, and her small but good collection of milk glass. Generally, the living room was reserved for when guests came to visit, not that that was often, especially not now. The den was the room where the Pattersons watched television or read in the evenings, after the dinner dishes were cleaned and homework was finished. It was probably the most snug room in the house with a thick, colorful rug, a bookcase that covered almost an entire wall, and three big armchairs, one really big, another sort of big, and the third, Rosie's, smallish. Just like the chairs for the three bears from the Goldilocks fairy tale, Rosie had noted when she was little. The comparison had often made her smile.

The kitchen, also on the first floor, was Rosie's mother's pride and joy. She loved to cook and had bought the best pots and pans and knives she could afford. Jane Patterson kept the kitchen spotless and the cupboards perfectly organized. Rosie had long ago memorized where every serving fork and can of tomatoes and jar of wild rice belonged. Behind the kitchen and leading out to the small patio and large backyard there was a small screened-in room where the Pattersons stored some of the spring gardening tools, as well as shovels and bags of rock salt for winter use. (The snowblower lived in the toolshed.) On the patio sat a wrought iron table and chair set, Mike Patterson's charcoal-fueled grill, and some of Mrs. Patterson's potted plants. In good weather, the Pattersons often ate dinner on the patio, though so far this summer no one had made the suggestion that they emerge from the security of the kitchen. That wasn't surprising.

A staircase off the living room led to the second floor, on which there were Rosie's bedroom, a bathroom in the hallway, and her parents' bedroom and private bath. Her mother had decorated both bedrooms with good faux-antique furniture and a few small genuine pieces. The chairs were upholstered in a cabbage rose print, and over each bed hung a ruffled canopy in the same print. Rosie had added her own small personal touches to her room, like a framed print of one of her favorite paintings. It was a portrait of the Princesse Albert de Broglie (whoever she was) painted by a French painter named Jean Auguste Dominique Ingres. Rosie thought the shimmering blue of the princess's dress was magical. Rosie had no talent for art, she could hardly draw a straight line, but she loved to study the paintings in her mom's art and design books and thought she might be developing what her mom called "a pretty good eye."

The basement of the Patterson home housed Jane Patterson's sewing room and a dressing room for her clients (Rosie's mom had a small tailoring business), Mike Patterson's at-home office where the family's computer was kept, and the washing machine and dryer. The basement was also where the boiler and all those other kinds of frightening "Dad machines" lived. Rosie had little if any idea of how any of them worked or what, exactly, they did, and that was fine by her. She was like her mother in that way. Stuff to do with gas and electricity and plumbing was stuff that men dealt with. Maybe that was a little old-fashioned, but that's the way it was in the Patterson house.

Rosie touched the glass of the living room window with one slender finger, as if that touch would bring her closer to the beautiful June morning just outside. The strengthening sun was drying what remained of the crystal-like dew. Two robins were hopping around on the front lawn, and she could hear the scolding cry of a blue jay somewhere not far off. The crows were silent at the moment and Rosie was glad for that. When she was little, their absurdly loud cawing had terrorized her. She had been convinced the birds were screaming in pain, not just going about the noisy business of being crows. But then, she had been an ultrasensitive child. Her mother often reminded her of that. And the past few months had further proved that her mother's opinion was correct. She was now an ultrasensitive young woman.

Though at this time of the day she couldn't see her reflection in the window in front of her, Rosie imagined that she could. (Imagining came easy to Rosie.) At times she wondered if there was some real connection between how you looked and your personality or character. It was a silly notion, and one that probably only found its truth in plays and novels where the villains were all short, dark, and ugly and the tragic heroines were all tall, pale, and beautiful. But what if it really wasn't a silly notion? In that case, Rosie thought, seeing herself in her mind's eye, her own appearance kind of proved her ultrasensitive personality and, as her mother often said, her "specialness."

First, there was her long, light blond hair that she usually wore in a single braid down her back. When her hair was loose, like when she had dried it after a shower, her father said she looked like Rapunzel. Then there were her big eyes, an unusual vibrant green surrounded by dark lashes. Since she was little, people had been telling her how beautiful she was. It had always made Rosie uncomfortable, strangers coming up to her and her mother on the street and saying things like, "Oh, my God, your daughter could be a model!" Why did people feel the need to comment on other people's appearance? Rosie thought it seemed kind of rude but was too polite to say anything like, "Could you please keep your comments about my body and my face to yourself? It embarrasses me." Plus, her mother had never asked anyone not to talk about her daughter's appearance—in fact, Rosie thought her mom kind of enjoyed hearing those comments—and Rosie wasn't the sort of girl to protest a parent's decisions. She just wasn't.

She was tall, too, and that was another thing that people often commented on. At her last checkup the doctor had estimated she would grow to be about five feet nine inches, which was a little taller than her mother but not as tall as her father. And she was really slim, which lots of girls at school had told her they envied. But Rosie had no interest in their obsession with thinness. She was thin because she was thin. So was her mother. It was no big deal, no better or worse than having red hair or brown eyes. Sometimes, in fact, Rosie wished she were totally average-looking or maybe even ugly so that people would see only what mattered about her, like the fact that she was smart and tried always to be good and polite and kind.

Rosie's attention was pulled back from the land of imagination and into the moment at hand as one of the neighbors, a nice older woman named Mrs. Riillo, came walking down the narrow sidewalk. Rosie began to raise her hand, intending to wave, but quickly dropped it. She didn't want to call attention to herself, standing alone at the window. Lately, she had begun to feel too much like the heroine of a novel she had read back in eighth grade. She had found the slim volume on a shelf in the den, stuck in between two of her father's fat mystery novels, almost as if it were hiding. In the story, a young woman not much older than Rosie was trapped in her home by her own fears and inhibitions. Her bedroom window provided her some small access to the outside world, while at the same time, with its heavy drapery that she could pull securely shut, the window represented the extreme isolation in which she chose to live.

It was a powerful story with no real ending, happy or otherwise, and it still haunted Rosie. She had chosen to write about it for an extra-credit assignment. Her English teacher had been more than a bit surprised at her choice—most of the other students had chosen to write about action and adventure stories—but she had given Rosie an A. Rosie almost always got As on her tests and assignments.

Mrs. Riillo was gone now, out of Rosie's sight. A neighborhood cat, an enormous shaggy tom named Harvey, was slinking across the front yard, his eyes riveted on the two robins. Rosie shut her eyes and hunched her shoulders as he leapt forward, intent on a kill. When she opened her eyes, slowly and just a bit, she sighed with relief. The birds had flown to safety and the cat was washing his face as if nothing had gone awry. She knew that cats were predators and that Mother Nature was not always pretty. Still, any kind of violence made Rosie feel queasy.

Satisfied that he was clean and presentable once more after his failed attempt at breakfast, the cat trotted off. Rosie sighed and for a moment felt a wave of restlessness overcome her. The day ahead stretched out for what seemed like an impossibly long way, offering far too much time to fill. The last term paper had been submitted and graded, and the last test had been taken and passed. Now what?

The final weeks of ninth grade had been packed with

activity, from writing those term papers to cleaning out lockers that had accumulated all sorts of interesting and sometimes slightly yucky tidbits. There had been the homeroom party on the very last day of class, complete with cupcakes and potato chips, and the trip up to Portland a few days before that to visit the museum and have lunch at Flatbread, the awesome organic pizza place with the huge brick oven. Judy Smith, a pretty, smart girl who everyone liked, had had a party in her backyard for most of the other freshman girls and a few of the boys. Mr. Smith had grilled red hot dogs and Mrs. Smith had made killer potato salad and brownies, and though it was still too cold for swimming, a few kids had brought their bathing suits just in case. In the end, Judy's aboveground swimming pool remained empty of all but a bobbing beach ball.

Well, Rosie had imagined all those details about the homeroom party and the class trip to Portland and Judy's party, because she hadn't gone to any of them. She could have participated in all three events. But she hadn't.

Here came Trudy Loren, a woman from the next road, walking her yellow Lab. Rosie stepped back a bit from the window, again reluctant to be seen watching the world go by. But Trudy was chatting on her phone, oblivious to the tall, thin girl behind the glass. In a moment, she was gone, heading in the direction of the park.

Rosie stepped forward and once again touched the glass with her finger. If this summer was going to be at all like last summer and the summer before that and even the one before that, she would have a lot of fun to look forward to. Sure, there was some reading to be done for school. Mr. Arcidiacono, who was going to be their tenth-grade English teacher, had given out a list of novels and nonfiction and instructed everyone to choose two books from each category, read the books through, and write a report on each one. For someone like Rosie who loved to read and write, the assignment would be enjoyable. And she would read way more books than the four suggested by Mr. Arcidiacono, anyway. She had always been a big reader, just like her parents.

But other than the reading assignment, the only responsibility facing Rosie this summer was to enjoy the warm and sunny weather. It had been a particularly long winter; by mid-May temperatures had barely reached fifty degrees. Everyone, even kids, not just grumpy, arthritic adults like their neighbor Mr. Newman, had been complaining about the cold and gray for so long it really had seemed as if this would be the year that spring never came.

Yes, if this summer was going to be like every other summer past, there would be trips to the beach, and lazy afternoons spent lying under the gingko tree in the backyard, daydreaming and planning an exciting, exotic future. There would be the annual trip to Chauncey Creek where they would get lobster rolls, and there would be a blueberry-picking excursion, after which they would make muffins and pancakes and pies with all the berries they had collected. And there would be trips to the green market and long bike rides and movies at the Leavitt Theatre in Ogunquit and . . .

Rosie pressed her lips together tightly and reminded herself that this summer would not be like last summer or like any of the summers before it. This summer would be a summer without Meg Giroux, Rosie's former best friend turned traitor. It was a strong word, "traitor," but Rosie thought it was the right one. Not that she would speak the word aloud, not even to herself, not even to Dr. Lowe, her therapist. Dr. Lowe wasn't supposed to judge her patient, but still, Rosie was afraid to appear vindictive.

Rosie consciously fingered the few thin, lingering scars on her left arm and then pulled the sleeve of her pink cotton shirt down over her hand. At that moment, as if summoned by Rosie's troubled thoughts, Meg, carrying a watering can, came through the front door of her home next door. Rosie quickly backed away from the window and turned toward the sanctuary that was her own home.

2

Jane rubbed the sponge in widening circles across the counter she had already cleaned that morning. In the past few weeks she had caught herself acting mindlessly, straightening pillows that had already been straightened, adding to the grocery list items she had already bought, even forgetting the day of the week. This was unusual behavior for Jane Ella Patterson. One of the things she prided herself on was her highly developed sense of purpose and organization.

The counter beyond clean, Jane rinsed the sponge and squeezed it until it was close to bone dry. The physical effort caused a dull ache in her right hand. She sighed and flexed her fingers. She wondered if she was developing arthritis. It would seem likely, given all the years of working with her hands. Well, if that was the case there was nothing much she could do about it. Her mother had developed severe arthritis in her fifties. Jane thought it might be an inherited condition.

Jane Patterson was about five feet seven inches on a good day, which was getting harder to find; she often caught herself slumping, and a muscle under her right shoulder seemed to have permanently clenched itself into a throbbing ball. Just after her forty-second birthday last summer, her normally perfect eyesight had begun to fail and she now wore prescription glasses for close work and reading. Wearing glasses didn't bother her; it was the cost of the prescription that was problematic. Both she and her husband were self-employed and that meant outrageous insurance costs. They weren't poor but they weren't rich, either, at least not by local standards. All you had to do was drive through certain parts of York County or the town of Ogunquit and you would find massive mansions overlooking the ocean and estates that went on for miles. But Jane loved her house on Pond View Road and enjoyed making it a home. Some women might balk at the term "homemaker," seeing it as old-fashioned and somehow demeaning. But Jane thought otherwise.

And her husband took pride in their home, too, and in the life they had made together. Mike was an accountant with his own small firm. He rented an office on the first floor of a large house on Riverton Road; a family practitioner worked from an office across the hall. On slow days Mike was able to come home for lunch, and when the roads were impassable due to severe weather, which happened several times each winter, he worked from his office in the basement. During tax season, when he regularly worked late into the night, the basement office became something of a bedroom as well. An acquaintance back in Boston had called Mike a workaholic. Jane thought he was just a very conscientious man.

Counter cleaned, lunch dishes long ago put away, laundry folded . . . What next? What could she do to distract herself from the nagging sense of failure that loomed over her like a thundercloud?

Jane went over to the fridge and straightened one of the photographs attached to the door by a magnet. Over the years the fridge had become the family portrait gallery. Jane ran her eye over the current display. Rosie's latest school picture, taken last September; a picture of the three of them at a Sea Dogs game up in Portland; Rosie at the age of four on Santa's lap. That was one of Mike's favorites. And then there was a photo that had been taken just about a year ago. It was—or at least it had been—one of Jane's favorites. The three of them had gone to Kennebunkport one afternoon to visit the galleries and shops. Totally by chance she and Rosie had come down to breakfast that morning wearing almost identical outfits: pink blouses, tan chinos, and white sneakers. The only thing that set them apart was Jane's wedding band and earrings and her shorter hair. In the picture, they were sitting side by side at a restaurant where they had stopped for a late lunch. Mike had called them his "beautiful twin girls." Now the smiling faces of their former, innocent selves mocked Jane.

She turned away from the photograph. Since Rosie was a toddler, people (Jane's mother Rosemary, for one, for whom Rosie was named) had been describing Rosie as her mother's Mini-Me. In Jane's opinion, her daughter was much prettier than she had ever been. Of course, she was prejudiced in Rosie's favor, but she really believed her daughter had a quality she had never had, what Jane liked to call a "specialness."

Rosemary Alice, her special little girl. Rosie was in the living room now, at the piano. Jane had coaxed her to practice. She had hoped that playing would bring her daughter some pleasure. But from the lackluster sounds reaching Jane's ear, it was clear that her heart was not at all into the music. In fact, Jane had noticed that for the past several months Rosie's interest in the piano had been waning. How much that had to do with what had happened to her daughter at the hands of those bullying girls, Jane didn't know.

A car horn sounded from the street out front and Jane flinched. *I should go back to work,* she thought, *at least for an hour.* She had accomplished her goals for the day but there was always something else that could be done, even if it was just re-ordering her collection of antique buttons or reviewing her schedule for the coming weeks.

And it would be a busy few weeks, what with it being wedding season. Jane had started her small tailoring business when Rosie was about four and finally in preschool. (The preschool had been at Mike's insistence. He was afraid Rosie wasn't learning to socialize with other kids her own age. Except for Meg, of course.) Her sewing room was in a sectioned-off part of the finished basement and contained two sewing machines, one of which she'd had since college, and a large worktable. Shelves along two walls contained neat rows of thread, bolts of fabric, and a collection of interesting and useful items Jane found at the better thrift stores, things like bits of old lace and lengths of brocaded trim. A dress form stood in one corner. Next to the sewing room was a changing room for clients. Mike had installed full-length mirrors in such a way that the client could see herself from every angle.

Much of Jane's business was taken up with minor projects, like alterations to dresses for special occasions or to suits for the office. Sometimes, though rarely, a woman would come by with a request for a jacket or a skirt or a pair of pants made from a pattern. Jane enjoyed those challenges; there wasn't a lot of thrill in hemming a skirt. As a child she had taught herself to sew on her grandmother's old machine, and she had been making most of her own clothes since she was in high school. Unlike her mother, Rosie had very little interest in clothes and absolutely none in sewing. Still, Jane liked to daydream about Rosie's far-off wedding. She imagined the two of them working together to design the dress and the veil and the handbag. She imagined—

The piano had gone silent. Jane's entire body tensed. She fought the urge to rush into the living room. Rosie was probably just stretching her fingers or taking a bathroom break. *There's no need to panic,* she told herself. *Rosie is not necessarily in trouble.* And then the piano sounded again and Jane sighed audibly.

That was the best thing about working from home, she thought now. She was almost always available for her daughter. When Rosie got home from school, Jane was there to ask about her day and put out a snack. When Rosie was sick enough to stay home from school, Jane was there to bring her homemade chicken soup and flat ginger ale. The situation had seemed ideal. She had considered their lives to be very close to perfect. Absolute perfection would have been another daughter or even a son, but no one achieved absolute perfection, Jane thought, no matter how hard she tried.

And Jane had tried.

Jane glanced again at the photograph of her and her daughter in their matching outfits. She knew that human beings were biologically wired to be fearful. It was a basic survival tool, but for Jane, especially after two failed pregnancies, fear had become her default mode. Not that she hadn't always been a somewhat high-strung person, prone to nerves and to what some (Mike, for one) would say were groundless terrors. That was the reason she had forced herself to become an exceptionally organized person. Organization was a way of staving off chaos. At least, you could tell yourself that it was.

But no amount of organized and disciplined behavior could entirely mask her basic fearful and cautious nature, and Jane was afraid she had passed that fearful and cautious nature on to her daughter. Clearly, Rosie was not tough and resilient in ways that perhaps she should be. If she had been tough and resilient, then . . .

For a moment Jane thought she was going to cry. She willed away the impulse, reluctant to have Rosie find her in tears. She wondered if the heavy sense of guilt she labored under would ever go away.

Sure, she worked from home and was almost always available to her daughter. Then how had she not known at the very start that something was seriously wrong? When she had begun to suspect that Rosie was unhappy, why hadn't she pushed harder for answers? She had attributed Rosie's unusual moodiness to mere adolescence, hormones wreaking havoc with her once generally sunny nature. It was normal for a fourteen-year-old to lock her bedroom door. It was normal for a fourteen-year-old to beg off activities in which she used to take pleasure. Though when Rosie had stopped going to the library each Saturday morning, her absolutely favorite activity, Jane should have known that something more than hostile hormones was going on. She should have known.

It was only back in May—just last month!—when Rosie's best friend Meg told Mackenzie Egan and her awful cohorts about Rosie's youthful trouble with bedwetting that Jane had finally seen the truth. And then she had learned about the bullying her daughter had endured, and about the harm Rosie had been inflicting on her body. The traces of those angry wounds broke

Jane's heart. They were a vivid and ugly reminder of her failure as a mother to protect her child. Even if the scars on Rosie's arm completely healed someday, they would never be forgotten.

Just like the memory of that fateful morning when Rosie refused to get out of bed to go to school. It was entirely out of the norm. Jane had asked her if she felt sick and Rosie just shook her head and said nothing. When after fifteen minutes Rosie still hadn't budged, Jane had actually raised her voice, demanding that Rosie stop fooling around.

And then, in a completely uncharacteristic action, Jane had yanked the covers off her daughter and been confronted with the brutal reality. Rosie's skinny arms, hugged around her skinny body. And the left arm scored with nasty red scars from her elbow to her wrist. Jane stood there, hands clutching the sheet and lightweight comforter, her head filling with an awful buzz. She was sure she was going to be sick all over the bed. Rosie lay still, her eyes wide open but staring at nothing, almost as if she were dead. And then Jane had dropped the covers and run from the bedroom.

Why had it taken so long for her to realize that something was terribly, terribly wrong, that her well-behaved, hardworking, always polite little girl was truly suffering? Why had it taken so long for her to realize that her only child was seriously ill and not playing an adolescent game?

Memories of that morning still made Jane feel sick to her stomach, but she couldn't chase the images away. In a way, she didn't want to forget. She remembered now with vivid recall the frantic call she had made to Mike at his office. He had raced home and, after looking in on Rosie, had called the school to tell them that she wasn't well and wouldn't be coming in that day. And then Jane and Mike had painfully learned the truth, at first in bits and pieces and then, in a torrent of words, finishing with what Meg Giroux had done to their daughter. Rosie had sobbed for what seemed like hours and then she had finally fallen asleep, utterly exhausted.

Over the following days there were meetings with the school's principal and guidance counselor, an appointment with the Pattersons' doctor to ascertain Rosie's physical health, and then the family interview with Dr. Lowe, psychotherapist, at her office in her charming old house in Kittery. It had been the most trying week of Jane's life.

Jane took the broom from the tall, narrow closet where it lived alongside a mop, bucket, and cleaning supplies. She had swept the kitchen floor after breakfast, but there always seemed to be stray bits of food or dust to catch. As she swept, methodically, starting in one corner of the room and working with short, rhythmic strokes, she thought back to Mother's Day. It had been a bittersweet occasion, coming hard upon the heels of Rosie's breakdown. Mike had done his best to make the day enjoyable—he had made Jane's favorite breakfast, eggs Benedict, and given her a lovely bouquet of flowers from her favorite local florist—but her heart had felt too bruised for celebration.

Of course she was glad that her daughter hadn't tried to kill herself, as so many bullied children did. Of course she was glad that Rosie genuinely seemed to want to get better. She went without protest to Dr. Lowe's office once a week, and while school was still in session she had kept up with her homework. The school administration had been very supportive. A teacher had come to the house to bring Rosie her final exams and to monitor her while she completed them. She had passed each class, even math, and most with flying colors.

There was a lot for which to be thankful. But there was also a lot to regret. True, Rosie had given her a beautiful Mother's Day card. But it had only partly reassured Jane that her daughter didn't hate her for not coming to her aid quickly enough against those awful girls. Jane suspected that someday, sooner or later, Rosie would lash out. She just had to be angry. But so far she had displayed nothing but sadness. At least, that was all that Jane could see. Maybe Dr. Lowe was seeing and hearing a different story.

Yes, Jane thought, emptying the meager contents of the dustpan into the garbage and returning the broom to its closet, it was too late for second-guessing, but it was not too late for self-recrimination, even though she knew that her job as a responsible adult was to focus on the future and on healing the damage done to her family.

That was what Dr. Lowe had advised. That was what her husband counseled, and that was what the self-help books she had been devouring in the past weeks recommended. "Try to have some compassion for yourself," Mike had said. He was a good man and generally gave very smart and thoughtful advice, but in this case, Jane found herself unable to really hear and accept it.

The one person who might have been able to help her heal, the one person to whom she might have listened, was the one person to whom she absolutely could not go. And that was Meg's mother, Frannie Giroux.

Jane sank into a chair at the round kitchen table. She felt tired and unhappy and her back was aching. She wondered if she should be taking an antidepressant. So far, Rosie was doing well without any medication. Her therapist had advised they hold off on a drug unless it was absolutely necessary.

Maybe I should make an appointment with Dr. Lowe, Jane thought. Or, if Jacqueline Lowe didn't think it was a good idea for mother and daughter to see the same therapist, with someone she could recommend. Jane had met alone with Dr. Lowe only once; it was common for her to have individual conversations with the parents of a new, underage patient. Jane wasn't sure what Dr. Lowe had learned from their session. Jane had cried a lot and was pretty sure she'd been generally inarticulate. What Jane did remember clearly was that Dr. Lowe hadn't judged or condemned her failure to detect Rosie's troubles earlier. Well, if she had judged or condemned her, she had kept her thoughts and opinions to herself as a professional was trained to do.

In fact, Dr. Lowe had been the one to suggest the books Jane could turn to for information about bullying, as well as about forgiveness and recovery. What Dr. Lowe couldn't have known was that Jane would read so obsessively, desperate in her desire to better understand Rosie's experiences through the previous winter and spring. And after absorbing a mind-boggling amount of information, some of it puzzling, some of it contradictory, Jane had come to the unhappy conclusion that she had sheltered her daughter too closely. She had raised a child unprepared to face the craziness of the world without falling apart. She was entirely to blame for Rosie's present situation. Not Mike. It always came down to the mother, no matter what anyone said to the contrary.

Jane wiped an invisible crumb from the table. The mother-daughter relationship, she had come to realize, was wonderful, but it was also a relationship famously fraught with jealousy and resentment and frustration. Why had she thought that her relationship with her own daughter would be exempt from trouble? Why had she thought they were so privileged or lucky, or, as Frannie with her belief in God would say, blessed?

Jane glanced over her shoulder. Through the window over the sink she could easily see the Giroux house. Her head began to tingle and she felt the blood rush to her face. It was a surge of anger that frightened her in its intensity. She turned away from the window and put her hands on her burning face. Would this awful rage ever go away? It came upon her several times a day, sometimes sneaking up on her full-blown, sometimes making its presence known with a tiny spark that, no matter how vigorously she tried to douse, eventually roared into a flame.

It seemed like a cruel joke that the two families should live next door to one another, that a symbol of what once had been a close, almost symbiotic relationship should now exist to mock her. She didn't want to remember all the good times the Pattersons had shared at the Giroux home, and all the good times Frannie and her children had shared at Jane and Mike's house—the family game nights, the holiday meals, the rainy Saturday afternoons when Mike would make popcorn and they would watch a funny movie. But the memories, like the scars on Rosie's arm, were there and not likely to fade away into oblivion anytime soon.

Jane rubbed her tired eyes. In some moments she found it hard to believe that she and Frannie had ever been friends. She wondered how she could have been so badly duped. She wondered how she could have allowed her daughter to be so badly deceived. She was as angry with herself as she was with Frannie and her daughter. And she was determined never, ever to forgive the Giroux family.

Jane got up from the table, went to the fridge, opened it, and stared inside. It was time to start thinking about dinner. She had lost weight since Rosie's breakdown (God, she hated that word, but what other word would do?), and it wasn't flattering. There were lines on her face that hadn't been there only weeks before, and her neck looked downright scrawny. Rosie's appetite, usually hearty, had also suffered. The last thing Rosie needed was for her depression to lead to anorexia.

With a sigh, Jane closed the fridge. She wished she were only being dramatic, thinking such a thing. But Dr. Lowe had told them that often kids who took to cutting were prone to developing eating disorders. Almost as proof, there was Rosie's disturbing weight loss, something Jane had been only marginally aware of over the past few months. And that was another crime. She couldn't help but wonder now if she had been willfully ignorant of that, too, simply unwilling to believe or to admit that her own child could be less than perfect.

If I turn my head, the problem will go away. If I pretend nothing is wrong, then nothing will be wrong. There was a bitter irony to it all, Jane thought now. If anyone should have noticed ill-fitting clothing, it should have been her. She could spot poorly fitting pants on a stranger at the mall, but she hadn't noticed sagging jeans on her own daughter.

Jane suddenly became aware that her head was throbbing and went to the kitchen drawer where the first aid kit was stored. She was taking ibuprofen at least twice a day lately, which was probably too often. But the headaches just kept coming, maybe because nothing in her world seemed solid or certain anymore. Everything had been put to question, every assumption and every comfort.

Thankfully, Mike would be home from work soon. He would spend some time alone with Rosie before dinner, encouraging her to work on a jigsaw puzzle with him or to play a quick, intense game of Scrabble. At times, Jane felt a tiny bit jealous of their relationship; she wanted to be the one doing puzzles and playing Scrabble with her daughter. But whenever that tiny feeling of jealousy emerged, Jane carefully squashed it. She knew that Rosie loved her, and anyway, it was so much healthier for a girl to have a good relationship with her father than to be virtually ignored by him, like Meg was virtually ignored by her father. Look at what Peter Giroux's neglect had wrought!

Jane picked up the vase of fresh-cut pink peonies that sat on the kitchen table and for the second time that day refreshed the water. Peonies were one of Rosie's favorite flowers, but so far, she hadn't commented on this bouquet. Her interest in so many once-loved things hadn't yet returned. Jane hoped that it did, and quickly.

The flowers rearranged, Jane again slumped into a chair at the table. Thus far in her life as a parent she had always felt as if she could handle whatever challenges cropped up, maybe with some help from Mike or even a dose of sheer good luck. But now, from the moment she got out of bed each morning until the moment she got back into it at night, she felt horrible, crippling doubt about her ability to shepherd her daughter through the remaining years of childhood and then safely into adulthood. And maybe she deserved to suffer from that doubt.

Jane heard the sound of a car coming up the drive toward the garage. Mike. She sighed in genuine relief. She always felt stronger and braver when Mike was around. She got up, almost knocking over her chair in the process, and hurried to the front door to greet him.

3

October 11, 2011

Dear Diary,

Today was pretty good. It's actually kind of fun being a freshman. I was sort of afraid at first that the upperclassmen were going to give us a hard time, but there's actually a kind of mentoring or big sister/big brother program where every ninth grader gets assigned a twelfth grader who's supposed to look out for them. My big sister is this girl named Carly. She seems okay, though she doesn't seem all that interested in being a mentor or a big sister. She forgot my name the other day and called me Rita. I didn't correct her, but Meg did. But so far everything's been fine, so it's no big deal. I have her class schedule so I know where she is if I need her for advice or something.

This is kind of interesting. Carly has a tattoo on the back of her neck. I think it's a flower, but I didn't want to stare (not that she would see me behind her!) or to ask her, so I don't really know for sure. I didn't even know you were allowed to have a tattoo in school. I mean, that you were allowed to show a tattoo. I'll never get one. I think they're kind of gross and it's supposed to hurt a lot when you get them. Why would I want to have someone stick a sharp needle or whatever it is they use into me? Meg says she's going to get one as soon as her mother lets her. She thinks maybe a small rose on her ankle or maybe a cross, if her mother won't freak out about the cross. Mrs. Giroux is pretty religious. She doesn't think you should wear a cross just as jewelry, which in some ways, I guess, is what a tattoo is. She says it's sacrilegious. Mrs. Giroux wears a cross but that's because she believes in Jesus.

Anyway, Meg's big sister is really into checking in with Meg and making sure she's doing okay. Her name is Tiffany and she says she's going to college in Florida because she hates the winters in Maine. I don't think she's been accepted into college yet—I'm not really sure how the whole admission process works yet—but the way she talks she's determined to throw away her parka and boots for good! I can kind of understand what she feels about hating the long winters, but I could never move so far away from my mom and dad, not even if I could come home for holidays. I'd miss them way too much.

Yesterday was my fourteenth birthday and Meg gave me a piece of polished rose quartz in the shape of a heart. (She said she got it in this fantastic store up in Portland called Stones and Stuff. She said this really nice woman named Heather owns it. I wonder when she got her mom to drive her to Portland without me knowing! That was pretty sneaky!) It's got a silver piece on top, kind of a loop, so I can wear it on a chain. I love it! Mom and Dad got me a new copy of the last Harry Potter book (somehow my old copy got lost, maybe when we stayed overnight in that hotel when we went down to Massachusetts for Dad's brother's wedding; anyway, now my collection is complete again, which is a big relief) and then Meg and her mother and Petey came over for dinner. We had my favorite, this chicken casserole with apples in it that Mom makes, and Mrs. Giroux baked a cake. It was chocolate inside with white icing. I had the best time. Everybody sang "Happy Birthday" (even Dad, whose voice is really terrible) and Petey gave me a crayon drawing he made of Meg and me holding hands. Sometimes I wish I had a little brother or sister, though when Meg is in a bad mood she says that being a big sister is a pain.

Meg is fun, though, even when she's in a bad mood, which she never takes out on me. I just know she'll be my best friend forever. Everyone in school says that about every friend they have—everyone is everyone's BFF—but Meg and I are different. I can't imagine us ever not being friends. It's, like, totally unimaginable. Mom says I shouldn't say "like" all the time. Imagine what she would say if she knew I just wrote it! But my mom would never, ever read my diary, so she won't ever know. That's one really good thing about my life. A lot of kids I know complain that their parents never give them any privacy. But my parents totally respect my privacy. They trust I'm not going to do something wrong or stupid, so they don't need to be poking around my room, looking for clues that I'm running wild or something.

Okay, I have to go and eat dinner now. Mom's making pork chops and this cabbage dish made with red currant jelly. The whole house smells really good. I should learn how to cook so I can help Mom out sometimes. Bye!

Your friend, Rosie

October 30, 2011

Dear Diary,

Meg and I went to an early Halloween party last night in the gym at school. I went as a medieval princess, complete with one of those tall, pointy hats with a veil attached, and Meg went as a bat. She complained the whole time that her costume wasn't good enough because she didn't have the money to put together a better one. I told her she should have asked my mother for help. Mom could have made her something fantastic. But Meg got all red in the face and told me that her mom had forbidden her to "go begging" to my mom for help. She told

Meg they didn't need charity. That seemed really weird and I was sorry I said anything. Since when is helping out a friend charity? Maybe Mrs. Giroux was just in a bad mood when she said that stuff. She knows that Mom really enjoys doing sewing projects for Meg. Why would it suddenly be charity?

Anyway, another interesting thing was that Mackenzie Egan and her friends were at the party, too, and they said hello to us. We've kind of known them since we were in first grade and they were in second, but they've never really noticed us before. They were dressed as Madonna wannabes from the eighties. I don't know where they found all of that tacky stuff to wear, these awful neon-colored hair ties and black lace pantyhose and big plastic jewelry! Jill had her hair teased about a foot off her head! I thought it was nice of them to come over and say hi and say they liked my costume, but Meg thought it was weird. Sometimes she's so suspicious!

By the way, Mackenzie Egan is really pretty. I don't think I ever noticed that before. She's kind of medium height but she has really long legs and really dark hair and bright blue eyes. In fact, she kind of looks exotic. I bet boys really like her.

The party was fun overall, though Halloween isn't my favorite holiday. (It's Christmas!) There was way too much candy and not enough other stuff to eat, like chips (not that Meg minded because she has a major sweet tooth!) and some spooky music (which wasn't really spooky; it was kind of goofy sounding) and some haunted-house-type stuff like a bowl filled with wet spaghetti that you stuck your hand into. You were supposed to think it was brains or guts or something. It all seemed pretty lame to me, especially the marshmallows made to look like blood-streaked eyeballs. Now, if a REAL ghost had shown up, that would have been awesome. I totally believe in a spirit world and would love to encounter a real ghost someday. When I can, which is not often because of homework and piano lessons and practice, I watch some of those TV shows about people's real-life experiences with spirits. Mom and Dad think the shows are all lies, but they don't forbid me to watch them. I think my favorite is PARANORMAL STATE and then maybe PSYCHIC KIDS. A lot of the kids on that show are made fun of by other kids in their school. If I knew a real psychic kid I wouldn't make fun of him at all. I'd have a lot of respect for him.

Anyway, I think the person with the best costume at the party was a boy who came as Captain Jack Sparrow. Meg thought the best costume was someone who came as one of the characters from the Transformers movies. She said it was totally accurate. I've never seen any of those movies—I don't get what's so interesting about machines and guns—so the costume didn't really impress me.

Dad picked us up at ten o'clock, which is the latest I've ever been out, and Meg spent the night at my house. There were some old, classic black-and-white movies on TV and we watched DRACULA with this Eastern European actor named Bela Lugosi. (Dad told me about the Eastern European part. I think he said Bela Lugosi was from Hungary, but I might be wrong.) I loved it—it was very atmospheric—but Meg thought it was silly and boring. She doesn't like old stuff like I do. Now I have to find a copy of the book in the library. Dad told me it's really scary. Also, I have to get a copy of FRANKENSTEIN, which I just found out was written by a woman (cool—and she was really young, too) and which supposedly isn't like the old black-and-white movie at all. I feel so bad for the monster in the movie. No one understands him and he's so alone. Dad says I'll feel even worse for him once I read the book because in some ways, the important ones, he isn't a monster at all. It's Dr. Frankenstein who's the monster.

Oh, and you should have seen Meg's little brother, Petey! He went to school dressed as Snoopy from PEANUTS. He's such a cute little boy. Sometimes I feel as if he's my own brother. I wonder what he'll be like when he grows up. I wonder if he'll still be nice or if he'll turn into one of those boys who pretend to be so tough and who make fun of everything like nothing matters.

It's like the only two things those boys can say are "Big deal" and "Who cares?" No. I think Petey will always be nice, even though his father isn't very nice. I probably shouldn't say that about a grown-up. I've always been taught to respect parents, even other people's parents, and other adults, especially teachers and police and all those other authority figures. But it's hard not to say or even think bad things about Mr. Giroux when his own ex-wife and his own daughter say them.

I just remembered something. Wow. I'd totally forgotten this, but when Meg and I were maybe in second or third grade Mr. Giroux took us on a hike in the woods. I can't remember exactly where but I do remember we brought lunch with us, peanut butter sandwiches and apple slices, and we ate sitting on a log by the bank of a pond. When we got back to Meg's house, Mr. Giroux surprised us by making s'mores. It was the first time I'd ever had a s'more. I didn't really like them—I hate marshmallows—but it was nice of him to do all that for us, so I ate two of them. It always pays to be polite. That's what Mom always says. Anyway, I wonder if Meg remembers that day. Maybe I should ask her. Or maybe it would only upset her and make her miss her dad more. She says she doesn't really miss him but I don't believe her. It's the way she says it, like she's trying to convince herself.

Okay, I should go now. I've got one more paragraph to write for English class and then I'm done with homework for the night.

Your friend, Rosie

4

The long metal chains that held the swing to the support rods squeaked as Meg kicked off halfheartedly. She knew she shouldn't be wasting time. There was still a lot to do before her mother came home from work, like vacuum the rugs in the living room and front hall and do a load of laundry and change the sheets on her bed and on Petey's. But she just couldn't make herself get up off that swing and do anything productive.

She wished the housework would magically do itself. Meg wished a lot of things would take care of themselves or go away or change. Like, she wished she were taller, not five feet three inches, where she had been stuck for over a year. She wished she were naturally thin, not grossly thin like runway models with their bones sticking out all over the place, just thin. She wished her hair were a richer shade of brown, or maybe even auburn. She fully intended to color her hair as soon as she was old enough to do it without getting in trouble with her mother. Mrs. Giroux didn't seem to believe in hair color; her own brown hair was pretty streaked with gray. It drove Meg a bit crazy that her mother didn't take more interest in her appearance. Lots of things had been driving Meg crazy for a long time now. Her mother said it was just hormones. Meg wasn't so sure.

Meg sighed, and for a moment was glad she was alone. It was hot, and swinging had made her sweat enough so that her glasses kept sliding down her nose. There just wasn't a cool way to push glasses back up your nose. Meg had tried in front of a mirror and every way just made you look stupid or like a definitely not cool kind of nerd. (She wouldn't mind being a cool nerd. Cool nerds grew up to make lots of money.)

Anyway, she wished she didn't have to wear glasses. The frames were okay, even though she'd had them now for three years and was dying for a newer, more stylish pair, maybe something in purple or blue. Worse, though, was that on really bright days she had to use clip-on sunglasses, as her family couldn't afford to buy a separate pair of prescription sunglasses. Most days Meg preferred to squint rather than to use the clip-ons, which, she was convinced, only old people used. She would love to be able to wear cool sunglasses, which you could get almost anywhere and which didn't have to cost a lot, either. She had seen some fantastic frames in Goodwill for three dollars! But she could only wear cool sunglasses if she could wear contacts, and that was another issue. Meg's mother only allowed her to wear contacts on special occasions, and there hadn't been one of those since Easter. According to her mother, regular old Sunday Mass didn't count as special enough for "wasting" the money on a pair of disposable contacts. And the only reason her mother had let her get contacts in the first place was she had promised to make a one-month supply last for a year. It was unfair and very frustrating.

Meg stopped swinging and kicked at the dirt with

her foot. Her whole life was unfair and frustrating. Once, in a fit of anger or maybe it was annoyance, her mother had told her to stop being so discontented with everything in her life. "Life is tough," she had snapped. "Get used to it." Meg remembered shouting back something like, "Why should I have to get used to it? Just because you have?" That exchange had not ended well. She had lost Internet privileges for a week and had to clean the bathroom floor for a month.

A slight squeak of a door hinge caused Meg to look up and across to the Patterson yard. Rosie was coming out of the door to the small screened-in room at the back of her house.

Meg lifted her hand in a wave. The gesture was automatic, though the shout of greeting she was about to call out died in her throat.

Rosie ignored her wave (or maybe, Meg thought, she hadn't seen it) and walked back to the toolshed at the edge of the Patterson property. She went inside and a few minutes later emerged with a large, empty clay pot in her arms. Again without acknowledging Meg, she went back inside the house. Meg heard the door closing firmly behind her.

Suddenly, Meg felt sad, and embarrassed, and very alone, sitting on that rusty old swing. There originally had been two swings, but somewhere along the line the chains on the other swing had broken. For over a year the useless swing had sat right where it had fallen, until Meg's mother got tired of asking Meg's father to either reattach it or take it to the dump. Finally, Mrs. Giroux had hauled away the broken swing herself. That was back when Mr. Giroux still lived with them and Petey was still a baby. Petey was a toddler when her father had left them. Or had her mother really thrown him out? Meg couldn't remember clearly the sequence of events or the messy details that had led to her father's final and for-good exit. Not that she missed him. Much. Not that she cared. Not usually. Now, if he had been anything like Rosie's dad . . .

The thought of Mr. Patterson, upright and kind, so vastly different from her own father, filled Meg with sadness. For as long as she lived she would remember the day her mother had made her apologize to Rosie; it was just after Rosie had left school a few weeks before the end of the term. And Meg had so wanted to apologize, so very much, but those moments when she stood in the Pattersons' living room in front of Mr. and Mrs. Patterson and the girl who had always been her best friend, her cheeks red and burning with shame, well, those moments had been the most awful moments in her entire life. She barely remembered what she had said exactly, and she thought that when she had stopped talking Rosie had mumbled something like "Okay," but she couldn't be sure. What she did remember very clearly was coming home and sobbing for hours alone in her room, a chair propped up under the doorknob so her mother couldn't come in. Not that she had tried.

Anyway, even if Rosie had accepted her apology, Meg didn't think Rosie really believed that she was sorry. Ever since then Rosie had been avoiding her, once even running back into her house when Meg came out of her own. Mrs. Patterson had frowned and glared the whole time Meg and her mother had been in that living room, and Meg was 100 percent certain Mrs. Patterson hated her now. Which was also awful because Meg had loved spending time at her house. She was a really good cook and was always so calm and happy, or at least she acted that way, and she let Meg try on some of her jewelry and the awesome clothes she had made for herself. And last year, for Meg's fourteenth birthday, Mrs. Patterson had made something special for her, too, a really cool top with a faux necklace sewn on the front. Rosie had thought it was too flashy, but that was because her idea of fashion was a comfy flannel shirt and also because she didn't read *Teen Vogue* and *InStyle* like Meg did. Not that she had a subscription to either magazine, but an older girl down the street did and was cool about giving each issue to Meg when she had finished reading it. Sometimes a page or two had been torn out but, as Meg had heard her mother mutter on occasion, "beggars can't be choosers."

Well, she certainly didn't consider herself a beggar, but she understood what her mother meant. "Don't look a gift horse in the mouth" was another way you could put it. Her mother was full of sayings like that. She said she had gotten them all from her parents. Meg had never really known her maternal grandparents. They both had died before she was two. She had seen pictures, of course, but looking at the pictures didn't tell her much about Harold and Eileen Donaldson, other than that they seemed pretty stern. But maybe they just hadn't liked having their picture taken. Her mother didn't like having her picture taken, but her father was always mugging for the camera. Like anyone would want a picture of him, with his missing front teeth and scraggly little beard and sagging stomach. Ugh.

A little yellow butterfly was fluttering around the kind of sad-looking roses her mother was trying to grow by the fence that separated their yard from the Pattersons'. Meg thought it would be nice to be an insentient thing like an insect, even if only for a day. All that mattered to an insect was that very moment, and the insect didn't even know that the moment mattered, just that the moment was . . . there. If she were a butterfly or even a mosquito she wouldn't be thinking ahead to the long summer months and wondering how the heck she was going to survive them. Because there wasn't much to look forward to this summer, not without Rosie's companionship. Not even the prospect of her fifteenth birthday in August excited her. There definitely would be no gift from Rosie or Mrs. Patterson, and certainly no handmade birthday card. And no birthday sleepover, either, where she and Rosie would try to stay awake all night but fall asleep by one or two o'clock. Gloomily, Meg wondered if anyone at all would send her a card. Her father usually forgot, though in past years Meg had overheard her mother on the phone reminding him that her birthday was coming up. So maybe it wasn't that he forgot to send her a card. Maybe it was that he just didn't want to. Petey would give her a card, something he had made with construction paper and glitter. Petey loved glitter.

The thought of her little brother brought a smile to Meg's face. Lately, the thought of Petey was the only thing that could. But the smile disappeared as rapidly as it had come. Since she had told Rosie's secret to Mackenzie and the others, which Mackenzie had then texted to almost everyone at school, Mrs. Patterson had refused to have anything to do not only with Meg and Mrs. Giroux, but also with Petey. Meg felt horrible guilt about that, but at the same time she felt angry that Mrs. Patterson could take out her anger on a totally innocent little boy. Maybe Meg deserved to be punished, but Petey certainly didn't. She was the one who had messed up.

How, how, how could she have been so awful? She had never planned to reveal Rosie's secret to anyone, ever. Her mother had taught her how important it was to keep your word as well as how important it was to keep a friend's secret. Unless, of course, it was a secret that could really get someone hurt, like a crime or something. And Rosie's secret certainly hadn't been dangerous. Well, only if it had remained a secret.

Meg would never forget that fateful day. She was in downtown Yorktide, window-shopping and trying to outrun a bad mood, when she spotted Mackenzie and Courtney and Jill standing outside the pharmacy. She had stopped in her tracks, her mind suddenly racing. Her feelings were a jumble of fear, frustration, and anger.

She was just so fed up with the whole situation. Rosie just never fought back when Mackenzie and the others bullied her. She never stood up for herself. Meg was so tired of trying to help and of being rebuffed. So many times she had been on the verge of taking matters into her own hands and telling her mother what was going on with Rosie and Mackenzie. It would solve everything, she thought. Her mother would tell Mrs. Patterson and then Mr. Patterson would step in and everything would come out into the light and . . .

And Rosie might never talk to her again. And Meg would have been branded a tattletale. And she might be dragged into whatever the Pattersons decided to do, like confronting Mackenzie and her father, Mr. Egan. . . . No, Meg had decided time and again, telling her mother would solve nothing. It would only complicate things. She had grown so angry with Rosie for putting her in this frustrating position. She felt like an accomplice to something wrong, but to what, exactly? To Rosie's self-destruction? That was sick. Rosie had pulled Meg into her nightmare.

And so, that day in downtown Yorktide, Meg had found herself walking toward the girls who had been making Rosie's life, and Meg's life, miserable for months. It was like some other Meg had taken over her mind and was operating her feet as she approached Mackenzie and her crew. She felt helpless to stop. She felt as if she were watching herself from a great distance, crying out, "No! Don't!" It was a terrible few moments.

And then she was standing in front of Mackenzie, Courtney, and Jill. She remembered Mackenzie sneering. "What do you want?" she had demanded, the emphasis on "you." Meg Giroux, loser friend of loser Rosie Patterson.

And then the words were coming out, almost but not entirely against her will. "Rosie Patterson used to wet her bed. Until, like, fifth grade."

The moment, no, the split second after she had spoken, Meg felt as if she were going to throw up.

"So?" Mackenzie had answered, looking to her cohorts and then back to Meg. "Why would we care?"

There was nothing Meg could say to that.

With a laugh to show just how pathetic they found her, the girls had walked away, leaving Meg standing rooted to the spot and still fighting nausea. How she made it home after that without getting hit by a car she couldn't recall. She did remember praying that nothing would happen as a result of her misconduct, that Mackenzie would just forget what she had told her and leave Rosie in peace. Once she was safely in her bedroom she actually got down on her knees like in church and begged God to hear her prayers.

But if God had indeed heard her prayers, He had chosen not to answer. The very next afternoon it seemed as if the entire school—at least, the entire ninth and tenth grades—knew that Rosie Patterson had wet her bed. And the only way that information could have gotten out was through Meg. There was absolutely no use in trying to deny her guilt. She had tried to apologize right then and there, at Rosie's locker, with kids swarming past, some of them laughing and pointing, but Rosie wouldn't even look at her. Even at the time Meg felt that it was more like Rosie couldn't look at her, that her shame and sadness were too great. Not anger. Meg would have preferred that Rosie punch her in the nose rather than look so . . . defeated. She had looked, Meg thought now, remembering, as if she had deserved the betrayal.

And that had been the last day of Rosie's normal ninth-grade life. She had completed her classes from home and missed out on all the end-of-the-year social events. Meg had participated in those events—a trip to Portland, Judy Smith's party, and the festivities at school—but without enthusiasm or interest. All she felt was shame. Her father had said nothing at all to her about the incident, even though Meg knew her mother had told him what had happened. Her mother had been seriously disappointed in her, though at least she had acknowledged that Meg's admitting her bad behavior right away was a good thing. Meg had accepted responsibility for her misdeed and her mother had forgiven her. But still, she felt lousy. It was good to feel genuine remorse, but it was not good to have done the thing for which you felt the remorse in the first place.

Meg looked at her hands on the chains of the swing and realized they were stained with rust. Somehow, to have dirty hands seemed appropriate, a symbol of her sin. She couldn't deny that she had betrayed her best friend to a bunch of thugs and yet, at the same time, she couldn't really believe that she had done it. Why had she been so stupid? What had she hoped to accomplish? The counselor her mother had made her see for a few weeks, someone from their church, Sister Pauline, a nun who wore jeans and T-shirts and earrings just like a normal person, had asked her that question more than once and other than the incredibly lame answer of "I don't know," all she could come up with was the almost as lame answer, "I wanted them to like me." It was all pretty pathetic, mostly the part she hadn't had the courage to tell Sister Pauline. That she had been mad at Rosie for not fighting back; that she had in some small way wanted to punish her friend for being . . . For being what? For being frightened. Yes, it was all pretty pathetic.

Well, whatever she had hoped to achieve, what she got in the end was no best friend and no nice and generous best friend's mother, and even Mr. Patterson didn't stop by anymore with his toolbox to see if anything needed fixing. Which meant that when something had gone wrong with the kitchen sink the week before, Meg's mother had had to call a plumber and spend who knew how much money she claimed not to have on a quick fix Mike Patterson could have done in five minutes and for free. Certainly Mrs. Giroux hadn't had the option of calling her ex-husband. Meg had known for years and years that her father was, in her mother's words, "pretty much useless around the house." Meg's opinion was that he was pretty much useless everywhere.

Abruptly, Meg got up from the swing and pushed it hard, jumping away as she did so. It flew wildly, the metal chains clanging against the structure's supports. Meg winced. She shouldn't be wasting time on a stupid swing set anyway. She would be fifteen in August, but sometimes she felt that she was still too much of a child. Judy Smith had a boyfriend. So did a few of the other girls who would be tenth graders in September. That was one of the things that had begun to frustrate Meg about Rosie back before all the bad stuff had started. Meg had wanted to talk about boys and maybe start dating, though she was pretty sure her mother wouldn't let her, not the way she ranted on about most men being bums. But Rosie hadn't been much interested in talking about guys or dating. She said that her parents wouldn't let her date until she was sixteen, maybe even seventeen, so there was no point in wasting a lot of time debating about who was the cutest guy in their grade or who was the hottest senior. They'd had a stupid fight, nothing major, but Rosie's lack of interest in guys and dating had pointed out to Meg that maybe their friendship wasn't as perfect as it had been when they were younger. Maybe they were growing apart a bit. The notion had not sat well with Meg. Although she had been annoyed with Rosie, the thought of life without her was too weird to contemplate. It was like trying to imagine your life without your right hand or something.

The swing had come to a stop and Meg headed back inside the house. She really had better get started on the housework. A lot of times her mother was in a bad mood when she got home from work. Finding the house a mess definitely wouldn't help. Not that she was afraid of her mother. Frannie Giroux's bark was way worse than her bite. It was just that Meg didn't like to be around anyone when they were in a bad mood. She had enough of her own bad moods to deal with, thank you very much.

Right before stepping inside the side door, Meg looked over her shoulder at Rosie's house. No one was in sight. Meg closed the door behind her. So what if Rosie wasn't really into boys or dating yet. So what if she preferred to watch an old black-and-white movie when Meg suggested they go shopping for makeup. Those things didn't really matter. What did matter was getting Rosie back into her life.

5

It had been one of those days. And in Frannie's opinion, there had been too many of "those days" lately. A traffic jam had come up out of nowhere, half of the office staff had mysteriously called in sick, and her intestines had been playing a game of Hacky Sack since noon. She had forgotten to bring in milk, and then had forgotten to ask Meg to pick up a carton, so at dinner Petey had had to drink orange juice. For some reason, this had struck him as a fate worse than death, which was odd, because Petey was the easy child. It was very unlike him to make a fuss about anything, but make a fuss he had. She would keep a close eye on him for the next day or two. Maybe he wasn't feeling well. Maybe some bigger kid at day camp was picking on him. The bullying epidemic loomed large in Frannie's mind these days.

Already in her worn and fraying flannel nightgown, Frannie left her room for the house's one bathroom. In a perfect world she would at least have a powder room on the first floor, but it was not a perfect world. Unflinchingly, she looked at her face in the mirror over the sink. Her eyes, once what her first boyfriend way back in high school had called chocolate brown, now looked downright muddy. Dark circles surrounded them and a spray of fine lines (Be real, she told herself, they're wrinkles) shot from the outer corners of both. Her complexion had muddied, too, in spite of using lots of moisturizer (generic brand, of course) each morning and night. She supposed she should have been using some product that claimed to lighten and brighten the skin, too, but it was too late now. Besides, what did it matter? She was pretty sure nobody really looked at her anymore, other than to see the cookie-cutter outline of Employee or Mother. And the last thing she wanted to do was date. No. Way. So what did it matter if Frances Giroux the person became invisible by the time she was forty? That was most women's fate, anyway, to fade away quietly. Frannie didn't have the energy to be one of those women who refused to go gently into social oblivion. Helen Mirren she was not.

Frannie sighed and turned to the process of brushing her teeth. She was only thirty-eight years old, but most times felt as if she were at least sixty. An old sixty, not a Helen Mirren kind of sixty-something. But unless a fairy godmother was going to magically offer her a free lifelong membership at a gym and an endless number of complimentary massages and facials, she was going to continue slogging along toward middle age with her wrinkles and sags and bulges. Amen. There were certainly more important matters with which to concern herself, like what had been going on with Meg. And like her own sense of responsibility and guilt.

Frannie turned out the light in the bathroom and walked back down the hall to her bedroom. As she passed Meg's room she noted that her light was still on. She hoped her daughter was reading something a little more substantial than a fashion magazine, like one of the books she was supposed to read for her new English teacher. Petey's light was out. He had fallen asleep right after dinner, another indication that something might be bothering him. *Or maybe,* Frannie thought, *I'm becoming a professionally nervous parent.*

She quietly closed the bedroom door behind her. Well, maybe she was right to be nervous. Their family situation often meant that Frannie didn't have the time to pay enough attention to her children, especially to her daughter, who was at that tender and often powder-keg age when the simplest incidents or the most innocent words could seem dire and dramatic and miscommunication between the old and young was the unfortunate norm.

Frannie pretty much collapsed into the bed she and Peter had bought when they were first married. Though she was bone tired, she knew within a minute of settling the light covers over her body that she would not be able to sleep for some time. Usually, she was snoring not long after her head hit the pillow (Meg had complained about the snores keeping her awake), but in the last weeks she had endured more and more near-sleepless nights. And a sleepless night did not make for a particularly easy day, especially not with Frannie's job. For the past ten years she had been employed as the office manager for a midsized lumber supplier and home improvement company called Le Roi Lumber and Homes. Appropriately enough, it was owned and operated by a family named King. The pay was decent and the job afforded her health insurance, which sometimes seemed more essential than the salary, like when you looked at what it cost to pay for a policy entirely on your own. But the hours were long and a few members of the office staff were incredibly incapable, kept on only because they were somehow related to the president of the company, Trip King, who wasn't exactly a rocket scientist himself. Still, she was thankful to have a job in the first place, especially with two children to support and little if any help from her ex-husband. Peter never had two nickels to rub together, and his asking for a loan and her refusing to give it was pretty much a monthly ritual. And on top of his fiscal irresponsibility, there was his general inability to be there for his children. His inability or his simple lack of interest or maybe even both.

Frannie sat up and adjusted the pillows behind her. How long had it been since she had replaced the pillows? She couldn't remember, which probably meant that it was time for new ones. These were probably full of dead skin and dust mites. Next time she found herself in South Portland—which could be quite some time; summer was her employer's busiest season and some weeks she found herself going in to the office on Saturday—she would stop in Marshalls or HomeGoods and see what was on sale.

She lay back down and sighed. Yes, Peter was useless in a situation like this, a family crisis. At least, he had been useless to date, and she didn't expect that to change. He wasn't a bad man, not really, just insensitive to emotional nuances, and also, she had to admit this, he was not the brightest bulb in the chandelier. And there was the cheating thing, too. Peter would never agree to go to therapy—not that he had the money for treatment—so Frannie had no idea if he was indeed a "sex addict." But he certainly had exhibited some seriously wayward behavior in the days of their marriage, and she wouldn't be at all surprised to learn he was still sowing his wild oats at the age of thirty-seven. Some women didn't mind a premature paunch and missing front teeth. Frannie knew she was being mean—like she was physically perfect!—but at that moment she didn't much care. She would admit such unkind thoughts to Father William when she next went to confession. But Father William had known Peter, albeit not very well. She doubted that deep in his heart he would condemn her for not thinking of her ex-husband with charity. Father William might be a priest, but he was a human being first.

Adjusting the pillows had not helped her to relax. And thinking about her ex-husband wasn't helping either, but she couldn't seem to stop.

To tell herself she should have known better than to marry the dubiously charming local boy with the spotty reputation didn't help matters. The fact was that she had married Peter when she was twenty-three and he was twenty-two. The following year she had given birth to Megan Christine. Almost eight years later, Peter Jr. had come along, unplanned, an accident, but welcomed. By then, the marriage was a sham, held together only by Frannie's willpower and the firm belief that divorce was fundamentally wrong and should be avoided at all costs. And then things had gotten really bad, with Peter losing his job and maxing out their credit card and taking up with a much younger woman with a drug habit, and reason and the instinct for survival had triumphed over her church's noble but unrealistic teachings. When Petey was barely two, Frannie kicked his father out of the house he was failing to pay for or maintain and began life as a single parent, which, in a way, she had been all along.

Maybe that was why Meg had acted so irresponsibly, Frannie thought now. Maybe she just hadn't been a good enough single parent. In all her reading she had yet to come across any study that identified kids from single-parent homes as necessarily more likely to bully or to betray a friend. Well, she hadn't yet come across such a study. Maybe that study was just waiting to hit her over the head with an accusation of failure.

Frannie looked over at the pile of books and magazines stacked on the night table. With few exceptions they were from the library, as her book- and magazine-buying budget was pretty pathetic. It was actually okay in this case because she didn't really want to keep all the information on such a grim topic as bullying in the house. It felt—contaminating.

The number of terms to learn and absorb was overwhelming—"relational aggression," "bullycide," "social contagion" (that was when nice kids joined in the bullying—was that what Meg had succumbed to, the disease of social contagion?), "potential defenders," "cyberbullying." So-called experts differed in their sometimes dubious, sometimes legitimate credentials as well as in their definitions of the types of bullies, though all seemed to agree about how a victim or a witness should respond to a bully. In short, walk away and tell an adult.

And the staggering statistics! Frannie had read in one of the magazines that every day an average of 16,000 children in the United States stayed home from school for fear of being bullied. Another source said that 30 percent of American kids were directly affected by bullying. Seriously, what the hell was going on? And the damn Internet wasn't helping matters, either. Children were being tortured in their own homes, the one place where traditionally they could feel safe and protected. It was insane. And it was criminal.

Of course, Frannie reflected, staring up at a new crack in the ceiling paint, the situation wasn't entirely hopeless. It seemed that every week someone was establishing an organization to educate students and their parents about bullying, how to prevent it, how to stop it, how to heal from it. And there were successful campaigns out there, like the "It Gets Better" effort. A band, Rise Against (Frannie had no idea who they were but had read about them), had teamed up with that campaign and had recorded a song called "Make It Stop (September's Children)" in which they called for the end of the kind of culture that fosters hate and bigotry. That had been after the rash of teen suicides in the fall of 2010.

Nickelodeon, which Frannie knew all too well from personal experience (if she never saw another episode of *SpongeBob SquarePants* it would be too soon) was very popular with kids and tweens, was running a two-year on-air public service campaign featuring some of the network's young stars. There were several activist groups in her own state of Maine pushing for a law to define and prevent bullying, and there was something called a "System-Wide Code of Conduct" that addressed bullying and harassment. Even the federal government was involved in the education effort. And not too long ago a New Hampshire boy had successfully petitioned the Boston Red Sox to make a video for the "It Gets Better" campaign in honor of his uncle, a gay man, who had recently died while traveling abroad.

That was all unarguably good stuff. But there were some aspects to the conversation surrounding the issue that worried Frannie. For example, some people in the anti-bullying industry were arguing that there was or should be no such thing as an "innocent bystander." They argued that it was every person's moral imperative to act to prevent, deter, or stop violence no matter the risk to personal health or happiness. That was a powerful ideal, but it was a tall order to expect a kid to act courageously when adults throughout history had failed—and continued to fail—to resist or criticize abuse. All you had to do was read the daily news to be reminded of human frailty. If you were really honest, all you had to do was look in the mirror each morning.

Frannie stretched her legs, toes pointed down, and felt instead of relaxation the beginnings of a cramp in her left calf. Quickly, she turned her toes up in the direction of her shins, hoping the cramp wouldn't fully materialize. It didn't. Good. Maybe if she exercised regularly her legs wouldn't cramp so often. Maybe if she exercised at all.

Like that was going to happen. Frannie sighed. Maybe what her daughter had done—betraying a friend's secret—would not be considered bullying by many people, but the results of her action, coming hard upon the terrorizing behavior of Mackenzie Egan and her gang, had undoubtedly pushed Rosie over the edge. Rosie had always been, from the very first, a quiet sort, a bit shy, a bit emotionally . . . delicate. Just like her mother, in fact. Before the girls were out of Pull-Ups, Meg had emerged as the leader of the two, the one who had walked first, the one who decided what toys they would play with, the one who jumped first into the pool while Rosie followed more carefully, using the ladder to ease her descent. Meg had given up her favorite stuffed animal, a plush little puffin named Puffy, by the time she was four. Rosie had carried around her favorite stuffed animal, a fluffy brown puppy named Harold, until she was eight. (Frannie had often wondered what sort of kid named a stuffed animal Harold. The answer seemed to be, a special sort of kid.)

No, Frannie decided again, her daughter should not be demonized. She was not evil. In a moment of adolescent weakness she had spilled a secret. She had done something wrong but not something demonic. She had confessed to Father William and had been absolved.

She had apologized to Rosie. What more could she do? There was no changing the past.

From her bed Frannie could see several lights on the second floor of the Pattersons' house. So, it looked as if she might not be the only one who couldn't sleep. It was probably Jane who was lying awake into the small hours. It was usually the woman who suffered the sleepless nights. Not always, but usually.

Frannie looked away from the Pattersons' house. She missed her best friend. She could barely remember her life before Jane Patterson. They had met almost fourteen years ago at a local mommy-and-me class. Jane had arrived on the first day carrying a new knockoff designer diaper bag; Frannie had arrived carrying a bag passed down from a neighbor who had used it for both of her children. It was old but clean and serviceable.

The women's differences, which were considerable, hadn't proved to be an obstacle to building a solid friendship. Frannie's mother had been a homemaker and her father had worked for a local utility company. She hadn't been able to afford college after high school, so instead, she had taken some classes in computer science and taught herself enough administrative skills to get and keep progressively decent jobs. She was smart and used to making do. Jane, whose mother had worked in an art gallery and whose father had been a lawyer, had grown up in a suburb of Boston and gone to a small arts-oriented college in New Hampshire. Later, she had earned a master's degree in the history of textiles. (That tidbit of information had amused Frannie for months. Imagine what her own parents would have said had she told them she was earning a degree in such a "useless" oddball topic!) Frannie loved the Red Sox with a passion. Jane couldn't even recognize a home run, though she did enjoy going to a Sea Dogs game as much as the next person. But Frannie suspected that for Jane, the outing was all about the chance to socialize and chat about what people were wearing, not about the final score.

And there were deeper differences than levels of education and a love of or indifference to baseball. Frannie, who had grown up in a fairly religious home, still considered herself a Catholic and attended Mass almost every Sunday and certainly on the holidays. At Peter's nagging insistence she hadn't forced a religious education on the children, though both Meg and Petey had been baptized and Meg had gone to an after-school religious education program so that she could receive her First Holy Communion. Anyway, there wasn't even a Catholic grammar or high school within ten miles of their home, not since the Church had hemorrhaged so much money in the past few years, paying off its emotional debts. Frannie had done her soul searching and had come to the conclusion that while the institution of the Church might be in many ways corrupt, and while some of its decrees were impossible for her to accept (No women priests? Come on! No gay marriage? What was that about?), there were plenty of good and faithful people, herself included, who should not be denied the solace and tradition offered by the community in which they had come to maturity. She had made her separate peace, which included requiring her children to accompany her to Mass whether they understood all that was going on or not.

Jane, on the other hand, considered herself an agnostic. She liked to say that she had been brought up in the First Church of Suburbia. She also claimed not to remember or maybe never even to have known the church's actual denomination. "Something vaguely Christian," she had said. "Nothing extreme. Nothing really memorable, either. No pomp, and certainly no circumstance."

"Was there even a cross?" Frannie had asked, slightly appalled, the first time Jane had talked about her past.

Jane had considered for a moment before saying, "I think so."

What the two women did have in common was intelligence, a devotion to family, a generous spirit, and, if Frannie was being honest, a real need for each other. That was enough to unite them and keep them together for almost fourteen years. The Pattersons moving into the house right next door to the Giroux family when the girls were about six further cemented the bond that had begun to form over hand-clapping games and diaper rash remedies. True, Mike and Peter had never been close. In fact, from the start Frannie had the impression that Mike only tolerated Peter for her sake. Certainly, after Peter had moved out, Mike hadn't spoken more than a passing word or two to him when he showed up to beg for a loan or to retrieve something important he claimed to have left behind. (That was really an excuse to make off with an object he could sell for some quick cash.)

And now, after all the two families had been through together—the childhood illnesses, Jane's miscarriages, the birthdays, the holidays, the first day of school, her own disruptive divorce and its aftermath—to have it all come to this horrible state of anger and betrayal and distrust sickened Frannie.

Frannie sighed and reached for the switch on the bedside lamp. If she had to lie awake well into the night, she might as well do it in the dark and keep the electricity bill within budget.

6

November 5, 2011

Dear Diary,

In the past few days, things have been kind of weird between Meg and me. This girl Jill Harrison, one of Mackenzie Egan's friends, told a bunch of people about a video that's going around online that's supposed to be really sexy. I'm not sure what Meg means by its being "sexy," like if it's a music video or what. Anyway, Meg asked me if she could check it out at my house because she didn't want her mom somehow finding out or her brother coming into her room while she was online. But when she told me about it I said no. Not just because my mom and dad wouldn't want me to watch the video but also because I just didn't feel right about it.

Meg was all, "But everyone is checking it out!" and I just laughed. Since when does she care about doing what everyone else is doing? Besides, I seriously doubt "everyone" is checking it out. Anyway, I said, "No, thanks," again and then she wanted to know if I was going to tell on her. I was totally shocked and really hurt, but I didn't say anything. How could Meg think I'd ever tell on her? I'm her best friend. I might not like something she does, but unless it's some sort of horrible crime—which Meg would never do, anyway—I'd never give her away! Never. Just like Meg has kept my big secret for years now and would never, ever tell anyone. I know that for certain, like I know that my name is Rosemary Alice Patterson.

Anyway, the long story short is that I guess Meg went ahead and checked out the video, but I have no idea whose computer she used or if she did it by herself or with someone else. I kind of want to know and I kind of don't want to know. I'm certainly not going to ask her! I think she's sort of mad at me for not going along with her or helping her out. I hope she's not but I think she is.

As for my big sister, I haven't seen Carly in weeks, except for glimpsing her across the cafeteria at lunchtime. But that's okay because I'm doing fine. Meg's big sister gave her a crinkly cotton scarf she didn't want anymore. I didn't even know that Meg liked scarves, but she's been wearing it ever since, so I guess she does. And it's orange, which I always thought Meg hated! I wonder if she just likes it because it was Tiffany's.

That sounds kind of mean. Sorry. I guess I'm still a little upset about the video incident. I shouldn't be because I know I did the right thing not letting Meg use our computer. But I am. I don't like to make anyone unhappy, and I guess that this time I did. Mom and Dad have always taught me that following your conscience isn't always easy. They were right.

Oh, this is news! In gym class I actually made a basket in basketball! It was the first time I ever even came close and this girl Kylie joked it would probably be the last time, too. She's probably right!

It's already been below freezing three times—at night—and it's only the beginning of November! Brrr. I don't like the cold that much, but I love the holiday season. I love all the decorating! Finding the perfect tree and then putting all the special ornaments on it is my favorite thing ever. We have one ornament from my mother's mother, my grandmother Rosemary. It's made of pink glass and has a kind of glitter all over it that looks like sugar frosting. It's my absolute favorite ornament. I hope that when I'm older and have my own tree, Mom passes it down to me. But if she doesn't want to, I'll understand.

This year for Christmas I'm asking for a hardcover copy of THE GOLDEN COMPASS. It's the first in a trilogy called His Dark Materials by a writer named Philip Pullman. I read it last summer and loved it. I kept imagining that I was Lyra, the heroine, though she's an awful lot braver than I am. Anyway, it was a library book, so of course I couldn't keep it. I'm going to read and someday own the other two books in the trilogy, too. The second one is called THE SUBTLE KNIFE and the third is THE AMBER SPYGLASS. How do people come up with such interesting titles? How can a knife be subtle? That sounds so interesting. Maybe someday I'll meet an actual writer and ask how they come up with titles and how they find their ideas.

I should go now. I really want to watch this special about the Vatican art collection on TV tonight, but I won't be allowed unless my homework is done. I am so going to Italy when I'm older. Mom went to Italy and to France for almost the entire summer between college and graduate school and I love looking at all the pictures she took, though I can hardly recognize her with such short hair. I can't wait to visit the Louvre in Paris and see the Mona Lisa up close and to see Michelangelo's statue of David, the original one, in Florence. And the food in France and Italy is supposed to be amazing and you know how I love to eat!

Arrivederci! Au revoir!
Your friend, Rosie

November 17, 2011
Dear Diary,

Thanksgiving is next week. Every time the holidays come around I think about how it would be nice to have a big fam-

ily. You see those commercials on TV with everyone gathered around a big table, kids and grandparents and aunts and uncles and cousins, and everyone's laughing and joking and teasing each other and it all looks like a lot of fun, people pretending to fight over the last crescent roll. (I love crescent rolls!)

I'm not complaining. I love my mom and dad. I just wish we had more family. I don't know why Mom didn't have more kids after me. I've never asked and I don't think I should, at least not until I'm older. Maybe someday she'll tell me on her own. Maybe she and Dad just didn't want any more children. But if that's the case, I wonder why.

My dad's brother and his wife live outside of Boston, but Dad and Uncle Rob aren't close and now that Uncle Rob and Aunt Jean have a baby—my cousin Alison, who I've never even seen!—they don't want to come to Maine, especially in the bad weather. At least, that's what Mom says. I guess I can understand that. Who wants to get caught on the road in a snowstorm? (Dad keeps all sorts of stuff in our car in case of an emergency in winter, stuff like blankets and flashlights and bottled water.)

I also wish I had a dog. I really want one but Mom says I'm too young for the responsibility of a pet (I am NOT too young! I'm fourteen!). Dad never had a pet, not even a goldfish, growing up so he just doesn't understand why a dog is so important to me. Sigh. When I'm an adult and living on my own I'll have three dogs and three cats and maybe a ferret. Unless cats eat ferrets, in which case I guess I won't be getting a ferret! I'll get all my animals from a shelter, of course. Just thinking about those poor animals in those cages, waiting to be adopted, breaks my heart. When those commercials come on TV, showing all those poor abused animals and asking for support for shelters, I have to close my eyes and put my hands over my ears. A few months ago Mom and I gathered up some old but clean towels (it was my idea after I saw an appeal in the paper) and took them to a shelter in South Portland. The shelter uses the towels as beds for the animals in their cages. Mom went inside with the towels while I waited in the car. I just knew I would start to cry if I went in with her and couldn't leave with a dog.

We got our history papers back today. Ms. Moore told me that I got the only A in the class. The only one I told about the A—aside from my parents!—was Meg because we always share our grades and stuff. She got a B+, which is also pretty good. She usually does way better than me in math class, even though I study like mad. I guess math just isn't my strong point. She's the only person I know who's actually looking forward to learning calculus! I'm trying to figure out a way to avoid it.

This is kind of weird. Meg told me that Ginny Doherty (a girl in her advanced math class) told her that Michael Perkins thinks I'm pretty. I don't believe it. Michael Perkins is really cute and besides, he's a sophomore. He could go out with any sophomore girl he wanted to, and lots of them are way prettier than I am. Like Mackenzie Egan, though I don't know if she already has a boyfriend. I've never seen her with a boy. I hope word doesn't get around about Michael Perkins thinking I'm pretty, because it has to be a lie. He's never even looked at me! I wouldn't want anyone to think I'm being stuck-up because a boy supposedly likes me.

Anyway, it was a pretty good week. I hope I get an A on the next history paper, too. I would hate to slip back a grade, or even half a grade. Ms. Moore would be disappointed, not to mention Mom and Dad. And me! One of my father's favorite expressions is "There's no excuse for laziness." I guess he's right.

About Thanksgiving again. I was hoping that Meg and her family would be coming here for dinner, but Meg told me they have to go up to Norridgewock for the day to see her father's older sister who is really sick. Meg's only met her aunt Linda once or twice but her mom thinks going to visit is the right thing to do because even though Mr. and Mrs. Giroux are divorced, they're still in some way family. And besides, this might be the last time they get to see Aunt Linda. She's got some aggressive cancer, which is very sad, especially because she's only around fifty. (Meg says that's old but it's not. I think the idea of older people frightens her in some way.) Meg's not happy about going, but unless she pretends to be sick on Thanksgiving morning, she's going to have to go. Besides, Mrs. Giroux is way too smart to fall for a lie!

So that means it's just Mom, Dad, and me for Thanksgiving. They don't have any close friends they could invite, and neither do I, other than Meg, of course, so . . . I wonder why Mom and Dad don't have other good friends. They're nice and smart and all and they each know lots of people through their businesses. But even the women in Mom's book club aren't really her friends. Two of them are clients and one woman she knows from back in Boston, though she says they weren't close. They took a class together once at the MFA, that's all.

I know why I don't have other good friends. Meg is the only friend I need.

You know what I just thought about? I wonder if Mom had a best friend growing up like I have Meg. She's never told me about anyone. Maybe I should ask her. But if something bad happened between them she might not want to talk about it, so maybe I won't say anything.

Oh, well. On Thanksgiving we'll watch the parade on TV, the big one from New York, and Mom will make her famous apple pie and those mashed turnips I love and we'll have a nice time. Dad's not so into the turnips, but he'll eat some for Mom's sake. And he'll have two pieces of pie! He has such a sweet tooth, just like Meg. Mom doesn't know this but I know that he keeps a box of Count Chocula in his office! He hides it in the bottom drawer of his desk. It's fun to have a little secret with Dad.

I have to go and do my homework now. Mr. Wall, our science teacher, gave us an extra-credit assignment that I'm going to finish before the weekend. Meg thinks I'm crazy to voluntar-

ily take on more work, but Mom and Dad are glad about it (they say any extra work might help me get into a good college) and I really don't mind. I probably don't do enough extracurricular stuff, though. Maybe I should be worried about that. But I really don't like sports. Maybe I should check out ways I could volunteer. There's some sort of nursing home in Wells. Maybe I could volunteer there. I like older people. I wish I had grandparents. The only problem is that Mom or Dad would have to drive me to the nursing home and back, and I don't want to cause trouble for them. I'll have to think about it.

But first—homework! See you soon.

Your friend, Rosie

7

Rosie went out into the backyard carrying a small basket of laundry to hang on the line her dad had strung up between the patio and a large oak tree in the middle of the yard. She went about clipping a pair of her mom's linen shorts to the line, unaware that Meg had come to stand at the fence that separated her backyard from the Pattersons'.

"Hi," Meg called out, startling Rosie into almost dropping a pair of her own clean, damp jeans onto the concrete patio. She finished attaching the pants to the laundry line and slowly turned around. She wasn't sure why she had. She did not return the greeting. She was determined not to talk to Meg. Besides, there was nothing she wanted to say.

"It's nice out today, isn't it?" Meg went on. "Not like yesterday. I thought it would never stop raining." She laughed then, a nervous kind of laugh.

Rosie turned back to her task. There was one final item to hang.

"I mean, we were afraid the basement would flood. But it didn't, so that was good."

Still, Rosie said nothing.

"Rosie, please talk to me."

Rosie whipped around, clutching a damp T-shirt in her fist. "I don't have to talk to you," she blurted, surprising herself by replying.

"I know you don't have to." Meg's voice quavered. "I just thought that, I don't know, you might want to."

"Why?" Rosie demanded.

Meg fidgeted with a thin braided bracelet around her left wrist. "Because . . . Because I said I was sorry and I meant it. I still mean it."

Rosie stood looking at her friend—her former friend—and could think of nothing else to say unless it was that the shirt Meg was wearing was a pretty color, like vibrant pink azaleas. But of course, she couldn't tell her that. Meg had totally messed things up for the two of them. Frustrated, confused, and a little bit angry, she quickly clipped the T-shirt to the laundry line, picked up the empty basket, and without a backwards glance went inside the house.

Rosie tramped down to the basement to return the laundry basket to its home on the shelf above the washing machine. And then she leaned against the machine, suddenly feeling too tired to climb back up to the first floor. Or maybe "tired" wasn't the right word. Maybe "confused" or "dispirited" was a more accurate way to describe what she was feeling.

Meg had apologized to her a few weeks ago and she had told Meg that she accepted her apology. But did that mean she had actually forgiven her? Maybe accepting an apology and forgiving a person weren't the same thing. If they were the same thing, then maybe she had lied to Meg. Maybe her "Okay, I accept your apology" had been just an automatic reply, the words she assumed everyone had wanted to hear. If that was the case, then those words hadn't solved anything and certainly hadn't healed any wounds.

Rosie put her hands over her eyes. Why was she the one who was supposed to make everything all right again? She wasn't the one who had broken a solemn promise to her best friend. She was the one who had been betrayed and humiliated in front of her classmates. It wasn't her responsibility to wave the magic wand so that everything could go back to the way it used to be.

Rosie dropped her hands to her side. Still, she couldn't help but admit to herself that part of her missed Meg. But every time she thought about the friendship she had lost—which was a lot of times—she tried ruthlessly to push the memories away. She couldn't help but feel that missing the friendship of the person who had betrayed her only proved that she was a loser. Her own weakness embarrassed her. She hadn't even admitted these feelings to Dr. Lowe.

Only months ago she could have written her thoughts in her diary and that would have helped her figure things out, but she had abandoned the diary just after Meg's betrayal. Somehow it had stopped feeling like a safe and private space. If Meg could tell her deep dark secret to those girls, who was to say she or someone else couldn't find her diary and expose all her thoughts to the world? Even if her thoughts weren't so unusual, they were still hers and hers alone. That meant something.

Her therapist, Dr. Lowe, had been urging her to start her diary again. She said that "free-form journaling" was supposed to help you name your anger. It was supposed to help you come to understand that anger and channel it somewhere else or whatever. But something was holding Rosie back from taking that step. Her old diaries, including the last one with the entries about

Mackenzie's campaign to torture her and the final entry about Meg's betrayal, were now kept out of sight in a plastic storage box under her bed. Sometimes, in particularly bad moments, Rosie thought she should burn the diaries in the living room fireplace or shred all the pages and dump them off the cliffs on Marginal Way. It would be as if the dairies had never existed. But she never acted on those impulses. Besides, to dump the torn pages in the ocean would be littering, and she could get in trouble with the police. Or maybe a wild bird or a fish would accidentally eat some of the pieces of paper and choke. That would be horrible. She could never live with knowing she had hurt an innocent animal.

Rosie touched the scars on her left arm through the sleeve of her cotton blouse, then abruptly pulled her hand away. She didn't like to feel the scars, but sometimes she couldn't resist the urge to affirm that they were still there. It was upsetting and it was another thing she had yet to talk to Dr. Lowe about. With a sigh, she pushed off the washing machine and went back upstairs and into the kitchen. Her mother was there, at the sink, washing out the vegetable bin.

"Do you want something to eat?" her mother asked.

"No," Rosie said, wondering why she hadn't just gone straight to her room. "Thanks."

"You didn't have much of a breakfast."

Rosie bit back an impatient remark. "I'm fine," she said.

Minutes of silence followed as Jane finished scrubbing the plastic bin and then reached for a paper towel with which to dry it.

"I saw you talking to Meg out back," she said when she had returned the clean bin to the fridge.

Rosie tensed but said nothing in reply.

Jane leaned against the sink and looked carefully at her daughter. "What did she say to you?"

"Nothing."

"She had to have said something."

Rosie sighed. Since when, she wondered, had her mother become so annoying? "Fine. She said they were worried about their basement flooding yesterday."

"That's it?" Jane asked.

"And she said that her apology was sincere."

"What did you say to her?"

"Nothing." Rosie took a dish towel from a drawer by the sink and started to dry the few already dry plates in the drainer.

"Do you believe that Meg is truly sorry?" Jane asked.

Rosie shrugged. She wasn't sure how to answer that question.

"You know, Rosie, you don't have to forgive Meg, but you might feel better if you did."

Rosie turned to face her mother. "How would I feel better?" she demanded.

"Well," Jane replied, "you would feel better in lots of ways. For one, studies have shown that when a person forgives someone who did something hurtful to them, her blood pressure goes down and she feels less anxious and more empowered."

"So?" Since when, Rosie thought, had her mother started talking like a textbook?

"So," Jane said, "it's a health issue, for one, physical and emotional. I'm sure Dr. Lowe can tell you more about it."

Rosie tossed the dish towel onto the kitchen table. "Are you sticking up for Meg?" she cried. "Next you're going to tell me I have to invite Mackenzie Egan over for dinner! Or ask Courtney Parker to stay overnight!"

"No, no, Rosie," her mother protested, "please. I'm

not sticking up for Meg and I'm not suggesting you have anything to do with Mackenzie Egan and her clique. I'm not. All I'm suggesting is that you think about forgiving Meg. You don't have to be her friend again. Just—forgive her."

Rosie didn't say anything for some moments. "Do I have to see Dr. Lowe every week?" she asked finally. The question was a bit of a test. Rosie wasn't entirely sure why she had asked it. She wanted to see Dr. Lowe every week.

"Yes," Jane said firmly. "Your father and I think it's a good idea. You like her, right?"

"She's okay." Rosie was lying. Dr. Lowe was more than just okay. But for some weird reason she didn't want her mother to know that. She wanted Dr. Lowe to be entirely her own.

"Do you feel she's helping you understand things?" Jane asked.

"Yeah," Rosie said. "I guess. Yes."

"Good."

Rosie looked closely at her mother. "You look like you want to say something else," she said.

Jane shrugged. "Just that, you know, I think we should understand that Mackenzie Egan must be a very sad person. Only people who feel bad about themselves feel the need to hurt other people."

"How do you know what Mackenzie feels?" Rosie shot back. "Did you read that in one of your books, about bullies feeling bad about themselves? Maybe she thinks she's so great that she has the right to make other people feel awful and left out."

"I don't think that's likely," Jane said calmly. "Look, Rosie, whatever the truth is about Mackenzie, she's not the one I care about. I care about you and I want you to be happy again."

Rosie looked away from her mother's searching gaze. "I'm going to my room," she said.

"Wait, Rosie. It's such a nice day out, especially after all that rain yesterday. Maybe we could take a drive to the beach. Or maybe we could—"

"No thanks," she said, already out of the kitchen. Once in her bedroom, Rosie shut and locked the door. She knew her mother meant well but lately, Rosie just wished her mother would stop trying so hard to make everything all right again. She knew her mother felt guilty for not having known what was happening to her. She had confessed as much. She had told Rosie that she more than anyone was to blame for driving Rosie to despair. *Fine. Let her feel guilty if she wants to. Now,* Rosie thought, *she should just leave me alone.*

And all that talk about forgiveness! No one could force her to be friends again with Meg. No one could force her to forgive. Dr. Lowe had told her that forgiveness was something she didn't owe to anybody other than herself. And that was a confusing enough idea to deal with right now, why she should need to forgive herself.

Rosie lay down on the neatly made bed and folded her hands over her stomach. She always made her bed, even on Saturdays and Sundays. She supposed she enjoyed the ritual of pulling the sheets tight and smoothing the comforter. Unlike Meg. Mrs. Giroux said that to get Meg to make her bed was like pulling teeth. Clearly, it was something unpleasant. But maybe Meg didn't like to make her bed because she was such a violent sleeper. In the morning the covers were in a giant swirl half-hanging off the mattress. Rosie, on the other hand, barely moved all night. Her father used to say she looked like an Egyptian mummy while she slept, completely still and limbs ordered. Meg would sometimes wind up with her head at the foot of her bed and her feet up on the headboard. Rosie had seen it.

Would she never stop thinking about Meg Giroux! Rosie sighed and turned onto her side. She wondered why she had responded to Meg earlier in the backyard. She had sworn not to say a word, but then she had. She had sworn not to think so much about her. Sometimes it felt that she was in control of nothing at all in her life. The cutting had made her feel better, more in charge, at least for isolated moments. But she was done with that. The memories disgusted her. Rosie put her right hand on her left arm in a gesture of protection, closed her eyes, and willed the memories to go away, at least so that she could get some sleep.

8

Jane scrubbed at the wooden cutting board with a green scratchy pad, vaguely aware that she had already scrubbed the board after breakfast. She would wear a crater into the wood if she went on this way, but she couldn't seem to stop. Cleaning didn't keep the sad thoughts at bay, but somehow it made them more tolerable. She wondered what Dr. Lowe would have to say about that. She would probably label her obsessive-compulsive or say that she was deflecting or burying her feelings. Well, that was just the way it was. Organization and discipline kept chaos at bay. Repeat continually.

Since her brief, somewhat heated conversation with Rosie yesterday afternoon, Jane had been feeling uncomfortable. When Mike got home from work she had told him about what had gone on between Meg and Rosie over the backyard fence, and then about her own failed attempt at—at what? What had she really been trying to say to Rosie?

Mike had considered for a while before saying, "I'm not sure it's the best thing for Rosie that she talk to Meg, but I'm also not sure it's the worst thing."

"But she was upset!" Jane had argued.

Mike, ever the rational one, had pointed out that Rosie's being upset at this early stage of her recovery was totally normal. She had a lot to be angry about.

"Look," he added, "she's going to come around on her own schedule, no matter what we want from her. And she's going to make her own decisions regarding Meg. I'm not sure we should be hovering over her, watching or directing. If she needs to talk to someone, she knows she can come to us. And she's got Dr. Lowe. Let's allow the doctor to do her job."

"But I feel so helpless," Jane had admitted, remembering that Rosie most certainly had not come to either of her parents the last time she was dealing with a difficult issue. "And so horribly guilty."

The look on her husband's face then had startled Jane. She had never seen such raw anguish there.

"I do, too, Jane," he had said. "Believe me. Some mornings I wake up and think it all had to be a nightmare. I wonder, where the hell was I, not to see my own daughter deteriorating before my very eyes? What kind of man lets down his own child that way? I know no parent is perfect, but right now, I would do anything to turn back the clock and be given another chance to prove I'm not the lousiest father ever."

They had hugged then and the conversation had drifted away, nothing concluded, only guilt confirmed. The depth of Mike's pain continued to haunt Jane. Until that moment he must have been hiding his grief for her sake, and realizing that made her feel even worse. She felt that she had been a failure as a wife and partner. She hadn't been there for him when he might have needed her, so absorbed was she in her own misery and self-blame.

Jane sighed and thoroughly rinsed the green scratchy

pad. She reached for two lengths of paper towel and went about drying the wooden cutting board, then carefully put the used paper towels into the trash.

Jane turned her attention to the toaster. No matter how many times she cleaned the tray, a few crumbs continued to lurk. It was probably her fault that Rosie hadn't wanted to talk that morning, Jane thought as she rinsed the offending toaster tray. "Fine" and "okay" weren't very informative responses. But she had pushed Rosie too far the day before, suggesting that she try to forgive Meg. Maybe Meg didn't even deserve forgiveness. In the course of her recent reading Jane had learned that some people argued that no one deserved forgiveness. They argued that forgiveness was a gift given freely from one person to another. But Meg was only a child, and no matter how angry Jane was with her, she found it difficult to say that Meg didn't deserve forgiveness. Meg's mother . . . Well, that was a different story.

At least I didn't quote Gandhi at my daughter, Jane thought as she returned the tray to the toaster. Teenagers just loved to be lectured! Gandhi had said, "The weak can never forgive. Forgiveness is the attribute of the strong." Those words had been haunting her for weeks. She wasn't sure if she agreed with them. If Rosie couldn't or wouldn't forgive Meg for her betrayal, did that really mean she was a weak person? And if Jane herself couldn't or wouldn't forgive Frannie and Meg, did that mean that she was also weak? Or did it mean that the standards of good behavior to which she held other people as well as herself accountable were admirably high?

Jane went to the small, narrow pantry Mike had built for her just after they bought the house. There was little doubt that every can and bottle and jar was in its proper place, but ascertaining that fact was always comforting. Her eyes roamed each shelf in turn, from left to right, slowly, so as not to miss anything. And while she confirmed the order of the pantry, she realized she had been glad to see Rosie express some much-justified anger after her encounter with Meg the day before. But at the same time, Jane absolutely didn't want her daughter to be provoked into negative feelings that might disrupt her healing process. Rosie had stayed locked in her room all yesterday afternoon and had refused to eat the dinner Jane had taken up to her on a tray. Even Mike hadn't been able to coax her downstairs with the promise of a game of Scrabble, or even with the suggestion they watch the original black-and-white movie version of *Wuthering Heights*. It was one of Rosie's favorite movies; she had asked for a copy of it on DVD for her tenth birthday.

Jane closed the pantry door. Except for a small glass bottle of vanilla extract that was on the wrong side of the bottle of almond extract—items read alphabetically from left to right—the pantry was in perfect order. She wished she knew what was being said in Dr. Lowe's office at that very moment. (Mike had an errand to run in Portsmouth, so he had taken Rosie to Kittery and would pick her up after her session.) But the sessions were inviolate. Short of some dreadful criminal revelation, their contents would remain between Rosie and her counselor.

Jane stood in the middle of the kitchen, hands at her side. There was work to do for a client and she knew she should be attending to it, but she just couldn't seem to make her way downstairs to her sewing room. Not until she went through with the mission she had set for herself.

Everything in her world might be in a state of confusion, but one thing Jane did know for sure. She did not want Meg accosting her daughter again. Well, maybe "accosting" was too strong a word to describe what Meg had done in trying to have a conversation with Rosie, but Jane was taking no chances. Even though Mike thought they should neither hover nor direct, Jane was fully prepared to do both. She would tell him what she had done later, when he got home from the office. Maybe.

Jane looked out of the window over the sink at the Giroux house. The house needed painting. And the roof didn't look quite right, either. It looked like it was sagging a bit over the living room. Mike would know about that, and about what it would cost to get it repaired. Even when Peter had lived there the Giroux house had begun to get run down. No matter how Frannie had begged, pleaded, and finally, nagged her husband to keep up with the basic maintenance, he had refused. Or maybe he just hadn't listened to his wife in the first place. Peter Giroux was the kind of man who believed that he was superior to all women, no matter how intelligent, simply because he had man parts.

Jane shuddered. She had often wondered why Frannie and Peter had gotten together in the first place, let alone married. Well, she hadn't known either of them when they had first met. Maybe Peter had once displayed some actual charm. She doubted it, but anything was possible. Anyway, it wasn't a question she could just come right out and ask Frannie, was it? "You married a jerk. Why?"

Jane turned away from the window and slid open the silverware drawer to ascertain that every fork, knife, and spoon was in its proper place. Satisfied, she closed the drawer and for the first time in ages actually noticed the small ceramic plaque hanging on the wall just above. Frannie had given it to her years ago. Inside a painted border of hyacinths were the words "Friends Are Forever." Without a thought Jane yanked the plaque off the wall. No, she thought, friends are not forever. This is a lie. She carried the plaque to the trash can, fully intending to jam it deep inside, but her hand hesitated. She couldn't do it. She hated herself for not having the nerve or the courage or whatever it was that would allow her to throw away the plaque for good. Instead, she stuck the small plaque in the back of the drawer where she stored the dish towels. Out of sight, out of mind.

No, Jane thought, closing the drawer tightly, friends were not forever, not when they betrayed you. Not when their children hurt your children.

Jane had not spoken to Frannie since Meg's awkward apology in the Patterson living room. Actually, it had been fairly easy to avoid Frannie. She left her house and came back to it every day at set times, at least during the week. Weekends had proved a bit more difficult. Schedules weren't as set, and they often changed. Jane felt slightly ridiculous peeping through the curtains before she left the house on a Saturday or Sunday, hoping that Frannie wasn't about to mow the lawn, hoping she wasn't about to get into her car to go to church.

But now, Jane thought, taking a deep breath and walking with determination out of the kitchen and to the front door, it was time for a confrontation. Meg had seen to that with her unwelcome presence.

The short walk from Jane's home to the Giroux home seemed like her own version of no-man's-land. Her stomach twitched and her heart began to race. How many times over the years had she made this journey with a light heart, anticipating the welcome that awaited her? Certainly too many times to count.

Frannie opened the door almost immediately. Jane couldn't help but wonder if Frannie had seen her coming across the yard. She looked more tired than usual.

There were dark circles under her eyes and her hair looked lank, as if it hadn't been washed in a day or two. Jane felt a flash of concern—only habit, she told herself—and tried to ignore it.

"Jane," Frannie said, offering a tentative smile. "It's good to see you."

When Jane didn't respond, Frannie gestured behind her. "Would you like to come in?" she asked.

"No," Jane said. She was aware that she was holding her arms stiffly by her sides and that there was a purposeful steadiness in her tone. "I'm here to ask you—to tell you—to keep Meg away from my daughter. She upset Rosie yesterday."

Frannie's brief smile died on her lips and Jane thought she saw her grip on the door tighten. "What did she do?" Frannie asked. "What did Rosie say she did?"

"Nothing specific," Jane admitted. "Meg just wanted to talk. But that was enough to upset Rosie for the rest of the day."

"I'm sorry that Rosie . . . got upset," Frannie said after a moment. "But maybe it would help if the girls did talk to each other. Seriously, Jane, maybe if we encouraged them to talk it all out, then—"

"No," Jane retorted. "I don't agree at all. I think they should have nothing to do with each other. So does Mike."

That last part was an outright lie, but Frannie didn't need to know that.

Frannie briefly put her hand to her forehead, as if to confirm a pain there. "I'll talk to Meg when she gets home from the library," she said.

Jane nodded and turned to leave. And there was Petey where he hadn't been moments before, sitting cross-legged on the Giroux front lawn, playing with some sort of plastic action figure.

"Hi, Aunt Jane," he said as she walked toward him. Petey had called her Aunt Jane since he could first talk.

Jane wondered if Frannie was still at the door, watching this encounter, or if she had retreated inside the house. She smiled awkwardly at the little boy. Of course she felt bad about being forced to abandon Petey because of his sister's careless actions, but she just didn't see any other way.

Jane willed a smile to her face. "Hi, Petey," she said, hoping he didn't hear the strain in her voice.

Petey squinted in the strong afternoon sun. Jane wondered if he had a pair of sunglasses, but doubted that he did. "I saw you talking to my mom," he said.

"Yes. I had something to ask her."

"Oh. Are you going home now?"

"Yes," she said. "I have a lot of work to do this afternoon."

"Okay."

Jane hesitated. She was torn between wanting to race away and to stay longer with the little boy. "How's day camp?" she asked, noting that his T-shirt was one he had been wearing for at least two years now. It was clean but tight and the neckline was a bit frayed.

Petey smiled, but Jane thought there was something guarded now in his smile. Or maybe she was imagining it.

"It's good," he said. "We're going to a pool tomorrow."

"I'm glad you're having a nice time. Well, I have to go home now, so . . ." With a little wave, Jane continued on to her own home. Her face felt heated. It might have been anger but more likely, she thought, it was shame.

Jane went straight to the backyard patio and sank into a chair at the small wrought iron table. She made certain that she chose a chair facing away from the Giroux property. She couldn't bear to catch another glimpse of Petey. She sighed and rubbed her forehead. The stand of bright orange daylilies and the profusion of pink and white lilies she had so lovingly planted and nurtured failed to boost her spirits as they so often did.

The confrontation had been even more difficult than Jane had imagined it would be. She hadn't expected to be moved by it. She thought she had thoroughly hardened her heart against Frannie. But it seemed that she still felt a bit of sympathy for her. Being a single parent was never easy, and it was even harder when a person didn't have any support from her ex-husband. Even when Frannie was still married to Peter she had shouldered almost all of the family's burdens, from financial to domestic. And yet, she had always made time for Jane and her family. When Jane had been sick during the pregnancies that had ended in miscarriage, Frannie had watched Rosie for hours on end, feeding and changing her right along with her own daughter. That sort of kindness and generosity was hard to forget.

Jane wished she could shake off the treacherous feelings of sympathy. To forgive Frannie for her part in Meg's actions would be tantamount to a betrayal of her own daughter. Wouldn't it? How did you parcel out the blame in a situation like this? Frannie might argue that she wasn't at all to blame for Meg's actions, but wasn't a parent always responsible to some extent for what her child did or said, or for what her child didn't do or didn't say? Except, maybe, in cases where the child was mentally unstable and unable to decide between right and wrong, which was certainly not the case with Meg. Meg had always been—or had always seemed to be—a levelheaded girl, responsible beyond her years. If she had ever felt any resentment or anger about her home situation, she certainly hadn't shown those emotions to

Jane, or, as far as Jane knew, to anyone. Maybe that was the problem. . . .

Jane pressed her lips together. No. She was not going to excuse Meg's behavior as the result of a difficult home life. Everyone faced pressures and trials. Besides, Meg didn't have it too bad. If Peter was less than a good father, at least Frannie was a . . .

With the tip of her finger she wiped absentmindedly at a tiny mark on the tabletop. It used to drive Frannie nuts, Jane's always wiping up the tiniest drop of liquid or endlessly sweeping away crumbs that were virtually nonexistent. Jane almost smiled at the thought. And she was forced to admit, however begrudgingly, that Frannie was, indeed, a good parent. She was hardworking and loving, never overindulgent but always thoughtful of her children's feelings. If she was sometimes a bit hard on Meg that was only because she felt she had to be, for Meg's own good. Frannie had never said as much, but Jane was pretty sure she worried about one of her children turning out to be like their deadbeat father. What sane mother wouldn't worry about something like that?

A deadbeat and a philanderer and quite possibly, an alcoholic. Jane shuddered as a feeling of relief spread through her. Relief and gratitude toward a god she didn't even believe in. She had been so lucky to find Mike, someone she could trust implicitly. To no one's surprise, Mike had never had much use for Peter. They were entirely different sorts of men, and their differences went much deeper than a collection of habits. Mike was intelligent and responsible and devoted to his family. Peter was none of those things. Mike was loyal to his wife. It was likely that Peter had never been loyal to Frannie, even in the earliest days of their marriage. Frannie had admitted as much to Jane, though anyone with eyes could have seen that Peter was worse than a tomcat. The amazing thing was that Peter had never tried to flirt with Jane, let alone seduce her.

No doubt that was because of Mike, who, though a peaceful man, was large enough to make some people think otherwise. Back before the divorce the men had survived each other's presence by sticking to neutral topics like lawn care and the weather. Any topics more challenging than that would have immediately shattered the illusion of neighborly friendship. Jane wouldn't have been surprised to learn that Mike was relieved when Frannie threw Peter out of the house. No more having to pretend civility for the women's sake. But whatever his feelings, Mike had kept them to himself.

That was another good quality he possessed, self-control and the sense of when not speaking was best. In spite of Mike's dislike of Peter Giroux, he had never let his sour feelings negatively affect his behavior toward the other members of Peter's family. Only a few nights before, Jane recalled, as they lay in bed, Mike had mentioned that he felt bad he hadn't spent any time with Petey in almost a month. They had argued in hushed tones about this, not wanting Rosie to overhear. Jane believed it was Mike's duty to keep away from the entire Giroux family. "You need," she had said, "to show loyalty to your daughter."

"I am loyal to my daughter," he had replied forcefully. "You don't ever have to doubt my loyalty to my family. But why should Petey be punished for something he didn't do?" Mike had argued. "It's bad enough his father has virtually abandoned him. Why should I walk away, too, just because his sister did something childish and wrong?"

The argument had gone around in circles, yet another conversation with no conclusion.

Jane sighed. She had so much work to do. A pair of pants needed hemming and the kitchen floor could use a cleaning, though she had washed it just two days ago. She was accomplishing nothing by sitting in the backyard obsessing over matters she could not change or influence. She went inside through the back door and locked it behind her. Then she checked to be sure that the front door was also locked.

There had never been a break-in in the neighborhood, at least as far as Jane knew. And she had never been overly conscientious about locking the doors to the house. Yorktide was not a high-crime town; the worst offenders were the occasional drunk driver and abusive husband—both horrors, but neither a real threat to the Patterson household. But ever since Rosie's trouble, Jane had felt generally insecure. She felt that her family was threatened in ways she could barely define. Locking the door was largely a symbolic gesture, ultimately futile as these days you could be threatened and even attacked right in your own home via the computer or cell phone. Still, it was a gesture Jane felt compelled to make.

9

December 9, 2011

Dear Diary,

Something weird happened this morning on the way to school. Mrs. Giroux offered to drive Meg and me for some reason. Anyway, she let us off a few blocks away to save herself some time, I guess. Or maybe she was just tired of Meg's complaining about having peanut butter and jelly again for lunch.

It all happened so fast I can't really be sure what exactly did happen.

I was about a block away from school by then and by myself because Meg had run ahead to try to catch someone in her advanced math class. She wanted to ask him something about the homework assignment. Anyway, Mackenzie Egan, Courtney Parker, Jill Harrison, and Stella Charron were passing me on my left and the next thing I knew, I felt what I thought was a shove or a shoulder bumping into me and then I was on the ground.

The left knee of my jeans ripped and my palms got kind of scraped, but the scrapes are not too bad. Mom can fix the hole in the jeans, so that's not really a big deal, either. I told Mom that I tripped on a crack in the sidewalk. It's not like that couldn't really have happened.

Later, I told Meg about it. She immediately got all freaked out and said that Mackenzie and her friends were bullies. She said I should totally ignore them all. She said that bullies want attention and that they go away when they get no reaction. I don't know if that's true. I can't remember if that's what we learned back in middle school when we had those classes about how to deal with bullies. Maybe I didn't pay enough attention. Why? I always pay attention in class. I guess it never occurred to me that I would be bullied.

And maybe I haven't been bullied. Maybe it really was an accident. Mackenzie laughed but sort of apologized to me and she called Courtney an idiot for having been clumsy and knocking into me. Jill and Stella said nothing and then all four of them just walked on toward school. But Meg is still suspicious. She thinks Mackenzie set the whole thing up and that Courtney banged into me on purpose. But why me? I've never done anything bad to any of them. I don't think I've ever even talked to any of them, certainly not to Courtney, not until that Halloween party, and they came up to us, not the other way around. Like I said, Meg can be so suspicious sometimes.

Anyway, I don't know if I can actually ignore Mackenzie and Courtney and Jill and Stella. They're so popular. At least, I think they are. They act like they are. I've decided after what happened today that I don't like them at all, but I would never say that to anyone, except for Meg. I mean, if it was really an accident, why didn't one of them ask me if I was okay?

I have to admit that after talking to Meg, I did wonder for about a half a second if I should say something to someone else about what happened, maybe to Carly or to Tiffany.

But then I thought, what if it really was an accident and I got Courtney into trouble for nothing? Then I'd be in a really bad situation and Mackenzie and the others would definitely hate me.

And what if it turned out that Courtney did knock me down on purpose? Then everything would be an even bigger mess. Because what would I do then?

And why would Carly or even Tiffany want to get involved in the first place? I'm only a freshman and they have all this important senior year stuff going on.

Besides, like I said, I really do think it was an accident. I've been in school with Mackenzie since forever and we've never even spoken before this year. Why would she suddenly want to cause trouble for me now? It doesn't make any sense.

I'm going to put it all out of my mind.

It's been snowing on and off for the past two days and the weather has been cold enough to freeze Duckworth Pond. Meg wants us to go ice-skating there on Saturday (she's always hoping we'll be there at the same time the boys from the high school ice hockey team are hanging out), but I'm not really in the mood to go ice-skating. I'm not really in the mood to do anything fun right now. I don't know why. But if she really, really wants to go, I guess I'll go with her. I mean, she's my best friend and was really upset about my falling (or, as she says, being pushed), so the least I can do is go skating.

I think I need to put some more Bactine on my palms. Some of the scrapes are kind of stinging. It's probably from holding this pen.

Well, I should go and do my homework. Mom and Dad never ask me if I've done it all before dinner, but I know they expect me to. And I don't want to disappoint them, so see you soon.

Your friend, Rosie

December 23, 2011

Dear Diary,

It's strange. Christmas is only two days away, but I just don't feel excited about it the way I used to. I wish I did feel ex-

cited. But I can't seem to fake it for myself, though I think I'm doing a pretty good job with Mom. She wanted us to bake cookies yesterday and I knew that if I told her the truth, that I didn't really want to bake Christmas cookies, she would be all upset, so I went along and pretended that I was having a good time. When we were done I didn't want to eat any, but I took a bite of one of the peanut butter cookies and when Mom left the kitchen to answer the door for the UPS guy, I threw the rest of it in the garbage. I felt bad about wasting food, but I just couldn't eat the rest of it.

I know she'll want to go to that Christmas concert at the Episcopal church, too, and I don't want to hurt her feelings, so I'll go with her. I don't know why she likes it so much anyway because she says she's an agnostic. I really like the carols, and even a lot of the hymns, especially "O Come, O Come, Emmanuel" (it sounds so haunting and it always makes me cry for some reason), even though I'm not really sure what most of them mean because I've never learned much about the Bible and theology and all. But this year . . . I don't know. I just don't care about going to the concert.

Meg's been going on about wanting a suede jacket for Christmas. She really thinks her mom's going to get one for her, but I saw in a catalogue my mom gets how expensive suede jackets are and I really doubt Mrs. Giroux can afford it. Still, I really hope Meg gets what she wants. She deserves good things. She asked me what I wanted for Christmas and I told her it was okay if she got me nothing because I really didn't want anything. That was a bit of a lie. There are a few small things I would like to get. The real reason I told Meg she didn't have to get me a gift is that I know money is really tight for the Giroux family. They shouldn't be spending their money on me. Besides, Meg bought me that really pretty rose quartz pendant for my birthday only two months ago.

I thought I saw Mackenzie giving me an odd look today at lunchtime, sort of a sneer. I was probably imagining it. Since that time when I fell I think I've been imagining stuff, small things, that probably aren't even real. Like after lunch today, when I was at my locker getting my books for the next class, I thought I felt someone watching me and when I turned around, Jill was right across the hall, staring at me. She didn't smile or say or do anything, just stared at me for another few seconds and then walked away. But it's not a crime to stare at someone, just rude. And like I said, maybe I was just imagining that she was staring at me. Why would I think that I'm so interesting? Mom's always taught me not to have a big head or to be full of myself.

I've always been a bit confused about that. I mean, Mom always likes it when someone tells me how pretty I am. But isn't that the sort of thing, getting compliments all the time, that leads you to being full of yourself or having a big head? Lately I'm realizing that there are so many things I just don't understand. Maybe life was always this complicated and I was just too young to understand. Or maybe life is always getting more complicated. If that's true, then how do you ever catch up with it?

I should go now. I still have to wrap Mom and Dad's presents. Usually, I have every present wrapped weeks ahead, but for some reason, this year every time I thought, "I should wrap those presents," I just couldn't do it. Seriously, sometimes it's like my brain just can't make my hands DO anything. It's never happened to me before. I wonder what it means. But now I only have two days until Christmas, so I really, really have to try to force myself to get those presents wrapped. I hope Mom and Dad like their gifts. I had a hard time figuring out what to get them. Finally, I got Dad a sweater and Mom a book about gardening. I saw that she'd circled an ad for it in one of our local papers about a month ago, so I hope she really wanted it and that she's not disappointed. I don't want her to think that I don't care about her.

I had a hard time choosing something for Meg, too. I mean, Meg always has a wish list a mile long, but I still couldn't de-

cide what to get her. Finally, I got her a DVD set of the second Twilight movie with outtakes and interviews and stuff. It's one of her favorite movies. It was kind of expensive but that's okay. I've been saving my allowance. I hope her mother doesn't also get it for her. Well, I kept the receipt, so I could always return it and get her something else.

Last night before dinner I went with Dad to find the "perfect tree." He loves searching for the tree. We got a nice fat one at a tree lot in town and it's out in the backyard. I think the man who sold it to us said it was a Scotch pine. We'll be putting it up in the living room tomorrow and decorating it like we always do. Mom will be sure I get to hang my favorite ornament on the tree, that pink one that once belonged to my grandmother. I'm not excited about it at all, though. Maybe it's just because I'm growing up. I don't know. I mean, I haven't believed in Santa Claus for a few years. (Neither has Meg, but we keep quiet about it for Petey's sake.) Maybe Christmas really is just a holiday for little kids. Maybe Mom and Dad pretend excitement around Christmastime just for my benefit. Maybe I should tell them they don't have to pretend anymore. I don't want them wasting their time for my sake.

Talk about wasting time! That's what I'm still doing. Good-bye, this time for real.

Your friend, Rosie

10

Meg didn't really mind picking Petey up from camp every day. It wasn't like she had anything else to do at three-thirty in the afternoon. Sometimes she walked to the church, but today she had ridden her bike. For some reason she thought more clearly when she was riding than she did when she was walking. And today she had something important to think about.

That morning, before she had left for work, Meg's mother had told her that Mrs. Patterson had demanded Meg not talk to Rosie. This news had made Meg feel angry and also a little bit sad. What did Mrs. Patterson think she was going to say to Rosie? What did she think she was going to do? Punch her in the nose?

Well, she supposed she had no right to be angry. She knew she had "blown her credibility" with the Pattersons. She had read that term recently in an article in *Time* magazine about some disgraced politician. Her dentist never had fun magazines, just serious stuff. In Meg's opinion, *Bloomberg Businessweek* did not help calm your nerves when you were waiting for someone basically to drill a hole in your head.

Meg turned the bike smoothly onto Main Street. The bike was secondhand; she and her mother had gotten it at a yard sale two summers before for twenty dollars. Her father, for once actually keeping his promise, had fixed it up enough so that it rode pretty well. And the brakes were in good shape, which was important. Meg just wished it looked a little newer than it did. And that it wasn't a weird shade of green, kind of like pea soup, which was good to eat but not so much to look at. But she didn't care enough about the bike's appearance to bother with painting it, and besides, if she was lucky she would find a newer model at another yard sale this summer.

Meg continued to ride through downtown on the sidewalk. Though technically you were supposed to ride a bike in the street, lots of people in Yorktide ignored that law, and as far as Meg knew, nobody had ever gotten arrested or fined. Anyway, she was careful not to go too fast and to watch out for old people or anyone on crutches or some little kid who wasn't paying attention. Once when she and her mother had been up in Portland, some skuzzy-looking guy on a bike had crashed into a tiny old lady on the sidewalk outside Renys on Congress Street. Mrs. Giroux had hurried right over to help the woman, but the skuzzy-looking guy had just taken off. That had happened years ago, but Meg still remembered how scared and kind of sick she had felt seeing the blood on the old lady's forehead. A police car was on the scene within minutes and it turned out that the cut on the old lady's forehead was minor, but Meg had a feeling that both she and the old lady would remember that incident for a very long time to come.

Meg glanced down at the Swatch watch on her left wrist. She was a bit early. There was time to window-shop. Nothing helped chase away negative thoughts or upsetting memories like window-shopping, unless it was actual shopping, but she couldn't afford to do that too often. She came to a stop in front of a small store called Annie's Boutique. It sold women's clothes and accessories. Now, for summer, there was a display of bathing suits, cover-ups, straw hats, sunglasses, and sandals. A pair of sandals right in the center of the display caught Meg's eye. They were flat and silver, with a thin strap around the ankle and a shiny blue stone on the strap that went across the toe. She would love, love, love to have a pair of those sandals, but she bet there was no way she could afford them. It seemed so unfair. Rosie could probably afford to buy them but she probably wouldn't bother; she didn't care about fashion all that much. Meg sighed and touched the glass of the window with a fingertip. She supposed she could try to save up for a pair, but by the time she had enough money to buy them, the store would probably be sold out.

"Grr," Meg said under her breath. "Grr, grr, grr." She was self-aware enough to recognize the mood into which she was rapidly descending. Her mother called it her Miss Grumpy Pants mood. She said it wasn't attractive. Most times, Meg didn't care. Like at that moment, slowly cycling on past the boutique and toward St. Teresa of Avila church and rectory. Who was around to even notice if she was being "attractive"? And why should Meg care what other people thought of her?

Well, no man—or woman—was an island. That was another one of her mother's favorite expressions. *And in my case,* Meg thought contritely, *yeah, I should care what other people think about me.* Because no one could get by alone. No person could survive without a community.

Her mother was right. She had told Meg she was lucky that her part in Rosie's breakdown wasn't known. If Meg had been publicly accused of bullying, even if she wasn't really guilty, no sane parent would have hired Meg to baby-sit her kids. And the Giroux family needed whatever money they could earn. It seemed like Meg's mother reminded her of that every single day. Meg glanced down at the ratty old sneakers she was wearing. As if she could ever forget. Her mother didn't even let them get a real tree at Christmastime because she said it was money down the drain. The artificial tree that they had been using for, like, forever, was sad and saggy, but nothing short of it falling on top of Petey could persuade Mrs. Giroux to toss it and buy a new one. Buy fresh flowers at Hannaford? No way. The dusty old plastic yellow tulips she had found at a garage sale would have to do. Throw away a pair of jeans because the hems were frayed? Why not just sew on a new hem, cut from a stray scrap of fabric? Her mom didn't need Jane Patterson's help to do that.

Meg pedaled on. Well, she thought, she might be poor now, but she fully intended to make a ton of money when she grew up and got out of school. She definitely wanted to go to college but was pretty sure she would have to go part-time while she worked a full-time job. Whatever. She would do it, and since she was really good at math and science and computers, she didn't think she would have too much trouble making a lot of money in some big career. No way would she wind up like her mother, who was really smart but stuck working a job that Meg had concluded was beneath her. Not that Mrs. Giroux had ever said that, exactly, but Meg thought she could read between the lines of her mother's reports at the end of each workday. And not winding up like her mother also meant not getting married to someone like her father. No. Way.

Lately, Meg had spent a lot of time wondering why

her mother had chosen to marry her father. She wondered what it was about him that had attracted her mom. It couldn't have been his intelligence or his character—neither of which he had much of—or even his sense of humor, which Meg had long since judged as juvenile. Beavis and Butt-Head were more sophisticated than her dad! Well, sometimes. Part of her wanted to come right out and ask her mom to explain why she had done what she had done, but another part of her was afraid to know the truth. Maybe, Meg thought, when she was older she would work up the courage to ask. There had to have been something good about her father to make Frances Mary Donaldson marry him. There had to have been. Meg had seen plenty of photos of her mom when she was young. She had been really attractive. She probably could have gotten any guy she wanted. But something had made her choose Peter Giroux.

Meg looked carefully both ways before riding her bike across the street to the opposite sidewalk. She passed the old-fashioned family-owned-and-run pharmacy and saw that no one was inside. She found it hard to believe that the Robbins family could make a living when all those big stores like Hannaford and Walmart had huge discount pharmacies. But maybe some people still liked the charm of a small local store. Personally, when Meg was a kid she had loved to go into Robbins Drugs and Sundries and buy a pretzel rod for a nickel or a giant gumball for ten cents. Her mom had been cool about little things like that years ago, before Petey was born. Maybe money hadn't been so tight with only one kid in the family.

Meg pedaled past the florist and then past the tiny salon where her mother used to get her hair cut, ages ago. For the past few years, Mrs. Giroux had been going to a salon out by the mall that hired beauty school students, some of whom, in Meg's opinion, were not very good at all. There were times when her mother came home from the salon and Meg itched to grab a pair of scissors. Anything she could produce, she was sure, would be more attractive than the disaster produced by those inexpensive but inexperienced students. How hard could it be to cut on a straight line?

Ahead, Meg could see the spire of the church. *Maybe,* she thought, *I should go to confession soon.* She didn't like having critical thoughts about her mother; even if it wasn't technically a sin, having critical thoughts was in some ways a betrayal. Honor thy father and thy mother. It was a commandment, so criticizing her mother probably was a sin after all. And Meg really did love her mom. She even wished she could spend more time with her, but knew it would be useless to ask if they could hang out, maybe go to the mall or just take a walk after dinner. What would be the point? Mrs. Giroux was always complaining about being so busy. And she really was busy, so busy that she seemed never to have time for anything fun. For example, a year or two ago, Rosie's mother had started a monthly book group and Meg's mother had gone to only two meetings before dropping out because she didn't have time to read the books. And if Mrs. Giroux wasn't busy, she was exhausted. She was usually in bed by ten every night and snoring loudly soon after. Meg couldn't remember the last time her mother had gone to a movie or had dinner out with anyone, not even Mrs. Patterson, her best friend. Correction, her onetime best friend. And Meg had ruined that.

About a block away from the church buildings, Meg spotted Mrs. Abbott getting out of her car across the street. Mrs. Abbott worked at the gigantic Goodwill store in South Portland and was a bigger busybody than anybody Meg knew, and in a small town like Yorktide, that was saying something. Meg said a silent prayer that Mrs. Abbott wouldn't see her. The last thing she wanted was to be asked questions about Rosie. The other day a checkout person in Hannaford, a young woman named Kari who Meg was pretty sure had a sister in Yorktide High School, had asked Meg if she knew why Rosie Patterson had missed the last weeks of school. Meg had thought she would pass out with embarrassment. She wondered if she was about to be publicly blamed for Rosie's breaking down. Before she could plan a careful reply, she was lying. "I don't know," she said. "I have no idea."

The checkout person had kind of smiled. Or maybe she had frowned suspiciously. (A guilty conscience, Meg thought now, remembering the girl's expression, needs no accuser. That was another one of her mother's favorite expressions.) "Oh," Kari had said. "I thought I heard that you two were best friends."

Meg had stammered something unintelligible and, grabbing the plastic bags of toilet paper and discount paper towels, darted out of the store.

Luckily, Mrs. Abbott didn't see her, or maybe, Meg thought, she had seen her and decided she didn't want to approach a teenager with a big scowl on her face. There were benefits to being grumpy. People often left you alone. Meg reached the church parking lot and parked her bike apart from a few mothers waiting to pick up their kids.

She recognized most of the women from church, but she didn't really feel comfortable going up to talk with anyone. Some Sunday mornings Meg grumbled about having to get up early enough to make the ten o'clock Mass, but usually she didn't much mind. The priest, Father William, gave pretty good sermons and Sister Pauline had been really nice to her when maybe she should have been angry. But then again, nuns were supposed to be nice and forgiving. One thing Meg knew for certain. There was no way she could ever be a nun, not with her short temper and general impatience with everything! Plus, she liked boys too much.

Meg lifted her hair off her neck and then let it flop back down. Why hadn't she brought a hair elastic with her? Because she had been preoccupied before leaving the house, hoping to catch a glimpse of Rosie coming or going next door. Pathetic. Maybe she had become like an island after all, alone and cut off from other people her own age. Her mother had never been able to afford to send her to a summer camp, but that had never really mattered, not with Rosie to hang out with. And as long as Rosie had been around, Meg had never felt the need to make other good friends, not during the summer, not during the school year. Now, without Rosie . . .

Meg roughly twisted her hair into a rope and knotted it so that it was semi-off her sweaty neck. Self-pity was lame. What was she complaining about? She had plenty to keep her busy all summer. She had those books to read for her English teacher and a lot of housework to keep her occupied. And then there was Petey to take care of. . . .

Petey's day camp was pretty inexpensive and a few of his friends from school were also enrolled, so his summer wasn't turning out so bad at all. Sometimes, but not too often, Meg felt a little resentful that Petey got so much more attention from their parents than she did, especially from their father. Not that Dad was a prize. But feeling a little resentful didn't mean that she didn't love her little brother. It was kind of hard not to. He was just an all-around good kid. Her mom deserved a well-behaved child, Meg thought, especially with Miss Grumpy Pants for a daughter.

Mom should have had a daughter like Rosie, Meg thought now, idly watching one of the waiting mothers chatting away on her cell phone, a daughter who was always sunny and willing to do her chores without grumbling. And Rosie would make a great sister. She had doted on Petey since the day Mrs. Giroux had brought him home from the hospital. Sometimes, Meg thought, Rosie had treated him more like a doll than a living, breathing child. Long after he was able to walk, Rosie had carried him around when they were together, kissing his cheek and telling him how much she loved him. Well, Meg thought now, as long as she hadn't tried to dress him up in ridiculous outfits. Meg—and her mom!—would have drawn the line there. She bet that Rosie missed Petey. But if she did miss him, why didn't she try to spend some time with him? Why had she cut him out of her life like she had cut out Meg?

Well, at least the entire Patterson family hadn't turned their backs on Petey. Just the night before her mother had told her that Mr. Patterson had asked if it was okay for him to take Petey miniature golfing, like he used to do before everything had gone wrong. Mike Patterson had admitted that his wife was totally against the idea, but he had urged Frannie to consider allowing him back into Petey's life.

For her part, Meg felt grateful to Mr. Patterson. Her mother said she was worried about angering Jane and causing trouble between the Pattersons, which might, somehow, hurt Petey. Meg thought her mom was being too cautious. Petey needed someone like Mr. Patterson, especially when his actual father was such a jerk. Not that she would ever say anything bad about their father in front of Petey. He liked his dad. He wasn't old enough to realize what kind of person Mr. Giroux really was. Meg, for one, didn't look forward to the day when Petey saw the grim reality of his father. She had been able to handle that grim reality when it had hit her in the face, but she was tough. Her mother had always told her that. She was strong. Well, Meg wasn't 100 percent sure she believed that about herself. Either her mother was lying or there was some truth to her opinion, somewhere.

With nothing else to occupy her time except uncomfortable thoughts, Meg found herself listening in to the conversation between the two women just to her right. Well, it was kind of hard not to listen in. They were talking really loudly about an outing they were planning together, a day at the outlet stores in Kittery with lunch at the Weathervane after. *It's weird,* Meg thought. *Those women could be adult versions of Rosie and me.* One was blond and tall, and the other was brunette and kind of short. The blonde was wearing low-key preppy stuff, knee-length shorts, a polo shirt, and sneakers, and the brunette was wearing more stylish stuff, a really pretty flower-printed chiffon blouse, white jeans, and high-heeled sandals. Meg frowned and moved her bike out of range of their chattering. There would be no more shopping trips for Rosie Patterson and Meg Giroux.

For the first time since she had apologized to Rosie, Meg realized that she felt a little bit angry with her. Maybe she had no right to be angry with Rosie, but she was. She had said she was sorry, and she was truly sorry. So why couldn't Rosie forgive her? Why wouldn't she? Even just a little bit, if only for Petey's sake?

If it was the other way around, she thought, if Rosie had told a secret about her, she would have forgiven

Rosie by now. At least, she was pretty sure she would have. And it just didn't seem fair of Mrs. Patterson to have gone to her mom and—

"Hi, Meg!"

Petey came racing out of the church's recreation room door, clutching something in his left hand. Like his big sister he wore glasses, but his eyesight was way worse, so his glasses had those awful thick lenses that made his eyes look like they were two fish swimming in two ponds. But even with that distortion, there was no denying that Petey was a really cute kid. His smile was what Meg's mother called infectious; it made you smile back even when you weren't in a smiling mood. His hair was much lighter than Meg's and he still had some of what her mother called baby fat. Other kids his age liked him, which pleased Meg. If anyone ever said or did anything mean to Petey, she thought she would go berserk. And she would probably wind up in jail for it. Then there would be two members of the Giroux family with a criminal record, Meg and her dad. She wasn't entirely clear on his criminal past, but she had found out that he had been caught stealing cigarettes from a convenience store once. Her mother had blurted that bit of information after a particularly infuriating phone conversation with him. "You might as well know," Mrs. Giroux had said when she had calmed down. "Better to learn the truth at home than on the street." And by "street," Meg had figured her mother meant one of Yorktide's busybodies, like Mrs. Abbott.

"Hey, Petey," Meg said as her brother came to a skidding stop in front of her. "What's up?"

"Look what I made for Mom." He held out a small square box made of Popsicle sticks and decorated with yellow glitter. Meg hadn't thought people still used Popsicle sticks for crafts. Glitter, she thought, would never go away.

"That's really nice," she told her brother. "I bet Mom will love it."

Petey nodded. "It's for her treasures."

Her mother's treasures. Meg doubted that her mother had any real treasures, certainly nothing her ex-husband or her children had ever given her. She did wear a tiny gold cross on a chain; it had once belonged to her mother, but Meg didn't think you should count a cross as a treasure. She thought of the Mother's Day just passed. She'd had the hardest time finding the right card. Every card seemed to imply that Mom had done a fabulous job of raising her kids and that those kids were happy and well-adjusted. Those kids were certainly not in trouble for having betrayed a friend and destroyed the friendship between the mothers. The messages on those cards seemed like a sham and a lie. Or maybe it was that the messages on the cards made Meg's relationship with her mother seem like a sham and a lie.

"Hey," she said now, "you want to get some ice cream?"

Petey's face assumed an expression of great seriousness. "I don't have any money," he said.

Meg laughed. "I do, silly. Come on. You can sit on my bike and I'll wheel you. Just don't take your hands off the handlebars, okay?"

So she would never get those cute sandals, she thought as she hoisted Petey onto the bike's seat and carefully stowed his treasure box in her saddlebag. It wasn't the end of the world.

11

Frannie had some errands to run after work, errands that she couldn't ask Meg to handle; Meg was too young to drive and the dry cleaners, for example, was too far away for Meg to get to easily on her bike. Not that Frannie often needed to go to the dry cleaners. It was just too damned expensive to get clothes cleaned outside the home. But certain items, like her one good summer suit and her winter comforter, couldn't be tossed into the washing machine. Jane's washing machine was bigger than hers and almost brand new. It could probably handle the comforter, but now there was no way Frannie could ask Jane for a favor.

Not so much longer now, Frannie thought as she pulled out of the parking lot behind the dry cleaners, before Meg would have her license. Somehow they would afford a decent enough car and she could rely on her daughter for more help with the chores than she could supply now.

As she drove along, past a fairly new housing development grandly calling itself Sea-mist Estates, Frannie tried to decide what she would make for dinner that evening. But a conversation she had had with Mike Patterson the day before pushed all thoughts of meat loaf and pasta out of her mind. Mike had called her from his office; Frannie had heard his assistant, Peggy, on another line in the background. He had asked how Petey was doing and said that he wanted her to consider letting him spend time with the boy again.

"I'll be honest, Fran," he had said. "Jane doesn't want our families to have anything to do with each other right now."

"I thought as much," Frannie had replied. "Jane came over and told me to keep Meg away from Rosie."

There was silence on the line for a moment and then, his voice tight, Mike had said, "I didn't know that."

Frannie had felt like a fool, though there was no way she could have known that Jane was holding something back from her husband. Before she could say something, anything, Mike went on.

"Whatever Jane feels about the girls is a separate issue. I'm concerned about Petey. And yes, Jane knows that but no, I haven't told her I was going to call you today."

Frannie had hesitated. Certainly, she agreed that her son did not deserve to suffer. In the past weeks Petey had asked, several times, when Mr. Patterson was going to take him miniature golfing again, and why Mr. Patterson hadn't suggested they play Wiffle ball, now that it was summer and school was out. Frannie had been hard-pressed to come up with an answer that would make sense to her son. She suspected he didn't really believe the excuse she had given him for Jane's absence in his life, that she was super busy with work. But in the end she had told Petey the same thing about Mr. Patterson. It wasn't technically a lie, but . . .

"I think," Mike had gone on, "there's a chance the

girls will work things out. But in the meantime, why should Petey suffer?"

By "the girls," Frannie had wondered if Mike had meant only Meg and Rosie. She hadn't asked Mike to clarify. In the end she had promised to think about his offer to pick up with Petey where he had left off weeks earlier. The fact that Jane was so adamantly against the notion was the real sticking point. If Frannie agreed to let Mike spend time with Petey, Jane's anger against Frannie and even against Meg might strengthen. And things between Jane and Mike might suffer. The last thing Frannie wanted was to be responsible for damaging someone's marriage, especially the marriage of two people for whom she had once cared so much. Who was she kidding? She still cared for Jane and Mike and wasn't happy to see either of them acting behind the other's back. That sort of thing could easily lead to trouble.

Frannie slowed for a light that had just turned red. She felt a twinge of anger against Meg as the cause of all the messiness. It was never pleasant to be angry with your own child, but she supposed it was inevitable. Your child was still a person, with free will and the ability to choose right from wrong. And sometimes, like every other person, she was bound to choose wrong. And you, as the parent, were bound to wonder if somehow you weren't ultimately responsible for that wrong choice.

The light turned green and Frannie continued on toward home. Yes, that was Bob Egan's car parked outside the Simmons' hardware store. It was unmistakable. No one else in the area drove an old Mercedes. And the vanity plates clinched the identification. MNYMAN. Money Man. Frannie suspected the car had been one of his wife's ways to flaunt their relative wealth and that the license plate had been her idea of witty.

Well, if Mackenzie Egan took after one of her parents, it was clearly her mother. The girl was what Frannie's ex-father-in-law used to call "a piece of work." Frannie remembered an incident that had taken place back when Meg and Rosie were in second or third grade and Mackenzie in third or fourth. Mackenzie had shown up at school wearing a face full of makeup, everything from lipstick to mascara and blush. She was sent to the principal's office to await the arrival of her mother. The word was that when Mrs. Egan saw her daughter she burst into peals of laughter and simply refused to accept that Mackenzie had done anything wrong. The principal, not amused, instructed Mrs. Egan to take her daughter home, remove the makeup, and return her for classes. Mrs. Egan had complied, but the very next day, Mackenzie showed up again in full war paint. Not once during the battle with the school authorities had Mackenzie so much as flinched. She had made her point. After that, her reputation as an "individual" was cemented. Frannie herself remembered feeling a bit of grudging respect for the girl.

Frannie waved to a man in a battered old pickup truck passing her in the opposing lane. Mr. Picken, both hands on the steering wheel, raised a finger in acknowledgment. He and his wife were good sorts, solid people and members of a local Lutheran congregation. They had raised six children on a farmer's earnings, no easy feat no matter what was going on with the larger economy. And all six of those children, boys and girls, had grown up to become as solid and self-reliant as their parents. Only two had moved out of state, which was also a bit of a miracle. One of those lived in a Boston suburb and worked in town as the manager of the women's department in a high-end department store and another was career military, stationed somewhere in the South.

Mrs. Egan, Frannie thought, should have taken parenting lessons from Burt and Betty Picken. Mackenzie's mother hadn't exactly been a model parent. Frannie remembered the time when both Meg and Mackenzie had been in Girl Scouts. The troop leaders had planned a camping trip and each girl was assigned an item of food to contribute to the evening meal. Mackenzie was supposed to bring the hot dogs. Patty Egan had sent her daughter empty-handed and otherwise ill prepared. One of the leaders had given up her sleeping bag for the girl. Another had driven back to the closest town and managed to scare up a few packages of frozen hamburger patties, which, it turned out, were gray and tasteless. At least half of the campers and all of the leaders refused to eat them. After that disastrous weekend, Meg decided being a Girl Scout wasn't fun after all. That was the end of her scouting career.

Mr. Egan was by all accounts a nice enough guy, Frannie thought, if a bit socially inept. He had a local reputation as a brainiac—that was Peter's term for Bob Egan; anyone with a higher education made him feel uneasy and intimidated—as he had gone to Harvard for graduate school and now taught economics at Barnes College.

Yes, the Egans had seemed an odd, mismatched couple, Patty Egan more interested in shopping and tanning salons than in sharing her husband's academic concerns. It was a mystery to Frannie why they had gotten together in the first place. It was probably a mystery to all the residents of Yorktide, one of many they would never solve.

Like why the levelheaded Frances Donaldson had married the delinquent Peter Giroux. Frannie sighed. Well, at least the entire Giroux family hadn't fallen apart as a result of the divorce. Not like what had happened with the Egans. When Mackenzie's mother had run off with that guy from Augusta a few years back, things had gotten bad, and fast, for her hapless husband and young kids. It was a small town, and everyone knew everyone else's business or thought they did. It wasn't an atmosphere a person like Bob Egan could handle, especially not when he found himself the focus of the gossip. Aside from the time he spent at the college, he had become almost a recluse. He let his membership in the country club where he had occasionally played golf lapse and even stopped going to Mass on Sunday. Frannie felt bad for Bob Egan, but she didn't know him well enough to offer a shoulder to cry on. Besides, she simply didn't have the time or the energy to take on another dependent. She figured that Father William had reached out to him. At least, she hoped that he had.

Mackenzie's older brother, Bobby—Peter's apt nickname for him was Booby—had gone really wild after his mother's defection. He had dropped out of school, gotten himself picked up by the local police a few times for minor infractions of the law, and, rumor had it, gotten an underage girl from a neighboring town pregnant.

Somehow, except for a few minor infractions, Mackenzie had managed to stay out of trouble, which was probably, Frannie thought, due to cunning and intelligence. Mackenzie was not a dumb girl. In fact, since first grade she had always been one of the best students, and sometimes, in spite of the occasional antics, even a teacher's pet. No doubt if her grades were poor, teachers and administration would take more critical notice of her, but as it was, Mackenzie presented as pretty self-sufficient and so was largely left on her own.

And that was the problem, Frannie thought, frowning as a car driven by a ten-year-old boy (okay, maybe a seventeen-year-old boy) screeched onto the road in front of her. Kids needed supervision even when they were doing everything in their power to convince you otherwise. But how could you supervise a child in every single situation? Like with Meg. Frannie was a bit worried that because Rosie was no longer her friend, Meg would throw all common sense to the wind when school started again and become involved with Mackenzie and her cronies. There were plenty of other, much nicer girls Frannie would rather see her daughter hang out with, but she couldn't be with Meg at school, guiding her social life, encouraging her to choose new friends wisely. Besides, though Meg wasn't a particularly contrary kid (well, not always), no one her age liked to do what her mother suggested she do. If Frannie did interfere (that's how Meg would see it), she would run the risk of totally alienating her daughter, and that couldn't be good.

Frannie slowed the car as the youthful driver ahead swerved a bit over the lane line. *When Meg gets her license,* she thought, *I am reading her the riot act before she hits the road. And if she crashes the car, that's it. I'm not buying her another car. She can walk or ride her bike everywhere until she's saved up enough money to buy her own car.*

Mackenzie Egan would probably have her own car before long, Frannie mused. If she didn't sucker her father out of his Mercedes. Yeah, it was a no-brainer to realize that it would be a bad idea for Meg to hang out with Mackenzie Egan. But Frannie honestly didn't know if it would be a good idea for Meg to be friends with Rosie again. She thought about Jane's unexpected visit the other day and how adamant she had been about the girls being kept apart. Jane was afraid for her child. Frannie could understand that. But it hurt her to know that Jane considered Meg a bad influence or a danger. Meg! True, she wasn't always full of happiness and light—in fact, she pretty much grumbled about everything—but she was hardly a monster. Frannie wondered what Jane was saying to her daughter about Meg. She wondered if Jane was painting a portrait of a hopeless juvenile delinquent, someone Rosie was better off without.

And let's face it, Frannie thought, happy to play devil's advocate for a moment, *Rosie really put Meg in a terrible situation for all those months, swearing her to silence.* In a way, she had made Meg complicit in the bullying from the start. Meg's spilling Rosie's secret was in some ways inevitable. Frannie didn't want her daughter having to go through that sort of thing again, and she might, if Rosie hadn't sufficiently learned how to stand up for herself. It was a puzzle. Frannie wished she knew what was best for her daughter, but she just didn't. How could anyone really know? Kids didn't come with operating instructions.

"Talk about freakin' operating instructions," Frannie muttered. Her home printer was on the fritz and the manual might as well have been written in Sanskrit for all Frannie could make of it. Well, maybe a broken printer was to be expected; it was over ten years old and had seen some heavy-duty use. After Mike's generous gesture, she supposed she could ask him to take a look at it. He had always been the Giroux family handyman and tech guy, even before her divorce from Peter. Peter's skills were limited, and his energy and focus were minimal.

Still, she didn't want Mike to think she was taking advantage in any way. She supposed they could survive without a printer until her next paycheck or even until the one after that, especially now that school was out and Meg wouldn't need to print out her book reports and other papers until the new semester began.

The lousy teenaged driver turned off onto a side road and Frannie sighed with relief. She wasn't a nervous driver but she was an alert one, and driving along behind an incompetent driver made her angry. Even if the kid wasn't technically incompetent, he had been acting stupidly behind the wheel, probably sending a text or surfing the Internet instead of keeping his eyes on the road.

Frannie frowned. Sometimes it seemed that 90 percent of the trouble in the world was caused by the Internet. A while back, before the whole episode with Rosie, she had begun to consider the pros and cons of monitoring Meg's being online. She had set time limits, of course, but she had stopped there. She did know for sure that Meg didn't have a Facebook page or a Twitter or an e-mail account, and that was because Frannie had forbidden Meg to get involved with that sort of social media until she was older. (How old was yet to be determined.) But what websites Meg visited, well, that was a mystery. Frannie knew it was easy to check the history of Meg's browsing, but she continually resisted the temptation. Still, with Petey being so young and impressionable, there was need for some vigilance.

It was complicated. Recently, she had read an article online about parents tracking their kids' computer habits. The writer had used the term "benevolent monitoring," which was what one woman had chosen to call her habit of checking up on her son's Internet history. "Spying," Frannie thought, was more accurate a term than "checking up on."

Was there really such a thing as "benevolent monitoring"? The term seemed a bit of an oxymoron, but viewed in the light of the concerned parent, maybe it made sense. Maybe it wasn't such a bad idea to keep tabs on your child's every movement. What would come next, Frannie thought wryly, a collar and a leash?

Yeah, it was complicated. She wanted her children to trust her. There was a fine line between overseeing and surveillance. Then again, you weren't supposed to be your child's friend before being her parent. That, Frannie believed. Still, she remembered how furious she had been when she discovered that her mother had been reading her diary. To a ten-year-old it had felt like the most horrible of betrayals, but her mother had justified her action by claiming that it was a parent's right to know absolutely everything about her child. Privacy was for adults only. It was something they had earned, if only by becoming adults.

After that, Frannie had stopped keeping a diary. For a while she missed writing in it every night, but what was the point when nothing you wrote down could be kept personal? You would be writing for an audience, not for yourself. As far as Frannie knew, Meg didn't keep a journal. If she did it was a deep, dark secret, a secret her mother was not going to try to ferret out.

Frannie's stomach growled. She hadn't eaten since breakfast, and that had been on the run, a stale granola bar munched on the way to work. She had planned on eating lunch like a normal person, but a crisis had arisen when the computer system had crashed and she had had to summon the off-site IT guy. By the time he had shown up and got the system up and running again, it was already three o'clock and Frannie was facing a backlog of work. So the ham and cheese sandwich she had made for today would be eaten tomorrow. If someone in the office didn't steal it. It had been known to happen, in spite of her name spelled out in big black letters on her reusable plastic lunch bag.

Her stomach growled again, loudly. A slight detour would take her past a McDonald's. She knew she shouldn't spend the money on takeout when there was a pantry full of food at home, but the thought of cooking anything at all, even of pouring a bowl of cereal or boiling water for pasta, suddenly seemed more than she could handle. She was only thirty-eight, but right then she felt as if she were seventy-eight. An old seventy-eight, not the Jane Fonda kind of seventy-something. Who did women like that think they were, Helen Mirren and Raquel Welch and God knew who else, setting the bar so high for the rest of womankind, the ones who did their own housecleaning and had more to worry about than what to wear on the red carpet?

So, Frannie thought, *does being tired really give me an excuse to overspend my hard-earned money on fast food? Is purchasing a meal loaded with grease and fat and excessive calories a responsible solution to my feeling too worn out to cook a healthy dinner for my children?*

"Screw it," Frannie said aloud. One meal of McDonald's hamburgers wouldn't kill anyone, and it wouldn't send the Giroux family into the poorhouse. She would get fries, too, and there was some ice cream in the freezer at home. Her stomach growled mightily at the prospect. Jane Fonda be damned!

12

January 5, 2012

Dear Diary,

A terrible thing happened to me today.

I still can't really believe it. I still keep thinking that maybe I'm having an awful dream, a nightmare, and that I'll wake up to find that nothing bad really happened after all.

But I know I won't.

I was on my way to the library after school. I was walking up through the small parking lot on the east side of the library when I saw them, coming around the back of the building. There are no windows on that part of the building, so later I realized that no one inside the library could see what was happening. They must have planned it that way.

Mackenzie and Courtney and Jill came up to me, kind of forcing me to stop. I don't know where Stella was or why she wasn't with them. It doesn't matter. The three of them stood really close, too close. I took a step back and they took a step forward.

They all talked at the same time, saying that my hair was beautiful and asking if they could feel it. I thought that was really weird and a feeling in my stomach told me that something was very, very wrong, but I didn't know how to say "no" or "go away and leave me alone" and then they were snatching my hat off my head. Jill held my shoulders and Courtney must have been hiding a pair of scissors in her coat pocket because I felt a hard tug and tried to break away but couldn't. Mackenzie just stood there, watching. Her face was totally bland, like nothing terrible was happening. And then Jill let me go with a bit of a shove and Courtney held up my braid and laughed. Before I could even react—scream or cry or whatever—she dropped my braid and they all ran off.

I don't know how I got home. My hat was on the ground and I put it on and then put up my hood over it. Luckily, Mom was out when I got to the house. She had left a note saying she had gone to see one of her clients and would be back by four-thirty. Dad, I knew, wouldn't be home until five-thirty, like usual. I ran upstairs and locked myself into the bathroom in the hallway. My heart was pounding like mad but I forced myself to look in the mirror. I started to cry then, the tears just pouring down my face. The ends of my hair were all jagged and uneven. The shortest pieces came down just below my ears and the longer ones came midway down my neck. It was a mess.

It just occurred to me that I don't know what happened to my braid. It could still be lying on the ground where Courtney dropped it. Or one of them could have taken it and I just didn't notice. . . . I feel sick to my stomach thinking about it. I feel sad for my hair. That might not make sense, but it's what I feel.

What will someone think when they find it there in the parking lot?

I lied to Mom when she got home. I've never lied to her, except for the time I told her I tripped outside school when I really hadn't, I'd been pushed down. But I just couldn't tell her what really happened. Then she would tell Dad and they would go to the principal and then everyone would know and I would be humiliated. She was kind of upset that I cut my own hair when she usually does it—that's what I told her, that I thought I could do it myself—and she didn't say anything while she was making everything even again. She says now that I have a "bob." The whole time I was trying super hard not to cry and I think Mom was, too. When Dad got home he looked kind of shocked but told me that I looked "fashionable" and "stylish" now. I know he was just trying to be nice. I knew what he was really thinking was, "Where did my Rapunzel go?"

The minute dinner (which I could barely eat) was over I told Mom and Dad I had a lot of homework, which wasn't a lie, and I went right into my room. I'm not coming out again tonight, either. And I'm not going to school tomorrow. I can't. I'll pretend I have a headache.

I wonder if Mom knows I was lying about my hair. But if she does, why doesn't she come right out and tell me she knows? Maybe she just doesn't care. She hasn't even asked what I did with my braid. Wouldn't she want to save it, like she's saved clippings from my hair since I was a baby? She has them all in a box. Each clipping is tied with a different-colored silk ribbon with a small tag identifying the year the clipping was taken. Meg thinks that's weird. Her mother never saved any of her hair.

I can't believe I just wrote that, about Mom not caring. Of course she cares. It's wrong of me to doubt that. It's just that . . . I don't know what I'm saying right now. I'm so confused.

One thing I do know. I'm not ever going to tell anyone what really happened, not even Meg. I just can't. Anyway, Meg was really disappointed about not getting a suede jacket for Christmas. Ever since then she's been sort of in a bad mood, so I don't know why she would care about what happened to my hair. I don't know why she would care about what happened to any part of me. Her life is so much harder than mine. At least my father lives with my mother and me.

Rosie

January 17, 2012

Dear Diary,

I didn't go to school today again. I know I can't take too many days off without Mom becoming suspicious or without my getting in trouble with the principal or the school board. But this morning I just felt so—I guess anxious is the word. I just couldn't go to school. I told Mom I had a really bad headache, which wasn't really lying because it turned out that I did get a headache around ten o'clock. Or maybe I got the headache as punishment for my having lied.

Mostly Mom left me alone—she had two clients come by today—which was good because I wanted to be alone. I read ahead in almost all of my textbooks and it won't be hard for me to do two days' worth of homework tomorrow night. Luckily, schoolwork comes easy for me. It's good that something does.

Mom still hasn't pressed me about what happened to my hair, so I guess she really did believe me when I lied to her about cutting it myself. I didn't know I was such a good liar. I don't think that being a liar is a good thing to be, but I guess I've become one anyway.

Like yesterday. At lunch, Meg asked me a bunch of questions again, like why hadn't I told her I wanted short hair and where did I get the idea to cut my hair when it was so beautiful long. I made up a story about having wanted short hair for a long time and other stuff I can't even remember now. I think she suspects that something is weird. She kind of looked at me funny, but she hasn't come right out and asked me what really happened. I don't know what I would tell her if she did. I think I would probably stick to my lies. I don't want to make everything worse than it already is.

Mom has a line she quotes whenever she hears about some politician or celebrity lying, which seems like every week. It's from Sir Walter Scott, but I'm not sure exactly from what poem. "Oh, what a tangled web we weave, when first we practice to deceive." I think I finally really understand that line now.

I feel so embarrassed and totally helpless. Every time Mackenzie or Courtney or Jill sees me in the hall or the cafeteria they make some comment on my hair. "What a cute haircut! Who's your stylist?" Stuff like that. So far Stella hasn't said anything to me. Actually, she usually looks away when the others make those comments. I'm not sure how close Stella really is to the others. But I don't want to find out. I wish they would all just disappear.

I wish I would just disappear.

R.

13

It was an absolutely perfect summer day, about eighty degrees with low humidity and a virtually cloudless sky. If you believed in omens, and Rosie kind of thought that she did, Yorktide's annual Independence Day celebration was going to be a lot of fun.

The Pattersons got to the fair at around eleven o'clock, after their traditional July Fourth breakfast of pancakes and bacon (sausage for Mr. Patterson) at the Maine Diner. The fair was pretty much the same every year. There was the rickety Ferris wheel (Rosie's mother had never let her go on that; she said it was too dangerous), and the carts selling hot dogs, and the vans selling greasy, sugary funnel cakes. Over by the bouncy castle for little kids, the volunteer fire department had set up a few small grills and were selling hamburgers; whatever profit the department made would go into a fund for local sick children. Near the firemen's table was another table at which a bunch of local women were selling their homemade desserts (there were lots of whoopee pies, of course) and preserves. Next to them a Baptist church group was selling coffee and tea. Some years there was a tiny petting zoo, but that depended on what local farmers were interested in bringing their animals. A quick scan of this year's fairgrounds told Rosie that there was no petting zoo, but for the first time a popular, longstanding duo, Lex and Joe, were booked to play blues and jazzy songs all afternoon; Rosie's father was psyched about that. And Rosie's mother was looking forward to seeing one of her favorite local jewelry makers, an artist who came to the event each year with a new supply of necklaces and bracelets and earrings made with beach glass and stones smoothed by the ocean's waves. Mrs. Patterson said that his prices were reasonable, so she usually bought herself something. Last year it was a silver necklace with a pendant made of bright blue sea glass. Rosie had heard that for some reason, blue was the hardest color of sea glass to find. It was a very pretty necklace.

It was too bad that fireworks weren't allowed at the fair, which went on into the night, but the neighboring town of Ogunquit was sponsoring its annual fireworks display down by the beach. Rosie was seriously hoping her parents would be into going. But it was unlikely. Her mother hated fireworks; if she was forced to be around them she flinched and covered her ears before the display even started, and she was always worried about stray sparks landing on her bare arms. Her father just didn't care about fireworks. He just didn't see the big deal. Most years Rosie had gone down to Ogunquit Beach with Mrs. Giroux, Meg, and Petey. Of course, this year that wasn't going to happen. With all that had gone on in the past weeks, Rosie hadn't realized just how much she missed spending time with Mrs. Giroux. She could be fun in a way that her own mother was definitely not, like when she slipped and said a bad word and then tried not to laugh at herself for saying it. She doubted that Mrs. Giroux missed her in any way, though. Why would she? Adults didn't miss children who weren't their own, right?

Anyway, Rosie figured that Meg might be at the fair, probably with Petey in tow. She hoped to see Petey and maybe even say hi to him, but that probably wasn't going to happen, either, given the current situation.

Only a few nights earlier Rosie had heard her parents arguing again about Petey. They were in their bedroom, talking in low voices, but Rosie, tiptoeing her way to the bathroom, had stopped and heard most of what they were saying. Basically, her dad was worried about Petey and wanted to start spending time with him again. But her mom was dead set against it.

Her mother had said that spending time with Petey Giroux would be betraying Rosie.

Her father had countered that the boy was innocent of all wrongdoing.

The argument had gone on long after Rosie had tiptoed back to her own room and closed the door. For at least another hour she could hear her parents' voices, occasionally raised and then hurriedly lowered, and then raised again.

Deep down, Rosie agreed with her father. She thought that her mother was being too harsh. But she wasn't sure she had the right to say anything to her father or to her mother, given the fact that she had been eavesdropping and wasn't supposed to know about their argument. Besides, she felt kind of guilty about being the cause of her parents' argument. Her parents never fought. At least, Rosie had never heard them fight before the other night. She would talk to Dr. Lowe about the Petey situation at her next appointment. She didn't want to be responsible, even in an indirect sort of way, for making someone, especially a child, unhappy. Dr. Lowe would probably help her decide if she should speak up.

"Hey, Rosie," Mr. Patterson said as they approached a garishly painted game booth. "Do you challenge me to make three perfect shots?"

It was that game where you had to throw a ball into a hole on a big board that was painted as a clown's face. The hole, of course, was his mouth. Rosie wasn't much for games, with the sole exception of Scrabble, a game she couldn't help but win even if she tried to lose for her father's sake. She didn't have an ounce of competitive spirit, which maybe was a bad thing. But she didn't see how that was going to change.

"No," Rosie said. "I don't challenge you. But you really want to try it, don't you?"

Mr. Patterson grinned and handed his money to the grizzled man inside the booth.

"Your father wants to show off his throwing arm," Mrs. Patterson remarked with a smile. "He was quite the pitcher in high school, or so he tells me."

"Hey," Mr. Patterson said, "I might be old but I'm not dead. Here goes."

In rapid succession, he sent all three balls right into the clown's mouth, surprising the grizzled man, who said, "Holy crap," and then, "Begging your pardon, ladies."

"Way to go, Dad!" Rosie said, patting her father's back.

"My hero!" Jane kissed her husband's cheek.

Mike claimed his prize, a stuffed pink rabbit—Rosie's mom loved rabbits—and the Pattersons moved off in the direction of the jewelry maker Jane wanted to visit. While her mom and dad considered the necklaces and bracelets and earrings, Rosie's eye wandered. Fairs were fun, she thought, for all sorts of reasons. The pageantry and the colors and the music were all exciting and made people feel good, like for a short time their troubles didn't matter. And somewhere underneath all the festivity, in a way Rosie was only beginning to identify and understand, there was an element of otherness, of danger, of things being not quite what they seemed. Carnivals, fairs, and the circus—they were all a little bit grotesque. It surprised Rosie that she felt drawn to that element of otherness. She was pretty sure that was something she wouldn't admit to her parents. They would only worry and think she wanted to get a tattoo or a piercing or dye her hair purple.

Her mom's laugh brought Rosie's attention back to the moment. As she turned to see what had pleased her mother, she caught site of two startlingly familiar girls. . . .

It was Mackenzie Egan and Courtney Parker. They were only yards way, standing together by the guys selling funnel cakes. Mackenzie's dark brown hair literally shone in the summer sun. She was wearing a floral patterned sundress that came to just above her knees and super-high wedges. A pair of enormous black sunglasses covered half of her face and she was carrying an equally enormous pink bag. If someone didn't know better, Rosie thought, they would think Mackenzie was a Hollywood star. Courtney was wearing what she usually wore in hot weather—a pair of super-low-cut jean shorts and a tight T-shirt that showed about three inches of her stomach. Courtney had gotten in trouble once for wearing that kind of T-shirt to school, but Rosie figured there was probably no dress code for a public festival. That was part of the otherness and the danger. . . .

Rosie quickly looked away from Mackenzie and her sidekick. She was pretty sure they hadn't seen her, at least, not yet. For some reason, she hadn't even considered that Mackenzie and her friends might be at the fair. She felt stupid now for not having thought about running into them. She should have prepared herself somehow. Or maybe she just shouldn't have come at all. Mackenzie and Courtney would laugh at her for coming to the fair with her parents instead of with some friends. They might even come over to her when her parents' backs were turned and say something nasty about—

A woman behind Rosie suddenly barked a command at her child. Rosie's entire body twitched at the harsh sound. Instantly, she felt and heard a loud buzzing in her ears, or maybe it was in her head. Her vision suddenly blurred and she felt incredibly hot, as if she was burning up from the inside.

Something weird was happening. Maybe she was having a panic attack. She tried to remember what Dr. Lowe had advised her to do in this sort of situation. She tried to imagine Dr. Lowe's round, pleasant face, her shoulder-length silver hair waved around it, her blue eyes bright and concerned. She tried to hear Dr. Lowe's voice, calm and reassuring. But the image failed to form and the voice remained silent.

"Rosie, what's wrong?"

This voice was very low and very distant. It might have been male or female, Rosie couldn't tell. She thought it sounded vaguely familiar but she wasn't sure about that, either.

"Oh, my God, Mike, I think she's going to faint!"

Yes, Rosie thought, hearing that very low and very distant voice. *I think I'm going to faint.* She became aware of hands on her arms and then, a moment later, a plastic cup of water being put to her lips. She felt some of the water dribble down her chin but managed to swallow a bit, too.

Slowly but surely her vision cleared and the awful buzzing in her ears stopped.

"I'm okay," she said, though she thought her voice still sounded a bit odd. "I'm fine."

"We should get you home," her mother said firmly. "Just in case."

"It was just the heat, that's all," Rosie protested, but she saw from the look on her mother's face that she, too, had seen Mackenzie Egan and Courtney Parker. There was no point in lying about the real cause of her distress.

"Even so," Mr. Patterson said, "we're going home."

Rosie fought back tears of shame. "I'm sorry I ruined your day. Dad didn't even get to hear the band."

Her mother linked arms with her and they headed toward the parking lot. "You didn't ruin anything," she said briskly. "We all had such a good time."

"Did you even get to buy a piece of jewelry?" Rosie asked quietly.

"Oh, I don't really need another piece of jewelry!"

"And I've had more than my share of junk food for one day," Mr. Patterson added.

Rosie managed a smile. It was true. Her dad had eaten two hot dogs, a funnel cake, and a whoopee pie. He had even bought a candy apple, in spite of the fact that her mom had warned him he could break a tooth biting into it. His teeth, Rosie was glad to see, had survived.

They reached the parking lot and Rosie, without looking back to the fairgrounds, slid into the backseat of her family's car. She wondered if Mackenzie and Courtney had watched her retreat. She wondered if they had seen her distress. *Well,* she thought wearily, *it's too late now.*

As her father pulled out of the spot and turned toward the exit, Rosie saw Meg standing with her mother and brother by the booth closest to the exit, almost as if they had followed the Pattersons to the parking lot. Even from this distance Rosie could see the look of concern on Meg's face, and on Mrs. Giroux's. Rosie thought that her eyes met Meg's for a second as her father drove past them. *But maybe,* she thought, slumping against the back of the seat, *I was imagining it.*

14

Jane sat in the ergonomic chair Mike had bought her, staring at the wall above her worktable. The collage she had constructed from photos torn from magazines and interesting bits of fabric she had collected over time was just a blur of color, lacking the creative inspiration it was supposed to provide. All she could think about was what had happened at the Fourth of July fair. A pleasant family outing had been ruined by memories made flesh. Mackenzie Egan and Courtney Parker. If there was a hell after all, Jane wished they would both go there.

She rubbed her tired eyes and wondered when they would be past all of this mess. When, she wondered, would the pain go away, hers and Rosie's and Mike's? When would Rosie be back to normal? Or, even better, when would Rosie be in a place where she wouldn't feel so vulnerable, ever again?

A life could be revolutionized in a matter of months. Just look at how her daughter's life had been so drastically altered in the course of one school year. The bullying could have been a lot worse, Jane realized that, but still, the results were bad enough. A happy fourteen-year-old girl didn't cut herself with a razor blade to make life tolerable. A happy fourteen-year-old girl didn't have to drop out of school weeks before the end of the semester. A happy fourteen-year-old girl didn't have a panic attack and almost pass out at a community fair.

And a happy forty-two-year-old woman didn't sit staring into space, brooding about what might have been.

When she and Mike had learned about the abuse, what could they have done differently? What could they have done that might have prevented Rosie from reacting so badly yesterday to the mere sight of the abusers?

Jane didn't really know. She had wanted to confront Mackenzie's father back in May, but Mike had convinced her that it would probably only be a waste of time. From what they knew, which, Jane had to admit, was largely hearsay, the girl was virtually on her own and had been even before her mother had run off with that lawyer from Augusta. Besides, who was Jane Patterson to give anyone parenting advice?

As for reporting Mackenzie and the others to the police, well, Rosie had been absolutely against that idea. Besides, there was no real, solid evidence—apart from Rosie's word—that Mackenzie and her friends were responsible for the harassment. Much too late Meg had admitted that she had known about some of it, but it could be argued—and it would be—that everything had been an accident or an imagined slight. Although how anyone could explain away the cutting off of Rosie's braid was beyond Jane's imaginative powers.

Wait. Courtney could swear that Rosie had asked her to cut it off. And someone would believe her. In times of stress, people were often eager to believe the most insane lies as truth, simply to be done with the trouble of having to think and to feel.

Jane shifted in her chair, though the discomfort she felt was entirely in her mind. Maybe she was one of those people who habitually avoided the truth when the truth threatened to be unpalatable. Maybe she just hadn't wanted to know the real reasons behind her daughter's strange behavior. Maybe she had been too afraid. Too often it was easier to ignore an unpleasant or a challenging reality than to face it head-on. Like when Rosie had come home that day with her hair chopped off and a story about having cut it herself. Deep, deep down Jane had known that was a lie, but she hadn't even had the courage to ask Rosie what she had done with the braid. Because then the unpleasant truth might have come out and the family would have been launched into chaos.

Jane rubbed the back of her neck, but the tension that had taken root there refused to budge. She remembered an article she had read online recently. (Whatever you might say about the Internet, it certainly didn't allow anyone to get away with claiming ignorance of a hot topic.) The article quoted a few experts who believed that single children, especially those who were very close to their parents, stood a higher chance of being bullied than children with siblings. It struck Jane as darkly ironic that forming a close relationship with your only child might actually put that child at risk in the larger world.

Sometimes, Jane thought, being a parent was the most frustrating job in the world. You were damned if you cared too much and damned if you didn't care enough.

But if there was one thing Jane knew for sure, it was that no matter the challenges, she was meant to be a mother. Since she was a little girl all she had really wanted was to someday start a family. But first had come college and then graduate school. It was not until she was twenty-three years old and finishing her master's at Cordette University just outside Boston that she met Mike. He was a few years older and working at a large accounting firm downtown. It was love at first sight. They were married within a year of their first date. Jane had no close friends (she never really had), so her mother had acted as her official witness. Mike's brother had acted as his witness, though after the wedding Mike and Rob had drifted apart for no reason Jane could discern.

For the first two years of their marriage, the Pattersons lived in a small, charming first-floor apartment in Boston's South End. Jane grew herbs and flowers in the tiny backyard and in the good weather they ate dinner there at a small plastic table. Jane had loved living in Boston. She regularly went to the Museum of Fine Arts and the ICA and the Isabella Stewart Gardner Museum. And the shopping was wonderful, even for someone like Jane, without a lot of disposable income. The vintage clothing shops were the finest she had ever seen, and the antique shops on Charles Street were stuffed with fascinating items.

But then Mike suggested they move to Maine, where he had been born and raised. He had grown homesick for what he called a simpler way of life. Cars that actually stopped for pedestrians. Natural beauty for the asking. An average workday that actually ended at five in the afternoon and not at nine at night. And, most important, neighbors who would go out of their way to help when you needed them.

In spite of her mother's protests, Jane had agreed to the move. At first, she found it difficult to adjust to life in semi-rural Yorktide. But she did have the experience of having been at college in a small New Hampshire town, so before long she settled into the local rhythms.

And because she wasn't the sort to flout conventions and bring attention to herself, Yorktide accepted Jane Patterson. When she wanted to go to a museum, she got in the car and drove north to Portland or, in the summer, to the Ogunquit Museum of American Art. When she needed an afternoon of retail therapy, she browsed the countless antique shops throughout York and Cumberland counties. In spite of what her mother had thought, southern Maine was hardly a backwater.

From the start the Pattersons had agreed to have at least two children. But it took a few years before Jane finally got pregnant and gave birth to Rosemary Alice. And then just after Rosie's first birthday Jane's mother passed away; her father was long gone, as were Mike's parents. Jane found herself feeling terribly alone in the world. To have another child seemed paramount. For the next few years she struggled to conceive again and to maintain a pregnancy, but it was not to be. What remained was a small family that developed into a very tight and self-sufficient unit.

But Jane wondered if their family unit had been in some ways too tight and self-sufficient. Maybe she had put too much pressure on Rosie to be her companion, when instead she should have been encouraging Rosie to make a wider circle of friends. But everything had seemed so cozy and perfect, just Jane, Mike, and Rosie, and right outside that tiny circle of two, Frannie and Meg.

Jane put her head in her hands and sighed. She would never forget the afternoon when Rosie admitted that she had kept quiet about the bullying because she had been afraid to disappoint her parents. Jane remembered feeling stunned, as if she had been physically struck. How, she wondered, had she been responsible for establishing a home in which her daughter, her only child, was more careful of her parents' feelings and expectations than of her own? It was horrible. It wasn't supposed to be this way.

And she had had no inkling of what was going on in Rosie's head all those months.

She remembered thinking that maybe she should have been reading Rosie's diary all along. If she had, she might have seen evidence of Rosie's distorted thinking. She might have been able to stop the abuse before it got too bad. But if Rosie had found out, Jane might also have lost Rosie's trust for good. Secretive behavior, like snooping in someone else's private space or like telling a lie, most often would out.

Jane took a sip of the now-tepid tea she had made almost an hour ago. In the past few weeks she had been wondering if bullying was really on the rise or if it had always been there in large numbers, just ignored or misunderstood. She tried now to recall any incident from her own childhood in which she might have been bullied. No, there was nothing, unless she counted that girl in grammar school who used to run up behind her and step on the back of her shoes, pulling them off. Jane had never told anyone about that, in spite of the scrapes on her heels caused by the girl's heavy shoes. She hadn't wanted to cause trouble.

Just like Rosie.

And then . . . There was another girl from grammar school, a pretty, sweet, dark-haired girl. What was her name? Try as she might, Jane simply couldn't remember that or anything else about her other than the fact that some boys and girls used to tease her about her weight.

One time . . . Jane shuddered as details of the memory came roaring back to her. How could she have forgotten this? One time a boy had grabbed the back of the girl's collar and shoved an unwrapped chocolate candy bar down her shirt. Jane had seen it happen. It was a warm day. The candy bar quickly began to melt against the girl's sweaty skin, staining her pale pink shirt with a thick streak of brown. And then . . .

Nothing. Jane couldn't remember what had happened next. Had anyone helped get the candy bar out of the girl's shirt? Jane knew for sure that she herself had done nothing, just like she had done nothing about her own unhappy experiences. She had been shy and self-effacing as a child, absolutely unwilling to call any attention to herself. And, it seemed, she had been unwilling to help another girl in distress because it might have directed the spotlight on her.

What Jane did remember was that the girl had not returned to school the following September. Jane's mother had learned that the girl's parents had enrolled her in a small, exclusive private school in another town where, they hoped, she would not meet with what everybody had then called "teasing."

In fact, Jane thought now, absentmindedly twisting a stray piece of ribbon around her finger, that poor little girl hadn't been teased, she had been bullied. She had been terrorized into leaving school and losing what few friends she might have had. It was a terrible story. Jane hoped it had a happy ending. But she would never know. Even if she could recall the girl's name, what right would she have to contact her, especially after having failed her so terribly? And besides, what could she possibly say to the now-middle-aged woman? "I was an accessory to your humiliation all those years ago. And I'm sorry." It was a true fact and a true sentiment, but neither would be very helpful. Better to let the past remain buried.

The phone rang, startling Jane out of her uncomfortable musings. Caller ID told her that it was one of her longtime clients, Mrs. Barnet. Jane's stomach sank.

"Hello, Mrs. Barnet," she said, her voice artificially bright.

"Jane," Mrs. Barnet said, without a greeting, "I'm calling about my dress."

"Of course. I'm sorry, Mrs. Barnet. It's almost completed."

"Almost? You said it would be ready by last Thursday. It's now Monday."

"I know," Jane said, "and I'm sorry."

"The party is this weekend."

"I know," Jane replied, mustering patience. "I assure you I'll have the dress ready for you to pick up the day after tomorrow."

"Well, let's hope so. I'll come by around ten Wednesday morning."

Jane thanked her justifiably testy client, replaced the receiver on its stand, and rubbed her tired eyes. Her ability to focus had suffered since Rosie's collapse. She had sewn Mr. Smith's buttons on Mr. Mendini's shirt and had misread the measurements she had taken for another client's skirt. Luckily, she had caught both mistakes before the clients had come for their clothing. Jane couldn't afford to be losing clients, especially relatively wealthy ones, not in this economy, not with wanting to send Rosie to a good college. With a sigh and great effort, Jane turned back to her work.

15

February 14, 2012

Dear Diary,

Today is Valentine's Day. It was one of the worst days of my life.

I don't even remember how it all started. Well, yes, I do, actually. It was right after homeroom. I was walking to my first class and when I passed this group of kids, boys and girls, they all burst out laughing. At first I thought one of them had told a joke or something but then it happened again with another group of kids farther down the hall and one of the girls whispered, but loudly, so that I could hear what she said. She said that I must be "desperate for sex." I was kind of shocked—well, a lot shocked—but I thought that maybe I'd misheard her. It was such an outrageous thing to say.

Then, at lunch, Meg told me that a boy in her advanced math class showed her a text on his phone. Supposedly, it had come from me, the only Rosie in school. Somehow, it had "gone viral," if that's the right term for what happened, which was that almost everyone with a phone had gotten the text, too, not only Roger Jackson.

The exact words are seared on my brain. I'll never forget them as long as I live.

"Roger, I love you with all my heart and soul. I dream about you every night. I want to kiss you. Love, Rosie"

It must have been written in text language with all those abbreviations, but those are the words Meg recited to me and she wouldn't lie about something like this. I sat there at the table Meg and I usually sit at for lunch and felt like I was naked, that's how exposed and embarrassed I felt. So many kids were looking at me and sniggering. I couldn't swallow a bite of food. Meg ate the oatmeal cookies Mom had packed for me.

I am devastated. That's not an exaggeration. When Meg told me what the text said, I almost passed out. Of course I would never tell a boy I loved him in a text message, even if I did love him!

The whole rest of the day was just awful. It was like this big conspiracy. No one came out and said anything like "Hey, Rosie, nice text!" so I couldn't just walk up to the kids who were giggling and say, "I never sent that text. It's all a lie." Maybe I should have done that anyway, but I didn't. And if I denied sending it, wouldn't some people just think I was just having second thoughts about having done it? There's some line my mom quotes about a lady protesting too much. It means that if you constantly deny doing something, you're probably guilty of doing it after all. At least, people are going to think that you're guilty.

I just didn't know what to say to anyone!

Later, when I was at my locker packing my books to go home, Mackenzie winked at me and gave me kind of a sly smile as she was walking by. I just know she sent that text to Roger and then, somehow, to everyone else in our class, but there's no way she'll actually admit it. I don't even know if there's a way you could prove that she was responsible.

Roger has always been nice to me before, but now he's furi-

ous with me even though I swore to him that I didn't send the text. But why would he believe me? Who am I? I'm not popular. I'm nobody.

He actually yelled at me after school and said I should leave him alone and quit stalking him and that he wouldn't go out with me even if I were hot, which I'm not. He said some more stuff, but I think I might have been in shock because I didn't really hear exactly what he was yelling. Finally, he just walked away and I just stood there. A bunch of other kids in our grade were watching and listening to the whole thing. I heard a few of them laugh and then someone, a boy I don't know, told them to shut up. Finally, I was able to walk away. If anyone said something to my back, I didn't hear it.

I feel so bad. I don't know what to do. Like I said, I just know it was all Mackenzie's fault, but I can't prove it, and even if I could, what would be the point? I don't think I would be brave enough to report her to the principal or to a teacher. I know I wouldn't be.

Why is she doing this to me?

Another weird thing is how Meg reacted to the whole episode. She said she couldn't understand why I got so upset. She said it was just a practical joke. She just couldn't see how humiliated I felt. How humiliated I still feel. No one's ever done anything really bad to her. Maybe that's why she can't be sympathetic. But she's my best friend, so she should at least try to understand how I feel. Right?

But maybe Meg is right. Maybe I did overreact. I shouldn't blame her for my own mistakes. Mom has always told me I'm a very sensitive person. It's true, I am. Maybe I do need to learn how to laugh off all the stuff Mackenzie is doing.

But I just don't see how I can do that.

How did all this happen?

R.

February 23–26, 2012

Dear Diary,

School is closed for a few days. I'm so relieved. I'm not going to think about having to go back.

Mom, Dad, and I just got back from a couple of days in Boston.

Meg said she was jealous I got to go to Boston. I think she was hinting that she wanted to come along, and I think that if I had asked Mom and Dad they would have said fine. But I wanted to be away from everything that reminds me of school. Even Meg.

Not that it worked. No matter how hard I tried to forget those girls and everything that's happened, I just couldn't. We went to the Museum of Fine Arts and there was this exhibit of medieval illuminations and even though it should have been really interesting to me because I love history, especially European history, it wasn't. I just looked at those tiny little illustrations in brilliant blues and pinks and greens and felt . . . nothing. I used to love the aquarium, too, but this time, it was like there was this heavy blanket over me or something, like everything around me was really . . . distant. Like all of my senses were dulled. It's hard to explain.

Of course, I pretended I was having a good time and I think Mom and Dad believed me, because neither of them asked questions or gave me funny, suspicious looks. I hate lying to them but if I told them how I'm really feeling, they would be so upset. It's better I keep everything to myself.

Like how I started cutting.

We learned about cutting in health class in a unit about stuff like eating disorders and depression and other bad things that can happen to young teenagers. At first it sounded horrible and gross, and I thought, there's no way I would ever do something like that. I've always hated the sight of blood. I was even really upset when I first got my period, though when I learned more about what was actually going on I was okay. Still.

I really don't know why I tried it. It's like, the idea got into my head and no matter how hard I tried to ignore it, the idea just wouldn't go away. It haunted me almost, following me around like a ghost. And then I stole one of Dad's razor blades from my parents' bathroom. And then I did it.

The oddest thing was that what I learned in class was true. It felt . . . good. At least, it didn't feel bad, like everything else feels these days.

I did it again after that.

I'm really afraid of Mom and Dad finding out and hating me or worse, kicking me out of the house. I'm such a disappointment to them already. I just know it. I bet they wish they had another child in place of me. Maybe even someone more like Meg, or even like Mackenzie. She's pretty and smart and popular. She's perfect. If I had any courage I would run away. But I don't. I'm a coward.

I don't know why I can't be homeschooled. I asked Mom and Dad about it. Turns out they are both seriously against homeschooling for all sorts of reasons. They asked me why I was asking about it and I lied and told them I'd heard someone in the cafeteria talking about someone they know who is homeschooled and I was curious. I really wish they would consider it because I really don't want to go back to school. But maybe it would just be too much work for Mom.

I couldn't cut when we were at the hotel. That was hard. Sometimes I wanted so badly to be alone so I could cut, but there was never a chance. Mom and Dad had booked a suite and it only had one bathroom. Even though I had my own room I was still afraid they would realize I'd locked the door and know something was wrong. So when we got home and Mom went out to the store and Dad went to check in at his office, the first thing I did was cut. Maybe it was all the worry and anxiety that had built up, I don't know, but it didn't work like it should this time. I just started to cry. For about half an hour I felt pretty hopeless, like I just couldn't continue to be alive, like I didn't know how to be alive, and that scared me. Then I heard Mom come home and somehow I managed to pull myself back together. At least, I managed to look like I was normal.

I know I should practice my piano, but I just don't want to anymore. But Mom and Dad pay so much money for my lessons that if I don't practice every day it's like I'm wasting their money and being disrespectful of them. And it's like I'm being disrespectful of Ms. Price, too. Mom told me that Ms. Price had cancer a few years ago and that she lost almost all of her money because of the cost of treatment. So if I give up piano lessons, I'm hurting Ms. Price and her husband, too. Mom and Dad taught me always to think of other people before myself. That's what I'm trying to do.

I am so tired.

R.

16

Meg had waited until Mrs. Patterson had left the house that afternoon before going through the pretty wooden gate Mr. Patterson had built in the fence that marked the boundary of their neat and well-kept backyard. Maybe she shouldn't be doing what she was doing. Maybe she shouldn't bother to care. But she did care.

The glass door of the screened porch was open, but the screen door was shut against bugs. Meg knocked loudly. After a moment, she knocked again. This time, she saw Rosie approach the door.

"I know you probably don't want to talk to me," Meg said hurriedly, "but I wanted you to know that I was really worried about you yesterday. I don't know if you saw me at the fair, but—"

"I saw you. When we drove away."

"I also saw . . . I saw who else was there."

"Yeah. Me, too."

"I kind of figured. So, are you okay?"

Rosie half smiled. "Yeah. It was stupid. I don't know why I got so upset."

"No," Meg said vehemently. "It wasn't stupid. That was the first time you'd seen them since . . ."

Rosie opened the screen door and stepped out onto the square of concrete. Her father's charcoal-fueled grill squatted to one side; along the other stood a row of her mother's potted pansies.

"Yeah," she said. "I guess that was it. I was just surprised."

"That makes sense. To be surprised, I mean. Mackenzie's such an idiot. They all are. And did you see what Courtney was wearing? Beyond tacky."

Rosie nodded. She had been thinking the same thing.

"I overheard my mom talking to someone on the phone once," Meg went on. "She said that Mackenzie's mother ran off with some guy from Augusta a few years ago and that her father's still a wreck about it. And she said that Mackenzie's brother is a loser. Well, actually, she called him a douche, but don't tell her I told you that. I heard he got arrested once up in Portland for being drunk on the streets. Gross."

"Yeah. Being drunk is gross no matter where you are."

"Yeah. And Courtney, please. I heard that her dad has been in jail, like, four times and that her mother is an alcoholic and that her younger brothers go to school wearing dirty clothes. No wonder she's always wanting to beat someone up and dressing like a tramp."

"Oh," Rosie said. "That's too bad about her family."

"Yeah," Meg went on, "and Jill, well, I don't know what her problem is other than for some weird reason she worships the ground Mackenzie walks on. And Stella, I don't know about her, either, but she seemed okay before she started to hang out with Mack—"

"Meg," Rosie interrupted. "What are you trying to say?"

Meg blushed. "I don't know. Sorry. It's just that I want you to believe me when I tell you I don't like those girls. I mean it."

"Okay. Um, did you go to the fireworks last night?"

"Yeah. I wasn't really in the mood, but Petey really wanted to go, so Mom and I took him. It was okay."

Rosie glanced over to the Giroux house. "Does your mom know you're here?"

Meg shook her head. "No. She's at work. Like always."

"Will you tell her you came over?"

"I don't know. I don't think she'd mind. . . ." But Meg wasn't at all sure what her mother would think about her having gone over to Rosie's. "I mean, I'm not doing anything wrong. Am I?"

"No," Rosie said. "Except that my mother might not like that we're talking."

"I know. She told my mom I wasn't supposed to bother you anymore. I waited until I saw your mom leave the house before coming over. Will you tell her that I was here and that we talked?"

Rosie paused before answering that question. "I don't know," she said. "Maybe not yet."

"Okay."

"It's not like I have to tell her everything."

Meg heard the new note of defiance in Rosie's voice and thought it was a good thing. "Right," she said. "I mean, it's not like we're Petey's age."

Rosie smiled. "Right. How is Petey, anyway?"

For a moment Meg wondered if she should mention that Mr. Patterson had asked to spend time with her brother. She decided against it. It wasn't her place to tell. Besides, maybe Rosie already knew.

"He's good," Meg said. "He likes day camp a lot. Can I tell him you said hi?"

"Sure."

"So, what books did you choose from Mr. Arcidiacono's list?"

"*Dubliners* by James Joyce, *Emma* by Jane Austen, and for the non-fiction, a biography of Elizabeth the First and a history of the last Crusade," Rosie said.

"Yow. The last Crusade? How many were there?"

"A lot, I think. I guess I'll find out. What did you pick?" Rosie asked.

"*The Great Gatsby, The Sun Also Rises, Up From Slavery,* and a biography of Ben Franklin. But I'm also rereading the Lord of the Rings trilogy."

"I love the movies, but I haven't read the books."

"I could lend them to you, if you want."

"Thanks." Rosie glanced over her shoulder, back at the house. "I should probably go inside," she said. "My mom will be home soon. She only went out to get some coffee. My father likes the kind they sell at Port City Roasters."

Meg nodded. "Right," she said. "Rosie? Thanks."

"Sure." Rosie smiled and then went back inside.

Meg half ran across the Pattersons' backyard, through the gate, and into her own yard. She felt happy. She felt relieved. Rosie had actually talked to her. They had had a real conversation. Meg felt tears prick at her eyes and furiously blinked them away. Her mother would be home from work soon. The last thing Meg needed was her mother seeing her eyes all red and swollen and asking questions about where she had been or what she had been doing all afternoon. Meg wanted to keep this very important moment to herself until things between Rosie and her became clear. And then, if everything was all right, she would shout it to the world.

17

The chicken was roasting in the oven, a pot of potatoes was boiling on the stove, and the green beans were rinsed and waiting to be steamed. Frannie ineffectually fanned her face with a dish towel and wondered what had possessed her to roast anything in this heat. She would love to have an air conditioner, central air preferably, but that certainly wasn't in the budget.

With a sigh meant for no one, she went to the sink and poured a glass of cold water. She thought about Petey, upstairs in his room, playing with an old Erector set he had inherited from the brother of a girl at school. The night before, as she was tucking him into bed, he had asked again why he wasn't allowed to go over to Aunt Jane's house.

Frannie had smiled and unnecessarily straightened the sheet over her son. "I told you before, Petey. She's very busy right now," she had said, hoping like mad that he would believe her lie. "She has some new clients and they're very demanding, so she needs to focus on work."

But Petey hadn't believed her lie. "Did I do something wrong?" he had asked, tears suddenly quivering in his eyes.

Frannie had hurriedly reassured him that he hadn't done anything wrong and that sometimes adults really did just get too busy to . . . She had talked herself into a corner. What was she going to say? Was she going to tell him that adults, like Petey's own father and like his own Aunt Jane, sometimes got too busy to be there for the children they claimed to love?

"I promise you, Petey," she had said, after kissing him on the forehead, "I'll never be too busy to be right here for you. Okay?"

It was a promise Frannie hoped she could keep, though she knew all too well that life could be unfair and random and that the most well-intentioned promises might have to be broken.

God, it was hot. Frannie ran the sweating glass across her forehead and thought again of Mike's offer to spend time with Petey. Really, the only thing standing in the way of her gladly accepting was Jane's stubbornness. She felt a flare of anger. Who was Jane to be punishing her son? How dare she act so righteously, as if she was perfect and everyone else around her was not? Frannie remembered a time when she and Jane had gone to Portsmouth to look for a birthday gift for Mike. Outside the parking garage they had encountered a homeless woman. It was hard to tell for sure, what with her tattered clothing, mangled hair, and dirt-streaked face, but Frannie thought she must be at least sixty. Jane had mumbled something disparaging about the woman, ignoring her outstretched hand and timid plea for a coin. Frannie, mortified by her friend's behavior, had given the woman all the change in her purse. Had Jane's conduct been so kind or generous or loving? It most certainly had not!

Be nice, Frannie told herself. *Treat others as you would have them treat you, with kindness and compassion and sympathy.* It was a commandment that was a lot easier to deliver than to perform.

Especially when it came to her ex-husband. She had tried again to talk to Peter about what had happened to Rosie, but from the start he had shrugged off the entire string of nasty behavior on Mackenzie's part as "just normal kid stuff." "It's the kind of thing that toughens you up," he had said again last night over the phone. "The Pattersons have always spoiled Rosie. They treat her like she's a princess or something. That's why she couldn't take some teasing."

"It was more than teasing," Frannie had retorted. "And what Meg did was probably even more hurtful to Rosie than what those other girls did."

Peter had sighed like a long-put-upon man. "Okay, Meg shouldn't have ratted out her friend. It was wrong. But it's not like it's the end of the world, for Christ's sake."

With supreme effort Frannie held her tongue, but internally she had fumed. Meg's bad behavior, she had decided after that conversation, was Peter's fault. Her daughter had learned from her father how to be mean and heartless and callous. She had learned how to disappoint and betray the ones she cared for.

And speaking of disappointing the ones you cared for, Frannie thought, it was time for her to remind Peter, yet again, about a promise he had made to their son. Frannie picked up the phone and dialed his number. With any luck he had remembered to pay his phonc bill. . . .

"Yo."

Frannie rolled her eyes. "It's Frannie. I forgot to ask you something yesterday. When are you taking Petey to the Sea Dogs game? You promised him you'd take him to a game this summer."

Peter groaned. "I know what I promised," he said. "I just haven't gotten around to buying tickets yet. A buddy said he could get me two for the price of one. I'm just waiting on him, that's all."

"Don't disappoint your son, Peter."

"Jesus Christ, Fran, lay off. I said I'm on it."

"You'd better be because—"

Frannie's ears were met with a dial tone. Not for the first time her ex-husband had eluded an unpleasant conversation by simply hanging up. Frannie sighed and put down the phone.

Meg came into the kitchen then, and yanked open the door of the fridge. "Who was on the phone?" she asked.

"Nobody."

"That means Dad. When's dinner?"

"When it's ready," Frannie said, feeling a twinge of discomfort. Did Meg really associate her father with "Nobody"? "Will you set the table?"

"Okay." Meg shut the fridge door and went over to the cabinet that contained the dishes. Frannie was a bit surprised. Lately, it had been usual for Meg to protest a request (a request that was not really a request but an order) with a sigh or a roll of the eyes.

"You okay?" she asked her daughter now.

Meg looked up from placing a fork next to a knife on a paper napkin. "Yeah. Why?"

"I don't know. You look . . . almost happy or something."

Meg shrugged. "Maybe."

"Well, I hope you are feeling happy."

"Thanks."

Meg quickly finished setting the table and loped out of the room.

Frannie sank into a chair at the kitchen table and pushed aside one of the plates Meg had put out. She noticed another scratch on the table's worn surface and remembered the table leg that had somehow grown shorter (what had Peter done to it, she wondered testily). They could really use a new table, one that didn't wobble and threaten the destruction of everything on top of it. The question was, how to afford it. She might be able to find something at a garage sale or in one of the local resale shops. It certainly didn't have to be beautiful, just strong and clean. Although, Frannie thought, it would be nice to have a new and beautiful piece of furniture for once. And with Peter no longer living in the house, it might actually stay beautiful for years!

Peter. His comments about Rosie, however crude, caused Frannie to think back to her own school days. She was absolutely sure she had never bullied another student. For one thing, it was wrong to hurt another person. The Golden Rule—that commandment again!—demanded that you Do Unto Others As You Would Have Them Do Unto You. There had been a pillow on the living room couch in her childhood home, embroidered with those very words. For another, if Frannie's parents had found out she had done something bad to another student, they would have seriously punished her. Her father had been fond of spanking and had sometimes used a belt. Her mother had liked to impose restrictions on food, television time, phone use—whatever she could find to restrict. Frannie didn't feel that her parents had been abusive, but they had been harsh, perhaps more harsh than was necessary, to get their lessons across.

No, Frannie was happy to conclude that she was innocent of any bullying behavior. And then something began to take shape in her mind, not clearly at first, but still, she absolutely knew it was a memory and not a fiction her brain was creating. And there it was. At the time it had seemed a small incident to her. . . . She must have been in the fifth or sixth grade, definitely not yet in high school because she could see herself in pigtails. It must have been lunchtime or recess because the schoolyard had been crowded with kids. A girl—definitely a girl—was laughing and pointing at another girl. A circle of kids gathered around the victim. Frannie couldn't recall who the victim was or why she was being laughed at. She did remember being part of that circle of kids, though, laughing along with the tormentor and her audience.

Frannie clutched her head. She was overcome by feelings of shame and embarrassment. Had she passed along to her daughter a serious flaw of character? Had her youthful participation in that poor girl's humiliation been an indication of something seriously wrong, something that would rear its ugly head in her daughter's lifetime? Even the Bible said that the sins of the father would be revisited on the sons, and that had to also mean that the sins of the mother would be revisited on the daughters.

The smell of something burning rudely dragged Frannie from her morbid thoughts. "Oh, crap!" she muttered, dashing from her seat and over to the oven.

The chicken, though slightly burnt, was salvageable, though the potatoes she had overboiled might be a little mushy. Lots of butter would make them appealing again. Neither kid would eat more than three or four green beans, so it didn't matter what she did to them.

Frannie began to slice blackened skin off the chicken, and as she did so, she took herself to task yet again. Here she had been blaming her ex-husband for something for which she might be responsible!

"Let she who is without sin cast the first stone," she whispered, dropping burnt chicken skin into the garbage.

18

March 10, 2012

Dear Diary,

Can things get any worse?

The answer to that question is yes, they can. They always do. And they probably always will.

Some of the girls at school have started to act as if I'm not even there. They're totally ignoring me. In Spanish class today Mrs. Moreno gave a girl in the front row a test to pass around, and when the stack of papers came to the girl in front of me, Larissa Flaherty, she reached way back and gave it to the boy sitting behind me. I was shocked. She's always been friendly with me before now. The boy behind me, Charles Lin, tapped me on the shoulder and gave me a copy of the test, and I thanked him and just pretended that nothing strange had happened.

I've gotten very good at pretending.

Then after lunch, this other girl I always thought was nice, Laura Bourdet, snubbed me. I said hi to her in the hall like I always do and she walked right past me without even looking at me. And on the bus on the way home, three other girls from one of our classes got on after Meg and me, and as they walked by us to their own seats, each one said, "Hey, Meg!" sounding really friendly, but said nothing to me. They didn't even look at me. It was like I wasn't even there. They always used to say hello to both of us.

Meg just sat there and didn't say anything about what had just happened. I waited for her to say something like, "That was so rude!" and get angry like she usually does when she sees someone getting hurt. But she said nothing. Like she hadn't even noticed what had happened or like she didn't even care.

But then, when the bus let us off outside our houses, I told her about what happened with Larissa Flaherty and with Laura Bourdet, and Meg said I had to tell someone about what was going on, our homeroom teacher or the principal, but I can't. How can I say that people aren't looking at me or talking to me and not sound like someone so full of herself that she complains about not being the center of attention? Besides, maybe I'm imagining everything, though Meg said that of course I'm not, and that Charles Lin, for one, was a witness and that she, for two, was another witness.

But I begged Meg not to tell anyone, not even Tiffany, even though Meg said she bet Tiffany would know how to handle things. And why would the principal care that some stupid freshman was being snubbed?

Meg kind of got impatient with me then. She said something like, "What did you do to them? You must have done something to make them mad at you!"

I was really surprised and also felt kind of sick. I couldn't say anything. I just went inside. Now I think that Meg is mad at me, too. But she just doesn't understand why I can't tell anyone about what's happening to me.

I don't know why all this stuff is going on. But I know that Mackenzie Egan is behind it. Why does she hate me?

Maybe Meg is right. Maybe it's because I did do something bad or wrong. Maybe this is all my fault. Maybe there is something wrong with me. That's why Mackenzie is making my life miserable. She could have decided to bully anyone else in school, but she chose me. It must be because I deserve it. Even Meg thinks so.

I was able to cut again after dinner. It helped a bit. It's like trading one pain for another. And the physical pain is way easier to deal with than the pain in my . . . I was going to say heart, but maybe I should say head, instead. I don't think people like me and my parents, people who are agnostic and don't pray or go to church, are supposed to believe in a soul. But if I do have a soul, I think that's where the pain might be worst. But that probably doesn't make sense. Once I thought that maybe I could talk to someone at Meg's church, maybe a priest, about souls and spiritual stuff, but then I decided I would only be wasting the priest's time. It's not like I go to Meg's church, so why would anyone care about my questions?

I got the second book in HIS DARK MATERIALS from the library, but I can't seem to start it. It's like suddenly I have no interest in it, which is odd because I was really looking forward to reading it. I think I'll just return it tomorrow so it's there for someone else who wants to read it. I don't want to be unfair.

R.

March 27, 2012

Dear Diary,

People are still ignoring me at school. Not boys. Just girls.

I remember seeing a documentary on TV about the Amish people, and it talked about how the community shuns someone who breaks a law of their church or someone who does something really wrong, like steal or have an affair. The person is forced to live with the community, but at the same time he isn't really an acknowledged part of it. I remember the presenter using the phrase "social avoidance."

I remember thinking how awful and frustrating and maddening that would be, having nowhere else to go and being vir-

tually invisible to everyone around you. It sounded like a cruel, cruel punishment.

I think I know a little of what that feels like now. It is awful and frustrating and maddening. I was right. It is a cruel punishment, especially for a crime I never committed. At least in the Amish community, the person being shunned actually chooses his punishment by refusing to apologize or change his wrong behavior.

But what did I ever do to hurt anyone? And if I did do something wrong, why won't anyone tell me what it was so that I can apologize?

I'm so tired lately. I go to bed as early as I can without making Mom and Dad wonder if I'm okay, but I still can't sleep for hours and when I do, it's never enough. I'm always tired, always. I don't know what to do. I thought about seeing if Mom had some old sleeping pills in her bathroom cabinet, but then I was afraid that she might need them and find out they were missing. I don't know if I could lie well enough to keep me out of trouble with her if that happened. She would be so disappointed in me. So would Dad.

And then they might find out everything.

I would die of embarrassment if anyone knew that I cut myself. I keep my sleeves pulled down and on days when we have gym I wear a long-sleeved T-shirt under my clothes. No one has said anything about why I always wear long sleeves, probably because it's still really cold and lots of other kids are still wearing their winter stuff. I don't know what I'll do when the weather gets warmer. My heart is racing really hard right now.

I'm back.

I had to put my pen down for a while and take some deep breaths. My heart isn't racing too badly now, but it still doesn't feel right. I've heard that young people can get heart attacks, too, not just old and overweight people. What would Mom and Dad say if I had a heart attack? I wonder if our health insurance would cover the cost of the hospital and medicine and all.

It would probably be a big disaster. It would probably be better if I just died right away.

Mom's going to call out soon that dinner is ready and I'll have to go downstairs even though I have no appetite. I don't care about food anymore. She'll watch me like a hawk watches a mouse and keep pressing me to eat more so I'll be forced to eat something. I don't think she knows I have to use two safety pins to help hold up my pants now. At least, she hasn't said anything to me, just that I don't eat enough.

She just called for me to come down.

I wish I never had to leave this room.

19

Meg sat at the kitchen table in the Pattersons' kitchen. It was a little after two in the afternoon. She had been pruning in the little Giroux garden when Rosie had come outside and called to her from her own yard. Meg had seemed happy to come inside and out of the hot midday sun. Rosie had never known Meg to be an enthusiastic gardener. Rosie wasn't that into gardening, either. She loved to look at flowers and enjoyed arranging them in a vase—she had put together the bouquet of miniature white roses that sat on the living room coffee table—but as for growing them, well, that didn't interest her so much.

"Do you want some chocolate milk?" Rosie asked. "For some reason my mom's been buying it lately. I think she's trying to get me to gain some weight."

"Sure," Meg said. "My mom never buys it. She says it's too expensive or something. Thanks."

Rosie got the carton from the fridge and poured two glasses of milk. "It's full fat. It's like melted ice cream."

"Yum. By the way, I haven't told my mom that we talked the other day," Meg said as Rosie handed her a glass.

"I haven't told my mom, either," Rosie said. In truth, she was a bit angry with her mother for having told Mrs. Giroux to keep Meg away. Rosie knew her mother had meant well, but it annoyed her to be treated like a helpless child. She had talked to Dr. Lowe about the incident and Dr. Lowe had assured her that her feelings were valid and that her anger toward her mother didn't make her a bad person. Just normal.

Meg took a long drink of the milk before carefully putting the glass on the table. "Can I ask you something?" she said.

"I guess."

"Why wouldn't you tell someone what was going on? Especially after what happened at Valentine's Day. Or when all those girls started to ignore you."

Rosie put her own untouched glass on the table now. She had talked about this with Dr. Lowe, and then, a little bit, with her mother. "I don't know," she said finally, which wasn't strictly true. "I was scared, I guess. I didn't want to make a bigger deal out of it. I didn't want everyone pointing at me."

"But didn't you want it to stop?" Meg asked. "The name-calling, the snubbing? And that disgusting text. I'm sorry. I guess I don't really understand."

"Of course I wanted it to stop," Rosie said forcefully. "I know I made a mistake in not reporting what was going on. But I kept imagining that Mackenzie would deny everything and not get in trouble and that then she would hate me even more. And then everyone, all the other kids, the teachers, and my parents would think I was a liar."

"Your parents are cool," Meg argued. "They would have believed you."

"Maybe." Rosie finally took a drink of the chocolate milk. She didn't think Meg would understand how she had felt that telling her parents about being pushed around would only result in their being disappointed in her.

Meg sighed. "It was all such a huge mess. You know, after I . . . after I did what I did, they didn't even look at me. It was like I didn't really exist for them. I was totally unimportant to them after I told them about—"

"Did you want to be important to them?" Rosie asked. The question was a bit of a challenge. "Was that why you told my secret?"

"No!" Meg cried. "I mean, I don't know what I expected. I just didn't want them to start bullying me, too. I just didn't realize that with people like that, well, I don't think anyone is safe. They could have started in on me, too, no matter how I had . . . how I had helped them."

"There's no honor among thieves."

"What?"

"It's something my dad says," Rosie explained.

"Oh. I think I understand."

Rosie finished her milk. If her mother really was trying to get her to gain weight, she thought, all she had to do was keep buying this stuff. It was delicious and in a weird way was helping her to get through this difficult conversation with Meg. Maybe chocolate did have some real, positive effect on people's mood, like the ads claimed it did.

"Can I ask you something else?" Meg asked now.

Rosie nodded. She could always choose not to answer Meg's question. Dr. Lowe was helping her learn how to say no. She was helping her to consider her own feelings, as well as the feelings of others.

"Why didn't you want me to say anything to someone, like my mom or Tiffany, about what was going on?"

Meg asked. "That might have taken some of the pressure off you."

Rosie's temporarily elevated mood plummeted. How could she tell Meg that she hadn't wanted her to speak up because a tiny part of her had felt that maybe she deserved the bullying? It was too embarrassing an admission to make. With Dr. Lowe's silent approval, she just shook her head.

"I was wrong not to tell," Meg went on, almost as if to herself. "It would have been the smart thing to do. It's what we're told to do in all those courses and pamphlets and stuff about bullying prevention."

Both girls were silent for a moment. And then Rosie became aware that she was feeling . . . angry. It felt weird. She had been sort of angry with Meg before, not often, but she had never actually acted on the anger. But now, she couldn't seem to stop the words from coming out of her mouth.

"You could have stood up to Mackenzie and the others for me," she said. "I would have stood up for you if you were the one being pushed around."

"Really?" Meg half laughed. "Those girls are bad, Rosie. No offense, but I'm way tougher than you are and even I . . . even I didn't try to stop them."

Rosie felt the blood rush to her face. "Well, if you were the one being harassed," she said, in a voice much louder than her usual, "trust me, I would have done something."

"You begged me not to tell anyone!" Meg cried. "I know I should have told but I was trying to keep my promise to you!"

"No, you weren't," Rosie snapped. "You were scared of Mackenzie."

Meg fiddled with her empty glass for a moment. "You

know what?" she said finally. "You're right. I was scared of her and of Courtney and of Jill and even of Stella a bit. I didn't want to be their victim like . . . like you were."

Yes, Rosie thought, her anger at Meg sliding away. *A victim like I was,* she thought. *So much of a victim that I took a razor blade to my own skin. So much of a victim that I wanted to die. And maybe I would have died if . . .*

"I guess I should get home now," Meg said suddenly, standing up from the table. "I need to pick up Petey from camp soon. Thanks for the chocolate milk."

Rosie half smiled. "Sure. Say hi to Petey for me."

At the back door Meg turned around. "Do you still hate me?" she asked, her voice a little bit wobbly.

Rosie was surprised. "I never hated you. I don't think I've ever hated anybody."

"Not even Mackenzie and them?"

"No. Not even them."

"I think I hate them," Meg said with a small smile. "And I'm the one who goes to church every Sunday."

Rosie smiled back. What could she say to that? She had never heard that going to church turned you into a perfect person. From what she understood, going to church was about trying to make yourself into a better person than the person you were when you came through the door. But maybe that wasn't right.

When Meg had gone, Rosie put their empty glasses into the dishwasher and went up to her room. Once there, she sat in the big comfortable armchair she used for reading and sometimes, for thinking. She had been lying to Meg when she said she didn't hate anybody, because there was one person she did hate. Well, maybe not so much anymore, but there was one person she had hated, and badly. And that person was herself.

Not that she had understood the self-hatred until Dr. Lowe had helped her to identify it for what it was. Dr.

Lowe had suggested that maybe, just maybe, Rosie was clinging to her anger over Meg's betrayal and Mackenzie's bullying because on some very deep level she had not yet accepted her own role in, her own responsibility for, what had happened. Not that she was in any way to blame for her victimization. But maybe, Dr. Lowe had suggested, Rosie was angry with herself for not having handled the bullying in another, better way. Like, by respecting herself enough to tell her parents after the very first incident last fall. And, Dr. Lowe said, before she could really and truly forgive her friend—if not those other girls—she would have to really and truly forgive herself. She would have to learn how to love and respect herself for who she was, flaws, strengths, everything.

She would even have to forgive herself for the cutting. She would have to say, "Rosie, I'm so sorry I didn't love you like you deserve to be loved." That idea had seemed frightening and kind of weird, but slowly and gradually Rosie had been coming to see the sense in Dr. Lowe's words.

Rosie absentmindedly touched the scars on her left arm, then, realizing what she was doing, took her hand away. It had felt odd, arguing with Meg before in the kitchen, but nothing terrible had happened, the world was still turning on its axis, and as far as she could tell, Meg still liked her and still wanted to be friends.

Rosie realized that she was smiling. She was actually glad that they'd had that argument or conversation or whatever it had been, exactly. She felt a little bit proud of herself and not even guilty for feeling proud. She thought that might be progress.

20

Jane pulled open the door to the dishwasher and slid her empty cup into the top rack. Her afternoon cup of strong black tea was a habit she couldn't imagine giving up. Her dental hygienist routinely scolded her as she worked to remove tea stains from her front teeth, but Jane was adamant. It was, she countered, her only vice. She had never smoked and she had given up drinking alcohol during the years she had struggled with getting and staying pregnant. Afterward, even a glass of wine with dinner held no appeal.

She began to close the door of the dishwasher when she spotted, on the other side of the top rack, two tall glasses, the bottoms of which were coated with what could only be chocolate milk. She wondered. Maybe Mike had come home for lunch or to pick up something he had forgotten to take to the office. Well, even if he had, that didn't explain the chocolate milk. Mike was lactose intolerant.

Jane heard Rosie coming into the kitchen and swiftly closed the door to the dishwasher. She turned to face her daughter and hoped her voice wouldn't betray her internal turmoil and suspicion. "Rosie?" she said. "There are two glasses in the dishwasher. Both have the remains of chocolate milk."

"So?" Rosie replied with a shrug. "You told me not to leave dirty dishes and glasses in the sink."

"I'm not worried about that. Was someone else here while I was out?"

Rosie's didn't answer at once. Instead she went to the sink and poured a glass of filtered water. "Are you spying on me?" she finally asked.

"Of course not," Jane protested. "I just want to know if someone came over while I was at the store. I know you would never let in a stranger, so—"

"Meg was here." Jane could not ignore the note of defiance in her daughter's voice.

"Oh," she said calmly, though the flash of anger that coursed through her was intense. She had told Frannie to keep Meg away from her daughter! She had demanded it.

"We've been talking a bit lately," Rosie went on.

"Oh."

"You don't sound very happy about it."

Jane thought that sounded like an accusation. She attempted a little laugh. "Well, I—I'm just surprised, that's all." Shocked was more like it.

"I thought you would be proud of me," Rosie said. "You're always talking about forgiveness."

"I know, and I am proud of you, of course I am." Jane put her hand on Rosie's shoulder and felt her daughter tense. She took her hand away.

"Then what's wrong?" Rosie asked.

Be careful, Jane, she thought. *Don't blow this conversation.*

"Nothing's wrong," she said. "Rosie, how do you feel about Meg? Do you want to be friends with her again?"

Rosie paused for a long moment before replying. "I don't know," she said. "I think so."

"As long as you don't feel forced to do anything you don't want to do, that's all that matters."

"No one is forcing me to do anything," Rosie said carefully. "I make my own decisions."

That, Jane thought, was Dr. Lowe's doing. "Good," she said.

Rosie picked up a home decorating magazine from the counter and began to flip through its pages.

Jane busied herself with making another cup of tea. The occasion seemed to call for it. She took a fresh cup from the hanging rack and a tea bag from the canister underneath. She poured filtered water into the teakettle and waited for the water to boil. And while she waited, she surreptitiously watched Rosie browsing through the magazine.

Whatever Rosie thought, Jane wished that she, too, could feel confident that Meg was truly sorry. She wished she could fully trust her. How exactly did you encourage your daughter to forgive while at the same time to exercise caution? Real friendship required absolute trust and was incompatible with doubt. Jane didn't expect easy answers, but she very much wanted them.

But wanting something didn't mean getting it, like her desire to keep Meg away from Rosie. That wish hadn't been granted, as maybe it was fated not to be. If you believed in such things, and Jane did though she wouldn't admit as much to her husband, you might say there was a powerful force working to bring the two families back together whether they liked it or not. Witness what had taken place the day before.

She had gone to Mike's office to pick him up (his car

was in the shop). His assistant was gone for the day, as was the family practitioner who worked from the office across the hall. Perhaps taking advantage of their being totally alone, perhaps suffering from a guilty conscience, Mike had told her that he had approached Frannie about spending time with Petey. Jane was furious with him for having talked to Frannie in the first place, as well as for having kept the conversation a secret from her for so long. Mike retaliated with his knowledge of her having kept from him the fact that she had demanded Frannie keep Meg away from Rosie.

The argument had rapidly escalated into one of the worst, most cruel fights of their marriage. Jane had accused Mike of being a dishonest husband and he had accused her of being a negligent mother. The fight had ended with Jane in tears and Mike stony and silent. If Rosie had noticed her mother's eyes later that evening, still slightly swollen and red, she had kept quiet about it.

They had apologized sincerely but were both still a bit tender. It seemed that the process of reconciliation had unexpected pitfalls and could cause collateral damage. Somehow, if only for a short while, Jane and Mike had become enemies, fighting on opposing sides of the war that was supposed to be about the two neighboring families. Well, war never made sense and there never was a winner, not really.

Jane took a box of imported Italian cookies out of the pantry; tea with a cookie was more comforting than tea without one. She wondered now if Rosie had told Meg about the cutting. Maybe Rosie hadn't yet told her but was planning on it. What if Meg repeated her original crime and told those horrible girls Rosie's latest secret? That kind of a betrayal could be disastrous.

Jane glanced at her daughter. She wondered if she should suggest that Rosie not mention the cutting to Meg.

But maybe her saying nothing at all about the issue was best. She didn't want to put ideas in her daughter's head, certainly not bad ones. And for the past few months, she thought, so many of her ideas had been bad ones.

The teakettle began to whistle and Jane poured the boiling water into her cup.

"I was thinking about making omelettes for dinner," she said then. "I bought some nice fresh goat cheese and I've got a big bunch of tarragon from the farmers' market. What do you think?"

Rosie nodded and closed the magazine. "It sounds good."

Jane smiled and watched Rosie leave the kitchen. If spending time with Meg was going to revive her daughter's appetite, it couldn't be an entirely bad thing.

Jane went to the fridge and began to gather ingredients for dinner. Whether she wanted it to happen or not, it seemed that progress was being made toward restoring some degree of emotional closeness between the Patterson and Giroux families. Jane brought the container of goat cheese and the bunch of tarragon to the butcher-block cutting board. She thought again of Mike and of how he wanted to be there for Petey. She supposed it couldn't hurt to talk to her husband again, especially in light of the development between Rosie and Meg, especially in the aftermath of their own dreadful fight. She really did want to make amends. Mike would be glad that she was trying to be more open and generous. He was a lot more courageous a person than she was, that was for sure. It was one of the primary reasons she had married him, his strength of character. Jane had always felt that she needed more protection from the world than most people. Mike provided that protection. She didn't know what she would do without him.

Jane took a bite of the cookie—hazelnut—and a sip of tea. Yes, she would tell Mike that she was okay with his spending time with Petey. She pretty much had to. But that didn't mean she wanted anything to do with his mother. Not yet. Maybe never.

Time would have to tell.

21

March 2012

Dear Diary,

A lot of girls are still ignoring me, but Laura Burdett said hi to me in the hall today. I was expecting her to walk right past me again, like she's been doing for weeks now, but she didn't. She actually stopped and said hi. She seemed kind of nervous, like maybe she was expecting me to be mad and yell at her or something for the way she's been treating me. But I just said hi back and continued to walk to my locker. She didn't actually apologize, but I think that's what she meant by stopping when she said hello.

I suppose I should care or be grateful that she said hello, but I feel too dead to feel anything. That doesn't make sense. I am too dead to feel anything. Anything besides despair. But if you're really dead, if your lungs aren't breathing and your heart isn't pumping, you're beyond despair. You're beyond happiness, too, but I'm already beyond happiness. So what's the big deal about death?

I was wondering. Maybe Mackenzie isn't behind all the bad stuff that has been happening to me. Or maybe she was, but now there's someone else who hates me just as much as she does. It seems entirely possible that someone else hates me.

Meg is acting odd around me, too. She hardly looks at me when we're together and at lunch she eats in about a minute and then says she forgot something in her locker or needs to finish homework and goes off to the library or wherever it is she really goes.

I think she's afraid that if she hangs out with me too much, Mackenzie and the rest are going to start tormenting her, too. Part of me can't blame her, I guess. I'm such a loser. I don't know why Meg ever wanted to be my friend in the first place. I wouldn't be surprised if she dumped me.

Social contagion. That term just popped into my head. I don't remember where I heard it, but I think it means when being around a certain person makes other people consider you the same as that person. Maybe that's not really the definition, but that's what Meg's probably afraid of, being considered a loser like me. I am socially contagious, like the lepers in the Bible. I don't know much about the Bible, but I know about the lepers. Everybody does.

I got another A in history and an A+ in English. Ms. Brown says I'm the best student she's ever had. At least I can handle schoolwork without being a failure. And as long as I keep getting good grades, Mom and Dad won't bother me with questions about how I'm feeling. I'm fine! I can say. I'm getting all As! What could possibly be wrong?

I really, really don't want to play the piano anymore, but I know if I tell that to Mom and Dad they'll both be sad, especially Dad, who always says he wished someone had given him piano lessons when he was a kid. I guess his family didn't have any money to spare. Mom had a doctor's appointment this afternoon and I told her I practiced while she was out. I feel bad about lying to her, but I don't know what else to do. I just couldn't bring myself to play a single note.

How did everything get so bad? I feel like everything is totally out of my control. Except for when I cut and then, for about a minute, I feel almost okay. But then the minute passes and everything is chaos again. I wonder if I'm addicted to cutting. I don't know if you can be addicted to it. But it can be so hard not to do it.

I am so sad all the time, every single moment of the day. I can't even cry. I want to but I can't.

Sometimes, I just want to go to sleep and not wake up. Beyond despair.

March 2012

Dear Diary,

Something really stupid happened. I mean, I did something really stupid.

It was an accident, I swear, I wasn't trying to kill myself. I was nowhere near a vein. I don't think I was. My hand just—I don't know, I pressed harder than usual, I guess. I don't really know how it happened, but it did. There was blood everywhere. It got all over my jeans and there was a big splash on one of the towels.

I almost passed out. I've always been squeamish. When I got my ears pierced when I was twelve I couldn't bear to change my earrings for almost a year. Mom had to do it. Anyway, luckily both Mom and Dad were out—Dad was already at his office and Mom had a dentist appointment—because I was in the bathroom for almost twenty minutes and if either of them had been home they might have found out about everything. I got the bleeding to stop and smeared antibiotic cream all over the cut and put a big bandage over it. I hope no one sees the outline of it through my sleeve. I'll have to wear my loosest blouses for a while.

I packed the stained washcloths and the towel and the bandage wrappers into a plastic bag and stuffed the bag in my backpack. I threw the plastic bag into a Dumpster a few blocks from school. (I had to make up an excuse not to walk or take the bus to school with Meg. I don't even remember what I told her, and it was only this morning. Maybe I'm losing my mind. Anyway, she didn't seem to care about walking or taking the bus alone.)

I don't know what will happen when Mom notices that the washcloths and the towel are gone. Maybe she won't notice. If she does I'll have to tell another lie and say that I don't know what happened to them. It will really bother her that stuff just disappeared from the bathroom and she'll search everywhere and drive herself crazy. I feel bad about that, but I just can't tell her the truth.

All day long I thought about what I would have said if someone had caught me. How would I have explained what I was doing? There is no way I could ever explain why I do what I do. My parents would be so horribly embarrassed I would have to run away or do something even more desperate. I still can't stop thinking about being caught. I should but I can't.

But I am going to make a declaration. That was the last time I'm ever cutting. Ever. I got so scared when I saw all the blood. I almost threw up, too. I will never, ever do this again. I can't. Please, don't let me! Please, if there is a god like Mrs. Giroux says there is, then maybe you can help me.

I think I'm going crazy. Is my life always going to be this way? Is it always going to be so bad? Because if it is, I just don't know how I can survive. I'm not brave or strong like other people. I'm just not.

I'm going to go to bed now. I know I won't sleep but I am so, so tired.

22

"My mom knows you were over at my house," Rosie said.

Meg winced. The girls were on the sidewalk out front of their homes. Rosie, who had wheeled her bike out of the Pattersons' garage, now got on it. It was newer than Meg's and in better condition. Mr. Patterson saw to that.

"How did she know?" Meg asked. "Did you tell her?"

Rosie grinned. "No. Not until after she asked. She's like Miss Marple."

"Who?"

"I forgot you don't read mysteries. Miss Marple is a detective in novels by this English writer named Agatha Christie. Anyway, my mom saw the two glasses we used in the dishwasher and asked me about them."

"Yikes. Was she mad?"

Rosie shrugged. "Not really. I mean, if she was mad she didn't show it."

"That's good. I mean, about her not being mad."

"I think," Rosie said, "that maybe she's scared. You know, that something will go wrong between us again."

"Nothing will go wrong, Rosie," Meg said seriously. "I swear."

Rosie half smiled. "So," she asked, "do you want to go to the park?"

Meg nodded and, taking their bikes into the street, they headed off in the direction of Yorktide Memorial Park. As they pedaled down Pond View Road Meg tried to ignore the fact that Rosie hadn't said, "I know nothing will go wrong."

But it was impossible to ignore. Meg felt a twinge of intense sadness. Rosie also hadn't wished her a happy birthday. Meg had celebrated her fifteenth birthday the day before with just her tired, distracted mother and her little brother. Her mother had picked up a small ice cream cake at Hannaford. There were no candles as her mother had mistakenly thought there were some left over from Petey's birthday in March. Petey had sung "Happy Birthday" in his high, piping voice, which had, for some reason, made Meg want to cry and go running to her room. She had fought back the tears and cut the cake to her mother's distracted applause. After they had eaten, and the rest of the cake was stowed in the freezer, she had escaped to her room where indeed she did cry tears of self-pity and of something else. Loneliness?

She still felt a bit raw after that sad little birthday party, yet she was happy that Rosie wanted to spend time with her today. Rosie didn't seem to want to punish her, either, which was something that Meg had worried about. Maybe she deserved more punishment for what she had done, but that didn't mean she was eager to suffer it. She wasn't a masochist.

They came to where the road narrowed for a stretch and, falling into an old habit, Rosie pulled ahead. Though her eyes were on the lookout for the occasional passing cars and rough road, Meg couldn't avoid noticing the short little ponytail sticking out from under Rosie's helmet. Meg still wondered about that. She had never entirely believed that Rosie had cut her own hair, but especially after all that had happened since then, she wasn't going to bring up such a potentially painful subject. Rosie would tell her what and when she wanted to tell her.

Look at her, Meg thought with a rush of affection. *With her slim neck and skinny arms and legs, she looks so vulnerable—so in need of my protection.* But that was nothing new. Meg had always considered herself the stronger of the two, ever since they were little kids. But, Meg told herself now, it would be a mistake to think of Rosie as inherently weak. Maybe she had acted fearfully over the past few months, but that didn't mean she couldn't become more courageous than she had been in the past.

Suddenly, as if the small rock under her tire had jolted the memory into consciousness, Meg remembered how she had come to feel that Rosie was being pathetic in her response to the bullying. She remembered how a sort of contempt had prompted her to tell Rosie's secret to Mackenzie and her tribe. A feeling of shame threatened to engulf Meg as she pedaled along behind her friend. She wondered if the shame would ever entirely go away, or if every time she thought about what she had done she would feel bad and embarrassed. Life might be kind of awful if that were the case.

Anyway, those thoughts, about Rosie having been pathetic in how she handled the bullying, those were thoughts Meg could never admit to anyone ever, especially not to Rosie. She hadn't even told Sister Pauline, though maybe she should have. According to some rule of the Catholic Church, a nun didn't have the power to offer absolution like a priest could, which was too bad and didn't make any sense, but Sister Pauline would probably know the right words to say to ease a sense of guilt. And she would probably have some good ideas about how to perform a penance that would really mean something. Meg had never understood how saying a bunch of prayers, like ten Hail Marys or fifteen Acts of Contrition, accomplished much of anything. But then again, there was a lot about the Catholic religion she didn't understand. Maybe someday she would ask Sister Pauline to fill her in. Not that she was going to become a religious fanatic or anything, but she was kind of curious. Curiosity went along with being smart.

Twenty minutes later, riding side by side again, the girls cycled into Yorktide Memorial Park. They got off their bikes next to an old-fashioned wooden bench with elaborate black iron arms at either end. The park was pretty big for a fairly small town. Besides large sections of grass where people could picnic or sunbathe, there was a playground with a jungle gym, a slide, a sandbox, and swings. Right now the playground was crowded with mothers and small children. Meg couldn't help but smile at the gleeful shrieks of the kids as they chased each other around the jungle gym or shot down the slide. A few of the kids were sitting more quietly in the sandbox, transferring sand from one plastic pail to another. Meg remembered how she used to love playing in the sand as a kid, especially on the beach. Maybe it was a universal thing, she thought now, kids and sand, like dogs and dirt and cats and mice. Or maybe, cats and string.

Beyond the playground there was a man-made pond in the center of which was a big fountain and in the middle of it, a little wooden structure, which, as far as

Meg knew, had no particular use, unless maybe it housed the mechanics for the fountain. In spring and summer the pond was home to paddling ducks and bobbing seagulls. In winter, it often froze hard enough to allow people to ice-skate on it. Not Meg. She preferred Duckworth Pond out by Wilson Farm. That was where the boys on the high school hockey team hung out, and some of them were really cute. Once, when she had fallen, one of the guys had helped her up. That had been awesome. Not that he'd stuck around to talk or anything, but still.

At the far edge of the playground there were a few other kids around Meg and Rosie's age. Some had their bikes with them and one boy had a skateboard, which made a loud smacking sound every time he let the front hit the concrete ground, which was, like, every other minute. Meg didn't recognize any of them, which was good; they probably went to another school. Nobody was going to come over to ask Rosie any embarrassing questions about why she had missed those last weeks of school. Meg had no idea how Rosie would handle something like that, but Meg was pretty sure that she herself would freak out in some way. And if she did something stupid like burst out crying, then her embarrassment would be so huge she would be forced to run away. Far, far away, like to California, where her mother's sister lived. She had never met her aunt Kathleen, but maybe they would like each other and Meg could live with her and . . .

Whoa, Meg told herself. *Don't be a drama queen!* If her mother had been able to read the direction her thoughts had just taken, boy, would there be trouble!

Not far from the wooden bench on which the girls were sitting there were raised beds of flowers and ornamental grasses. They weren't as elaborate as the ones in the Public Garden in Boston, but they were still beautiful. Meg remembered the Public Garden so clearly, though the last time she had been in Boston was when she was nine and she and her mother and Rosie and her mother had driven down for the day. Actually, she remembered the whole day clearly, not only the gardens. They had had a lot of fun, mostly at the aquarium and on the Swan Boats, especially when a seagull had landed on the boat right by Meg's feet. Mrs. Patterson had shrieked, but Meg and Rosie and Mrs. Giroux had thought it was pretty funny. Meg's mom had given the bird the rest of the soft pretzel she had been eating and the bird had flown off, satisfied. Mrs. Patterson had gone on a rant about rabies. Some man on the boat had laughed and then his wife had shushed him.

Anyway, here, in Yorktide Memorial Park, there were literally walls of rhododendron, with their dark, glossy green leaves and bright pink flowers. The super old lilac trees were no longer in bloom but the black-eyed Susans were, as well as a big mass of some tall purple flower Meg couldn't identify. That wasn't unusual. She didn't exactly have a green thumb. In fact, she never could understand why people got so excited about growing their own flowers when you could buy them at the grocery store or, if you had the money, at a florist.

Meg became aware that she and Rosie were sitting close enough for their arms to touch if one of them moved even just a little bit. Just like old times, sort of. Meg had a feeling that if her arm accidentally touched Rosie's arm, Rosie would yank hers away.

But maybe she wouldn't yank her arm away. In some ways, Meg realized, they had become strangers to each other. They hadn't really talked in months, not like they used to talk. She felt a bit nervous now, sitting there side by side. She wondered if the relationship would still be there, the real relationship, not just a chatty, polite thing conducted over the backyard fence. "Hi, how was your day?" "It was okay. How was yours?" "Okay. Gotta go!"

There's only one way to find out, Meg thought. *Start talking and see what happens.*

"How were your allergies this year?" she asked, looking to the profusion of wildflowers for conversational inspiration.

"Not too bad," Rosie replied. "I think it had something to do with the weather being so cold for so long. I guess. Or maybe I'm growing out of them. I read on the Internet that you can grow out of allergies."

"That would be good. Remember that year when you could hardly go outside for, like, all of May?"

"Yeah. That was horrible. My nose was as red as Rudolph's!"

Meg laughed. "Well, I wouldn't say it was that bad!"

"Did Tiffany get into a college in Florida?" Rosie asked after a moment.

"Yeah. I mean, I haven't seen her since school ended, but before that she told me that she was never coming back north."

"Not even to see her family?" Rosie asked, surprise in her voice.

"I don't know. That's what she said."

"I don't think I'd ever want to live far away from home."

"Really?" Meg asked, reminded of her earlier, panicked thoughts. "I think it might be kind of cool to move far away. Maybe California or maybe even someplace in Europe, like, I don't know, Amsterdam. You could start your life over and be anyone you want to be."

"Who do you want to be?"

"I don't know. Just . . ." Meg laughed. "Not this me."

Rosie shrugged. "Well, when you get older you'll be someone else. Not entirely, but you'll definitely be different. We all will. That's the one thing you can always count on. Change. For a while I forgot that, but it's true. Nothing ever stays the same."

Which meant, Meg thought, that bad things might get better. Or worse. "What happened with Carly?" she asked, eager to drop the subject of change. "I mean, do you know if she's going off to college?"

"I don't know anything about her. I don't think we even talked after Thanksgiving last year."

"Yeah. She wasn't really into the big sister thing, was she?"

Rosie laughed. "Not really."

A guy riding a red mountain bike caught the girls' attention. Meg guessed he was about seventeen. He wasn't wearing a helmet, so she could see his face, which she thought was pretty cute. And his legs were long and muscled. That was good, too.

"Do you still like Justin Bieber?" Rosie asked as the guy rode past.

Meg shuddered. "Ugh. I am so over him."

"Me, too. Not that I was really into him in the first place. He kind of looks like a girl. Not that there's anything wrong with that. And he's kind of short. Shorter than me, anyway. I suppose that shouldn't matter to me, but for some reason it does. I know the only thing that's supposed to be important about a person is what's on the inside, but . . ."

"Yeah," Meg agreed. "I'm not sure I'd want to go out with a guy a lot shorter than me. I mean, what if I wanted to wear heels? Anyway, now I like Robert Pattinson. His eyes are sooooo gorgeous and he's sooooo moody. Maybe not in real life, though. Anyway, I've loved the Twilight movies for years, but I never really got how gorgeous Robert Pattinson is until now."

"Yeah. He's pretty cute. And I definitely like vampires more than werewolves. All that hair is gross!"

"Blah! And werewolves probably stink."

"Oh, you know who else is cute?" Rosie said. "The guy on that show *Psych.*"

Meg frowned. "Which one? There are two guys."

"The goofy one. The one who pretends to be a psychic. His name on the show is Shawn."

"He's okay. But he's kind of old. He's probably thirty or something."

"Yeah," Rosie said, "but he's so cute. And he's so funny and witty. I definitely like a sense of humor. And I think I might like older guys. I mean, when I'm old enough to actually date."

"But you wouldn't date a thirty-year-old when you're sixteen, would you?" Meg asked, her eyes wide with disbelief and just a bit of horror. A thirty-year-old guy was almost old enough to be her father! Ugh.

Rosie shrugged. "I don't know. I think it might be illegal. I mean, for the guy. And there's no way my parents would allow it!"

Meg laughed. "I can't even imagine what my mom or your parents would say if either of us brought home an older guy!"

"I don't want to imagine it! I think my mother would freak out even more than my father." Rosie leaned forward and reached into the small saddlebag behind the seat of her bike.

"So, here," she said, handing Meg a pink envelope. "I got this for you. Happy birthday."

For a tiny moment Meg was confused. Well, not exactly confused, but . . . surprised, even stunned. It happened to her whenever something beyond wonderful occurred, that momentary feeling of disbelief. And then it came to her that, yes, Rosie was actually giving her a birthday card. After all that had happened between them, Rosie was wishing her a happy birthday. She thought she was going to cry and was seriously glad she had worn her clip-on sunglasses.

"Thanks," she managed to say, hoping Rosie didn't hear the quaver she heard in her own voice.

Meg took the envelope and opened it. She read the card, with its simple message. It wasn't hand made and it didn't say the word "friend," but it was a card. It was a start. It was a big start.

"Sorry it's a day late," Rosie said.

"Oh, that's okay." Meg slipped the card and its envelope into her own saddlebag. She usually threw cards away after about a week, but this card she thought she might keep for a long time. "Thanks, again."

"What did your mom get you?"

"She got me two new tops," Meg said. "They're okay. One's a little tight, so I might have to return it. I doubt I'm going to lose weight! Petey made a card out of construction paper and about a pound of glitter. My dad, of course, did nothing."

"Oh. Sorry."

Meg shrugged. "It's okay. It's not like I expected to hear from him or anything." Though, she thought, it would have been okay if he had sent a card.

They sat quietly for some time. Meg began to feel, just a bit, like it really was the old days when they could sit side by side and just look out across the water or stare up at the clouds and not have to talk to communicate.

She thought about the weekend Mr. and Mrs. Patterson had taken the girls to a lake somewhere in New Hampshire. It was during the summer Meg turned ten. She and Rosie had spent the days swimming and playing tag and eating ice cream. In the evening they had sat on the dock, legs dangling over the edge, Rosie with her nose in a book, Meg watching the sun as it set and the fireflies as they dipped and darted. When it got too dark for Rosie to read, they would walk back up to the small cabin Mr. and Mrs. Patterson had rented and play board games and cards and eat more ice cream. Meg was convinced she would never forget that weekend, no matter how many great and exciting things happened to her in the future. It was as near to perfect as she could have imagined. Of course now, at fifteen, her idea of an absolutely perfect weekend away would be one that included cute guys to look at and lots of shops to browse through.

The thought of shopping made her think of one of her favorite stores, Stones and Stuff. It was where she had bought the heart-shaped rose quartz pendant for Rosie's fourteenth birthday. Meg shot a quick glance at her friend. It had been months since Rosie had worn that pendant. Meg wondered if she ever would wear it again. Or maybe she had thrown it away, back when Meg had betrayed her. She hoped not. She didn't feel brave enough to ask. *Now who's the coward,* Meg thought wryly.

Thinking about the heart pendant reminded Meg yet again of her own less-than-spectacular birthday. Her mother had asked if she wanted to have some friends over. Meg hadn't even given the suggestion a moment's thought. She had no good friends other than Rosie. The idea of asking a bunch of people she barely knew to celebrate her birthday with her seemed beyond lame. And the weird thing is that people would have come. There were always girls who would say yes to an invitation to a party, even if they didn't really like the person giving the party. It was a chance to dress up and maybe get a goodie bag from the hostess and maybe, just maybe, get to play a kissing game if the birthday girl was cool enough to invite boys.

Well, Meg liked boys a lot, but she didn't feel cool enough to invite them to her house, not yet, and besides, even if she did invite some boys, she doubted any of them would come. There were way prettier and nicer girls at school. And her grades were really good, especially in math and science, and sometimes that turned boys off. It was unfair, but there was no way she was going to pretend to be stupid just to get a guy!

Anyway, she wanted to tell Rosie how the idea of having a party without her was unthinkable, but something held her back. She thought it might embarrass Rosie at this point in their new relationship—if it even was a real relationship. Besides, she didn't want to make herself sound so emotionally needy. Even though she was.

"Do you want to stay here for a while?" she asked after a time. "Or do you want to ride down to Little Harbor and watch the boats?" She was feeling lazy and would prefer to just sit there, but she wanted to let Rose decide what she wanted to do. Rosie had opinions, too, and she seemed to be getting better at voicing them. Now Meg had to get better at listening to those opinions. That's something her mother was always reminding her about, that other people mattered as much as she did. She knew that, of course, but still, sometimes it slipped her mind.

"Let's go to the harbor," Rosie said. "I love watching the boats coming in and going out. There's something so peaceful about it. And kind of romantic, too, in the capital 'R' kind of way. It makes you think of adventures in foreign places." Rosie smiled. "Even if the boats are only going out to fish."

Meg stood. *It will do me good to get more exercise,* she thought. *If I lose a pound or two, maybe I can keep that top Mom bought me.* "Cool," she said. "Let's go."

23

Frannie stood at the small counter squeezed between a wall and the fridge, chopping vegetables for a salad. Her dream kitchen would include an entire island just for prep work. She frowned down at the knife in her hand. It was missing its tip. The dream kitchen would also include a new set of knives and maybe some decent copper pots, too.

Meg was leaning against the sink, eating Oreos. Frannie had counted four so far and if history was any precedent, at least four more would follow. Ah, she thought, youth. When stuffing cookies into your mouth had virtually no ill effects. Unless you counted cavities as an ill effect, and with no dental insurance . . .

"Save some of those cookies for your brother," she said now.

"I know. I will."

"You kids are going to eat me out of house and home."

Meg sighed and put the open packet of Oreos back in the fridge. "You always say that."

Frannie shrugged.

"Mom? Don't be mad at me, okay?"

Frannie's stomach clenched. *Don't be mad at me, Mom. I robbed a bank. Don't be mad at me, Mom. I accidentally burned down the house. Don't be mad at me, Mom. I've joined a cult and as part of my initiation I am required to kill you.* "That's a pretty tough thing for me to promise," she said carefully, "when I have no idea what you're going to say."

"I know," Meg admitted. "It's just that, well, Rosie and I have been spending some time together. Talking and stuff."

Frannie put down the knife she was using and faced her daughter.

"Does Rosie's mom know about this?" she asked.

"Yeah. Rosie says she doesn't mind."

Frannie wasn't too sure about that, but as long as Jane didn't take out her anger on Meg, things might be okay. Or not. Jane might be a protective mother, but that didn't mean Frannie wasn't one, too. And if anyone came after one of her children, Frannie wasn't sure she could be trusted not to go crazy.

"You know," she said now, "just because you apologize to someone doesn't mean they have to accept the apology. And even if they do accept the apology, it doesn't necessarily mean that all is forgiven. Not right away, in any case."

Meg frowned. "Do you think Rosie doesn't really forgive me?"

"I don't know what Rosie feels," Frannie admitted. "All I'm saying is that you shouldn't be surprised if there are a few bumps in the road ahead for both of you."

"Do you not want me to be friends with Rosie?"

"Now, did I say that?"

"No," Meg admitted. "But it's all kind of confusing."

Frannie smiled what she hoped was a smile of support. "I know. Welcome to life, kiddo."

"Mom," Meg said, rolling her eyes, "I'm not a kid. I just turned fifteen."

"I know. It's just an expression."

"Still."

"Sorry," Frannie said. She thought about how Peter had neglected Meg's birthday again this year. Meg hadn't even mentioned the glaring absence of a card on the small living room mantel over the fireplace that hadn't worked in years. Meg was right. She was no longer a kid. She hadn't been for a long time.

"Hey," Frannie said, "you know that I'm proud of you, don't you?"

"I guess."

"Don't guess. Know it."

Meg smiled and loped out of the kitchen.

Frannie wiped her hands on a clean dish towel. She really was proud of her daughter. It took courage to pursue Rosie's friendship after having betrayed it so badly. And it took courage on Rosie's part, too, to give Meg the benefit of the doubt. Even if nothing came of it in the end, there was a lesson to be learned from the girls' attempt at reconciliation.

Incidents in Frannie's own life had taught her that both girls and grown women could be their own worst enemies, indulging grievances and petty jealousies, at times reveling in animosity. The boss at one of Frannie's first decent jobs was a case in point. Frannie flinched as the memories came leaping back.

Mrs. Monroe had found that every little thing Frannie did was wrong. The staples were put too close to the corners of the page. The blue ink she used was not as professional as black. Only the very top button of her blouse was to be left undone. This last edict had really puzzled Frannie. Mrs. Monroe was seriously into showing her own cleavage. Maybe, she remembered thinking, there was a different dress code for bosses. But if that was the case, shouldn't the boss be the one required to dress more conservatively?

Anyway, Frannie hadn't been seeking an inordinate amount of praise. All she had wanted was to be treated with respect and to have her work, which she knew was good, acknowledged as good. The other office staff seemed to escape Mrs. Monroe's notice. Why was she being singled out for criticism? Frannie had wondered, her stomach fluttering with nerves as she walked into the office each morning.

One day one of her coworkers, a pleasant, older woman named Martha Klein, suggested they have lunch together. Normally, Frannie brought something to eat from home, but she was feeling so lousy and so uncertain of her talents, such as they were, that she had gladly accepted Ms. Klein's offer. When they were seated in a booth at a local diner, Ms. Klein, with a kindly smile, said, "You know why Mrs. Monroe is so hard on you, don't you?"

"No," Frannie said, taken aback. She hadn't been sure the other staff had noticed. "Why?"

Ms. Klein had laughed. "Oh, dear, it's because she's afraid of you! And probably jealous, to boot."

"Afraid of me? Jealous? But why?" The idea had thoroughly surprised her.

"For one, you're young and attractive," Ms. Klein explained. "For a woman like our boss, that's a big threat. And for two, you're smart and hardworking, certainly smarter than the rest of us. She looks at you and sees someone who could easily steal her job and probably her husband. Silly woman."

"But that's crazy!" Frannie had cried, then, embarrassed, she said more softly, "I don't want her job. Or her husband!"

"It's not really about you, dear," Ms. Klein had explained, patting Frannie's arm. "Thc trouble lies with Mrs. Monroe. I'm sorry to say there's not much you can do about it but grin and bear it, learn as much as you can at the company, and then move on. She'll never promote you, you know. I've worked for women like her before."

So Frannie had taken Ms. Klein's advice and moved on to another job as soon as she could. Mrs. Monroe had not been sorry to see her go.

And then at her third or fourth job—Frannie couldn't remember which now, as those early jobs all had been pretty much equally similar and boring—there had been a woman named Elaine Blair. Elaine was slightly older than Frannie. She loved to tell silly knock-knock jokes and to go out for beers after work at a local Mexican food chain. She wore wacky jewelry—feather earrings and necklaces made out of chunky plastic beads—and her long and pointy nails were always painted scarlet.

Frannie and Elaine had hit it off immediately. Before long they were having lunch together every day in the company's break room or, on nice days, on a small stone bench outside the building, sometimes swapping half a sandwich for a yogurt or an apple for a banana. One night they had even gone out to a singles bar, though Frannie was already with Peter. She had been Elaine's wingman, occupying the "loser friend" in chitchat while the "cool guy" danced with Elaine. Frannie had really believed they were close friends as well as coworkers, and she was happy about that. It had been a long time since she had had a close friend, not since high school, really.

Not long after Elaine had gotten a promotion that

Frannie had been in line for, one of the midlevel managers, a man in his early forties, had caught up with her one evening in the company parking lot. "Look," Fred had said, "maybe it's none of my business. But you seem like a nice person and I feel I should warn you. Stay away from Elaine Blair. You don't want to be friends with her."

Frannie had actually laughed. "What? Why?"

"I can't tell you who told me," Fred went on, glancing quickly over his shoulder, "but Elaine has been telling your boss that you steal from the supply room and leave early when he's not in the office."

"I don't believe you," she had replied, stunned now and angry that someone would accuse her friend of such bad behavior. "Why would you say such a thing?"

"I have no reason to lie," Fred said. "I just thought you should know the truth so you can watch your back. Look, everybody knows you should have gotten that promotion, not Elaine."

"But I'm happy that Elaine got the promotion," Frannie protested. "She's my friend."

Fred shook his head. "It's your funeral," he said. Then he walked off to his own car.

Frannie hadn't wanted to believe that Elaine had betrayed her, but Fred had planted a seed of doubt. After an uncomfortable few days she worked up the nerve to confront Elaine. Elaine hotly denied she had spread false rumors about Frannie. She said she was hurt by Frannie's accusation. Frannie had believed her and apologized. She had felt like a fool for believing Fred's lies.

But then, only a few days after that, Frannie was in one of the stalls in the women's bathroom when she overheard Elaine whispering to the receptionist about another coworker, accusing her of crimes similar to the ones she had accused Frannie of committing. The truth had hit her hard.

Despite Peter's protests that she "suck it up" and his declarations that "business was a bitch" (like he would know, never having worked in an office), Frannie had immediately begun to look for another job. From that day forward she said not another word to Elaine. It seemed safer not to, and besides, Elaine didn't seem to care. She had gotten what she wanted, the promotion. And from that day forward Frannie had been wary of becoming too close to anyone in the workplace. Maybe she had been too cautious, overall. But it was too late now to change the past.

Frannie leaned against the sink, suddenly feeling tired. She wondered if either Mrs. Monroe or Elaine Blair could be fairly accused of having bullied her. Whatever the proper word for their behavior, each had acted with malice. Why was there such a terrible and embarrassing tradition of women behaving badly to other women? Of girls going mean and wild? Frannie remembered Jane telling her once about an old English play called *Women Beware Women.* The title still haunted Frannie. She didn't exactly know what went on in the play, but she had a pretty good idea that the characters weren't swapping helpful investment tips over cappuccinos or sharing recipes for casseroles over cups of tea.

Ugh, and the preponderance of those awful reality TV shows that perpetuated the stereotype of the backstabbing, face-scratching woman—catfights, indeed! Frannie had often wondered to what degree those shows reflected reality. She was a bit afraid to learn the answer to that question. Thank God Meg found the shows as repulsive as she did.

That's it, Frannie decided, standing away from the sink and draping the dish towel she had used to dry her hands over its edge. In the spirit of sisterhood—of women caring for women!—she was going to make a gesture of reconciliation to Jane. The term "sisterhood" might be outdated (the feminist movement was, what, forty years old, and Gloria Steinem was almost eighty!), Frannie didn't really know, but it sounded right for her purposes. Jane had always been more like a sister to her than her own, biological sister had been.

Frannie fetched a note card and pen from the drawer that held an assortment of miscellany, and sat down at the kitchen table.

It wasn't really a difficult note to write. First, Frannie wished Jane a happy birthday; Jane would be forty-three on the fifteenth. Then she simply told Jane that she missed their friendship, that it had been one of the best things in her life, an anchor as well as a source of pleasure. She apologized again for Meg's misstep and for any part she might have unwittingly played in fostering Meg's bad behavior. She hoped that Jane could find it in her heart to at least try to rebuild the trust that had once flourished between them. She signed the note "with love" and sealed the envelope. She would slide it under the Pattersons' front door after dinner.

And then she would wait. She would have to be strong enough to take her own advice and give Jane time, as much time as she needed. And she would have to prepare herself to accept whatever answer Jane gave in return. Even if that answer dashed all hopes of a reunion.

24

April 2012

Dear Diary

I'm not sure what day it is, exactly. Not that it matters. Every day is as awful as the next.

Today in school something bizarre happened. I was walking to Ms. Moore's history class and suddenly, I just stopped walking. I mean, I was suddenly just frozen, my legs, everything. Something like that never happened to me before, going all—I was going to say numb, but it wasn't like that.

I've heard about something called locked-in syndrome, where someone who has a brain injury is alive inside but unable to communicate with anyone on the outside. It sounds like the most lonely and unbearable situation ever, to be thinking and dreaming but unable to tell anyone that you're thinking and dreaming, and maybe even hearing people talk about you and saying things that are wrong, like you can't hear them when you actually can. Maybe what happened to me was something a little like that.

I guess I was just coming out of the . . . trance . . . when Charles Lin from Spanish class came over and touched my arm. He asked if I was okay because he said I looked kind of pale. He asked if I felt faint and wanted to go to the nurse's office. I was able to shake my head and then to say no, I'm fine. I don't think he really believed me, but after a moment he nodded and walked off.

I can't imagine my life in the future. I mean, I used to be able to create these amazingly real scenes about my life, but lately, nothing new comes into my mind. I remember the scenes I've already created—like the one where I'm living in a big castle in England, perched right on a cliff overlooking the ocean, with lots of dogs and cats and a big black horse in the stables—but I can't really enjoy the scenes anymore. I can't walk into them like I used to. It's like my imagination is totally gone. Maybe that doesn't make sense. I don't really know what I'm saying lately.

If I stay this way, the way I am now, I'll never be able to—I don't really know what I was going to say.

I can't DO anything.

This diary is my only friend. Maybe Meg is still my friend, but somehow, it doesn't feel like it anymore. But maybe that's because I'm so dead inside.

If I can't trust myself to be sure of anything, how can I trust anyone else? Except this diary. And maybe that doesn't make any sense.

I've kept my promise not to cut again, though sometimes it's really hard to resist the temptation. I keep thinking, someone, help me be strong, please. But I don't know who it is I'm asking. Maybe nobody.

Probably it's nobody.

R.

Dear Diary

April, another day

I tried to find that book I read a few years ago, the one about the girl who never leaves her house, the one I wrote a book re-

port about. It wasn't on the shelf in the den where I thought it would be. I went through every single book on every single shelf, reading the titles out loud to be sure I wouldn't miss it, but it was nowhere. Then I went back and did it all again. Still nothing.

I wonder what happened to that book. I just had a bizarre thought. What if I imagined the book? What if it never really existed and I made the whole thing up in my head and wrote that report about a fantasy?

Would that make me officially crazy?

Probably. But who would care?

I have nothing else to say.

25

Rosie and Jane were in the kitchen. They had just finished lunch. Jane had made tuna salad sandwiches on whole wheat bread with lettuce and tomato and Rosie had devoured hers in minutes. Her appetite had definitely returned. She no longer had to hold her pants up with pins.

"I'm curious," Jane was saying, putting their empty sandwich plates in the dishwasher. "I know you and Meg are getting close again. Have you told her about the cutting?"

Rosie hesitated a moment before answering. She wasn't sure she wanted to talk to her mother about what was going on with Meg. Their new relationship seemed very private and also, somehow delicate. "No," she admitted finally.

"Oh. Do you think you will tell her?"

"I don't know," Rosie said noncommittally. "Maybe."

"Okay." Jane wiped her hands on a clean dish towel. "There's something else I've been wanting to ask you about. Your father wants to spend time again with Petey."

"I know. I mean," Rosie said hurriedly, "I kind of figured he would."

"Well, what do you think about the idea?"

"I think it's a good one. Definitely."

"Okay," Jane said. "Good. I'm so relieved."

Relieved? Rosie watched as her mother wiped the counter on top of the dishwasher for the third time. Had she really thought her daughter would want to punish an innocent little boy? Rosie very much wanted to ask her mother to explain why she had been so reluctant to let her father spend time with Petey. She didn't entirely believe the excuses she had overheard her mother claim, that the Pattersons' loyalty to Rosie forbade them from being nice to Petey. She was beginning to realize there were a lot of things about her mother she didn't understand. That was probably a part of growing up, she thought. Realizing that your parents were real, individual people. And sometimes, they were people you didn't always agree with or even always like. But that was okay.

Mrs. Patterson folded the dish towel neatly and placed it next to the sink. "To be honest," she said then, "I didn't really want your father to—"

The doorbell rang then, cutting off whatever it was she was going to say. Rosie was disappointed. Her question might have been answered without the need for it to be asked.

Jane looked at her watch. "There's my client," she said. "She's here for a fitting."

Jane left the kitchen and went to open the front door. Rosie went up to her room with the intention of cleaning out her closet. Usually, she kept it neat and organized, but since the awful hair-cutting incident back in January she had been lazy about some of her routines. Well, that had been due to the depression. She had been "lazy" about living, come to that. Getting through each day with her mind intact had been her priority, not a neat closet.

Rosie peered into the closet now. She was sure there had to be some old, forgotten toys she could donate to Goodwill the next time Meg's mom was going shopping there for packets of slightly irregular underwear for Petey or new clothes for herself and Meg.

Rosie bit back a smile though there was no one to see. Everyone who knew Meg even a little knew that it killed her (that was Meg's expression) to have to buy most of her clothes secondhand. Which was one of the reasons she worked as hard as she did to earn money. Like this afternoon, Meg was baby-sitting for a family with three children under the age of ten. The very thought of shepherding three small children all afternoon—playing with them, giving them their snacks, putting the youngest down for a nap—exhausted Rosie. She didn't know how Meg did it. Of course, Meg would say that she did it because she had to do it. Brand-new clothes weren't the only things hard to come by in the Giroux household. Rosie knew she was lucky not to have to work yet. She knew she was lucky to have parents who could afford to give her piano lessons and take her for weekends in Boston or vacations north to Montreal.

The closet was far less of a disaster that Rosie had feared—for donation there was only an old board game she had forgotten about and one good blouse she realized she had outgrown—and she was done with reorganizing before long. What to do now? It had begun to rain pretty heavily, so the option of reading beneath the big old pine at the back of the property held no appeal. Instead, Rosie decided on the next best thing and settled in the big comfortable armchair by the bedroom's window.

But after reading a few pages of *Emma,* she realized that she couldn't concentrate. It had nothing to do with the book, which she was thoroughly enjoying. She hadn't known that Jane Austen was so funny, and that she could create such incredibly horrible characters, like Mrs. Elton. It was just that since she had been seeing Dr. Lowe, she had a lot of things to think about. She was coming to realize that her life really was in her own hands, and that meant responsibility as well as freedom and opportunity. She was coming to realize that she owed it to Rosie Patterson to make decisions based on what was going to be best for her and not on what she thought might be best for someone else.

Like, there was still the issue of the piano. She was about 99 percent sure that she didn't want to pursue lessons, but she still hadn't worked up the courage to be honest with her parents about that. She knew she was just being cowardly, even silly. After all, it wasn't like she was committing a crime, wanting to give up piano lessons. And as Dr. Lowe had pointed out, not everyone was destined to be a professional musician. In fact, more and more Rosie thought she might want to become a writer. Which was a bit odd because she still wasn't ready to start keeping another diary.

Rosie looked over to her bed and imagined the plastic box of diaries underneath it. The pages of those little books held evidence of so many painful emotions—sorrow, confusion, isolation, shame. But, and Rosie had been shocked when she had first realized this, anyone reading through those pages would find very little evidence of anger.

Anger, she was coming to acknowledge, was not

something a member of the Patterson family "did." If her mother or her father ever felt angry when each was alone, Rosie couldn't say. But she could testify to the fact that her parents didn't fight. Well, if they did fight, it was when Rosie wasn't around, or when they thought she wasn't in earshot, like when they had argued over her dad spending time with Petey. And they had never, ever raised their voices to her. They certainly didn't believe in corporal punishment. In fact, Rosie couldn't remember ever having been punished in any way! Maybe she had never done anything worth punishing. But what kind of normal child didn't get into trouble every now and then? That, Rosie realized, was a topic for her next session with Dr. Lowe.

Well, whatever sort of child she had been, normal or not, Rosie had never been comfortable feeling anger or expressing it. Since she was a little girl, being around people yelling or fighting had always made her almost physically ill. Once she had been at Meg's house, years ago, when Meg's father had come by and gotten into a big shouting match with Meg's mother. Rosie remembered being absolutely terrified. Meg had shrugged it off. "They're just letting off steam," she had explained. "It's nothing."

"But they sound so furious with each other," Rosie had said, the pit of her stomach whirring with tension.

Meg had just smiled. "They are. But they'll get over it."

Rosie was only now learning that while it wasn't fun to feel angry, it was normal and often, it was healthy. Feeling angry about an injustice done to you meant that you had good self-esteem. Feeling angry about an injustice done to someone else meant that you were a good, empathetic person. What you did with that anger, how you acted on it and channeled it, those were the important things. It wasn't okay to go around screaming, kicking, and throwing punches. It was okay to confront the person who had done the wrong and make your objections known. Dr. Lowe had been telling her that the right kind of anger was responsive, not reactive. Responsive meant being in control of the anger and acting appropriately. Reactive meant letting the anger rule and acting inappropriately.

Rosie heard the doorbell ring again and wondered if her mother had scheduled another client appointment. Or maybe it was UPS, here to deliver the new part her father had ordered for the lawn mower. She got up from the armchair and ran downstairs. As was her habit, she peered through the glass panel to the right of the door. She was surprised. It was a girl from school, someone she knew only by sight, someone whose name escaped her. For a moment, Rosie hesitated. She supposed she could run back up to her room and pretend that she hadn't heard the bell. Her mother would probably answer the door on the next ring. And then she thought for a moment and realized that she didn't feel in the least bit afraid. There was no need to run away. She pulled open the door.

"Hi," Rosie said. Now she remembered the girl's name. Kristin Walsh. They were in the same grade but didn't have any classes together. In fact, Rosie knew almost nothing about her, other than that she was one of the school's best athletes. She was just about the only girl in her grade taller than Rosie.

"Hi," Kristin said, tucking a stray strand of blond hair behind her ear. "I'm here to meet my mom. I just got out of basketball practice. . . ."

Rosie stepped back into the living room and gestured for the girl to follow. "Sure, come in. She's with my mom, in the basement. I mean, in my mom's sewing room."

"Thanks."

"They should be done soon, I think. I mean, they've been down there for a while."

"I'm Kristin Walsh," the girl said. "We go to the same school."

"Yeah. I'm Rosie Patterson. Where do you play basketball when school's out?"

"The summer league uses the courts at Parkside Recreational Center. It's pretty much just around the corner from here."

"Oh." Rosie hadn't been to the rec center in years, not since she and Meg had taken a pottery class there one summer. She almost smiled at the recollection of how awful their pots had come out. Of course, their mothers had said the pots were beautiful, but mothers were supposed to lie about that sort of thing.

"You know," Kristin said now. "I didn't see you around the last few weeks of school. But things were pretty crazy."

"I know." Rosie hesitated and then said, "I kind of got sick."

Very lightly, Kristin touched Rosie's arm. "Oh," she said, "that's too bad. I hope you're feeling better."

Rosie smiled. "Yeah, thanks. I am."

She heard the basement door open and the voices of Mrs. Patterson and Mrs. Walsh. A moment later the women were in the living room. There was no way Rosie could miss the sudden look of concern on her mother's face.

Mrs. Walsh greeted the girls and thanked Mrs. Patterson. Then she and her daughter walked down the drive to where their car was parked.

"Bye!" Kristin called out, turning and waving once before she slid into the front passenger seat of the car.

Rosie waved back and closed the door.

"Are you okay?" her mother asked.

"Yeah," Rosie said. "Fine. Why?"

"That girl, Mrs. Walsh's daughter. Was she one of—"

Rosie shook her head. "No, no. I hardly know her. We don't have any classes together. And she's on the basketball team. All the athletes hang out together. We never even talked before today."

"Did she say anything to you about . . . anything?"

Rosie laughed and didn't know why. She felt a bit angry and didn't really know why about that, either. But she would think about it. She would use some of the techniques Dr. Lowe had taught her for figuring out her emotions. "Mom," she said, "nothing happened. I'm fine. Kristin's really nice. You don't always have to . . ."

Rosie hesitated. How could she say what she wanted to say without offending her mother? *Mom, stop treating me like I'm a three-year-old. Mom, back off. Mom, you have to let go!*

"What?" her mother prodded. "I don't have to always what?"

"Check up on me," she said finally. "I'll tell you when something's wrong, okay? You have to trust me."

"I know." Jane's voice was a bit quivery. "I'm sorry. It's just that all that time you were suffering and you didn't say anything and I didn't know and I should have known and—"

Rosie reached out and took her mother's hand. "But I'm different now, Mom. Really. I know you're just looking out for me. But just—just try to trust me."

"I will. I promise."

"Thanks. Did everything go okay with Mrs. Walsh?"

Jane rolled her eyes and laughed. "She changed her mind again about the hem on that dress she plans to wear to her high school reunion. It's lucky she's so pleasant, otherwise I'd have to shake her."

Rosie laughed, too. "Now, Mom. Patience is a virtue."

"Yeah," Jane said. "One I don't seem to have a lot of anymore!"

26

Jane had made meat loaf for dinner and Rosie had eaten all of her portion, as well as all of her salad. She had turned down dessert, as Meg had promised there would be ice cream cake at her house. It seemed someone at Frannie's office had had a birthday and there was half a cake left over, which Frannie had brought home for the kids.

"But why didn't the birthday boy or girl take it home?" Jane had asked her daughter. Rosie had shrugged. "Meg said her mom's taking the cake is payback for all the time people have stolen her lunch from the fridge in the break room."

Jane wasn't sure that the concept of stealing-disguised-as-payback was something a parent should be teaching her child, but she had said nothing.

Jane finished loading the dishwasher while Mike flipped through the most recent issue of *The New Yorker*. Earlier that day, after having talked again to Frannie about becoming part of Petey's life and assuring her that Jane had come around, too, he had taken the little boy to one of the miniature golf courses along Route 1 in Wells and then for lunch at Bob's Chowder House out on the marsh. The Patterson family had talked about the outing at dinner, like it was a usual, commonplace event. Things were inching toward normalcy, and to Jane, it felt uncomfortable. And the fact that it felt uncomfortable made her feel even more uncomfortable. Mike and Rosie were progressing toward a full reconciliation. Why wasn't she?

"It feels so odd," she said now, "Rosie's being at Meg's house."

"It used to feel normal," Mike said, looking up from the magazine. "Maybe it can be again."

"But what if . . ."

"Jane, Frannie's there. She'll keep an eye on things. Not that I believe anything bad will happen."

"I suppose."

"What movie are they watching?" Mike asked.

"The movie about that surfer who lost her arm to a shark."

"Hasn't Rosie seen that at least twice already?"

Jane shrugged and came to sit at the table with her husband. "It's a favorite with a lot of the girls. It's certainly inspirational, though it gave Rosie bad dreams the first time she saw it."

"I'm not surprised." Mike looked back at the article he had been reading, but Jane interrupted him. She needed to talk. "Mike?" she said. "Aren't you afraid that Meg will betray Rosie again?"

Mike closed the magazine and laid it on the table. He appeared to give his answer some thought before saying, "I'm a parent. I'm always concerned about the welfare of my child. I always want her to be safe and happy. But as far as trusting Meg . . . I have faith in her. And I have faith in her mother. I really don't think Meg would have sought Rosie out if she intended to hurt her again. She's not manipulative. She's not vindictive by nature."

"But it could happen," Jane pointed out. "She could hurt Rosie again."

"Anything could happen, Jane. An entirely new bully could start an entirely new reign of terror. Or not."

Jane had to admit that Mike had a point. But still. "As far as I know," she said, "Meg hardly had any counseling. That time she came over to apologize to Rosie, Frannie mentioned that Meg was going to talk to a nun at the church. But I don't know if she ever did or for how long. Meg could succumb to whatever pressures made her betray Rosie in the first place."

"And Rosie could succumb to whatever fears stopped her from telling us what was going on with that Egan girl," Mike retorted. "There comes a time when you have to trust that your child has learned a lesson. Which is not to say we abandon her to the wolves, so to speak. Of course we have to be vigilant, but we have to be trusting at the same time."

"Being a parent is just awful sometimes." Jane got up from the table and retrieved an envelope from the drawer at the end of the counter.

"Look," she said, handing it to Mike. "Frannie slipped this under the door last night."

Mike took a card from the envelope, opened it, and read.

"She wants to reconcile," he said after a moment. "She sounds sincere. And a bit sad."

"I know."

"What did you tell her?"

Jane sighed and sat down again. "I slipped a note under her door this morning. I thanked her for the card and the birthday greetings. But I told her I can't go back to being her friend. I just can't, Mike."

Mike returned the card to its envelope and gave it back to his wife.

"Are you sure?" he asked.

Jane looked down at the envelope in her hand. "I think so," she said. "Yes."

They sat in silence for a few minutes, each occupied with their own thoughts. Finally, Mike was the first to speak.

"You know I'm not a violent man," he said. "You know I hardly ever get angry, not really. But whenever I see that loser Peter stopping by next door I want to pop him one. Not just for how he neglects his wife and kids but for being so damn lazy. And stupid."

"But what does that have to do with me and Frannie?" Jane asked.

"Just this. Frannie is not Peter. She's a good person. I don't know, Jane, but I think it might be a good idea to establish some sort of positive relationship with her again."

"Good for Frannie, you mean."

"And good for you," Mike said. "And for the girls. Look, if Rosie and Meg are going to be hanging out together again, even if it's only occasionally, it seems to be a smart idea for their mothers to be on friendly terms. Plus, you'll be showing them a good example."

Jane smiled ruefully. "The girls are the ones showing Frannie and me a good example."

"Sometimes it's easier for young people to be brave. They have way less emotional baggage than adults. There's way less in the way of simply doing the right thing or taking a risk."

"Yes," Jane agreed, wondering about the weight of her own emotional baggage. Like the fact that she still missed her mother terribly, and still felt guilty about having moved to Maine and leaving her alone in Boston. "That's true."

"What does Rosie's therapist say about the girls reuniting?" Mike asked.

"Rosie won't tell me," Jane said. "She said she doesn't have to tell anyone what goes on in her sessions, and she's right. It's frustrating, though, not to know." Frustrating, Jane thought, and annoying. She couldn't admit to Mike that she was a little bit jealous of the relationship between Rosie and Dr. Lowe. Maybe more than a little bit jealous.

"We have to trust that Dr. Lowe knows what she's doing," Mike said now. "And I think that Rosie's showing some improvement. She seems less distracted and moody. She even suggested we play Scrabble the other evening. She hadn't shown any interest in Scrabble for months. She would only play when I forced the issue."

Jane smiled. "Did she beat you?"

"Of course. She can't help it."

"And her appetite is coming back," Jane added.

"Thankfully."

"You know, she hasn't told Meg about the cutting."

Mike raised an eyebrow. "No, I didn't know. I hope she realizes there's no reason for shame."

"Oh, I think she knows that. I suspect she just doesn't know how far she can trust Meg yet."

"That's probably wise," Mike said, "to move slowly. Let Meg prove her loyalty before rewarding her with secrets."

Jane got up from her seat and came around behind her husband to give him a hug. "Why," she asked, "is trust so terribly hard to achieve? That's a rhetorical question."

"Good," Mike replied. "Because I certainly don't have

any answers to that. On a lighter topic, we haven't talked about what you want to do for your birthday."

Jane shrugged. "Oh, I don't know."

"Why don't Rosie and I surprise you?" he said. "You deserve a nice surprise."

Jane wasn't sure about that but she gave her husband another, tighter hug. "That would be very nice," she said. "Thank you."

27

Dear Diary

Another day

I don't know if I can make it until the end of school.

I don't know if I can make it until morning.

Dear Diary

Another day

These last few days have seemed like a lifetime. A bad, painful lifetime.

Sometimes I think it would be nice just to go to sleep and never wake up.

Maybe if I believed in God I could pray to him to make me die in my sleep. But I don't know if you're allowed to ask God for death.

Anyway, it doesn't matter because I don't believe in God. So even if God is out there, he wouldn't listen to me, someone who thinks he doesn't exist.

28

Meg turned on the lamp on the table beside the black leather couch in the Stehles' large, beautifully furnished living room. She had only sat for baby Benjamin once before and had been happy when Mrs. Stehle had called to ask if she was free this Saturday night. *Yeah, like I ever have plans,* Meg had thought, as she gladly accepted the job. The baby was a sweetie, and the other time she had sat for him he had woken only once and was quickly lulled back to sleep by some gentle rocking. The Stehles paid well and their house was gorgeous. Meg wasn't sure exactly what Mr. Stehle did for a living—she knew that Mrs. Stehle didn't work—but whatever it was, it had gotten him a huge home complete with a finished basement and an in-ground pool.

Meg smiled down at a framed photograph of little Benjamin. He really was a cutie, with his enormous eyes that looked as if they were going to be dark brown. She had always been good with kids, so baby-sitting was a no-brainer way for her to make money. Still, unlike some girls she knew from school, Meg had no plans for having kids of her own someday. The way she figured it, she had plenty of time to think about kids later, after she had finished college and maybe grad school and after she had established a good career. Having a husband to help raise the kids would be smart, if he didn't turn out to be a lazy bum like her father. So choosing a husband wisely was also on her far-off agenda. But who knew? Maybe she would never get married and never have children. From what she could tell, life might be a whole lot less stressful without a husband and kids. Maybe it would be lonely, but it might be better to be lonely than to be miserable. Time would tell. That was another one of her mother's favorite phrases. Actually, she had heard Mrs. Patterson use it, too.

Meg picked up the TV remote from its stand on the marble coffee table. The Stehles had a fifty-inch flat-screen TV attached to a wall and a fantastic selection of channels, unlike the Giroux family. They had only basic cable. It was a money issue, of course. Sometimes it was so boring being poor! She selected the guide and scanned for something she might want to watch. She selected a station she wasn't familiar with just for the heck of it and caught a commercial for a documentary on the nationwide bullying epidemic. Meg hit the power button and put the remote back into its stand.

Maybe, she thought, TV wasn't such a good idea right now. She tried to shake off the feeling of shame that had come sweeping over her for what seemed like the millionth time in the past month or two. It took some serious effort. She wondered if she would always feel ashamed, even if it were just a little. Maybe full atonement just wasn't possible.

Well, whatever the deal was with atonement, Meg suddenly realized that she was seriously thirsty. She had ridden her bike to the Stehles' house and the heat and humidity had been really awful. She went to the kitchen for a glass of water. The kitchen was what was called "state of the art." Mrs. Stehle had told her that the first time Meg had come over to watch Benjamin. There was an indoor grill and a big, shiny espresso machine and a double sink. (Meg wasn't even sure what you were supposed to do with two sinks. Why wasn't one enough?) Meg was sure her mother would die of envy if she saw the massive fridge with its automatic icemaker. The room almost looked as if it had never been used. The granite counters were spotless, the grill was immaculate, and there was not a crumb in the sink. Meg bet Mrs. Stehle had a housekeeper. You didn't have manicured nails like Mrs. Stehle did and do your own housework.

Meg got her glass of water with ice and walked back into the living room, past a formal dining room with a table big enough to seat at least twelve people. Meg did a quick count. Yes, there were twelve chairs set around the table. A massive, modern-looking chandelier hung over the exact center of the table. Meg thought of the old, chipped light fixture that hung too low over the wobbly table in her own kitchen and winced. Not that there would ever be a reason for it, but Mrs. Stehle was not ever going to step foot in the Giroux home, not if Meg could help it.

Being surrounded by the accoutrements of success, or at least those of physical comfort, made it impossible for Meg not to contrast Mrs. Stehle's life with her mother's life. Here was one obvious example: The Stehles traveled. On a side table there was a framed photo of Mr.

and Mrs. Stehle on a tropical beach somewhere; the palm trees were brilliant green, the sand shining white, and the water bright blue. Mrs. Stehle was wearing a tiny pink bikini and really looked like a model, with her fantastic figure and long blond hair. Her hair, Meg thought, was probably professionally dyed. You didn't get those cool tones from an at-home kit! At least Meg didn't think you did.

Her own mother, with her graying hair, had never traveled farther north than Greenville and Moosehead Lake or farther south than Hartford, Connecticut, and that was only once, for someone's wedding ages ago. And as for wearing a bikini, well, Meg loved her mother, but she would not want to see her in a bikini! Mrs. Stehle probably went to a gym a few times a week. That just wasn't going to happen for Mrs. Giroux. But God, if only her mother would dye her hair!

Meg sighed, though there was no one to hear her. She thought about how fantastic Mrs. Stehle had looked earlier that evening. She had been wearing a form-fitting lime green linen dress that came just to her knee and nude pumps with heels that were easily four inches high. Her wedding set had maybe ten round diamonds around a big sparkly emerald-cut diamond. Meg had felt almost dizzy looking at it. Mrs. Stehle had gushingly told Meg that her husband was taking her to MC Perkins Cove for dinner and then on to the Ogunquit Playhouse to see a production of *My Fair Lady*. Mr. Stehle had come into the living room then and Meg had almost gasped out loud. He was so handsome and neat and really fit, like Ryan Reynolds or another one of those Hollywood guys, maybe that other Ryan. They had left the house soon after and driven off in a sleek black car that Meg thought was a Lexus. Even the name of the car was hot! She was psyched to ride in that car later, when Mr. Stehle drove her and her bike home.

Meg wondered if her mother would still be awake to see her get out of Mr. Stehle's awesome car. She kind of hoped that she wasn't. It might make her feel bad. No one drove Frannie Giroux around in a cool car. No one took Frannie Giroux out to dinner at a fancy restaurant. No one took her to the theater, either, not even to see a movie. No one bought Frannie Giroux a big leather couch or an in-ground pool or diamond jewelry. Meg thought about what Rosie and her father had done for Mrs. Patterson for her birthday. They had taken her for lunch at some fancy Italian restaurant down in Portsmouth and then to a crafts fair. *Mom will be lucky if I can afford to take her to Arby's this year,* Meg thought grimly, and maybe a stop at a garage sale if they each had only one soda at lunch. That would save about three dollars.

Meg knew that you weren't supposed to compare your life to the lives of others and she was pretty sure it was a sin to feel jealous of what other people had. Right, there was a commandment that said, "Thou shalt not covet thy neighbor's goods." But sometimes it was awfully hard not to covet someone else's stuff, especially when they had so much of it!

And how did people get stuff? By working for it! By being smart and energetic. By being ambitious. Meg gently, with one finger, touched a delicate purple glass vase on an end table and frowned. Her father seemed proud to have no other ambition than to party and lose jobs as soon as he got them. Meg didn't really know about her mother. Maybe she once had had plans and dreams. Now she didn't seem to have the time or the energy for anything other than getting by.

Sometimes she wondered why her mother couldn't

go back to school at night for a degree. You saw those ads on TV all the time for Kaplan and those other online universities. Meg was sure that some of them were bogus, but probably not all of them. It would be a way for Mrs. Giroux to better herself, get a bigger job, and make more money. But it was not something Meg felt she could suggest to her mother. It would sound too much like criticism, and that was the last thing her mother needed. Even Meg, Miss Grumpy Pants Complainer Person, knew that.

Meg sighed and looked across the room at the large oil painting that hung above the couch. Mrs. Stehle had told her that it was an original work by a local artist named Judy Sowa. Maybe someday she would be rich enough to take care of her mother. She could buy her mother nice clothes and expensive art. She could take her mother on a cruise on one of those monstrously huge ships that offered every luxury you could possibly imagine, like pools and tennis courts and lectures by famous writers. She would buy her mother massages and pedicures and order her the most expensive dishes on the dinner menus. And maybe one day she would get her mother a real diamond. Certainly, her father had never given her mother any jewelry other than the cheap gold wedding band she no longer wore. Meg often wondered why her mother didn't just throw it out. She just didn't understand how it could have any sentimental value. Maybe she just didn't want to understand. The idea of her mother still having some romantic feelings for her father struck Meg as . . . grotesque.

Earlier in the day her father had come by the house, just shown up without warning, even though Mrs. Giroux had repeatedly told him not to. He had asked for Petey, said he wanted to hang out with his son. He had almost blown a gasket (Meg didn't know what a gasket was, but she knew how to use the phrase) when her mom had told him that Petey was out with Mike Giroux.

Meg smiled at the memory of her frustrated idiot father. She hadn't seen him—she was listening from the kitchen—but she sure had heard him. Everyone on Pond View Road had probably heard him.

"I'm here for Petey," he had announced when Mrs. Giroux had opened the front door. He hadn't even said hello to her.

"Well," her mother had replied, "he's not here for you."

"Why not? Where is he?"

"He's with Mike Patterson. They went to a country fair in Falmouth."

"What the hell?" her father had said, his voice rising with indignation. "I'm here now."

"I'm aware," her mother had answered dryly. "Peter, you can't just show up at any time and expect your son to be available to you. I've told you this."

"Why not?"

"Because you have no legal right to, how about that?"

That was true, Meg had thought. Her mother had full custody of her and Petey.

"Well, I don't like him spending time with that guy. Who does Patterson think he is?"

"Well, too bad if you don't like it," her mother had retorted. "Because I say Petey can spend time with him. Mike Patterson is a good role model for Petey and a good friend to the family."

There was silence for a long moment and then Mr. Giroux had said, "Are you saying I'm not a good role model?"

"Duh, Dad," Meg had muttered, almost hoping he could hear her.

The stupid conversation had gone on like that for a while, until finally her mother had booted her dim-witted ex-husband out the door.

Meg snapped back to the moment. She thought she had heard a sound from the baby's bedroom. Dreams were fine, she thought, as she rushed to check on little Benjamin. But actual, well-laid plans were better.

29

Frannie sat on a brightly upholstered chair in the waiting area reserved for women scheduled for a mammogram. She had only been able to get an appointment midafternoon, so she had worked through her lunch hour to justify leaving the office at three-thirty. Getting a mammogram wasn't something she liked to do—who did?—but it was something she took very seriously. Her grandmother and an aunt had both gotten breast cancer while they were in their fifties. Frannie had had a scare once, and so for all those reasons she was vigilant about self-exams, too. Like her mother had always said: You never know. It was a grim mantra by which to live your life, but it was better than expecting good things and being continually disappointed.

Frannie sighed. It was impossible not to be plagued by gloomy thoughts while you were waiting for two of the most sensitive parts of your body to be sadistically squished. In spite of the pleasantly decorated room, with several thriving green plants, stacks of magazines with pictures of rich desserts and beautiful homes on the covers, and classical background music wafting from unobtrusive wall speakers, the spectre of sickness and death was not far off.

Who, Frannie wondered, glancing around at the other women waiting, all strangers to her, who would take care of the kids if she got sick and then, God forbid, died? Once she could have counted on Jane and Mike for some degree of support. Not anymore, at least, not in the big matters. Mike might be willing to be a friend to Petey and pleasant to his mother and sister, but without his wife's full support . . . The bottom line was that without the Pattersons, there was no one. Jane's note in reply to the one Frannie had slipped under her front door had made it clear that a friendship between the two women was out of the question. Though Frannie had half expected Jane's negative response, it had hurt and disappointed her all the same.

Face it, Frances Mary, she told herself now. *You're alone in the world.* It was true. Her parents were long dead. She was estranged from her only sister, who lived in California. And even if they weren't estranged, she doubted that Kathleen would want anything to do with taking in two orphans, especially two kids she had never even met. Responsibility wasn't really her strong suit. Besides, even if for some bizarre reason she did want to take in Frannie's kids, she had sworn she would never move back to the "gloomy northeast." That would mean further uprooting Meg and Petey's life by sending them out to the West Coast.

Frannie continued her silent survey. She had no brother. Peter's older sister was dying, and both of his parents were in a nursing home, barely aware of their own names. In short, there was no family except for Peter, and even if by some miracle he wanted to raise the kids after her death, there was no way Frannie would allow it. So, where would Petey go? There was no way he was going to be raised by a borderline alcoholic like Peter and his string of bimbo girlfriends. And Meg . . . Frannie suspected that no matter what happened to her mother, Meg would be on her own as soon as she legally could. Meg was tough. Which was not to say that Frannie didn't worry about her daughter. That very toughness could become a problem, and God only knew what the emotional and psychological results of Meg's having such a lousy father figure would turn out to be. Maybe Meg would decide never to marry because of Peter's bad example as a husband. Maybe she would marry at seventeen, desperate for male attention. Neither scenario seemed particularly healthy, though if she could choose her daughter's path she would choose the first one over the second, and neither over almost any alternative.

Absentmindedly, Frannie picked up a cooking magazine from the low table to her left and placed it on her lap, unopened. There was certainly no one at work she could turn to for help with her children. Sure, she was on friendly terms with a few of the women, but there was no one she could call a real friend. Her relative isolation was her own fault, Frannie realized. After those early bad experiences in the workplace, first with her boss from hell, Mrs. Monroe, and then with her backstabbing colleague Elaine Blair, she had never gone out of her way to make friends at the office. Plus, she was always so busy, running the household alone, and besides, for fourteen years she'd had Jane. Her entire social world had been centered on the Patterson family. The three people next door to her on Pond View Road had been her entire social network. Jane and Frannie had even scheduled their annual mammograms for the same day and time! Now, of course, that was no longer possible.

Frannie felt a sudden wave of anger come over her. Why was Jane continuing this ridiculous stalemate? What was she hoping to accomplish by refusing to reconcile? Punishment. That had to be it. She wanted to continue to punish the entire Giroux family, but to what end? Revenge?

She tried to imagine herself in Jane's position. *In all honesty,* she asked herself now, *would I have forgiven Rosie and Jane if Rosie had betrayed Meg?* She would like to think that she would have. Her religious tradition told her that she was obliged to forgive. Forgiveness was a cornerstone of the Catholic creed. The sacrament of confession offered absolution for your sins, the priest acting for God himself. Or maybe the priest was acting for Jesus. She really wasn't sure. But either way, he could offer absolution.

Who was it who had first said that to err was human but to forgive was divine? That was setting a pretty high standard of behavior, but it wasn't at all a bad idea. A person could try. It never hurt to try.

Frannie sighed aloud and quickly looked around the waiting area. No one seemed to have heard her. Or if they had, they were too occupied with their own worries to care about her dramatics. Good.

Of course, Frannie thought now, *if I had re-married, there would be someone to care for Meg and Petey if something bad happened to me.* Assuming, of course, that the second time around she chose wisely, and assuming, too, that the man wanted to legally adopt her children. Marriage was still an option. She wasn't even forty. But . . . Frannie mentally inventoried her body, and try as she might, she just couldn't see any nice-looking guy finding her physically attractive. Sure, other things mattered, like intelligence and kindness and humor and . . . But guys didn't care as much about those things as they did about a flat stomach, big perky breasts, and a perfect butt.

Come on, Frannie, she thought. *You're selling guys short. Not all of them are idiots.* Look at Mike Patterson, for example. He was a good man. He was the very definition of upstanding. And Rob Costello, from church. His wife had lost a leg in a terrible car accident and he was still totally devoted to her, even though other injuries meant she would never walk again. He knew what really mattered in life: love and commitment. And then there was Father William, though of course he was out of the running as a spouse. Still, he was a really good man, too, totally devoted to his parishioners. He routinely visited the elderly who couldn't get to church, and in what little free time he had volunteered at a homeless shelter up in Portland. She would much rather Petey look to Father William as a role model than to his own father.

Frannie looked down at her empty ring finger and tried to imagine a pretty ring around it, something solid but unostentatious, maybe a platinum band with a small but good diamond, something she could leave to Meg in her will. Instead, she noticed another dark, slightly scaly spot on one of her knuckles. No. Dating just wasn't going to happen. She didn't have the mental or emotional energy to make herself vulnerable and attractive to anyone else. Her kids would have to survive without a new father and she would grow old and die alone and . . .

"Mrs. Giroux?"

Frannie looked up from the hand she had been staring at and smiled weakly at the nurse who had come to fetch her.

It's Ms. Giroux, she silently corrected as she put aside the magazine and followed the nurse out of the waiting area. Not that it really mattered.

30

Tuesday

One of them, I don't remember who, Mackenzie or Courtney or maybe even Jill, whispered at me as I passed them in the hall that I was a slut. I didn't even care. I still don't care.

What's wrong with just giving up? Why do I have to keep trying to smile and get through each day like I'm normal like everyone else? I'm not like everyone else. I'm way worse. I'm pathetic.

Tuesday, again

Nothing touches me. Nothing . . . gets through. I look at a flower and I know—I remember—that it's one of my favorite flowers, like a peony, but I feel nothing. I feel dead inside. If you can feel being dead.

31

"Grrrrr!"

The girls were hanging out in Rosie's bedroom. Meg was sitting cross-legged on the bed and Rosie was curled up in the big comfortable armchair by the window.

"What's wrong?" Rosie asked, a smile playing about her lips. Meg could be so dramatic.

"Everything. But for one, why can't I look like Kate Middleton? Look at this picture!"

Meg held up the issue of *People* magazine she was reading for Rosie to see.

"She is pretty."

"Pretty? She's beautiful. I hope I marry a prince someday, or at least a guy with lots of money. Not that I'm going to sit around waiting for some guy to take care of me. I'm going to make a ton of money on my own first. I saw what happened with my mom and dad."

"That's smart," Rosie said. "To make your own money and have your own career. That's what I'm going to do, too."

"Yeah, and one of the first things I'm going to do

when I have money is have plastic surgery to make me look beautiful like Kate Middleton!"

Rosie rolled her eyes. "You're totally pretty. I don't know why you can't be content with who you are."

Meg laughed. "That's easy for you to say! You're gorgeous. And you don't even have to work at it!"

Rosie hesitated. She knew she would probably sound like Dr. Lowe, giving advice, but maybe that wasn't such a bad thing. "You'd probably be happier," she said, "if you appreciated all the stuff you do have instead of focusing on all the stuff you don't."

Meg grunted. "Like what stuff do I have?"

"A nice house, for one."

"Yours is nicer."

"Meg!" Rosie laughed. "You're impossible. And you have a cute little brother. And a pretty cool mother. And I know you hate your hair, but I think it's really nice."

"Well," Meg said grudgingly, "I don't hate my hair. I just don't like it all that much."

"And you're really smart. That counts for a lot."

"Yeah, okay, but why can't I want more?"

"No reason. Just, come on, Meg, can't you be nice to yourself for once?"

Meg raised her eyebrows. "So, you really never feel bad about yourself?"

For about a half a second Rosie considered telling Meg about the cutting. But she just wasn't ready to reveal that awful secret. Not yet.

Instead, she laughed. "Are you serious? Do you think if I had had any real self-respect I would have let Mackenzie and the others get to me like they did?"

"That wasn't about not having self-respect," Meg argued. "That was about fear. You were afraid, and for a good reason. I think Mackenzie is a psycho. A social deviant. Whatever she is, she's not normal. And Courtney's a thug. She'll probably grow up to be a professional hit man. Hit person, whatever. Jill's just pathetic."

"Well, I still let them get to me rather than taking control like I should have."

Meg looked back at the magazine. "I really wished I looked like Princess Catherine," she said.

"I don't think she's a princess yet. She's the Duchess of Cambridge."

"And her hair is awesomely fabulous!"

Rosie laughed. "Why don't you call yourself Megan, Duchess of Yorktide? It might make you feel better."

"Ha." Meg closed the magazine and tossed it toward the bottom of the bed. Rosie thought she suddenly looked serious or thoughtful.

"What's wrong now?" she asked.

"Nothing," Meg said unconvincingly. "It's just, I don't know if I should ask you something."

"You can ask. I might choose not to answer." *No,* Rosie remembered, *is also a valid choice.* Dr. Lowe had taught her that bit of wisdom.

"Okay. Are you, you know, worried about going back to school?"

Rosie had known that at some point this conversation was going to happen. *It might as well happen now,* she thought. "Kind of," she said. "Yeah. I'm kind of embarrassed, too."

"You so shouldn't be! Mackenzie's the one who should be embarrassed. Though I bet you anything she's not."

"Yeah. But I mean, having to leave school early like that, before finals . . ."

"You know what?" Meg said. "If anyone says or does anything bad to you, I swear I'll—"

"No," Rosie interrupted. "You don't need to be involved. I'll be okay. I think I've learned how to take care of myself. At least, I know more now than I did a few months ago."

"Good."

Rosie looked out the window at the backyard her parents tended so lovingly. Everything was so very lush and green at this time of the year. It was hard to feel really down or sad when that seriously blue hydrangea was in bloom. Rosie turned away from the window. Maybe she wasn't ready to tell Meg about the self-harming, but she realized she was ready to tell Meg one of the other things she had been keeping a secret. "You know," she said, "there's something I haven't told you about the stuff that happened to me."

Meg's expression darkened. "Oh."

"My hair."

Meg jumped off the bed and almost fell over her sneakers, which were lying in the middle of the carpet. "Oh, no, Rosie! Oh, I knew it. I just knew it! I had such a feeling that something was wrong about it all and I couldn't force you to tell me but . . . Those . . . those little shits!"

"Meg!" Rosie cried, feigning shock. "Good thing your mother isn't here."

"Trust me, she would call them something much worse."

"Yeah." Rosie thought of all the times she had heard Mrs. Giroux curse and then apologize for it, sometimes with a laugh. "Probably. By the way, Stella wasn't involved. I don't know why she wasn't there, but she wasn't."

Meg plopped back down on the bed. "Do your parents know?"

"I told them after I told Dr. Lowe," Rosie said. "They wanted to confront all the parents but I begged them not to. I was just so—I was just so tired."

"But it was such a violation!" Meg cried. "God, it was almost like a rape! Sorry, but that's the way I see it. Those creeps can't get away with this! With everything! They have to be punished! They should be thrown out of school!"

"The big stuff didn't take place on school property," Rosie pointed out. "And I can't prove that it was Mackenzie who sent the text on Valentine's Day, or that it was her who told people to act like I wasn't there."

Meg frowned. "I bet you could report them to the police for assault. Courtney should be thrown in jail and then someone should lose the key."

"Maybe. Probably. But I don't want to."

"Doesn't your therapist tell you to report them?"

"That's not how it works," Rosie said with a smile. "Therapists don't tell you what to do."

"Well, doesn't she suggest you report them?"

"We discuss my options and the possible ramifications of those options," Rosie explained. "And then I make a decision."

Meg made a sound of disgust. "I still think you should rat out those bitches."

"Meg!"

Meg shrugged. "Witches. Whatever. They need to be taught a lesson."

"Revenge usually backfires. Unless it's in the movies."

"I'm not talking about revenge," Meg corrected. "I'm talking about punishment. There's a difference."

"Well, whatever. Hey, do you believe in karma?"

"I don't know," Meg admitted. "I'm not really sure how it works. I mean, what if you do something bad to someone but then you're really sorry you did it and apologize? Does that mean you still might be punished later on or in another life? Does it mean you're going to come back as something gross, like a honey badger?"

"I don't really know how it works, either," Rosie said. "But think about 'crime and punishment.' They don't always go together, do they? There's a good chance that nothing bad will ever happen to Mackenzie, even though she caused other people pain. That's just the way life is. Sometimes it's totally unfair and random. And sometimes it's not. Or it doesn't seem to be. Sometimes good people get rewards and bad people get punishment. But you can never tell what's going to happen."

"Life shouldn't be that way," Meg said, "unfair and random, I mean. But I guess there's not always a lot you can do about it."

Rosie faked a big sigh. "Right. Like, why is Kate Middleton married to a prince and living in a castle and you're stuck on Pond View Road with me?"

Meg laughed. "Yeah, exactly like that!"

32

Jane parked her car on Sommer Street just off Main Street in downtown Yorktide. The weather was perfect, warm but not too hot, and dry as a bone, which was unusual for summer in southern Maine. The good weather had helped put her in a lighthearted mood, that and a pleasant chat with a good client she had happened upon at her favorite farmers' market where she had bought ten ears of fresh corn and a variety of greens. If history was any precedent, she thought, smiling, the corn would be gone by morning. Mike was crazy for fresh corn. Actually, so was she, and Rosie could hold her own, too.

Jane was now on her way to browse through a few of the stores in town. She had decided to buy a little treat for herself, nothing major, just a little something. Retail therapy, she thought, was a fine thing, as long as it was used judiciously. That wasn't a problem for Jane. She prided herself on having a high level of self-control. Anyone who knew Jane Patterson could vouch for her sense of discipline and order. Not once since her wedding had she blown her self-imposed weekly budget.

She turned the corner of Sommer Street and onto Main where she came to a sudden halt, her lighthearted mood blown away like dandelion fluff in the wind. Frannie was standing about halfway down the block, on the curb by her car. Her head was bent over her old leather bag, the one she had bought at a thrift shop right after Meg was born. At a guess she was looking for change for the parking meter just to her right.

The women hadn't spoken since the day Jane had gone to the Giroux house to demand that Frannie keep Meg away from Rosie. A lot had happened since then. The girls had begun the process of reconciliation. Mike had argued for kindness toward Petey. Frannie had written that note apologizing and asking for Jane's renewed friendship. And Jane had . . . She had clung to her anger and disappointment and pride. That was the truth, and it wasn't pretty.

For a half a moment Jane considered ignoring Frannie, walking on by without a word, pretending that she didn't see her. But she just didn't have the stomach to snub someone, especially someone with whom she had once been close. She could turn around and walk back to her car. Frannie might never even know she had been there. But Jane remembered the sincerity of Frannie's note, and allowing a better impulse to direct her next move, she took what quarters she had out of her coin purse and walked toward Frannie.

"Hi," she said when she was a few feet from where Frannie was standing.

Frannie looked up from digging in the bottom of her bag. Jane could see new lines around her eyes (she wasn't wearing sunglasses) and thought that her expression looked strained.

"Hi," Frannie replied. Then, with a nervous laugh, she held up the old leather bag. "I know I have some change in here somewhere. I think it might have slipped into the lining. . . ."

Jane held out her hand. "Here, I have three quarters if that will help."

"Oh, no," Frannie said, "that's okay. I'm sure I—"

"No. Take them."

Frannie put out her hand and Jane dropped the coins into her palm. "Thanks," Frannie said. "That's nice of you."

Jane was glad to be wearing dark sunglasses; they allowed her not to meet Frannie's eyes. The thought of making eye contact at such a small distance frightened her. And it confused her. For a half a moment she was tempted to ask if Frannie was free for a cup of coffee. And then she was blurting, "This doesn't mean we're friends. I'm just being a good neighbor."

"Okay," Frannie said with another nervous laugh.

She's uncomfortable, Jane thought. *Why did I say that?* And then, more words were coming out of her mouth, again without real intent. "You know that Rosie was cutting herself this past spring," she said.

"What?" Frannie stumbled slightly, as if proving her shock. "No, of course I didn't know."

"She was self-harming," Jane went on, unable to stop, as if some demon puppet master were controlling her. "That's how badly those girls got to her. All of them. She used one of Mike's razors."

Frannie put her hand to her chest. "Oh, my God, Jane," she said, "I had no idea. I'm so sorry."

Jane didn't respond. Suddenly she felt sick. So much for self-control and discipline. She had used that awful information about Rosie's ordeal as a weapon. And she had betrayed her daughter by revealing something that wasn't hers to reveal. Essentially, she had done to Rosie what Meg had done to her. Jane realized that she couldn't risk opening her mouth to speak. She would probably only sob. Or throw up.

"Is she . . . Is she feeling better now?" Frannie asked.

Jane nodded, desperate to be anywhere else but standing by that curb in full view of the town. Her shame and distress were so great she felt that anyone passing by would know exactly what she had done and brand her as a . . . as a bully.

Frannie looked away from Jane's face. "Well," she said, "I have to run. I have a dentist appointment. Thanks again for the quarters. And again—I'm so sorry. About Rosie."

Though she wanted to run away, Jane stood completely still, as if rooted to the sidewalk, and watched Frannie Giroux walk off. Her old friend had gotten grayer, she noted. The observation gave her no pleasure at all. She realized that in addition to feeling guilty she felt very sad.

The impulse to do a good deed had been real and then she had destroyed and invalidated her act of minor kindness. Why had she said what she had about not being friends? She should have simply accepted Frannie's thanks and walked on. And why had she blurted the awful truth about the depths of Rosie's despair? The answer was painfully obvious. She had wanted to punish Frannie, and to imply that Meg, too, was guilty of having pushed Rosie over the edge and into mentally ill behavior.

Jane was ashamed of herself. She had wanted Frannie to feel bad about herself and about her child. What did that say about her? That she was a mean-spirited person. That maybe Rosie wasn't the only one who should be talking with a therapist.

A car passed by, loud pop music blaring from its open windows. Jane flinched, whether from the surprise of the noise or her own embarrassment, she couldn't say. She had just behaved like one of those disgraceful women on those reality shows like *Real Housewives* or *Mob Wives.* You didn't have to watch them, and Jane didn't, to be aware that they were absurdly popular. Who were these women living lives where vindictive, spiteful behavior was considered the norm and even encouraged among so-called friends? Well, just how true to life those shows were, Jane couldn't really say. Were women really so horrible to each other as a matter of course? She didn't want to think that they were, but suddenly, a memory of something that had happened back in college was making itself heard.

One of her suitemates, a girl she had liked enough to consider a friend, had stolen Jane's boyfriend. Jane had been devastated. She had been in love with Derek. At least, she thought she had been. Of course, not all the blame for Jenna's success at luring him away could be laid at her door—Derek had made the decision to cheat—but still, it was mean and nasty of Jenna to have betrayed another woman, especially a woman she lived across the hall from.

Jane cringed as the memories came flooding back now. She would never entirely forget walking into the suite and finding Jenna and Derek kissing on the couch. She had been absolutely shocked, so stunned she had just stood there and stared at the two, unable to speak. After a long moment, they had become aware of Jane's presence and Derek had shot to his feet and stumbled toward her, spouting excuses and explanations. Jenna had stayed on the couch, her expression smug, complacent, and triumphant. Jane had pulled away from Derek's pleading hands and literally run out of the room and then out of the building. She had kept on running until she felt sick to her stomach and been forced to stop.

It had been really hard for Jane to accept the fact that Jenna had shown such blatant disrespect for a friend's romantic relationship. And the most confusing part of the entire episode was that only a few weeks later, Jenna had dumped Derek. Had she even cared for Derek at all, or had she stolen him away just to cause another girl pain? Whatever the case, Jane had learned a bitter lesson about trust and about choosing friends wisely. She had not forgiven Derek, in spite of his determined attempts to apologize and win her back, and she had not forgiven Jenna, either, though Jenna didn't seem to care. She hadn't apologized and she hadn't seemed upset by Jane's giving her the silent treatment for the rest of the semester.

Another car passing by on Main Street, this time one with a problematic muffler, shook Jane back to the present. To this day she hadn't forgiven Jenna Marsh for what she had done to her back in college. Maybe that was all right. But was it all right that she still hadn't forgiven Frannie for a betrayal that wasn't even her direct doing?

Jane suddenly felt very, very tired. She had come into downtown Yorktide to indulge in a little personal shopping, but now shopping was the last thing she wanted to do. Besides, she didn't deserve a treat. Her earlier good mood completely gone, Jane walked slowly back to her car on Sommer Street and drove directly home. There was a floor to wash and a hall carpet to spot clean and a kitchen cupboard to rearrange and put back into perfect order, all before Mike came home for dinner.

33

Dear Diary
I have nothing to say.

Dear Diary
I have nothing to say. Again.
Except that I hate myself.
Like that should be a big surprise.
There's nothing about me to like. There never was.

34

Meg finished slathering sunblock on her legs and arms. She loved the look of a tan, but her mother had drilled into her head the dangers of sun exposure. "And we can't afford for you to be getting cancer," she had said. What did that mean, Meg wondered, that if she did get sick her mother would abandon her on a lonely stretch of highway and let the moose take care of her?

"Want some?" Meg held out her tube of sunblock.

"No thanks," Rosie said. "I put a ton on at home. It's supposed to be more effective if you put it on before you go out."

Meg shrugged and put the tube back in her canvas beach bag. The bag had once belonged to her mother, about a bazillion years ago, back when she had been single. *How expensive can a canvas beach bag be?* Meg wondered, brushing ineffectually at an old stain on one of the handles. Really, it was time she talked to her mother about getting a new one. Maybe something with a jaunty nautical look, like something Ralph Lauren would design. Only it would have to be a knockoff of a knockoff of a knockoff.

Meg sighed at the thought and looked at her watch. It was just eleven o'clock. Mr. Patterson had driven them to Ogunquit Beach on his way to a meeting in Portland. He told them he would be back in the area around three. When they were ready to leave later in the day, Rosie would call him on her cell phone and he would come to pick them up. Meg frowned to herself. She couldn't imagine her own father ever being so thoughtful.

"I can't believe my mother still won't let me have a cell phone," Meg said now. "It's insane! You can get these great deals, like a family plan or whatever. It's so unfair. And what if I needed to call nine-one-one? What if I was running for my life away from some creep? What if I crashed my bike on some lonely road?"

"It does seem a little . . . irrational," Rosie agreed. "Maybe your mother will surprise you with a phone when we go back to school."

"Huh. Maybe. But I doubt it."

"Anyway," Rosie said, "if it's any consolation, I'm not allowed to use mine except for emergencies. Or, like, calling my dad when we want to be picked up later."

"That's all I'm asking! Maybe your dad could talk to my mom. . . ."

"No way. He would think it was interfering, which it probably would be."

"Whatever," Meg said with an exaggerated shrug. "You're probably right."

The beach was crowded, which was not unusual for a hot, bright summer afternoon. If you listened closely, you could hear accents from other parts of the United States as well as a fair amount of French Canadian. A lot of people considered Ogunquit Beach as one of the most beautiful in the country. Meg hadn't been to many other beaches, certainly none outside of Maine, so she couldn't say if she agreed with that assessment. But it definitely was beautiful and more dramatic than York Beach, with the cliffs along Marginal Way in sight.

Rosie was wearing a new unadorned, navy one-piece suit her mother had ordered for her from an L.L.Bean catalogue. Over it she wore a kind of sheer navy long-sleeved blouse. Meg assumed that was Mrs. Patterson's idea, as Rosie wasn't usually into making a fashion statement. Meg was wearing last year's two-piece. It was slightly faded from sun and salt water, washed-out pink rather than hot pink. Her mother had picked it up at Goodwill for five dollars. She remembered her mother bragging to Mrs. Patterson about the price. It still fit, though Meg was conscious of her thighs, which she thought were too big, and thought that maybe next year, when the suit would definitely be too worn out to wear, she would look for one with those boy-shorts bottoms. That might be a good look for her figure. Or maybe a one-piece with really high-cut legs would be more slimming. *If Mrs. Patterson was still talking to me,* Meg thought, *she could help me choose a flattering bathing suit.*

Meg settled back on her elbows to watch the people around them. That was one of the best things about being at the beach, the chance to people watch. A bunch of older teenagers, boys and girls, were camped out a few yards to the right. As far as Meg could tell, every single one of them was wearing earbuds. Meg thought that the guy in the Hawaiian print bathing suit was really cute but hoped he didn't accidentally look in her direction because the last thing she wanted was for him to notice that she liked him. Okay, she was wearing her clip-on sunglasses so he couldn't see her eyes, but he still might be able to tell (she wasn't really sure what kind of powers boys had when it came to sniffing out girls who liked them!) and she would be incredibly embarrassed. What would she do if he came over to her? Yeah, right. Like he would leave those beautiful girls in their brand-new bikinis for a dull-looking girl with big thighs in an old, faded bikini. *Get real, Meg,* she scolded herself, looking away.

A few yards to their left there was an old couple in pretty heavy-duty beach chairs, complete with what looked like a mini-cooler attached to the left arm of each chair. Meg looked harder. Well, she had thought they were old people, but now she realized that they might not be. Their skin was leathery and so brown . . . Meg quickly looked away. It was kind of disgusting, she thought. And probably they were going to get cancer. But it was their choice to roast themselves until they looked like burnt hot dogs, so who was she to protest.

In front of the toasted couple there was a young family. There was a mom, a dad, a toddler in a bright blue bathing suit, and a baby wearing an enormous sun hat, propped up well under the family's umbrella. The mom and dad seemed to be really enjoying their day at the beach. They laughed a lot and the dad had already kissed the mom on the cheek twice since Rosie and Meg had arrived. Meg frowned. Like that would ever have been her family.

Not far from the family, two middle-aged men were camped out with chairs, a cooler, and a big wicker picnic basket. Meg squinted. There was something familiar about them. She thought that she knew them from somewhere . . . And then it hit her. She didn't really know the men, but she had seen them in Ogunquit and Yorktide a few times. She thought they might be a couple. She remembered once . . . Meg winced. She had been with her father for some reason, shopping in Hannaford. Maybe her mom had been sick. Anyway, those two men were ahead of them in the soup aisle. She remembered her father poking her with his bony elbow. "Look," he'd hissed loudly. And then he'd pointed at the two men and said something too awful for Meg to repeat to herself, even silently. One of the men must have heard Mr. Giroux because he had turned around and frowned at them. She had been so embarrassed she thought she would die right there by the canned soups. Hopefully, she had changed enough in the three or four years since then that neither of the men would recognize her. She didn't know if she would have the nerve to apologize on behalf of her idiot father.

Meg deliberately looked away from the men and was mercifully distracted by a new group of sun worshippers who were beginning to unload their beach gear not far from where Meg and Rosie were planted. There were three girls about eighteen or nineteen, none of whom Meg recognized. *Probably on vacation,* Meg thought idly. Maybe up from Massachusetts or New Hampshire for the day. The tallest one, the one with long blondish hair, began to take off her cover-up, and Meg silently gasped. The girl was wearing a skimpy neon yellow two-piece. *If I looked like that,* Meg thought, *I would die before wearing that out in public.* What was she thinking! That girl so didn't have the body for that bathing suit!

Meg reached across to Rosie and tapped her arm. "Look over there," she said softly. "Those three girls. Can you believe the tall one is wearing that bikini! She's way too fat for it. She's enormous. She's like, Fatty McFatster. Ugh."

Rosie snatched her arm away. "You shouldn't make fun of people, ever!" she hissed. "You, of all people, should know that!"

Meg cringed. "Okay, you're right," she said. "I'm sorry. Really. I don't know why I said that. It was stupid."

"Yeah. It was."

"At least I didn't say it to her face."

"The point is that you said it," Rosie argued. "Everyone has critical thoughts sometimes, but you're not supposed to say them aloud, to anyone. It's cruel."

Rosie was right, Meg thought with a sigh. *And here I was condemning my father for being cruel.* She glanced again at the tall girl. Actually, she really didn't look so bad in that bikini. And she seemed to be having a good time, laughing with her friends. Meg wondered. Maybe she had reacted so meanly and so critically because she was always complaining about her own body. How often had she called herself Thunder Thighs? *Making fun of that girl,* Meg realized, *was a way to make me feel better about myself. A really stupid way.* She wouldn't be surprised to learn that her father had insulted those men in the grocery store simply because they were better dressed and in far better physical condition than he was. And, oh. They had all their teeth.

Meg gathered her courage and looked over to Rosie. "Are you always going to be kind of mad at me?" she asked.

Rosie sighed. "I don't know. Maybe a little."

"Oh." It wasn't the answer Meg wanted or expected to hear. She was glad she was wearing the dorky clip-on sunglasses because that way Rosie couldn't see the tears stinging her eyes.

"I mean, I hope not, but I guess I can't promise anything yet."

"Okay," Meg said. "I understand."

"Do you?"

Meg managed a smile. "Yeah. I think I do."

"Anyway," Rosie said, "I shouldn't have yelled at you like that. I'm sorry. Maybe I overreacted."

"It's okay."

"I mean, to be honest, I was just looking at those people over there, the ones in the fancy chairs, and thinking about how bad they looked, all leathery and wrinkled. They kind of look like lizards. No offense to lizards."

"I was thinking the same thing!"

Rosie smiled. "I guess neither of us is perfect."

Rosie picked up her book, some huge, hardcover novel, and seemed instantly engrossed. Meg, pretending to be interested in the latest issue of *Elle,* let her mind wander.

Her mother had warned her there might be bumps in the road to a complete reconciliation with Rosie. She had told her that if she really wanted the friendship, she would have to be patient and let Rosie forgive fully on her own schedule, whatever that might be. You couldn't compel a person to get over her pain. You could only hope for it. And maybe pray for it.

Meg watched a father and his daughter, maybe about nine or ten years old, walking down to the water. The father laughed at something his daughter said and put his arm around her shoulder. Meg thought of her own father. She wondered—again—if he cared at all about her. And then she wondered when she would stop caring what he felt or didn't feel. She wondered if he would ever apologize to her for being a lousy dad, for never taking her to the beach, for forgetting her birthday year after year. And if he did apologize, she wondered if she would be able to forgive him and mean it. At that point in her life, she wasn't at all sure that she could.

Meg sighed. She was really beginning to understand

what her mother meant about reconciliation being hard. Even when you really wanted to forgive and forget, you sometimes just couldn't, not right away.

Meg mindlessly flipped to a new page of the magazine. At church the Sunday before, Father William had talked about compassion. On some days Meg found her mind wandering during the sermon, but this time, she had paid close attention. Father William said that to be compassionate toward a person was to think about him as someone independent of your feelings about him. It was to realize that his reality was separate from what you in your reality thought him to be. The priest's words had struck Meg, especially when he had said that being compassionate wasn't about being cowardly or about being naïve. It was about being fearless and powerful and about using your imagination. That last part had really intrigued Meg. Imagination. So it wasn't just something you used in writing or art class. Imagination was a tool you could use in the real world to understand differences and to mend rifts between people.

Meg glanced across at her friend. She wished Rosie could use her imagination and put herself in Meg's shoes for a moment. It might help her to understand why Meg had acted the way she had, why she had turned on her best friend. But Rosie didn't seem to want to do that. Or maybe she wasn't able to do that. Not yet, anyway. And Meg had no real idea what Dr. Lowe was telling—well, advising—Rosie to do as far as her friendship with Meg was concerned. For all Meg knew, Dr. Lowe was advising Rosie to stay far, far away from her.

Rosie's voice brought Meg back to the moment. "Penny for your thoughts?" she asked, closing the huge novel around a bookmark with the picture of a yellow Lab puppy printed on it.

"Oh, nothing much," Meg lied. "Except that maybe it's time for ice cream."

"In your world, it's always time for dessert."

"I know."

"But I wonder if they sell Fudgsicles up at Fancy That. I could definitely go for a Fudgsicle."

Meg smiled and got to her feet. "That would be awesome. I'll go and find out."

35

Frannie sat at her desk in her cubicle at Le Roi Lumber and Homes. She might as well have been at the zoo or at home in bed, she thought, for all the attention she was paying to the numbers on the computer screen before her. The surface of her desk was cluttered with loose papers, thick file folders, and the usual paraphernalia of an office desk—stapler, tape dispenser, an old green mug that held pencils and pens. To the right of her computer sat a framed photo of Meg and Petey taken by Mike Patterson at last year's Christmas by the Sea event in Ogunquit. Or maybe it had been taken the year before. Lately, Frannie couldn't remember such trivia. Next to that photo sat the small box Petey had made her earlier that summer at day camp. Paper clips probably didn't count as treasures, but they were as close as she could come. Petey's last class picture was in a small frame on the other side of the box. She knew for sure it was last year's picture because the date was printed across the bottom. Reminders like that were helpful to an aging and stressed-out mind.

All day Frannie had been thinking about Jane's small

favor, which had seemed genuinely given, and then about the appalling news Jane had blurted just after giving her the quarters. Poor Rosie. To have suffered a bout with cutting seemed too awful to even contemplate. All afternoon memories of Rosie as a little girl had bombarded Frannie, so vivid that they had actually caused her to wince. Rosie with her two bright blond braids and old-fashioned pinafore dresses. Rosie clutching her rag doll and watching as Meg climbed halfway up a pine tree in the Giroux backyard. Rosie on her last birthday, when Meg had given her that heart-shaped rose quartz pendant. She had been so happy and cheerful that day. She had been so innocent.

Frannie absentmindedly fiddled with a stray paper clip. Jane had seemed almost stunned after telling her about the cutting. Frannie hadn't been able to see her eyes behind her dark sunglasses, but she wouldn't have been surprised to learn that Jane had been working furiously to hold back tears.

She wondered if Meg knew about Rosie's cutting, but it was certainly not her place to tell. Besides, she would rather that Meg not know that awful detail of Rosie's experience. She suspected that knowing her friend had resorted to self-harming behavior would only make Meg feel even guiltier than she already did. And that would negatively affect the girls' friendship. And so far, that renewed friendship seemed like a good thing. At least, Frannie hadn't heard about any major explosions between them, and Meg hadn't been stomping around the house or hiding in her room crying.

Abandoning the paper clip, Frannie picked up a pencil and idly tapped it against the edge of the desk. She strongly suspected that Jane was having a harder time recovering from the events of the past months than Rosie was, and in a way, that wasn't surprising.

Rosie might be what Peter would sarcastically call a delicate flower, but she was resilient in a way that Jane, over the course of the years, had proved not to be. Like that time when one of Jane's clients, a woman everyone in town knew was unhinged, had threatened to sue Jane over some bogus mix-up involving a pair of capri pants. There was no possible way that Wacko Millie Murphy had had a real case, and Mike had dealt quickly and efficiently with the situation, but the minor bump in the road had left Jane literally prostrate for days. Frannie couldn't help but imagine what would have happened if she had reacted so hugely to a minor crisis. She could hear her mother's voice in her head, telling her to "Snap out of it!" and her father's voice telling her to "Stop dwelling on your own problems and pay attention to the problems of other people!" And what would Peter say? Something to the effect of, "Jeez, Fran, get a freakin' life."

It didn't take much imagination to relate Jane's fragile nature (Frannie knew that an unkind person would say her overly dramatic nature) to her being an overprotective mother, especially once it became clear that Rosie was going to be Jane's only child. And, in Frannie's opinion, since then Jane had relied far too heavily on Rosie as her companion. Disturbingly, Peter shared her opinion. In his words, Jane had stifled her daughter. Well, Frannie thought, every once in a blue moon even the dumbest person was right about something.

On the matter of Peter, she had gotten a call from him that morning before she had left for work. He had asked for money. Again. Just a loan, he said. Just for a week or maybe two. Frannie had become so bored with this ridiculous routine. Most times she couldn't even bother to get mad at him. He was always going to ask for money and she was always going to say no.

She couldn't even wish him married to someone with deep pockets because to wish Peter on another woman was to betray her own sex. Besides, being married to another woman probably wouldn't stop Peter from appealing to his ex-wife for funds. Peter was not at all acquainted with the notion of shame, let alone that of propriety.

Frannie was distracted from her musings by a peal of feminine laughter from across the room. Marlene Gervais. She always seemed to be laughing or smiling. Frannie might have found it annoying if Marlene had been faking her sunny nature. Well, if she was faking it, she was a consummate actress. And it wasn't as if she had such an easy life. She, too, was a single parent and her son had some form of autism. She and her two kids—the other was a girl—lived with Marlene's mother, and everyone knew that Marlene's meager salary supported the entire household. Still, Marlene seemed to find joy in her life. Frannie wanted to dislike her colleague but just couldn't. What she could do was to be a little bit jealous of her ability to see the glass as half-full.

Frannie stared at the columns of figures on the computer screen. At the moment, they made little if any sense; no more sense, she thought, than what had become of her life. How, she wondered, had her life become so—so small and joyless? She had been a relatively happy child. Her teen years had lacked a lot of the trauma some of her friends had experienced. Maybe that was due to having such strict parents. Acting out had been unthinkable. Even the years of her lousy marriage hadn't been entirely terrible because she had met Jane Patterson and that had made up for a lot of what was lacking in her home life. Now she didn't even have a friend with whom she could celebrate the negative results of her mammogram.

I'm not exaggerating my isolation, Frannie told herself, as if to be sure that it was true. There was nothing in her life in which she took real pleasure. Nothing. The last time she had tried to do something just for herself was when she had joined Jane's book group. But what with her job and the two kids and the house and yard work, she just hadn't been able to keep up with the reading. She supposed she could have gone to the gatherings anyway and sipped wine and nibbled cheese and listened to the other women debate plot development and character motivation, but that had seemed kind of dishonest so she had dropped out of the group. Jane had been disappointed and had tried to argue her out of leaving, but in the end she had given up and accepted Frannie's decision.

Frannie squeezed her eyes shut and then opened them wide. The numbers on the screen were still meaningless. She wondered if she should talk to Father William about getting involved in one of the church's social societies. She would simply have to make the time to "have fun." Sister Pauline was nice, and she had a degree in counseling. Maybe she could give her some advice about how to jump-start her life. Maybe. Or maybe, Frannie thought, sitting up straight in her seat, she should just stop bitching and moaning, and learn to accept that this was her life and that's all there was to it. Deal. Life's tough, get a helmet. How many times had her father said that to her as she was growing up? Many, many times. No wonder she had never set her sights very high. She had been discouraged from the first, taught to keep her head down and her complaints to herself.

Frannie firmly pushed away the trace of self-pity that was attempting to make a comeback and looked hard at the screen of her computer.

"Frannie!"

Her boss's booming voice made her jump in her chair, which made her realize just how flimsy and non-ergonomic the chair was. So much for his promise to get her a new one. Not that she had really believed him. Trip King wasn't known to be a man of his word. Like, for last year's office Christmas party he had promised a platter of shrimp. Of course, there was no platter of shrimp, only a plastic plate on which sat crumbling cubes of processed cheese food and a pile of store-brand crackers.

"Yes, Mr. King?" she said, plastering a smile on her face.

"Do you have those new budget figures for me?" he asked.

"Done in ten minutes," she said, trying not to notice the food stains dribbled down his tie. The man did not know how to use a napkin. *His dry-cleaning bill,* she thought, *must be astronomical.* Unless he made his poor wife hand-wash his ties. She wouldn't put it past him. And what was up with that name anyway? Trip. More like Drip.

"Nine would be better," he said, turning and walking off in the direction of his office.

Frannie turned back to her computer. The columns of numbers on the screen now made sense. As her parents had repeatedly told her, the devil found work for idle hands and a wandering mind didn't pay the bills.

36

Dear Diary

Thursday, I think

I had to cut again.

Diary

Another day

Still here. I don't know why. I'm not worth anything to anybody.

I heard somewhere once, maybe in a book or on TV, that some people can will themselves to die. I wish I could remember more, like who those people are and how they do it. But I think maybe they're special, like shamans, or mediums, people who communicate with the spirit world, and that's why they can will themselves to die when they know their life here is over. And I think they probably believe that they're going somewhere else even better than Earth and the human world.

I wish I believed in a heaven, the kind that Mrs. Giroux believes in. I wish I were one of those special people who can see and communicate with another world beyond this one. But clearly, I'm not one of those special people. I used to believe in ghosts. Now, I don't believe anything except that life is awful.

Why did my mother ever go on about my "specialness"? What did she mean by that, anyway? Maybe she meant it to mock me, like when you call a tall person Tiny or a fat person Slim or a stupid person Genius.

I got an A on my latest history paper.

37

The early afternoon was slightly overcast when Mrs. Patterson dropped off Rosie and Meg in downtown Ogunquit. She was on her way to visit a client who was temporarily unable to get around easily due to a broken leg. She had been polite to Meg during the drive, but it was clear to Rosie that her mother was still not comfortable with the idea of the girls hanging out together. Meg, for her part, had been unusually quiet. Rosie had tried to fill the uneasy silence with chatter about a really fun episode of *American Pickers* she had watched the night before. She doubted her mother or Meg had really heard her.

"I'll call you when I'm finished with Mrs. Romane," Mrs. Patterson had told Rosie before driving away. "Have fun and be careful. Hold on tight to your bag. There are a lot of strangers in town this time of year."

Rosie, hiding her annoyance, had promised she would hold on to her bag. When, she wondered, would her mother ever stop warning her about every little potential danger? Pickpockets, bag snatchers, unexpected rain showers, rabid squirrels, and stray dogs. Probably never. In Rosie's admittedly limited experience with adults, she had kind of concluded that they didn't much change, at least, not in big ways.

The girls strolled through the tiny downtown and drifted in and out of the shops. Rosie bought a couple of cashew turtles in Harbor Candy Shop and Meg bought a bag of dark chocolate nonpareils, half of which she ate before they had left the store. After a while they ambled down Shore Road to the mouth of the path that led to the Marginal Way, which would in turn lead them into Perkins Cove.

The Marginal Way was a popular footpath about one and a quarter miles long. It was very narrow in some spots, which was probably why bikes and Rollerblades weren't allowed. Dragonflies seemed drawn to the flora along the path, and on this hot summer day, they flew past the girls in dizzying loops. The sound of cawing seagulls was at times almost deafening. Still, Rosie liked hearing the big white-and-gray birds going about the business of their lives. (Where did they nest? Rosie often wondered. She had never seen a seagull's nest.) Pine trees, twisted by years of wind off the ocean, clung to the edges of the rocky cliff, and hardy purple and yellow wildflowers sprang from tiny deposits of sandy soil between the steel-gray rocks. Rosie's mother had taught her to identify the bayberry and bittersweet bushes, but she had no trouble recognizing the bushes of pink and white roses. Here and there along the Marginal Way benches had been installed in memory of someone who had loved the town or the ocean or both. To the girls' left was the Atlantic Ocean. To their right were massive, well-kept houses with long, perfectly manicured lawns stretching out before them.

"How much do you think that house cost?" Meg asked, pointing to a three-story pile made of brick and stone with a wraparound porch and what looked like a more modern, attached three-car garage.

"I have absolutely no idea," Rosie admitted. "A lot. Maybe millions?"

"Yeah. And there's probably just some weird old couple living in there, dressed in rags and rambling around a bunch of empty rooms."

Rosie glanced at her friend. "What in the world would make you think that?"

Meg just shrugged.

A few minutes later the girls were forced to slow their pace. They had caught up with a group of middle-aged people, two men and two women. And by middle-aged, Rosie meant that they were older than her parents but not old enough to be, say, her grandparents. The two women were dressed a lot alike, both in bright-colored capri pants, white T-shirts, and white sun visors. And the two men were dressed alike, too. They were wearing khaki pants, striped polo shirts, and the kind of hat Gilligan wore in that old goofy TV show. Rosie found herself wondering about the four of them. Maybe they had been friends for ages, maybe even since high school or college. Rosie could see the glint of a yellow gold wedding ring on all four of them. Maybe they had been in each other's weddings and gone on vacations together when their kids were little and—

"Playing tourist is fun," Meg muttered under her breath, ending Rosie's speculations. "Except when you get stuck behind a bunch of people walking, like, in slow motion."

Rosie shrugged. "Why does it matter? We're not in a rush."

"You are just way more patient than I am."

"I'm aware. Why don't you try to enjoy the view of the water?"

Meg made a face. "I've seen the ocean a thousand times."

"But it looks different all the time! Sometimes it's blue and sometimes it's gray and sometimes it's as flat and shiny as glass and—"

"It's just water, Rosie."

Rosie laughed. "Wow, you are in a bad mood!"

"I'll be in a better mood when we get off this stupid path!" Meg said darkly.

Finally, as if sensing the grumpy adolescent behind them, the two middle-aged couples ushered Meg and Rosie past them. Rosie thanked them. Before long the girls had reached Perkins Cove, which was jammed with vacationers and day-trippers.

"Shopping!" Meg announced. Rosie followed her into a really good jewelry store called Swamp John's. Meg spent close to a full ten minutes pretty much drooling over a silver bangle bracelet. Finally, Rosie pulled Meg away from the display case, still moaning about how much she wanted the bracelet and how unfair it was that she couldn't afford it.

"Why do you go into jewelry stores if it's only going to make you miserable?" Rosie asked when they emerged into the sunlight. "It seems, I don't know, counterproductive."

"Because I get ideas for what I'm going to buy when I have a lot of money," Meg explained, with a final look over her shoulder at the store's display window.

"I only see you get frustrated. You know, they had some nice necklaces made with beach glass. You could probably afford one of those, if you saved up a bit."

"Beach glass!" Meg cried. "No. Way. I want real stones, like aquamarines and diamonds and rubies!"

Rosie decided to let the subject of jewelry go away.

Just yards away a giant tour bus was letting off a group

of elderly men and women just outside a restaurant called Jackie's Too. Well, there were mostly women, Rosie saw after a moment, and they were filing inside the restaurant for lunch. Rosie thought it was nice that older people could get around and visit different places instead of being cooped up in their retirement villages or in some awful nursing home. She had never understood why some people thought being old meant being boring or useless.

"I don't ever want to be old," Meg said as the last of the group disappeared into the restaurant. "Ugh."

"What's so ugh about being old?" Rosie asked.

Meg shuddered. "Just—everything."

"Maybe those people are happy," Rosie said. "I mean, it's a beautiful day and they're out for lunch by the seaside. How miserable could they be?"

"They could be super miserable."

"Are you saying you'd rather die when you're young?"

"No, not young," Meg said. "Just not . . . old."

"Well, I hope I live to be old. Maybe not one hundred, but at least into my late eighties. There's so much I want to do!"

Meg frowned. "You do realize, don't you, that people in their eighties have brittle bones and all sorts of icky skin tags and blotches. You are aware that half the time they can't remember their own names and have to eat only bland, mushy foods because they have no teeth and their stomachs are rotted. And cataracts. They can't even see without, like, having an operation to vacuum out their eyes."

Rosie stared at her friend and then grinned. "I don't think cataracts are 'vacuumed out.' Anyway, wow. You're in a really, really, really bad mood today! Did you fall out of bed again?"

Meg just shrugged.

"Well," Rosie went on, "I'm not going to worry about stuff like brittle bones or senility. I want to enjoy today, right now, this very moment."

"Is that what your therapist tells you to do?"

"Advises me to do," Rosie corrected. "And, yes, it is. You should try it sometime."

Meg nodded over Rosie's shoulder. "Here's something you can focus on this very minute. Stella Charron."

"What about her?" Rosie asked. She felt a momentary flicker of panic but managed to tamp it down. She was only a victim if she let herself be a victim. That's what Dr. Lowe had told her.

"She's coming our way."

Rosie turned and for a moment didn't recognize the girl walking toward them. She had gotten an entirely new haircut, something Rosie thought was called a pixie cut—Meg would know for sure, she thought—and she was wearing ragged cut-off jean shorts and a cotton top with long, bell-shaped sleeves and lots of intricate embroidery. The design looked Indian, Rosie thought. The whole outfit was really different from the sort of clothes Stella used to wear, preppy stuff like polo shirts and chinos. It was all a bit puzzling.

Stella came to a stop a few feet away. "Hey," she said, sticking her hands in the back pockets of her shorts. "Can I talk to you guys?"

Meg looked to Rosie. Rosie nodded.

"Okay," Meg said.

Stella smiled and came a bit closer. "I just want to say that I'm really sorry about what happened. I swear I didn't even know about some of the stuff Mackenzie did until it was over. Like . . ." Stella's cheeks flushed. "Like what happened with your hair, Rosie. But I still should have said or done something to stop them. I'm sorry."

Rosie nodded. It was a moment before she could trust herself to speak without crying. This was something she had never, ever expected. "Okay," she said then. "Thanks."

Meg glanced again at Rosie before asking, "You're not friends with them anymore?"

Stella laughed a bit nervously. "I never was their friend. And they weren't my friends, either. Mackenzie and Courtney and Jill don't know anything about friendship. All they care about is, I don't know, power. And making people feel bad. I don't really understand what it is they want. Maybe they don't, either."

"Then why did you hang out with them?" Rosie asked. She didn't know why, exactly, but she believed that Stella really was contrite and not trying to fool them into anything.

"I don't really know," Stella said with a shrug. "I mean, things were kind of weird at home for a while. My little sister got sick and my parents sort of checked out as far as I was concerned. I guess I just went a little crazy for a while."

"Sorry," Meg said. "Is your sister okay now?"

"Better. Thanks. And my parents finally remembered I'm alive, too. Anyway, I can't believe Mackenzie even wanted me around. I was never really part of that group." Stella laughed. "Actually, she liked the fact that I had a bunch of money to spend on stuff. I wound up paying for her almost every time we went to a movie. Do you know how many pairs of those stupid plastic glittery hoop earrings I bought her, the ones everyone was wearing last year? Like, twelve or something like that."

Meg winced. "Yikes."

"I know," Stella agreed. "I was totally used. But I kind

of let myself be used, too. It's actually pretty embarrassing when I think about it. But at the start, Mackenzie made me feel so special, like I actually mattered." Stella gave an exaggerated shudder. "Ugh. It freaks me out to think about it."

Rosie knew all about memories that freaked you out. And many of hers, she wasn't ready to share. She didn't know if she would ever be.

"And I have to confess about something else," Stella was saying. "Back around Valentine's Day I gave Mackenzie the money to buy a prepaid phone. She told me that her cell was dead and that her father wouldn't get her a new one. I had no idea she was lying or that she was going to use the prepaid phone to send that text to everyone about Rosie and Roger. I swear. I kind of figured it out after, and I was so mad I confronted her. I asked her if she'd lied to me."

"What did she say?" Meg asked.

Stella shook her head. "She totally denied everything. And I didn't get the phone back. And, like, the very next day she was using her regular phone. I felt really bad about it all. I'm sorry, Rosie. If I had known what she was going to do I wouldn't have given her the money in the first place, I swear."

"It's okay," Rosie said. "Thanks for telling me."

"So, did you believe that Mackenzie was telling the truth?" Meg asked sharply. Rosie thought she sounded like a lawyer for the prosecution. "Did you believe that she wasn't responsible for the text?"

"No," Stella admitted. "I knew she was lying but I pretended to believe her. I was still too under her thumb to break away. I guess I was scared she'd do to me what she'd done to Rosie."

Meg blushed and nodded. "I think I understand."

"Anyway," Stella went on, "after school got out I finally went to my mother and told her about who I'd been hanging out with and all. She helped me understand a lot of stuff. She said that being friends with people like Mackenzie is the same as being in an abusive relationship, like what sometimes happens in marriages. The bully is always blaming the victim for his own cruelty, then apologizing, and then being cruel all over again."

"What do you mean?" Meg asked.

"Like, the bully husband hits his wife and then says, 'See what you made me do? You made me hit you.' Then he apologizes, but of course he doesn't mean it. And then he hits her again."

Rosie shook her head. "That's just awful."

"You're never happy," Stella went on. "It's like, you know something bad could always happen, so you learn not to trust things when they seem okay. Because deep down you know that they're not okay, ever."

"It sounds terrible," Meg said with a shudder.

"It is. I think it's worse for Jill and even for Courtney than it was for me. They seem to really need Mackenzie. I only thought I did."

"Aren't you afraid that Mackenzie's going to do something bad to you," Rosie asked, "now that you're not hanging out with her anymore?"

Stella shrugged. "A little bit, I guess. But if she even looks at me weird I'm telling my parents and anyone else who will listen. I am so over all that craziness. I feel like that wasn't even me all those months. It's like I became someone else."

"Speaking of becoming someone else," Meg said with a smile, "what made you get such a radical haircut? I mean, it looks great, but it's so totally different from what you had before."

Stella put a hand to her short hair. "I know. My mother was kind of freaked when I told her this is what I wanted.

But I was tired of long hair and I just wanted a big change, in all sorts of ways. This is like a symbol of starting over for me."

"It looks really good," Rosie said. "It suits you."

"Thanks. My dad says the clothes make me look like a hippie. But I like it. I've seen plenty of pictures of hippies and I think they look cool." Stella looked at her watch. "Well, I should be going. I'm just here to pick up some candy for my mom." Stella pointed in the direction of Perkins Cove Candies. "She has a major sweet tooth and she really loves the gummies they sell there."

She waved and walked on in the direction of the candy shop.

Meg raised her eyebrows. "Wow," she said. "That was . . . weird."

"Do you believe her?" Rosie asked. "That she's sorry. Do you believe that she's not friends with Mackenzie Egan anymore?"

Meg thought about her answer for a moment. "Yeah," she said finally. "I do. Do you?"

"Yes," Rosie said. "I do, too."

38

Jane sat with her back ramrod straight and her hands at ten and two, just like she had been taught all those years ago in driver's education. The girls were in the backseat, sharing observations about what they were passing (cute guys behind the wheel of a car was a favorite) and occasionally laughing at some inside joke or an amusing bumper sticker. At times the giggling was shrill.

At least, Jane thought, they weren't each plugged into some electronic device, ignoring each other. She would never understand how two people could sit side by side and each be completely occupied with someone or something else on a screen. Why not just stay home alone? She could probably blame her age on the puzzlement this caused her, but she had a strong feeling that even if she were much younger, she would not be one of those super-plugged-in people. Clearly, though Rosie was computer savvy, she had no interest in spending a good part of the day with something stuck into her ear. Meg, on the other hand, was dying for an iPhone. *Good luck with that,* Jane thought. As far as she knew, Frannie still hadn't gotten Meg a regular, basic phone, which, in Jane's opinion, made no sense at all. It was a safety issue, pure and simple. Not that she could argue the issue with Frannie, but maybe Mike could say something to her. She would talk to him about it that evening.

Traffic along this stretch of Route 1 was light at this time of the morning. Jane was glad. Not that it gave her an excuse to let her mind wander, but at least she didn't have to be as tense as she was when traffic was heavy or when she was forced to drive alongside a massive truck or trailer. She hoped that when Rosie got her license, which wouldn't be long now, she wasn't as fearful behind the wheel as her mother. *Time would tell,* Jane thought, glancing in the rearview mirror at her daughter.

Rosie had told her about meeting Stella Charron in the cove. Jane had heard something about the Charrons' younger daughter being ill. She was glad to learn that the little girl was doing well. And if Stella Charron was being honest with Rosie and Meg, and the girls thought that she was, then she was indeed a brave young woman for apologizing for her part in the bullying.

A car sped by in the left lane and Jane's hands on the steering wheel tensed. Yes, she thought, courage wasn't her strong suit. Case in point—she still hadn't told Mike about her encounter with Frannie on Main Street. She thought that she might never tell him. She was too ashamed, and she was pretty sure Mike would be angry with her for having betrayed Rosie's personal business. She wasn't afraid of Mike's anger—he would never hit her or even raise his voice at her—but she was desperately in need of his good opinion and approval. Sometimes, in the middle of a sleepless night, she would lie awake wondering if someday he would realize how disappointing a person she was and decide to leave her.

Well, she thought, hopefully this outing would in some cosmic way make up for her poor judgment in her encounter with Frannie. And hopefully, she had learned a bit of a lesson from Stella's bravery. She had definitely learned a lesson from a six-year-old boy. Petey had come by after camp the other day with a bouquet of Queen Anne's lace (and some weeds) plucked from the side of the road.

"My mom says you're very busy," he said when Jane opened the door to his timid knock. "I know I'm not supposed to bother you, but I wanted to give you these. I know you really like flowers."

The tears had sprung to Jane's eyes as she reached out to accept the little bouquet. *God,* she thought, *he could be the son I never had.*

"I didn't mean to make you cry!" Petey said, alarmed.

"Oh, these are happy tears," Jane assured him, smiling and wiping her cheeks. "Thank you, Petey. Does your mom know you're here?"

"No. She's still at work. Meg's on the computer. I just came over."

How alone he is, Jane had thought. She had ushered him in for a snack, and before too many minutes had passed he was munching an oatmeal cookie and chattering on happily about day camp and how they had gone swimming at the Y and how they were putting on a puppet show next week. He was excited because he would be operating a marionette in the shape of a cat. Petey liked all animals. Once Jane had caught him offering a peanut to a squirrel in their backyard. He said he thought it looked hungry.

She had felt so happy sitting at the kitchen table with Petey. It was such a simple but such an important happiness. How, she wondered, could she have chosen resentment over love, especially where a child was concerned?

She had no good answer for that. There was no good answer.

After a while Jane had walked Petey home. Meg was horrified to realize that he had left the house without telling her. She had also seemed very embarrassed and had apologized profusely to Jane.

"I hope he didn't bother you," she said, when Petey had gone inside and up to his room.

Jane, too, had felt awkward and embarrassed. "Not at all," she assured Meg. "It was a pleasure to see him. I hope the cookies I gave him don't spoil his appetite for dinner."

Meg had smiled. "Oh, I don't think that will be a problem. Thanks again."

And they had parted. It had been on the tip of Jane's tongue to say, "Tell your mom I said hi," but she had caught herself just in time. First, she wasn't sure that Meg would want her mother to know that Petey had gone over to the Pattersons' and that Jane had brought him home. And second, Jane wasn't sure Frannie would want to accept a greeting from her. Best just to leave everything the way it was for the moment.

But things had changed thanks to Petey's unexpected visit and Jane's brief exchange with his sister. Unwittingly, Petey had created an opportunity for Jane to take her courage (such as it was) and her maturity in hand. That evening, via Mike, who had gone over to the Giroux house to see if he could fix their printer, she offered to take the girls to Old Orchard Beach for the day. Reluctantly or not, Mike hadn't said, Frannie had given her consent.

"Okay, girls," Jane said now, turning on to Old Orchard Road. "We're here." She parked the car in a small lot across the street from the Palace Playland. With exclamations of "Awesome!" and "Psych!" Rosie and Meg clambered out of the car. Jane followed with less enthusiasm.

Palace Playland was a major attraction for locals as well as for families on vacation. It was New England's only beachfront amusement park, which gave it some cachet. While the girls were well past spending time on the rides in Kiddie Land, they could choose from the "family rides" like the inevitable bumper cars and the Wave Swinger and the carousel or the classic Ferris wheel. Or, and this would be Meg's preference, they could go on the "thrill rides" like the Galaxi Coaster, the Pirate, or the Power Surge. Jane's preference would be that they stick to playing safe games like the roulette-style Spin-N-Win, but she wasn't naïve enough to think that was going to happen.

Not far from the amusement park, the Pier jutted out five hundred feet over the ocean. It was lined with overstuffed shops selling a variety of inexpensive souvenirs, including T-shirts, sunglasses, and visors. There were also five restaurants and five bars. Jane remembered that Frannie and Peter used to enjoy going to one of the bars. Jane wondered when Frannie had last been to her favorite stomping ground and figured that it probably wasn't since Peter's dismissal. She had certainly known better than to ask Jane to join her! Jane didn't like hanging out in bars.

The beach was wall-to-wall people for what looked like its entire seven miles, as was the water for what looked like seven miles out. No one could actually swim, though plenty of people seemed to be having fun just bobbing and splashing around. Jane shuddered. Looking at the mass of bodies crammed together made her think about germs and fungal infections and kids peeing on each other's feet.

The hordes of skimpily dressed teenaged girls annoyed her, too. Tight skirts that were indecently short, short shorts that looked more like underwear, tank tops that exposed more skin than they covered. Jane couldn't help but feel the girls were demeaning themselves without knowing it and that the boys, with their baggy shorts worn down almost below their butts, were taking full advantage of the girls' pathetic need to please them. She would never allow her own daughter to dress that way. Never. *But I'm lucky,* Jane thought. *Rosie isn't that kind of girl. She has no need to flaunt herself. She knows better.*

Like she knew better than to keep the bullying a secret. Like she knew better than to take a razor blade to her arm. Jane swallowed hard. You could never tell what might happen in life. Never. She wasn't superstitious, but still, there was no point in tempting fate by being absurdly sure of your own good luck. After all, look what had happened to Rosie this past school year. Never in a million years would Jane have imagined her daughter not only the victim of bullies but also someone who engaged in self-harming. Never.

Complacency was dangerous. She would try to remember that.

Once actually inside the grounds of the Palace Playland, Jane did her best to hide her distaste. But it was difficult.

"Oh, my God," Meg cried, pointing toward a man carrying a massive stuffed animal. "Look at that giant yellow monkey! I would so love to win that for Petey!"

Jane forced a smile. Frankly, she couldn't stand anything about the place, from the giant yellow monkeys to the greasy fast food. She knew she was being a snob and a prude and maybe overly fastidious, but there it was. Meg loved everything about Old Orchard Beach, especially the scarier rides in Palace Playland (she had always been a bit of a daredevil), and Rosie liked what she called the pageantry of it all (she said it reminded her of what a medieval fair might have been like, without the bear baiting, of course, old people and young people having fun together). So Jane bought each girl a hot dog and a funnel cake and a bunch of tickets for the rides, and refrained from openly criticizing the style, or lack thereof, of the majority of the crowd. Old Orchard Beach was definitely more Frannie's scene. She was far more tolerant of—well, of people than Jane. For example, Jane thought, wincing, she would laugh at the sight of the guy over by the stand selling fried dough. He was wearing a baseball type hat with a big foam hot dog perched on top.

The girls decided to go on a ride called the Orient Express. Jane waited in a rare spot of shade, thankful for a moment alone. (As alone as anyone could be in a teeming crowd of revelers.) She spotted the girls climbing into their car (or whatever it was called) and waved. Both girls waved back and Jane smiled. She was finding that interacting with Meg was not as difficult as she had imagined it might be.

The ride began and Jane thought back to earlier visits to Palace Playland and Yorktide Memorial Park and Ogunquit Beach and York's Wild Kingdom, all the places she and Frannie had taken the girls when they were little. Jane waved again but this time only Meg waved back. She wouldn't be surprised if Rosie's eyes were clamped shut.

Meg's personality had always been big, not bossy but determined and decided. More than once when the girls were small Meg had come to Rosie's rescue, like the time they were at the playground and that boy had tried to take Rosie's tricycle. Rosie had stood there, tears welling in her eyes, but before Jane could rush to the rescue, Meg had walked right up to the boy, who was bigger and older than she was, and demanded he give it back. Maybe it was the shock of a smaller, younger girl standing up to him, but the boy had immediately released the bike. And then there was the time Rosie had ventured higher than she ever had on the jungle gym and suddenly, been too scared to come down. Again, before Jane could lift her to the ground, Meg had scrambled up to where Rosie stood clutching a bar and basically talked her slowly down, taking each careful step by her side.

Then what, Jane thought now, *had made Meg turn against the friend she had loved since before she had even known what the word meant? What had changed inside Meg? What pain or misery or anger had caused her to lash out at Rosie, the person she had always protected?* Jane felt at a complete loss to understand. She wondered if even Meg understood her own motives, then or now.

Jane spotted the girls again as the ride whipped past. She had to look away when Meg raised her hands high above her head. Rosie's hands looked riveted to the safety bar. Over time, Jane realized, peering up again at the ride, she and Meg had become friends of a sort. Unlike Rosie, Meg had a real interest in fashion, and she definitely had an eye for style. Jane had enjoyed sharing her passion with Meg, passing along items she no longer needed or wanted, like a purse or a sweater, pointing out styles in catalogues and magazines. Vaguely now she recalled having promised to teach Meg how to sew. But she had never made good with that promise, had she? Maybe, she thought, now was the time to offer lessons. Maybe soon.

And she was surprised by that thought. The idea of finally offering to teach Meg how to sew had come to her unbidden. Maybe it was an indication that she was ready to begin the process of real forgiveness, at least where Meg was concerned.

Jane watched now as the ride came to an end and the girls came loping toward her.

"That was awesome!" Rosie exclaimed.

"Really?" Meg said. "I thought it was kind of lame. Well, not lame, exactly, but not super exciting. Not as good as the Galaxi Coaster."

"Well, nothing's as good as the Galaxi Coaster!"

"Meg," Jane said, interrupting the analysis of the rides, "the back of your neck is getting a bit burnt. I have some sunblock. . . ." She rummaged in her bag and produced a tube.

"Thanks, Mrs. Patterson," Meg said. "I totally forgot to bring any."

"Mom is always prepared," Rosie said with a smile. "She's a grown-up Girl Scout."

It was true, Jane thought. She always carried a tube of sunblock in her bag, that and a bottle of ibuprofen, a small spray bottle of Bactine, a few Band-Aids, and of course, a pack of tissues. How many times had she come to Frannie's rescue over the years when Meg, taking a physical risk, had skinned a knee or scraped an elbow? *Interesting,* Jane thought. She couldn't remember Meg ever crying when she had gotten hurt. Rosie had bawled at the slightest bump or bruise. *But maybe that was partly my fault,* Jane thought. She had always come running to the rescue, panic and alarm clear in her expression and attitude. Maybe Rosie had learned by example that the tiniest incident should be blown up into a tragedy.

Meg handed the tube of sunblock back to Jane and Rosie announced they were going to try their hand in the arcade. "But I thought you didn't like to play games,"

Jane said. Rosie shrugged. "I don't, really. But I guess sometimes it can be fun."

Jane opted to wait outside. The din of the rattling and ringing machines in the dark, almost subterranean space made her nerves twitch. The darkness made her worried about pickpockets. She had never ridden on the New York City subway and if she had her way, she never would. She had found Boston's clean and well-lit T system challenging enough.

Jane perched on a bench across from the arcade, but only after wiping the seat with a tissue. She hoped that no one decided to sit next to her. She doubted she had much to say to just about anyone else at the park, especially, she thought, not to someone like that woman with the massive multicolored tattoo on her chest and those horrid big round ear plugs in her earlobes. She was greedily consuming a triple-scoop ice cream cone, and the melting ice cream was running down her hand and arm.

Jane felt her stomach lurch and looked away from the woman. Her attention was almost immediately caught by a familiar figure standing by a mechanical fortune-telling booth. His back was to her so she couldn't be sure, but . . . The man turned a bit so that she could now see his profile. Yes, it was Peter Giroux! The slouch was unmistakable, as was the paunch. And he was with a much younger woman—a girl, really—in tiny shorts and super-high wedges. Jane prayed to a god she didn't believe in that Peter and the girl would be long gone before Meg came out of the arcade. And she prayed that Peter didn't spot her on that bench. It would be just like Peter Giroux to make his way over to flaunt his new girlfriend in front of Jane, assuming that she would run back to Pond View Road and tell Frannie about his latest prize. Only, Jane would never do such a thing.

She watched with distaste as Peter rubbed his potbelly, as if proud of it. *Poor Frannie,* she thought, *to be saddled with such a man for the rest of her life.* Because as the father of her children he would always, always be a part of Frannie's life, even if only in memory, even if he chose to entirely abandon Meg and Petey. Jane had a surprisingly strong urge to get off that bench, march right over to where he was standing with his friend (ha!), and . . . And what? Tell him what a jerk he was? Slap him in the face? With an enormous feeling of relief she watched Peter and his gal pal head in the direction of the parking lot. She could only hope they would get in a car and drive far, far away. Or maybe into the ocean where they would drown and never cause Frannie or Meg or Petey trouble ever again. The force of that last, nasty thought took Jane by surprise.

"Mom?"

Jane jumped at the sound of her daughter's voice and finally noticed Rosie and Meg standing in front of her. "Oh," she said. "Hi."

"We've been standing here for, like, three minutes."

"Maybe two," Meg corrected.

"Whatever. You looked like you were in a trance or something."

"I did?" Jane attempted a smile. "Sorry. I was just thinking about something."

Rosie shrugged. "We want to do the Pier now, okay?"

Jane stood and tried to hide her reluctance behind another smile. "Sure," she said.

An hour later, the Pier "done," the girls climbed into the backseat of the car, not much worse for wear in spite of sun, spine-shattering rides, and bad food. Jane, on the other hand, felt weary to the bone. *It's good to be young,* she thought. *Except when it's not,* she added, thinking of Petey. Like when you think you're responsible for an adult's bad behavior.

Traffic was fairly light on the way back to Yorktide, and Jane was glad for that. She was always highly aware of the enormous responsibility she shouldered when another person's child was in her car. She owed it to Frannie to keep Meg safe and to return her in sound condition. Until last year, Jane hadn't let anyone but Mike or Frannie or the school's bus driver (and that with protest) chauffeur Rosie around. Maybe, in retrospect, she had been overly cautious. Maybe that sort of behavior had further set Rosie apart from the other kids at school. Maybe that had marked Rosie as different and vulnerable and . . .

"Thanks, Mrs. Patterson," Meg said from the backseat, interrupting Jane's dark thoughts. "It was really nice of you to ask me to come along."

Jane noted Meg's choice of words and was at a loss as how to reply. "You're welcome," she had finally said, hoping her voice held steady. It would have to suffice for now.

39

Dear Diary

Friday

Thank God school is over for the week.

I realized that Mom was right. It's a good thing I don't have a dog, not because I'm too young but because I'm an idiot. I would probably only forget to feed him and then he would die. Then I'd be arrested for animal cruelty and go to jail where I would rot away until I died.

Disgusting.

Dear Diary

I remember when the weekend was something I looked forward to. Why? Was one day better than another? Now every day is the same. Too long and too sad.

Meg asked me if I wanted to go with her and her mother to the outlets in Kittery. I said no. She didn't ask me why.

Dad wanted the three of us to go to dinner at some expensive restaurant in Perkins Cove Saturday night. A special treat, he said. I told my parents I wasn't feeling good, which wasn't really a lie, and to go without me. They did.

Why would I want to shop? Why would I want to get dressed up and go to a fancy dinner? Why would I want to do anything?

Why would anyone want to do anything with me?

Meg and her mother and Mom and Dad all probably asked me to join them out of pity.

They shouldn't have wasted their time.

I am so tired that my whole body is shaking. But I won't be able to sleep. I checked Mom's medicine cabinet but there weren't any sleeping pills. I went through her dresser drawers just in case, but there was nothing. Maybe the doctor across the hall from Dad has something in her office. But I don't know how I could get past her receptionist.

Maybe I'm just stuck being awake for the rest of my life.

40

Meg was sprawled on the couch in the living room, waiting for her father to come by and fetch Petey. She had been thinking about what Stella had told her and Rosie the other day in Perkins Cove. She had had no idea life around someone like Mackenzie could be so miserable. And she was thinking about how nice it had been of Mrs. Patterson to take them to Old Orchard Beach. Meg had felt a little awkward around her at first, but Mrs. Patterson had been really nice, offering her sunblock and buying her food, and by the end of the day things had seemed pretty normal, almost like old times. Not quite, but almost.

The doorbell rang and Meg sighed. She wished that her mother was home to deal with Peter Giroux, but her mother was at work. Of course.

Meg opened the door. "Hi," she said. Her father was dressed in his usual sloppy way—baggy jeans, a T-shirt proclaiming that he braked for hotties, and dirty sneakers. He badly needed a haircut, and by the looks of his dirty fingernails, Meg guessed he could probably use a shower. She had pretty much gotten used to the two missing teeth, though when he had first lost them to gum disease Meg had felt embarrassed to be seen with him. Whose fault was it that he hadn't been to a dentist in, like, twenty years? His own, that's whose fault it was.

"Hey, whassup, Megarino?" he said, smiling hugely as he loped past Meg into the house.

Meg felt her face get hot. She hated when he called her that, and all those other stupid nicknames he came up with. But long ago she had stopped begging him to use her real name. He never listened, so why waste her time? And she had long since stopped being afraid of him. Her father's bark was much worse than his bite. It was the only halfway good thing about him.

"Where's my kid?" Mr. Giroux asked, scanning the living room as if Petey was hiding behind a piece of furniture. More likely, Meg thought, he was looking for something he could steal and then sell. Her mother had warned her to watch her father carefully when he came to the house. They were already missing a silver candlestick Frannie had inherited from a great aunt. "He ready yet?"

"He's upstairs," she said. "He'll be down in a minute."

"Don't want to miss the opening pitch. Yo, Petey!"

Meg flinched at her father's shout.

Petey's still almost girlish voice floated back. "Coming, Daddy!"

A complete silence followed, which, Meg thought, was nothing unusual. Her father never had anything to say to her. But she had something to say to him.

"Why didn't you send me a birthday card?" she asked.

Her father widened his eyes in an exaggeration of surprise. "It was your birthday? Oops. Sorry, Megorama. Guess I just forgot. Got a lot on my mind these days."

Yeah, Meg thought, like how to pay for a keg of beer

and how to get a new girlfriend, someone who didn't know about your lack of a steady job and the family you'd left behind. "You're so busy you can't even remember your daughter's birthday?"

Peter put his hands up in protest. "Hey, cool down. Chillax. What's the big deal?"

"The big deal is that it was my birthday."

"Jeez, I'll make it up to you next year. I promise."

"I don't believe you," Meg shot back. "You always break your promises."

Peter Giroux's face took on a mean expression. "That's no way to talk to your father," he growled.

"Why not?" Meg challenged. "I'm only telling the truth."

"I kept my promise to take your brother to a Sea Dogs game, didn't I? Hey, Petey!" he called again. "Hurry up, let's go!"

"That's only because Mom reminded you, like, a hundred times."

"No," Peter spat out. "It's because your brother doesn't give me crap. He has some respect for his old man. You're way too much like your mother, Megarrific."

Meg felt as if she had been slapped. She felt as if she would cry. But there was no way she would give her father that satisfaction. Instead, with every effort of her will, she said, "I'll take that as a compliment."

Before her father could reply Petey came racing down the stairs, his too-big baseball cap askew. "I'm ready, Daddy!" he cried. His face was shining with excitement.

"Hey, looking good, Petey." Peter guided his son toward the front door.

"Have a good time, Petey," Meg said, watching them leave the house. "Don't eat too much junk food."

"Okay," Petey said. "But can I get ice cream, Daddy?"

"You can get all the ice cream you want," he said loudly, almost, Meg thought, in defiance of her caution to Petey.

Her father shut the door behind him without a word of farewell to his daughter.

Her father and brother were barely in Peter's much-abused, heavily rusted car before Meg, still standing in the living room, began to sob.

41

Frannie was in the dairy aisle in Hannaford. Since when, she thought, frowning at the display in front of her, had everything become so expensive? And since when had yogurt come in so many varieties, styles, and flavors it could take you a week to choose one? Frannie grabbed the carton of yogurt with the cheapest price tag and placed it into her cart. Maybe it was high fat, or maybe it was low fat. Maybe it was prune flavored or maybe it had those probiotics, whatever they were, that helped regulate your digestive system. Whatever. Her time was too precious to waste agonizing over dairy products.

And she was tired, even more so than usual. She had been up until all hours the night before, reliving the afternoon and evening. Because when she had gotten home from work she had found Meg sitting on the couch in tears, and it didn't take a rocket scientist to figure out that Peter had had something to do with Meg's distress.

"What did he say this time?" she had asked her daughter, sitting beside her and gently putting an arm around her shoulders, half-expecting Meg to pull away.

But Meg hadn't pulled away. "Nothing," she had mumbled. "The same stuff."

"Yes," Frannie had replied with a sigh. "Your father is predictable."

"And he calls me those stupid names."

"Yeah. He used to do that with me, too, before the divorce. Franerific. The Franstigator. It was beyond annoying."

And after a moment Meg had blurted, "Sometimes I hate him!"

The force of Meg's declaration had surprised and saddened Frannie. She had never made excuses for or tried to hide her ex-husband's bad behavior from her daughter. At the same time she didn't want Meg to actually hate her father. But the hate was partly her fault. She hadn't taught her daughter to respect her father because she hadn't found anything in him worth respecting. Maybe she should have lied about Peter, painted him as a good man and a loving father. No. That would have been impossible. Meg wasn't stupid.

"Don't say that, Meg," she had said then, not angrily.

"Why not? You hate him."

"No," Frannie said, truthfully. "I don't. At least, not anymore. Mostly I feel bad for him. He can't help but be the way he is."

Maybe that statement wasn't the truth (change was usually possible, but Peter was too lazy to even try to change) but at any rate, it had been the end of the conversation. A bit later, when Meg had washed her face with cool water, Frannie had persuaded her to go out to dinner, just the two of them. They went to the nearest Applebee's, and by the meal's end, Meg had recovered enough to smile, just a bit, and to thank her mother for "hanging out" with her. Frannie had been touched by Meg's thanks. To have a teenaged daughter who actually wanted to hang out with her mother . . . Well, that was special.

Frannie wheeled the cart in the direction of the cereal aisle. She hoped the store wasn't out of the generic brand of the cold cereal Petey liked. Mostly, when you bought a box of cereal you got half a box of air. *You might as well buy generic air,* Frannie thought. *It's cheaper.*

And speaking of cheapness . . . Peter had returned Petey two hours later than promised and without the five-dollar bill Frannie had given her son in case of an emergency. Petey had been exhausted but seemed happy enough, babbling on about details of the game and how they had met Daddy's friend Buster there and how after the three of them had gone somewhere for pizza. A few artfully casual questions had unearthed the fact that Peter had taken his son to a pub, not a walk-in pizza joint, but as long as he hadn't driven back to Yorktide drunk she couldn't really complain. When he had dropped Petey off he had seemed completely sober. Unless he had become very good at faking sobriety . . .

Frannie snatched the last box of Petey's favorite cereal from the shelf and headed on to the condiment aisle. The Giroux family was out of mustard. Petey liked yellow mustard. Meg liked honey mustard. Frannie was partial to Dijon. She scanned the prices for the generic brand in each flavor. For whatever reason, the yellow mustard was cheapest, so yellow mustard it would be. Frannie tossed the plastic bottle into the cart. Sometimes it was just downright boring to shop on a tight budget, even though it took more brainpower than simply grabbing what was closest or packaged in the brightest container. Witness her experience in the dairy aisle!

Overwhelmed by yogurt. Was this what her life had become?

Frannie moved on to the paper goods aisle and wheeled the cart past the selection of holiday cards, wrapping paper, and small stuffed animals. *Obviously,* she thought, *this is an aisle my ex-husband isn't familiar with.* When no birthday card had shown up for Meg she had called Peter, though what she had hoped to accomplish by calling him was anybody's guess. Characteristically, he had given several ridiculous excuses for having forgotten or ignored his daughter's birthday, excuses he had to know Frannie wouldn't believe. Like that his psychic buddy had told him it would bring bad luck if he sent a card to his daughter this year. Or that he'd bought a card weeks ago, really, and had mailed it right away, so it must have gotten lost or something, goddamn postal service.

Frannie tossed a six-pack of paper towels into the shopping cart, followed by a twelve-pack of toilet paper. She wondered if other people's kids went through as much toilet paper as hers did, but she certainly wasn't about to take a survey and find out. Maybe she should tell Meg and Petey just how much toilet paper cost. . . . But regulating toilet paper struck Frannie as the one economy she couldn't bring herself to make. She had to maintain some sense of dignity.

At least Peter wasn't living with them on Pond View Road. Talk about excessive use of toilet paper! Frannie almost smiled at the thought. But Peter was a bum and didn't deserve a smile. She had never apologized for his careless and sometimes cruel behavior, and it was too late to start. Meg was too old now to believe that her father really cared about her but was just forgetful when it came to birthdays and other holidays. She had lost what naïveté she had ever had early on. Maybe that was common for children in a single-parent home with a careless absentee parent like Peter. It would be interesting to see how Petey matured and if he, too, would realize before long that his father was a severely limited man. But the father-son relationship was so very different than the father-daughter relationship, and Peter had always shown a marked preference for his second child. It was unfair, but that was the way it was.

Maybe, Frannie thought, she would ask Meg if she wanted to talk to Sister Pauline again. It might help if Meg could talk about her father to an adult other than her mother. Frannie sighed and put the jar of fancy pickles she was contemplating back on the shelf. No one really needed fancy pickles. Pickles weren't even supposed to be fancy. They were only cucumbers, after all. They were supposed to come in a wooden barrel and be sold on the sidewalk for a nickel!

She wheeled her laden cart to the front of the store and scooted over to the shortest line. Just ahead of her was a young mother. Her child, surely less than a year old, was strapped into the seat of the shopping cart. The young woman was obese. The tank top she was wearing strained across her back, outlining every bump and stitch of her bra. Her hair was lank and unkempt. A large tattoo of a snake or a dragon ran down her left arm and there was a black and red tattoo of a skull on the back of her neck. The woman was trying to pay for her groceries with food stamps. Without actually eavesdropping, Frannie could tell that something was delaying the transaction.

Thank God, Frannie thought, the Giroux family had never had to rely on food stamps. Some families simply had it a lot worse than her own family did. "There but for the grace of God go I." Or, in other terms, the Giroux family had gotten lucky, pure and simple. She wondered what chance that little baby in the cart ahead of her had of breaking away from his parents' troubled world and making a better life for himself. If his parents didn't have access to opportunities for education, how would he get access to them? Who would save him from repeating a pattern of poverty and all the problems that stemmed from it?

Frannie knew she should be grateful for what she and her children had and not dwell so much on the negatives, like not being able to justify the purchase of a silly magazine or a fancier brand of peanut butter, or even three types of mustard at once. *No wonder,* she thought, *my daughter is a Miss Grumpy Pants. She got it from me! I should be more like Marlene from the office.* She was a person to emulate, always looking for the positive in any situation, even the difficult ones like having a son with autism and a mother who was rapidly losing her eyesight.

Finally, the young woman ahead of Frannie was able to complete her purchase and wheel the cart out to the parking lot. Frannie began to unload the contents of her cart onto the conveyor belt. It would take a miracle to transform a bitching and moaning Frances Giroux into a happy and grateful Marlene Gervais, she thought. But miracles had been known to happen.

"Would you like to donate a dollar to children's cancer research?" the smiling woman behind the checkout counter asked, pointing to a sign posted against the cash register. The sign advertised a statewide charitable organization.

"Yes," Frannie said, reaching into her bag for her wallet. "I would be happy to."

42

Sunday

I have nothing to say.

Still Sunday

Why did I even bother to open this diary? I even bore myself. It's all a sick joke.

43

What Stella had said the other day in Perkins Cove about her experiences with Mackenzie, Courtney, and Jill had given Rosie a lot to think about. So a couple of days after the trip to Old Orchard Beach, which had been lots of fun though she knew her mother hadn't really enjoyed it (she hadn't said anything but her discomfort was written all over her face), she decided to go online and read up on the whole topic of bullying. She knew some stuff, of course, from the anti-bullying and bullying prevention programs at school, but clearly, Rosie thought, there was an awful lot she didn't know or hadn't paid enough attention to.

The family's computer was located in her father's small home office in the basement, near her mother's sewing room. Rosie sat down at the desk and went online. There was so much information, a lot of it repetitive and some of it contradictory, but her father had taught her good research skills. She knew how to locate the better sources and how to spot the sites that were ill conceived and badly written. Her dad had taught her that websites like that were likely to contain faulty or downright wrong information and were a huge waste of time.

After over an hour's worth of reading, Rosie was beginning to realize that what Dr. Lowe (and even her mother) had suggested about Mackenzie Egan was probably right. Mackenzie was not inherently evil but weak and maybe even afraid. Quite possibly she was the child of a home in which she had learned early on that nobody, certainly not a parent, was to be relied upon for anything. In a deeply uncertain world, this child had learned that it was better to attack before you were attacked. It was better to seize control before control was seized from you. It was better to watch people suffer than to suffer yourself. It made a kind of sense, really.

From what Rosie knew of Mackenzie Egan's home life, which admittedly wasn't firsthand information, she thought it likely that Mackenzie's bullying tactics were in reality a damaged or twisted sort of self-defense mechanism. She wondered if this scenario held true for Courtney and Jill, too. It didn't for Stella, who, by her own admission, had just been looking for a place to feel welcome when things at home had gotten bad.

Rosie exited the last site she had been reading and put the computer to sleep. She wasn't sure if what she was feeling now toward those girls was actual compassion, but whatever it was, it felt right. Not that she was going to be stupid and actually approach them and say, "Hey, let's be friends!" There was a line between compassion—if that was the right word—and self-protection. You could learn how to turn the other cheek, but you didn't have to present your face to be slapped.

The door to the basement opened and her mother came down the stairs, carrying a basket of dirty clothes and towels.

"What are you up to?" Jane asked after putting the basket on top of the washing machine.

"I've been reading up on bullies and bullying," Rosie said. "But I'm done for the day."

"Was any of the information helpful?"

"Yeah. It's just that there's so much information. There's a lot to sort through."

Jane came over and perched on the edge of the desk. "It's certainly an important topic."

"Yeah," Rosie agreed. "You know, Mom, I can't help but wonder what Mackenzie will think of my being friends with Meg again. I wonder if she'll think I'm stupid."

Jane frowned. "I'm pretty sure Mackenzie won't know what to think. If she can't understand true friendship, then she definitely can't understand forgiveness."

"I guess that's true."

"Anyway, you shouldn't worry about what Mackenzie thinks."

"Oh, I'm not worried," Rosie said. "Just curious. I feel like I understand more about people like Mackenzie now, but there are still some things I don't understand. I think she must be a very lonely person deep down."

"I think you're probably right."

"I suppose I should feel sorry for her in a way."

"Do you?" her mother asked.

"I don't know," Rosie said after a moment. "Yeah, I guess I do."

Jane smiled. "I guess I do, too."

Rosie considered. She had been wanting to talk to her mother about something important, and now seemed like a pretty good time. "Mom?" she said. "Why can't you and Mrs. Giroux be friends again?"

Her mother's smile faded and she hesitated before answering. "It's—it's a difficult situation," she said.

"Is it because Mrs. Giroux doesn't want to be friends?"

Jane fiddled with a button on her blouse. "No. That's not it. In fact, she sent me a very nice note around my birthday. She basically asked if we could sit down and talk. The reason we're not friends again is because I'm just not ready to—"

"To forgive her?" Rosie said after a moment of her mother's silence. "But she didn't do anything wrong."

Jane shook her head. "I'm just not ready to be friends again. That's all I can really say, Rosie. I'm sorry."

Rosie shrugged. "Okay. But that's too bad. You guys used to have so much fun together. She would have liked coming to Old Orchard Beach with us the other day. If she could have gotten off work, I mean. She loves cotton candy. And we could have stopped at that place she used to like on the Pier. She said they had free popcorn."

"I know."

"She must have some vacation days," Rosie said, aware that she was pressing her mother. "Though Meg says she hasn't taken any this summer."

"Yes," Jane said. "I suppose she has some vacation time."

Rosie remembered something her mother had said only a moment before. If Mackenzie couldn't understand true friendship, then she couldn't understand true forgiveness. Rosie wondered if the same held true for Jane Patterson. Did her mother really not understand true friendship? Had she never really understood it?

"Meg says her mother hardly ever smiles anymore," Rosie said now, watching her mother's expression closely.

Jane abruptly stood from her perch on the desk. "I'd

better get to that laundry," she said, turning away. "It won't wash itself."

Rosie knew her mother had deliberately changed the subject, but that was okay. She wouldn't push her mother any further, at least, not yet. Instead she groaned. "You always say that! Laundry won't wash itself. Dinner won't cook itself. Blouses won't iron themselves."

Jane laughed from the vicinity of the washing machine. "And I'm always right!"

44

Saturday morning found Jane at the wheel of the car again, the chaperone of another excursion. This time Rosie and Meg were less interested in spotting cute guys or funny bumper stickers. Meg had a copy of *Allure* magazine, and from what Jane could hear the girls were debating the coolness factor of the latest crop of nail colors. She caught the word "peridot," which she knew was a semiprecious stone, and the interesting phrase "Hello there, beautiful." Since when, she wondered, did Rosie care about nail polish? Well, as long as she was enjoying herself and not debating what tattoo or piercing she was going to get . . .

A minivan packed with kids in soccer uniforms trundled by. Jane caught a quick glance of the smiling mother behind the wheel. She looked as happy as Jane was troubled. She had been deeply embarrassed by the conversation in the basement with Rosie. The last thing any parent wanted was for her child to be disappointed in her, and Jane would bet money on the fact that Rosie was, indeed, disappointed in her failure to make peace with Frannie.

Later that night, after Rosie had gone off to bed, she had talked to Mike about her conversation with Rosie. She had gotten the distinct impression that he was getting a little frustrated with her inability or unwillingness to make peace with Frannie. Not that he said as much, but Jane had known him a long time. Mike didn't need to spell out what he was thinking. It was all over his face, if you had the skills to read it. And Jane was highly sensitive to signs of Mike's disapproval.

Honestly, she could understand her husband's frustration, even if a very small part of her was upset with him for not taking her side on the issue. By refusing to accept Frannie back into her life she was depriving her daughter of so much, like, for example, the annual mother-daughter afternoon at Chauncey Creek in Kittery Point. They had kept the tradition for the past five years, rain or shine. Frannie always brought the homemade macaroni salad that Rosie loved and Jane always brought the homemade sugar cookies that Meg loved. The adults shared a lobster and the girls usually got lobster rolls. Last year, Jane and Frannie had caught the girls watching—and pretending not to watch—the strong young men hauling nets and lifting large wooden crates off the boats and onto the dock. They had shared a smile over that.

But this year there would be no excursion, no shared smiles, and no holiday routines like taking Petey to the mall in South Portland to get his picture taken with Santa Claus, and making cupcakes with green icing for St. Patrick's Day. There would be no annual shopping trip to Freeport or Kittery for back-to-school clothes, and no movie Saturdays. So much was lost now. . . . And she was the one person standing in the way of it all returning.

So, in another attempt to assuage some of the guilt

she felt about not befriending Frannie, Jane had offered (via Mike, though she knew using him as a go-between couldn't go on forever) to take the girls to Portland for the day. In Jane's opinion, Portland beat Old Orchard Beach by a long mile. For one, there were no dangerous amusement rides or dark, noisy arcades, though there were the occasional shirtless guys who really should have been at the gym instead of displaying their poor excuses for abs and their lewd tattoos. *Well, no place is perfect,* Jane thought now, *city or country, uptown or downtown.*

"Mom?"

Jane wasn't comfortable talking while driving. It distracted her. Rosie must have forgotten that.

"Yes?" she said.

"Would you ever wear green metallic nail polish?"

"Never."

Shouts of laughter came from the backseat. "I so know you wouldn't," Rosie said. "I just thought it would be funny to ask."

Jane smiled. She was so, so happy that her daughter was laughing again and being silly like a young person should be. Only weeks ago . . .

No, Jane thought, sitting up even straighter. *No bad thoughts now.* Instead, her mind drifted back to the moments just before they had left their house on Pond View Road. Something, maybe sheer nostalgia, had compelled Jane to retrieve the plaque that Frannie had given her from the drawer where she had stashed it out of sight earlier in the summer. She had read the words on the plaque out loud. "Friends Are Forever." Frannie had given her the plaque for her birthday about a year or two after they had met, and until Jane had yanked it down, it had hung on the kitchen wall where the family could see it every day.

Purposefully, Jane removed the small watercolor painting she had hung on the nail above the silverware drawer and replaced it with Frannie's gift. It seemed like a small act of commitment to . . . to what, she wondered. Maybe to the future. Maybe even to the past, if that made any sense. What once had been should be honored, especially if it had been good.

Jane, Rosie, and Meg arrived in Portland around ten-thirty. "Art first," Jane decreed when they had parked the car on Free Street. "Shopping later."

With a little grumbling from Meg they went to the Portland Museum of Art where they viewed an exhibit of New England–based artists in the main gallery. Downstairs, by the café, there was the museum's impressive collection of antique glass and art glass, which Meg, who had ignored the work on past visits, suddenly found "mind-blowing." Rosie seemed really struck by the white marble statue of Ulysses S. Grant in the Gillian Rotunda. Meg thought the interactive learning tools in the McLellan House were interesting.

Later, while the girls examined the books and one-of-a-kind jewelry and glass ornaments in the gift shop, Jane sat on a bench in the Great Hall and remembered. She and Frannie had come to the museum one day about three years earlier to see an exhibit of Depression-era photographs of native Mainers. The show was moving and in its own way, beautiful. Afterward they had gone to Bessie's diner for lunch (Frannie's choice; she craved the egg salad on white toast) and then had spent some time strolling along the waterfront. Frannie had declared the day a mini-vacation and Jane, too, had enjoyed herself immensely. But that was in the past, Jane told herself, smiling vaguely at an old, very well-dressed woman sitting down beside her.

After the girls had bought some postcards from the

gift shop, Jane led them down Congress Street toward Monument Square. Along the way, they stopped in a variety of stores. In Renys, Meg bought her mother a bright purple summer-weight scarf for four dollars. "She never wears bright colors," Meg said. "I'm going to make her wear this. She needs a change." Jane silently wished Meg luck with changing her mother's habits. She remembered the time she had suggested—tactfully, she hoped—that Frannie spruce up her look by wearing a different shade of lipstick; she had been wearing the same orangey pink color for years and Jane thought it was not at all suited to the skin tone of a woman in her mid-thirties. But Frannie had stubbornly stuck to the color until mercifully (to Jane's thinking) it was discontinued.

Jane shook off the memory of that awkward conversation—maybe she shouldn't have tried to change Frannie; Frannie had never tried to change her—and focused on choosing a new garden spade and a pair of gloves. Rosie picked out a navy T-shirt for her father. "There's just no way my dad is going to wear anything other than tan, navy, and maybe, if he's feeling really daring, brown," she said as they were checking out. "Ever."

Meg snorted. "At least his clothes are clean. I don't think my dad ever does laundry. Ever." Jane winced at that remark.

Rosie wanted to visit the store where Meg had bought her the rose quartz pendant, so they stopped in Stones and Stuff and met the owner, a very friendly woman named Heather with beautiful dark, curly hair. Rosie bought a chunk of citrine for three dollars. She loved the sunny color. Meg bought a small but real uncut ruby for fifteen dollars. It was a big splurge and Jane quietly suggested that Meg seriously consider her purchase. What would Frannie say to such an extravagance? But she didn't protest further when Meg handed over her cash with a huge smile on her face. Everyone needed to treat herself on occasion. And those occasions for Meg and her mother were rare. For a moment Jane wondered if she should have bought the stone for Meg. But Frannie might not have liked that at all, and given the situation between the mothers, Meg might have felt awkward about it, too.

Across the street in a resale and antique store called Encore, Meg and Rosie gazed openmouthed at the racks of beautiful old furs from the forties and fifties and fancy dresses from the sixties and seventies and investigated the trays of gaudy, gorgeous, and sometimes costly costume jewelry. On a shelf over the front counter Jane spotted an intricately beaded antique purse almost identical to one Frannie had inherited from a great aunt, the same one who had left her the pair of silver candlesticks. She wondered if Frannie knew the bag's twin was being sold for a whopping fifty dollars. Not that Frannie would part with a family heirloom, but she might be interested to know its market value, just in case times got even tighter.

Jane sighed and turned away from the display. Frannie might as well be with them here in Portland. Every single thing—the museum, the purple scarf, the antique beaded purse—had triggered a memory. Someone didn't actually have to die to haunt another person. Certainly, Jane realized that now.

After twenty minutes or so, Jane dragged the girls back onto the sidewalk and directed them down to Exchange Street. Making it from one end to the other took close to forty-five minutes as the girls insisted on going into just about every single clothing, shoe, and jewelry shop on each side of the street. Eventually, they made their way past Fore Street and down to Commercial Street, which ran along the water's edge. In big rains the street had been known to flood, but on this sunny summer day it was dry as the proverbial bone and packed with visitors in shorts and sneakers and baseball caps.

"Look," Jane said, pointing. A cruise ship was in port, one of the many ships that made a stop in Portland each year between August and mid-October. The city benefited from the trade the passengers brought, though Jane was at a loss to understand just who, exactly, could afford a cruise in the current economy.

"It's insanely big," Rosie said with a shudder. "I mean, it's actually kind of terrifying."

"I think it's awesome," Meg said, squinting up at it through her clip-on sunglasses. "I can't wait to go on a cruise someday."

"Not me," Rosie said. "All I would think about is the ship sinking out in the middle of nowhere. I saw *Titanic,* you know. I can't think of anything worse than drowning. Unless it's burning to death."

"Like flying in a plane is any safer than being on a ship?" Meg laughed. "You could crash in the middle of nowhere and yeah, burn to death! At least if you're shipwrecked there's a chance you'll survive. Not everyone died when the *Titanic* hit that iceberg. Some people were rescued."

Rosie shrugged. "Still. I'll take a plane over one of those . . . behemoths . . . any day."

"What's a behemoth?" Meg asked.

"A behemoth," Jane explained, "is an animal described in the book of Job. Scholars think the writer was describing a hippo. Today people use the word to describe something huge and cumbersome."

"You know way more about the Bible than I do," Meg

said. "All I know is what I've heard someone read in church."

Jane shrugged. "It's a good book. I studied it in college. Anyway, I have to say I agree with Rosie on this one. Though I would like to go on a tour of a cruise ship. As long as it's safely docked."

"I'm going to take my mother on a cruise someday," Meg said, reluctantly turning away from the monster of a ship. Jane forced a smile. She wanted to say something like, "That's nice of you," but couldn't make the words come out of her mouth.

Jane took the girls for lunch at the Portland Lobster Company, a bit farther down the street and right on the water. They sat on stools at a high table from where they had a clear view of the bar area, where a skinny young guy with a scraggly little beard was playing guitar. "He is so cute," Meg whispered and sat enthralled, mouth open, her chicken wrap barely touched. Rosie spent much of the time petting the furry mixed-breed dog that had come with the people at the next table. When the dog settled down for a nap at their feet, Rosie watched the water taxis and the touring and whale-watching boats coming in and out of the docks.

Jane ordered a bucket of steamers. Meg said they looked gross, and then apologized for insulting Mrs. Patterson's lunch. Secretly, Jane agreed, they did look gross, but they tasted delicious. While she ate she judged the clothing of fellow diners. Of course, if Frannie were at the table with her, she would have someone with whom to share her observations. The cut of that woman's sundress was perfect; that girl's shorts fit badly but could be saved. True, Frannie wouldn't be much interested in talk about cut and fabric, but she would listen amiably as a good, comfortable friend does, and then, when Jane was done critiquing, she would talk about her own concerns (the idiots at the office, Peter's latest antics), and Jane would listen in turn. *That's what friends do,* she thought. *They listen even when they might not want to. They endure and tolerate; they accept and they share.* Jane tried to shake off the heavy feeling of loneliness that had suddenly overcome her. There was scientific proof that people got sick when they were deprived of love and affection. But you didn't need to be a scientist to know that. Just human.

The guitarist finished his set (Jane had to admit that he was pretty talented, though she wished he was wearing shoes rather than sandals) and Meg was finally persuaded to finish her lunch. Afterward, Jane suggested they go across the street to a store called Asia West. The girls made a dash for the jewelry cases and Jane wandered among the furniture until the sight of two women, clearly good friends, chatting about something that was making them both smile sent her across the store. At Rosie's urging, Jane bought herself a woven tote bag the color of gingko leaves for ten dollars and the girls each got a beaded bracelet from Indonesia for six dollars. Rosie's was mostly blue. Meg's was mostly orange.

"I really feel like I'm on vacation!" Rosie said when they emerged into the bright sun, shopping bags in tow.

"I know," Meg said, "isn't it great! I wish we could come to Portland all the time."

"At least once a month. Could we, Mom?"

Jane mentally estimated the cost of lunch out and shopping and museum admission, not to mention gas and parking, and blanched. A monthly expedition was out of the question. "We'll come more often than we have in the past," she said. "How about that?"

They strolled farther down Commercial Street, stopping in the gift shops geared for summer visitors, until finally, exhaustion seemed to embrace all three at once. They turned around and began what now seemed like an overly long and hot walk back to where Jane had parked the car up on Free Street. The girls walked ahead, talking nonstop. Jane walked behind, lost in her own thoughts, thankful for the peace. She was a little bit tired of listening to countless exclamations of "Awesome!" and "Oh, my God!" and "I so have to have this!" That last was exclusively Meg's. It seemed that every time an interesting item caught her eye she would "literally die" if it couldn't be hers. Jane had never met anyone so covetous, but she thought it indicated Meg's desire to live with items of beauty rather than an unhealthy desire to own things for the sake of owning things. At least, she hoped that was the case.

She smiled now, watching Rosie grab Meg's arm as Meg started to cross against a light. They would have their old argument there on the curb. "But there are no cars coming!" Meg would point out. And Rosie would retort, "But you never know what could happen." In so many ways they were Jane and Frannie in miniature. . . .

The light turned green and the girls moved on, Jane following. She had enjoyed herself in Portland, and it was obvious that the girls had, too, but she had missed Frannie. A lot. If she could only get over her own inflated sense of pride . . .

But was it really pride that stood in the way of reconciliation with Frannie? If so, that was pretty pathetic. Pride, it was said, went before a fall. You didn't have to grow up a Catholic to have learned that lesson.

Well, maybe pride (which might simply be another term for stubbornness) was a factor, Jane thought, but maybe once again she was allowing fear to dictate her behavior. Fear of a repeat of the emotional loss she had already sustained. What if Frannie changed her mind and didn't want Jane back in her life after all? She didn't know if she could stand to lose Frannie twice. That was a new and sobering realization.

They reached Free Street, found the car, and climbed inside. The forty-five-minute drive home was uneventful. The nail polish debate seemed to have been decided on the way north. Peridot had won as the coolest new color. When Jane pulled up to the Pattersons' garage Meg thanked her again and hurried into her house, eager, she said, to present her mother with the scarf she had bought her. She said nothing about the little ruby and Jane thought that Meg was likely to keep that purchase to herself for a while, a secret treasure. Jane and Rosie walked around to their own front door.

"Thanks, Mom," Rosie said as Jane put her key in the lock. "This day was just—"

"Let me guess," Jane interrupted. "It was awesome!"

Rosie rolled her eyes, but she was smiling. *And it would have been even more awesome,* Jane thought, stepping inside, *if Frannie had been with us.*

45

Dear Diary

My Final Entry

I've said before that a particular day was the worst day of my life, especially since last fall. I've said that a lot.

It turns out that I was lying. Today was the worst day of my life. Beyond a shadow of a shadow of a doubt.

I can't even put down on paper what happened. What the person I thought was my best friend did to me. How she betrayed me. I'll never get over it. Ever. Everything is gone now. Nothing matters anymore.

So if nothing matters then I'm going to go ahead and say it.

Meg broke a solemn oath she made to me years ago. She told my big secret. She told Mackenzie Egan that I used to wet the bed at night. And Mackenzie told everybody in the entire school.

I can't face anyone ever again. I feel like dying.

I want to die.

Rosemary Alice Patterson, age 14

46

Meg was sitting cross-legged on the living room couch watching the local evening news. It was boring. Nothing really exciting ever seemed to happen in Yorktide and its neighboring towns. Big deal, a guy was caught driving drunk. Like that was news? It happened every day! Some idiot was smoking in bed and the bed caught fire. Nobody was hurt, which was good, but come on, Meg thought. Why can't something really interesting ever happen here, like some sort of spying scandal, something big? That was another reason for moving far away when she got older, to begin a new life in a place where interesting things took place and—

Meg abruptly uncrossed her legs, reached for the remote, and pressed the volume button. The announcer, a woman with curly red hair, was hinting at the next story, or whatever you called it. Teasing it. And it was a bad story. Not exciting or interesting. Just bad.

The show went to a commercial. Meg shot to her feet and called out, "Mom! Get in here, fast!"

Frannie appeared a half a moment later, holding a damp dish towel. "What is it?"

Meg pointed to the television. "Listen. The news is back."

They did listen. After a moment, Frannie dropped the towel to the floor and put her hand to her mouth. "Oh, my God in heaven," she said. "I know that family from church."

"Me, too."

Together they watched and listened to the brief report. A boy named Kenny Ray, aged twelve, from a neighboring town, had shot himself in the head in a failed suicide attempt. A note found near his bleeding and unconscious body explained that he was no longer able to stand being a target of bullying by some of the boys at his school. They hated him, the note said, because he was gay.

School officials were being questioned, as were fellow students and neighbors of the family. The parents claimed they had known nothing about the bullying. Their son had never complained to them.

"He's such a good boy," his mother said, tears streaming down her face, her hands clutched to her chest. "Why would anyone want to hurt him?"

His father, a tall, spare man in a work shirt and jeans, was clearly unable to speak. He stood behind his wife, his head bowed, his mouth tight.

When the report was over and the announcer moved on to a lighter news item, Meg turned off the television.

"This is a disaster," Meg said forcefully. "This is wrong, wrong, wrong."

"Isn't there an older boy in the Ray family, too?" her mother asked, still staring at the television though it was no longer on.

Meg nodded. "Yeah. I think he's in college now. He was a big athlete in high school. I remember seeing his picture in the paper, like, every week."

Frannie now sank onto the couch. "I feel sick to my stomach," she said. "Literally."

"Violence is sickening," Meg agreed. "Physical or verbal or psychological. I hope the police find the creeps who taunted that boy. And then I hope they—"

"Remember what you just said about violence, Meg."

"Yeah. I know. But there can be justice without violence."

Frannie opened her mouth to speak, but the sound of Petey tramping down the stairs from the second floor made her close it again. Petey came into the living room and looked closely from his sister to his mother and back again. "What's wrong?" he asked.

Meg didn't know what to say. She looked to her mother for guidance.

"Nothing's wrong," Frannie said, feigning a smile.

"Oh," Petey said. "Is Daddy coming over?"

Meg was convinced by his expression that he hadn't really believed it when his mother said that nothing was wrong. Petey was not dumb. And children had an instinct for trouble.

"No," Frannie answered. "I don't think so. Why?"

Petey shrugged. "No reason. I just miss him, that's all."

Meg glanced down at her mother. She looked awful, her face ashen, her eyes strained. Meg thought that maybe her mother could use some time alone to process the awful news they had just heard. "Hey," she said, as brightly as she could manage. "I have an idea. Why don't I take Petey to the park for a while? There's some time before dinner, right, Mom?"

Frannie looked up at her daughter. Her eyes were suddenly bright with tears. "Right," she said. "Just be careful."

"Don't worry, Mom," Meg said, reaching for her little brother's hand. "You can count on me."

A moment later they were out the door and headed toward Yorktide Memorial Park. Petey was quiet, as if affected by the suddenly strange mood that had come over the Giroux house after the evening news. And lies didn't sit well with children. Meg knew that for a fact.

She held back a sigh. The world was such a scary place. She supposed it always had been, and maybe in a lot of ways more dangerous than it was now, at least, more dangerous than the world was for a twenty-first-century teenaged girl living in one of the most privileged countries in the world. She didn't have to worry about tsunamis or famine or volcanoes. She didn't have to worry about civil war. At least, she hoped that she didn't. The first civil war sounded horrid enough. Those pictures of wounded soldiers and the prisoners of war were pretty unbearable to look at. But she could still be worried about crime and financial ruin and one person bullying another person until that person finally snapped and tried to harm herself—or kill himself.

Meg felt Petey squeeze her hand.

"Hey." She smiled down at him.

"Mom looked sad," he said.

"Oh," Meg said, keeping her tone light, "I think she's just tired. You know she works really hard."

"Maybe Daddy could help her with some stuff."

"Mmm. Maybe." How did you tell a six-year-old child that his father was a lazy bum? You didn't tell him.

"I'm going to go on the slide," Petey announced. "Gregory at camp says he goes down the slide head-first."

"He does, does he? Well, you're not doing that!"

"Why not?"

"Because it's way too dangerous," Meg said, pushing aside memories of her own headfirst slides. Just because she had been a daredevil didn't mean that Petey should be one, too. Do as I say, not as I do. That was another one of her mom's favorite expressions. Meg thought it might become one of hers, too, at least where Petey was concerned.

Petey shrugged. "Okay. Hey, maybe I could help Mom with some stuff. I'm getting pretty strong. Maybe I could help her mow the lawn!"

Meg bit back a smile at the thought of her little brother struggling with the heavy, old mower her mother had bought ages and ages ago. "That's really nice of you," she said, "to want to help Mom. Though maybe instead of mowing the lawn you could help her load the dishwasher. I know she hates doing it."

Petey smiled and nodded.

Brother and sister walked on. Meg thought she could feel a tiny hint of fall very vaguely in the air. If it was her imagination, so be it. She was tired now of summer (it had been a difficult one, albeit productive) and ready to move on. Fall brought a fresh start, with a new school year and—

Meg was caught short by an image of Mr. and Mrs. Ray. She saw all too clearly Mrs. Ray's tear-streaked face and Mr. Ray's grimly set mouth. Fall would not bring a fresh start for them. It would bring only more grief. She wondered if they could ever move on and recover from this awful thing that had happened to them. By all accounts they were a loving family, but they had somehow failed to protect one of their own, maybe not through any fault or negligence. Maybe it had just happened. Like Rosie had said that afternoon in her bedroom when Meg had been moaning about not looking like Kate Middleton. Life could be random and unfair.

Right there on the sidewalk, Meg felt overcome with a fierce love. She loved her family beyond words. And she would do anything and everything in her power to protect her brother, and her mother. She didn't mind taking on more responsibility. Like her mother had always told her, she was tough. Megan Christine Giroux was strong. She really believed that now.

"I see the park!" Petey cried.

"Wanna skip?" Meg asked.

"Sure! I'm a way better skipper than you!"

"Are not!"

And together, still hand in hand, they skipped on toward the park.

47

Later that night, after the dinner dishes had been cleaned and put away and Petey had gone off to bed, Frannie poured herself a glass of red wine. She hardly ever drank—she didn't have time to be tipsy—but this night, she felt she deserved just one glass before bed. Nothing else helped her sleep these days, not praying or counting sheep, not even warm milk. Maybe wine would work.

Glass of wine in hand, Frannie sank onto the living room couch and sighed. Her thoughts were tumultuous, an unpleasant mix of sadness and anger and frustration. She hardly knew the Ray family, but somehow, their tragedy had brought her closer to them, or them closer to her. As a parent it wasn't hard to put herself in Maria Ray's shoes and know something of what she must be feeling right now. You didn't have to be the most sympathetic or empathetic person in the world to feel connected to the Rays' tragedy.

And, not surprisingly, the Ray family's tragedy brought to mind—as if it had ever been far off—Rosie's own story, and what she had endured at the hands of those girls for all those months. And, of course, of what Jane, as a parent, had gone through once she had finally learned the truth. Maybe, Frannie thought, Jane's refusal to befriend her was understandable, even reasonable, after all.

Still, Jane's refusal to communicate had pretty much made any friendly gesture Frannie might make toward Rosie impossible. It was a weird situation. Somehow, Frannie had become the pariah of the bunch, the only one left out of the Patterson-Giroux dynamic. It was unfair, but Frannie felt helpless to change the situation. She remembered that saying: When God closes a door He opens a window. Something like that. But for the life of her she could see no open window, no way to salvage a remnant of the past, no way out of the isolation that seemed to engulf her.

Frannie took a sip of the wine. She so wanted to talk about the Ray family's recent tragedy with someone, but with whom? There was no comfort to be found with Jane anymore. And Peter, of course, would be no help. He never had been good at listening to an expression of grief, let alone with offering sympathy or consolation. Frannie remembered when her parents had died, within months of each other. The depth of her pain had blinded her to the extent of her husband's emotional distance. Later, after she had passed through the initial intensity and shock of her loss, she realized that aside from an occasional pat on the shoulder, Peter had left her entirely alone in her moment of need.

When they were first married, and for some time after that, Frannie had decided that Peter's inability to comfort was simply due to his being a "typical man," thoughtless and obtuse. After a while she had had to face the fact that he was actually an incredibly self-absorbed person. To a great extent, other people didn't exist for him. And in Frannie's experience, people like that didn't demonstrably change.

She took another sip of wine. *Okay, yeah,* she thought, *so I feel terribly isolated. Big deal.* This was not a time to pity herself when others in her community were experiencing much greater pain. That poor family. Frannie had told Meg not to watch the news in the next few days when Petey was around. She didn't want him to hear about the Ray boy, ask questions, and be confused by whatever answers she or Meg could muster. Frankly, Frannie wasn't at all sure what she could say to Petey that wouldn't scare him. She didn't get the local daily paper at the house, so he wouldn't find out about the Ray boy that way, and Frannie doubted the tragedy would be talked about in front of the kids at Petey's day camp, especially since some of the kids were bound to know Kenny Ray, at least by sight. So, hopefully, Petey was safe for the moment.

Frannie heard a creak on the stairs and looked up to see Meg descending. She was wearing a pair of pajama bottoms and a T-shirt.

"I thought you were upstairs for the night," Frannie said as Meg came into the living room. She felt momentarily guilty to be caught drinking a glass of wine. But nothing in Meg's manner or expression betrayed disapproval. I'm not her father, Frannie told herself. And Meg knows it.

Meg shrugged and sat next to her mother on the couch. "Nah. I couldn't really get involved in my book. It's really good, but I can't stop thinking about that poor family."

"I know what you mean. I feel as if I've been hit by a train. Utterly flattened. And I've hardly even spoken to the Rays. Just friendly, Sunday-morning coffee hour small talk."

"Did you know their younger son was gay?" Meg asked.

"No," Frannie said. "I suspect they didn't, either. Well, unless he had told them. But if he had already told his parents, he could have turned to them for help when the bullying got bad. Unless they had rejected him, which I find hard to believe. They seem so nice. The poor boy must have felt so awfully alone."

"Yeah. Mom? What if Rosie . . . What if she had tried to kill herself?"

For a moment, Frannie thought she might be sick, and with an unsteady hand she put the glass of wine on the small table by the side of the couch. "But she didn't try to kill herself," she said forcefully. "Remember that."

"But she might have. And then . . ."

Frannie put her hand on her daughter's arm. "Don't even think it, Meg. Please."

"I can't help it," Meg protested. "Then I would have been responsible for killing her."

"No. A person who kills herself makes her own decision. It's a bad, terribly sad decision, but it's her own."

Meg was silent for a long moment. Finally, she said, "I'm not so sure about that now. At least, not when it's a young person committing suicide. I know sometimes I act like I know everything, but I don't. No one my age does, especially someone who's depressed."

Frannie thought about that. "Okay," she said then. "Honestly? I'm not so sure about that, either. I'm not so sure that a young person's decision to take her own life is her decision alone. Or that she's really responsible for that decision. But I don't want you to be blaming yourself for something that didn't happen and that might never have happened."

"I'll try," Meg said. "Seriously."

A crunch on the gravel-covered front walk caused

Frannie to turn her head and peer out the open living room window.

"What . . . It's Jane and Rosie," she said. "I wonder what's going on. Jane hasn't been over here since . . ."

Frannie got up from the couch and opened the door before Jane or Rosie could knock.

"I'm so sorry, Frannie," Jane said immediately. "Will you forgive me?"

In reply, Frannie reached forward and hugged her old friend. Jane hugged her back just as tightly.

"Come inside," Frannie said then, her voice a bit strangled, and wiping a tear from her eye.

Once inside the women hugged again, and now tears flowed copiously.

"Come on," Meg whispered to Rosie. She gestured toward the kitchen. "Let's give them some privacy." Rosie nodded and followed.

After all the weeks of silence between them, Frannie half expected the words to flow fast and furious, accusations and apologies, regrets and revelations, but neither woman said a word. *Right now,* Frannie thought, *what we most need is the powerful simplicity of touch.*

Some moments later, Frannie couldn't have said exactly how long, the girls returned to the living room. Slowly, the women released each other.

"You guys okay?" Meg asked, a slight smile playing on her lips.

Jane just nodded. Frannie held out her arms for Rosie.

"I've missed you," she said as they embraced.

Rosie smiled. "Thanks, Mrs. Giroux. I've missed you, too."

"We heard the news about that young boy just now," Jane blurted, having found her voice. "One of Mike's clients called him about something totally unrelated and mentioned the tragedy."

"Yes," Frannie said. "Meg was watching the evening news earlier. That's how we found out. Let's sit down, all of us."

Jane and Frannie sat on the couch. Rosie sat in the plush corduroy chair and Meg perched on its arm.

"It could have been anyone's child," Jane said, her voice raw. "It was almost mine. It just as easily could have been yours, too."

Frannie nodded. "Yes. But it wasn't Rosie and it wasn't Meg, so let's at least be grateful for that."

"Why did we escape without further tragedy?" Jane went on, as if to herself. "I know there's no real answer to that. I just keep thinking how unfair and random it all seems. . . ."

Frannie saw Meg and Rosie share a look. "Life is unfair and random," Meg repeated.

Jane shook her head. "I'm so ashamed that it took this awful thing to happen before I could reach out to you again. Frannie, will you ever forgive me?"

"Don't be silly," Frannie said, her voice a bit quivery. "There's nothing to forgive. We've weathered a rough patch, that's all."

Jane managed a wan smile. "You're being too nice. I don't deserve it. You should be angry with me."

"I was angry. But I'm over it." Frannie shrugged. "Anger does nothing for the complexion."

Jane laughed. "And neither does holding a grudge, believe me."

Rosie cleared her throat meaningfully. "It's great that you two are friends again. But right now, there's something else we need to focus on—what happened to that family. We have to do something, Mom. I'm not just standing by. No freakin' way."

"Excuse me?" Jane asked, eyebrows rising.

"Whatever. Everyone says it. Anyway, what are we going to do?"

"I don't know. Not yet, anyway." Jane turned to Frannie. "Have you heard anything new? Is the boy . . . Is he still alive?"

"Yes," Frannie said. "He's in critical condition but alive. I got a call earlier from a woman I know from church. Mrs. Kneeland is very close to the Ray family. She went over to the house as soon as she heard the news. She spent a few hours trying to comfort the parents. I doubt she had much success. Still, it was good of her to be there."

Jane shook her head. "The poor thing could have died. He could, I suppose, be paralyzed. It's just so awful."

"Where did he get a gun?" Rosie asked.

"His father is a hunter," Frannie explained. "Mary Kneeland told me that every one of Jack Ray's guns is registered and kept locked away. But a lock can always be picked."

"He must have felt so desperate to do something so brutal," Rosie said quietly. "I wanted to die but I didn't want to actually kill myself. I guess I don't really know how bad he was feeling. It must have been so much worse than I ever felt."

"His parents must be devastated. They must feel so responsible. . . ." Jane couldn't go on and pressed a tissue to her already tear-swollen eyes.

"Maybe we can take up a collection for the Rays at church," Meg said suddenly. "Do you think they'll let us? Isn't suicide a sin if you're a Catholic?"

Frannie frowned. "Yeah, like homosexuality is a sin. Please. But he didn't actually kill himself, so . . . I'm not sure how we can do it, but we'll collect money somehow. Father William and Sister Pauline will help. No one in his or her right mind is going to condemn a child in trouble."

Jane nodded. "And who knows what kind of insurance the Rays have, if they have any at all. The hospital bills could ruin them."

"Maybe we could take Mr. and Mrs. Ray some food, like casseroles," Rosie suggested. "Stuff they can just heat up."

"Good idea," Jane said. "I'm sure the last thing they want to do is cook. I hope there's someone close to them who can make sure they eat and get some sleep."

"Mary Kneeland said that she'll take charge of that sort of thing," Frannie said, glad to see Jane rallying to the cause and not entirely lost in memories of her own despair. "She lives just next door. And she called the Rays' older son at college. He's been doing a summer semester. He's on his way home now."

"Good." Jane sighed. "We have a lot of catching up to do," she said to Frannie.

"Yeah," Frannie said, "we do. But not tonight. This whole thing . . . I'm exhausted. It's been a terrible few months, hasn't it?"

"Yes, it has," Jane said, getting up from the couch and putting her hand out for Rosie's. "Try to get some sleep. We'll talk tomorrow."

"That sounds good. Good night, Jane, Rosie."

Frannie closed the door behind the Pattersons and then leaned against it. She almost couldn't believe that what had happened in the past half hour had really happened.

She had almost come to accept as fact that she and Jane would never again be friends. It had been a bitter thing to accept, let alone to contemplate. But now . . . more than anything, Frannie realized, she had just wanted things on Pond View Road back to normal.

Meg broke into her thoughts as if she knew exactly what they consisted of. "So, Mom, how do you feel about Mrs. Patterson apologizing?" she asked. "Are you glad?"

Frannie didn't need to think about it. "Yeah," she said, pushing off the door. "I am glad."

"Good. You know, there are going to be some bumps along the road. . . ."

"Stop quoting me to me."

Meg grinned. "Just teasing. Really, Mom, your advice helped me be patient with Rosie."

"Thanks. I'm glad. It's weird being a parent, Meg. You never know if what you're telling your kid is going to help or harm in the end. You set out with the best of intentions, but . . ." Frannie shrugged.

"Well, you did good this time, Mom."

In response, Frannie yawned hugely. Meg laughed.

"Yeah," Frannie said. "We should get some sleep."

"Agreed. I suddenly feel completely exhausted."

Frannie put her arm around Meg's shoulder and together they walked up the stairs to their bedrooms.

48

"Hi!" Stella called as she climbed out of her mother's car. "Sorry I'm a bit late. Can you believe I almost overslept on the first day of school!"

Meg laughed. "Getting detention would not be a cool way to start the school year."

"I've been awake since five this morning," Rosie admitted. "I guess I was just too worked up to sleep. I hope I don't have bags under my eyes."

"You look great," Stella assured her.

The three girls had planned to meet at the foot of the steps to Yorktide Memorial High. They wanted to start the new school year together. It had been Rosie's idea, seconded by Meg. Stella had enthusiastically agreed. *In a way,* Rosie thought, *all three of us are recovering from an injury. Why not show each other support? And why not show anyone who cares to know that we survived?*

Stella's hair had grown in a bit since Meg and Rosie had last seen her in Perkins Cove, but she said she was having it cut again soon. Rosie noticed a few kids in their grade kind of stare at Stella as they passed and went up the stairs. But that was probably because she looked so different than she had back in May. A long floaty top and a chunky beaded necklace were a far cry from a polo shirt and penny loafers. Meg wore a cool pair of jeans that Jane Patterson had hemmed for her and a purple zip-up hoodie over a pink T-shirt. Her mother had given her a cell phone—finally!—and Meg kept finding excuses to take it out of her bag and text and take pictures. Rosie had no idea who she was texting. She half suspected that Meg was pretending, but she wouldn't call her on it. Meg had wanted that phone so badly and for so long.

Rosie wore the heart-shaped rose quartz pendant Meg had given her for her last birthday. It was the first time she had worn it since about January, when things had gotten so really awful. She had gained back all of the weight she had lost last spring, largely thanks to her mother's efforts in the kitchen, and wore a brand-new emerald green cotton sweater, a white blouse, and chinos.

Mrs. Patterson had been fighting back tears since the night before and had tried to insist that she drive Rosie to school instead of letting her take the bus or walk like a normal person. Thankfully, Rosie's father had stepped in and convinced his wife that Rosie would be perfectly fine getting to and from school the usual way. Really, Rosie thought, sometimes her mother treated her like she was a child. That was going to have to change. She was going to have to show her mother than she was perfectly capable of taking care of herself. Mostly.

Rosie spotted Kristin Walsh and one of her fellow teammates starting up the stairs to the school. She waved and Kristin waved back with a smile.

"You know Kristin Walsh?" Meg asked.

"Not really. I met her for, like, two seconds one day this summer. Her mom's one of my mom's clients."

"She's supposed to be pretty nice," Stella said. "And she's an awesome basketball player. I bet she'll get a scholarship to college."

"Wow," Rosie said. "Yeah, she seemed pretty nice when she was at my house."

Meg nodded toward the curb where a woman was getting out of a Jeep. "There goes Ms. Broccoli," she said. "She's going to be my advanced math teacher. I heard she's really tough. And that she hates jokes about her name."

"You'll ace the class," Rosie said. "You always do."

But Meg actually looked worried. "I think I might actually have to try this year."

Rosie then spotted Charles Lin, the nice boy from her ninth-grade Spanish class, the one who had stopped to ask her if she was okay the time she had kind of frozen in the hall. He saw her, too, and waved. She smiled and waved back.

"You're waving at a guy?" Meg asked. "You, Rosie Patterson?"

Rosie shrugged. "He waved first."

"My mom heard that Charles and his parents went to China this summer to visit family," Stella told them. "I would love to go to China someday."

Meg nodded. "Me, too!"

"I want to go to every country in Europe first," Rosie said. "And that might take a long time!"

"And a lot of money," Meg pointed out. "You'd better write a lot of best sellers someday."

Rosie laughed. It was a beautiful morning, sunny and a little bit cool. Seeing Kristin and Charles this morning seemed like a good omen, a promise that this school year would be different, that she, herself, would be different. There really was a future ahead of her, though only months before she had seen her life as bleak and meaningless and yes, better off ended.

How much had already changed in her life, and for the better!

"We'd better go in," Meg said, checking her phone for the time.

Stella nodded. "And you'd better turn off your phone. The school's cracking down on cell phone use in a big way. My mom told me. I'm pretty sure we'll hear about it in today's assembly."

"Yeah," Rosie said, thinking of how she had suffered from cell phone abuse, "your mother would be really furious if you had your phone taken away, especially on the first day of school."

"Tell me about it!" Meg turned the phone off and tucked it deep into her backpack.

"Okay, everybody," Stella said. "Let's do this!"

And side by side the girls climbed the stairs to Yorktide Memorial High and began the journey that was tenth grade.

49

Journal Entry for August 28, 2012

Today was the first day of sophomore year, tenth grade.

My therapist has been telling me since the stuff that happened with Mackenzie and the others back in the fall and spring that I should try to write a diary again, only she called it a journal. From the beginning she's said that writing out what's going on in your life and how you're feeling about it can really help you understand things. But I didn't want to understand things. Maybe I couldn't.

That is, until now.

This is the first entry in my brand-new journal. I decided to call it a journal and not a diary. It seems more mature. Anyway, this is the first entry about what's going to be my brand-new life. And here's the thing I learned about life this last summer. No matter how much good stuff there is, there's always the possibility of bad stuff, too, just that you have to try not to let the bad stuff contaminate the good. That's hard to do, but you kind of have no choice if you want to live, and I do want to live. Like I told Meg back when we were in Perkins Cove one day this summer, the day we ran into Stella, there's a lot I want to do in my life, so I have to live to be old!

BTW: In some cultures around the world, old people are really respected, but not here in the United States. People (not all people) just make fun of them or ignore them. I wonder why that is. It's not fair at all. I was at the store the other day with Mom and I saw this little old man being shoved aside—literally!—by some middle-aged guy who wanted to get something on a shelf in the cookie aisle. It made me furious, but I was too scared to go up to the guy and say something. He was pretty big and mean looking. But I did go over to the little old man after the big guy had moved off and asked if I could reach something for him. He was nice and asked me if I could get him a box of Fig Newtons and then he thanked me. I wish I could have done more.

Maybe elder care (I think that's what it's called) is a field I could work in when I'm an adult. I'm not sure what kind of degree that would require. Though I think I also want to be a writer. (Meg acts like it's a done deal that I'm going to be a writer! She says I act like one. I'm not really sure what she means by that.) Maybe I could combine the two somehow. . . . We'll see what happens!

About my old diary. I'm kind of curious to read it again and see just how my mind was working and what I was feeling all last school year. But I'm also kind of scared to do it yet and Dr. Lowe agrees that it might not be time to "revisit"—that's her word—those sad months yet. Maybe, someday, I'll decide I'm ready. Until then, all of my old diaries will stay in that plastic box under my bed.

Here's something interesting: Today, when Meg and Stella and I were at my locker, Mackenzie and Courtney and Jill came around the corner and started to walk down the hall. I have to admit my stomach clenched a bit but I just went on talking to my friends, and Mackenzie and the others just walked by. No one said a word and no one even looked at us! When they were out of sight the three of us burst out laughing!

Oh, and I ran into Kristin Walsh in the hall after lunch. She stopped and we chatted. She said I should come to some of her basketball games. I kind of laughed and told her that I didn't really know anything about sports and she kind of laughed and said, "So come and learn!" So maybe I will.

So far things between Meg and me have been going well. We've had some arguments, but Dr. Lowe has been trying to help me understand that disagreements within a relationship are normal and that it's smart to "embrace the differences." That's her term. Also, I've learned that although forgiveness can be really hard, it's definitely worth it. At least, most times it is. With Meg, it was totally worth it.

Oh, and get this—Mom is going to give Meg sewing lessons. Meg's super excited because if she learns to sew she can make her own clothes, especially some of the stuff she couldn't afford if she had to buy it in a store. As for me, I'm glad she won't be complaining so much anymore! Don't tell her I said that! Anyway, she told me she's saving up to have that little ruby she bought the last time we were in Portland wrapped. That's when thin silver or gold wire is laced around a stone, with a loop on top so you can wear it on a chain. (My rose quartz pendant isn't wrapped. It's actually a big bead.) Mom said she would contact that jewelry guy she likes, the one who comes to the Fourth of July fair, and ask him if he knows anyone local who could do that for Meg. Meg is determined to wear a "real piece of jewelry" as soon as she can. I guess her definition of "real" is different from mine!

I don't know what's going to happen with Stella and me. Meg thinks she's pretty nice and so do I, but I think it's going to take time for us all to really trust each other. That's okay. I have the time. Last week Stella loaned me a book of poems by Emily Dickinson, which I thought was really nice of her. She said she thought I would like them. They're kind of hard to understand at first, and some of them are kind of bizarre, but I really do like them. Stella was right. The lines really stick in your head and the poems are even better when you read them out loud. I'm going to go online after dinner and look up information about Emily Dickinson's life. I know a little but I'd like to know more. That famous portrait of her, the old black-and-white photograph, is so haunting. I wonder if anyone has ever felt her spirit in the house she lived in for so long. I wonder if you can visit that house. It's in Massachusetts, so it's not too far away. Maybe I'll ask Mom and Dad if we can go there someday.

And I'm also determined to talk honestly to Mom and Dad about not wanting to keep up with piano lessons. Wish me luck.

Oh, and another thing I'm going to talk to Dr. Lowe about is what to say when people tell me I'm so pretty or beautiful, or when they comment on my hair or my weight. I don't ever want to be rude but I do want to be able to let a person know when they're doing or saying something that makes me uncomfortable. Wish me luck on that, too!

One last thing. There's a new guy in our class. He transferred from some school in New Hampshire. He seems kind of shy. Plus, he has really bad acne, the kind that you can't really cover up. Last year I would have been nice to him in a kind of distant way because he was new and didn't know anybody, but now I know that he might need some real friends. So I introduced myself today and he's actually less shy when you talk to him. If I see even the slightest bit of someone bullying him—his name is Josh—I'm going straight to the teacher and the principal and Mom and Dad. Meg and Stella swear they'll do the same thing. No more standing by while someone gets hurt. Ever. One thing I really found out this past year is that it's not enough just to think good thoughts about people. You have to do good things for people. You just have to.

Oh, wait! One more other last thing, and it's important! That boy, Kenny Ray, the one who tried to kill himself, is doing okay. I mean, he's not 100 percent at all, but Mrs. Giroux found out through Mrs. Kneeland that he's in stable condi-

tion. That's a big relief. Mom's still taking food over to the Rays' house once a week. I've been helping her to make casseroles and stews, dishes that are easy to reheat and that fill you up. Lots of people are taking turns helping them out in whatever way they can, like one of the neighbors is taking care of mowing the lawn. Small stuff, but it's important the Ray family know people are there for them.

Oh, one more other last, last thing! I decided I don't want to wear my hair super long again like it was last year. It's grown out a bit past my shoulders now, and once it gets a little longer I'm keeping it there. No more Rapunzel. Meg showed me some articles from one of her fashion magazines about how to wear hair that length, and I'm kind of excited to try some styles. I guess I partly got the idea from Stella—about being a new me. Not that a haircut is going to change the important stuff, but like Stella says, for her it was a symbol of bigger change, change that took place inside.

Oops, gotta go. Mom's calling that dinner is ready. She made pasta with carbonara sauce, which is so awesome and I am so starved!

Your friend,

Rosie

In bestselling author Holly Chamberlin's poignant new novel, a mother and daughter escape to a beautiful coastal town in Maine to find healing in the wake of heartbreaking loss.

The journey to Yorktide, Maine, was always a happy one for Frieda and Aaron Braithwaite and their two daughters. Frieda loves her mother's old farmhouse, and the girls have grown closer there, sharing a bedroom and spinning stories into the night. But that was before—when tragedy was something that happened to other families.

Since the car crash that claimed the lives of her husband, and their younger daughter, Frieda has struggled emotionally and financially. Bella, now seventeen, is withdrawn and wary, and Frieda fears losing her too.

At her mother's urging, Frieda decides to return to Yorktide with Bella for the summer. Bella gets a job in a local shop, and little by little edges her way back into the world. But it's the unexpected connections they make—with a former schoolmate, a troubled teenage girl, and Frieda's estranged father—that will spur them to find healing amid bittersweet memories, and discover if their bond is strong enough to guide them back to hope once more.

Please turn the page for an exciting sneak peek of Holly Chamberlin's
HOME FOR THE SUMMER
coming soon wherever print and e-books are sold!

Prologue

"I can't believe we have to go home already. It's so unfair."

Frieda Braithwaite smiled at her older daughter across the breakfast table in the resort's main dining room. Bella's brownish-blond hair was pulled away from her face into a ponytail, emphasizing her high cheekbones and large blue eyes. "Bella," she said, "we've had seven days of fun in the sun. We've eaten fantastic food and danced until dawn. Well, almost. I don't think there's anything unfair about that. The only unfair thing is that your grandmother couldn't come with us."

"Poor Grandma." Ariel, Frieda's soon to be fifteen-year-old daughter, pushed a stray curl of hair from her face. It was a futile effort. Ariel's long red curls obeyed no one. "It would have been so great to be here with her. She was so excited about the trip. But I guess it's not easy to travel with a broken leg."

"And when you're confined to a wheelchair." Aaron Braithwaite shook his head. "If your grandmother were less of a heroic sort . . . But that's Ruby Hitchens for you."

Bella sighed dramatically. "It stinks about Grandma's accident, but I still wish we could stay here for a few more days. I mean, it could be forever before we get the chance to come back!"

"That doesn't make sense," Ariel pointed out. "But I know what you mean. This really was an awesome vacation. Thanks, Mom and Dad."

Frieda looked to her husband with fondness. "It's your father who deserves the thanks. He was the one who moved heaven and earth to get this week away from the firm."

Aaron put his hand over his heart and bowed his head. "I'll happily accept praise and adulation, but don't forget it was your mother's idea to make Bella's sixteenth birthday into something really special. And next year," he said, turning to Ariel, "we'll do something really special for your sixteenth birthday."

But Ariel didn't seem to have heard her father; she had her nose in the guidebook she had started studying weeks before the vacation. "Oh, wow," she said suddenly. "I don't know how I missed this! There's a museum of Jamaican culture in the next town. It says they've got pieces dating back to pre-Columbian days. OMG, they even have stuff from the "Redware people." That's before the Taino tribes settled here. And they've got artifacts from the Spanish invasion and the English invasion and pieces from the Maroon culture, too. Please can we go?" she asked, looking up from the guidebook.

Bella laughed and rolled her eyes. "Ariel, you are such a dork. How can anyone possibly be interested in looking at a bunch of dusty old clay pots?"

"I doubt the pots are dusty," Ariel said matter-of-factly. "They're probably kept in glass cases to prevent people touching them. And the cases probably have a specially controlled atmosphere to help with preservation. And I'm sure there are lots of other things on display besides pots."

Bella rolled her eyes again and reached for her juice. "Yeah," she said. "Like broken pots."

Frieda looked at her watch. "I don't know, Ariel," she said. "We have to be at the airport by noon to return the rental car and catch our flight. It's already almost nine thirty."

"Wait a minute. There might be time," Aaron said, checking his own watch. "When does the museum open?"

Ariel glanced at her guidebook. "Nine."

"And the airport is only about forty minutes from here. Frieda?"

Frieda shook her head. "We'd be calling it pretty tight, Aaron."

"Nonsense," Aaron argued. "Look, clearly Bella has no interest—"

"Uh, yeah!"

"So why don't you two stay here, catch some last rays, and I'll take Ariel to the museum. The luggage is in the trunk and I've already checked us out, so that's no worry. I'll text you when we're on our way back and then we'll head right out to the airport."

Frieda looked at Ariel's face, shining with excitement. She had been such a good sport about coming to Jamaica even though Ariel and the sun didn't play well together and, with her keen interest in history and art, she was more suited to galleries stuffed with antiquities than to sunbathing and surfing. And Aaron was a responsible man; if he thought they could make it to the museum and back in plenty of time for the family to catch their flight home to Massachusetts, then why object any further?

"Sure," Frieda said. "Sounds like a plan. You two have fun."

"We will!" Ariel jumped up from her seat. "Thanks, Mom. I'm so psyched."

"Then we'll be on our way," Aaron said, rising from his own chair.

"Be careful and don't forget to drive on the left side of the road."

"You worry too much, Frieda." Aaron smiled and leaned down to give his wife a kiss on the lips.

Frieda, who had just taken a bite of toast, gave him her cheek instead. *I am so lucky,* she thought as she watched her husband and daughter walk out of the dining room hand in hand. *I am so lucky to have this beautiful family.*

"Sometimes I don't know how Ariel and I are related," Bella said when they were alone. "Pots? Seriously? What's interesting about a pot?"

"You know," Frieda said, "we'll probably be going to Paris next year for Ariel's sixteenth. I'm thinking you might want to get used to the idea of looking at old pots and oil paintings and religious statuary and historic buildings."

"Blah." Bella shuddered. "At least that's a whole year away."

When they had finally finished breakfast—Bella decided to have another helping of scrambled eggs from the buffet—Frieda and her daughter left the dining room and settled in the comfortable open-air lounge not far from the resort's reception area. Potted palm trees stood between prettily cushioned chaises and low tables made of glossy rattan. Bella put on her sunglasses and buried herself in her iPhone. Knowing Bella's obsession with the Internet, Frieda had made sure that the resort was equipped with Wi-Fi before booking a reservation. An unplugged Bella was not something either of her parents wanted to be around for more than a few hours. As for Frieda, she turned to reading Iris Murdoch's *The Sea, the Sea* on her Kindle.

Absorbed in the novel, lulled by the warm breeze and the sound of the gently swaying palms, Frieda was oblivious to the passing of time until a child's gleeful shout brought her to the moment. She checked her watch. It was almost eleven. *Aaron and Ariel really should have returned by now,* she thought with just a trace of annoyance. *If they missed their flight . . .* Frieda took her phone from her bag and sent Aaron a text. *Where r u?* He didn't reply. Well, Frieda thought, maybe the museum was a dead zone, and she knew that Aaron refused to text while driving, so if they were on the way back to the hotel . . .

Rapidly Frieda typed Ariel's cell phone number and sent the same message she had sent to her husband. But Ariel didn't reply, either.

"Who are you texting?"

Frieda looked up from her phone to find Bella watching her.

"Your sister," she said. "But she isn't answering."

Bella snorted. "Ariel is such an airhead. You know how she's always losing her phone. She probably dropped it somewhere and doesn't even know it's gone."

"Be fair," Frieda said. "She doesn't lose her phone. She just misplaces it."

"Whatevs. Try Dad."

"I did," Frieda told her. "But you know he won't answer if he's driving." *But why wouldn't he ask Ariel to reply?* Frieda wondered. A sharp sliver of worry stabbed at her belly.

"Well, they'd better be on the way back," Bella said. "I want to be home in time to watch The Bachelor tonight. If we miss our flight because of some boring old museum I will so kill Ariel."

"We won't miss our flight," Frieda said. "Don't be dramatic."

Bella looked back to her phone, but Frieda couldn't resume her reading. In spite of the fact that Aaron thought she worried too much, she wasn't a person prone to panic. Still, she didn't like that neither Aaron nor Ariel had responded to her message. Their silence didn't feel right.

"I'll be back in a minute," she said, rising from the comfortable chair and moving out of her daughter's hearing. She called Aaron's cell phone; when he didn't pick up she left a message on his voice mail. "Hey, it's me. Where are you guys? It's getting late. Call me." She then called Ariel's cell phone; when Ariel didn't pick up, Frieda left a message on her voice mail, this one delivered in a voice that was just a little tense. "It's Mom. Please call me, okay?"

Frieda could feel her face constricting in a frown as she walked back to where Bella was waiting.

"You called them, didn't you?" Bella asked, removing her sunglasses.

"Yes," Frieda admitted. "But the calls went to voice mail."

"We are so going to miss our flight!" her daughter complained loudly. "It's after eleven! Why don't we just meet them at the airport? Send Dad another text and tell him we've gone ahead."

"They'll be here," Frieda said firmly. Of course they will, she thought. Of course they will. There's the potluck dinner at the Andersons' tomorrow night. They'll want to see the pictures of our vacation. And Aaron's got that big presentation on Friday and Ariel has a violin solo in the school's concert on Wednesday. Of course they'll be back. They have to be.

"It's eleven fifteen, Mom." Bella was pacing now, her purple flip-flops slapping the floor.

Maybe, Frieda thought, *they should leave for the airport.* She could give a message to the clerk at the reception desk for Aaron and Ariel and entrust their plane tickets to her as well. She could leave another voice-mail message telling Aaron she and Bella had gone ahead. But what then? She couldn't get on the plane not knowing what had become of her husband and daughter. What can I do? she asked herself. What is there I can do?

"Mom," Bella moaned. "Come on. We could get a cab or maybe the resort bus could take us. If we don't leave now . . ."

Frieda shook her head and stared down at her phone as if willing it to ring.

"You don't think anything could have, you know, happened to them?"

Frieda looked up at her daughter, whose expression had suddenly and drastically morphed from one of annoyance to one of concern. "Of course not," she said with a lame attempt at a smile. "They probably just got caught in traffic."

But by eleven thirty Frieda was sick to her stomach with fear. It was now too late to get to the airport in time for their flight. She fought back the panic she was afraid might overwhelm her. She had to keep a clear head for Bella's sake.

"I'm going to talk to the clerk," she said, her throat dry. Bella followed her to the reception desk, where Frieda briefly explained the situation.

"I'm not sure what I can do," the clerk replied kindly. "I'm sorry."

A burst of loud laughter followed by voices speaking in the local patois caused Frieda to flinch. She just wanted to be back home, safe and sound in their house on Maple Drive. The Braithwaite family. All four of them. She wanted them to be home.

"Can you call the museum?" Frieda pleaded. "Maybe they're still there. Maybe my husband just lost track of time."

"I'm scared, Mom," Bella said, her voice trembling. "Dad never loses track of time. He's the most punctual guy ever."

Frieda said nothing. She couldn't. She stared at the young woman as she placed a call to the museum. She listened to the clerk's questions and to her maddeningly uninformative replies. After a moment, the clerk hung up.

"Yes," she said. "An American man wearing a blue shirt and glasses and a girl with red hair were there, but they left about a half hour ago. Would that be your husband and daughter?"

Frieda nodded and swallowed hard. "How long would it take to drive back to the resort?" she asked.

The clerk shrugged. "At this time of the day, ten minutes?"

Bella grabbed her mother's arm. "Mom, what are we going to do? Something's happened to them, I know it!"

Mindlessly, Frieda shook her head. Something has happened. Something has happened. And then the glass doors of the reception area slid open and two uniformed police officers walked into the lobby.

"Oh no," Frieda murmured, grabbing Bella's hand. "Please God, no."

"Mom!" Bella cried as the officers walked toward them, their faces set. "Mom! What's going on?"

"Mrs. Braithwaite?" the taller of the two police officers asked.

Frieda could only nod. She was aware of little whimpering sounds coming from Bella and of a roaring in her own ears. She was vaguely aware that the clerk had come out from behind the desk to stand just behind them.

"Mrs. Braithwaite," the officer went on, his voice gentle and low. "I'm afraid I have some bad news for you. Perhaps you would like to sit down."